SHELLY THACKER

HIS FORBIDDEN TOUCH

His Forbidden Touch

Stolen Brides Series, Book 2

"A fun and erotic 14th-century romp... loaded with non-stop adventure."
– *Publishers Weekly*

"It is stories like this one that keep so many of us reading romances."
– *The Oakland Press*

"Shelly Thacker has a unique and dazzling talent."
– Lisa Kleypas, *New York Times* bestselling author

"The adventure is thrilling and the sensuality is breathtakingly erotic. A must read for anyone who loves a well-written, wonderfully rich and fulfilling romance."
– Tanzey Cutter, *Old Book Barn Gazette* and *TheBestReviews.com*

"Shelly Thacker has the gift of bringing readers straight into her adventurous, heart-pounding romances and keeping them highly entertained and completely captivated. This fairytale romance will sweep you off your feet. This is an author who has made an indelible mark on romance. Exceptional. 4 1/2 stars (highest rating)."
– Kathe Robin, *Romantic Times*

The Stolen Brides Series:

One falls through time and finds herself married to a dark stranger…one may never reach her royal wedding if she can't resist her rugged protector…one is abducted by a mysterious swordsman and swept away to a secret island paradise. Three regal brides are about to discover that falling in love with a warrior is the most dangerous adventure of all.

Book 1: ***Forever His*** – Gaston and Celine
Book 2: ***His Forbidden Touch*** – Royce and Princess Ciara
Book 3: ***Timeless*** – Hauk and Avril

And coming soon, an all-new edition of the prequel,
Falcon on the Wind – Connor and Laurien

This book is a work of fiction. Names, characters, places, and incidents are either products of the author's imagination or are used fictitiously. Any resemblance to actual events, locales, business establishments, or persons, living or dead, is entirely coincidental.

Publishing History

First edition published by Avon Books

Digital edition published by Summit Avenue Books

Second Print edition published by Summit Avenue Books,

ISBN: 978-0-9887298-1-0

Cover design by Kim Killion of Hot DAMN! Designs
www.hotdamndesigns.com
Print Design by A Thirsty Mind
www.athirstymind.com

Publishers interested in foreign-language translation or other subsidiary rights should contact the author at www.shellythacker.com.

Dedication

To all the Thacker Backers, past and present,
who have blessed my life with their enthusiasm and kindness.

Fearful that they might betray
The love that they had come to share,
They always took the greatest care
Not to let anyone detect
Anything that might be suspect…
But lovers can't be satisfied
When love's true pleasure is denied.

~ Marie de France
"The Nightingale"
Twelfth century

Prologue

Châlons, near the French border
1302

Fire lit the night sky, devouring the forest like a hungering dragon that would not be sated. A treacherous wind lifted the flames higher, until it seemed they might swallow even the stars and moon. That fierce draught of air whirled up the mountainside, howling around the palace walls, carrying ashes that rained down on Princess Ciara as she ran across the bailey.

Her velvet cloak billowing behind her, she darted through the crowd of servants and peasants who were gathering up scythes and pitchforks to use as weapons. Burning cinders stung her face, her hands, but she barely noticed. Beyond the massive stone curtain wall that guarded the castle's perimeter, she could hear the metallic crash of blades and lances, war hammers and shields.

The war was ending. With the enemy victorious.

She felt each blow as if it pierced her own heart. After seven years of battle, the Thuringians had come within striking distance of the palace itself. And the men of Châlons could not hold back Prince Daemon's ruthless mercenaries for long. Her father and his knights were outnumbered five to one.

Dear God, please protect them. Please watch over him.

Her eyes and throat burning, she kept running, past the storage sheds and granary, their thatched roofs ablaze; past the stables and mews where milkmaids and serving women were trying to rescue the castle's valuable animals. She circled around the keep toward the front, choking on the sharp taste of pure fear.

When she reached the main gate, she found herself in the middle of a deafening tumult. Guardsmen and archers thronged the parapets, rushing up and down scaling ladders, carrying weapons and torches and cauldrons of some sort, their leaders shouting commands. The night blazed with firelight, so bright that the billowing smoke from the forest beyond glowed eerily, like a dragon's breath.

She searched for one particular face among the mail-clad warriors, felt a stab of panic when she did not see—

"Saints' blood!" a familiar male voice boomed from behind her. "What do you think you are *doing* out here?"

Ciara turned to see her brother atop one of the towers that flanked the drawbridge, and she exhaled in relief. As he came down from his position and stalked toward her, his tone and his mien had warriors scrambling to get out of his way. "I told you to stay inside!"

"I *was* inside, Christophe. But I could see the fire from my chamber window, and I thought I should—"

"Disobey my commands as quickly as possible, and walk into the middle of a battle?" He came to a halt barely a foot away, towering over her. "Without consulting me?"

Ciara almost gulped. At twenty-three, Christophe was four years older and a full foot taller than she was. He made a most imposing presence, wearing his chain mail, his helm, and his most severe scowl.

"I *am* consulting you," she pointed out, rushing onward before he could interrupt. "I cannot remain in my chamber with my books and my music while everyone else defends the palace against the enemy. I came to see what you would wish me to do."

"I wish you to go back inside the keep. At once."

She darted aside when he tried to take her elbow. "I cannot *help* anyone if I am inside," she insisted, thinking that should be obvious, even to a male brain. When he reached for her again, she grabbed his arm instead, lowering her voice so that only he could hear. "And I will not sit by and do naught while our kingdom comes down around our ears."

"By God's breath, Ciara, if I have to lock you in a tower—"

A barrage of arrows interrupted his threat, singing over their heads and striking the dirt with lethal-sounding *thwacks* just inches away. Christophe grabbed her and pushed her toward the curtain wall as the bailey erupted in battle cries and curses—and several shouts of pain.

"You foolish girl, do you see now?" He flattened her against the stone, protecting her with his broad-shouldered body as more arrows rained down from the sky. "This is not a game! And it is no place for a woman. You must go back inside where it is safe."

Ciara could not reply, her heart pounding so hard it seemed to fill her throat and block her breath. She stared past him to the spot where a quartet of sharp-pointed shafts protruded from the ground.

The very spot where she had been standing seconds ago.

An instant later she heard a great roar—the sound of dozens of ancient pine trees snapping like twigs—and knew that one of the castle's most important defenses was gone.

The forest where she and her brother had played as children was being reduced to ashes.

"Christophe," she whispered brokenly, "there *is* no safe place. Not anymore."

He remained silent, not bothering with false words of reassurance. They both knew it was true.

A second later, he abandoned royal protocol and hugged her tight, in full view of their subjects. Closing her eyes, Ciara buried her face against his silk surcoat and let the tears come, not caring that his chain mail bit into her cheek.

For a moment, in the midst of the fire and desperation and despair, there was only the two of them. Not prince and princess, but brother and sister. Afraid and in need of the comfort that only love could bring.

"God's mercy, Christophe," she said tearfully, "Father is out there. If the enemy has gotten this close, it must mean that he and his men—"

"Nay, little sparrow, do not underestimate our father. He is one of the two most brilliant military tacticians ever born in Châlons. He knows he can elude them. That is why he insisted I…"

He did not finish, but Ciara knew what he had been about to say. She had heard the heated argument between her father and brother yestereve, when they had clashed over which of them should go forth with the palace's knights. Father had ordered Christophe to stay behind, where he would be safer.

As heir to the throne, he was too valuable to risk.

"We are not finished yet," Christophe said fiercely, his arms tightening around her. "Our ancestors built this castle on the most inaccessible peak in the heart of Châlons for a reason. In three hundred years, no enemy has breached these walls, and none ever will."

"But no enemy has ever come so close," Ciara whispered.

As if to underscore her words, the sounds of the battle on the mountainside grew louder. She could hear the war cries now. And the screams of the wounded and the dying.

Several leaders of the palace guard came running up to ask for orders, and Christophe gently set her away from him. Ciara turned her face toward the wall, wiping at her tears. They both knew they had to conceal their own fear and uncertainty, had to provide a brave, calm example for their subjects.

Christophe addressed his men, his deep voice crackling with authority once more. "I want you and you to go to the rear of the castle, gather up everyone who is still outside, and get them into the keep. If any of the men back there can wield a weapon, send them to me." He motioned one of the other warriors forward. "Escort the princess to her chamber and see that she—"

"Christophe, you are the heir to the throne. Father was right." Ciara placed her hand on his arm as she glanced at the night sky, which now glowed red on all sides of the castle.

Her heart pounded wildly. "You are much more important than I. You are the one who should be escorted to safety. I will go, as you wish, but I beg of you to come with me."

"Nay, Ciara. My duty is here. I must see to the gate and the drawbridge. That is the first place they will attack."

Their gazes met, his light brown eyes, so much like her own, reflecting the full depth of his love and concern for her.

"Be off now, my little songbird," he murmured, using one of his favorite nicknames for her and tugging lightly at the long braid that hung down her back. "Châlons has only one princess."

"And she has only one brother," Ciara whispered desperately.

Suddenly the ground shook, so violently it knocked her off her feet. It felt as if the mountain were a sleeping giant that had just awakened.

"What was *that?*" she cried.

Christophe uttered a vicious oath. "Catapults. Sweet Jesus, they are attacking the gate with catapults. How in the name of all that is holy did they get them up the slope?" He reached down and grabbed her arm, pulling her to her feet, turning to the guardsmen. "Back to your posts. *Now.* I will see the princess to safety myself."

"But Christophe—"

"No more arguments, Ciara. Do you know what Daemon's mercenaries will *do* to you if they capture you?"

The images that filled her head at his words were enough to silence her.

Holding fast to her arm, he ran along the curtain wall, staying out of reach of the arrows that now rained down among the searing ashes in a deadly storm. Ciara looked back over her shoulder, at the towers that supported the gatehouse. "Why can we not get inside that way?"

"Because the drawbridge towers have all been sealed from the inside," he explained tightly, "so that each can be defended like a miniature keep. A trick I learned from the second of Châlons' most brilliant military tacticians—my old friend Royce."

A hail of arrows thwacked into the dirt in front of them and Christophe yanked her to a halt. "I only wish he were here now," he added under his breath.

Ciara barely remembered her brother's best friend, except that he had disappeared suddenly and mysteriously four years ago. But she did not have time to ask any more questions, for Christophe led her across the open bailey at a dead run, heading straight for a mural tower at the rear of the keep.

They reached it safely, and he tore open the door that led inside. "Go to the secret chamber in the east wing, Ciara. Seal it behind you."

She nodded, trying to summon a brave look and failing utterly.

He brushed a cinder from her cheek and tucked a loose strand of her brown hair back behind her ear. "There will be peace, Ciara, I promise you. One day this will be my kingdom, and I swear that Châlons will know peace and freedom once more." He hugged her again, tightly.

She did not want to let him go. But he had his duty to attend to, and she…

She could do naught but hide and hope. And pray.

Releasing her, he gave her a brief smile before he turned and ran back across the bailey, into the fire-ravaged night, heading toward the front of the palace.

"God be with you, Christophe." She watched with her heart in her throat as he circled along the inside of the curtain wall, trying to stay beyond the reach of the arrows.

Then suddenly the ground shook again. And this time a whole section of wall gave way.

With Christophe beneath it.

She stared in mute horror, seeing it happen by the unearthly light of the fire that painted the night bloodred. Rock and mortar rained down on him. It was over in the span of a heartbeat. One moment her brother was there, the next he was gone. Simply gone.

Buried beneath a crushing mass of shattered stone.

"Christophe!" she screamed, leaving her place of safety, running across the bailey, crying out his name again and again.

She was halfway across the open ground when Prince Daemon's mercenaries came swarming through the breach.

Chapter 1

Alone in her father's solar, Ciara huddled deep in a corner of the stone window seat, an open book in her lap, a single tallow candle flickering beside her. Bright winter moonlight gleamed through the stained glass, spilling a pattern of blues and reds and greens across her velvet skirts and the rush-strewn floor.

Slipping off her jeweled coronet, she rested her forehead against the window, her breath fogging the frosted panes. Through one of the clear triangles of glass, she could see the mountainside stretching away into the darkness, the stars sparkling on a fresh blanket of snow...and the newly repaired curtain wall.

The stonemasons had finished it only days ago, after four months of work. They had affixed a small brass cross to mark where Christophe…

A sob escaped her, welling up from a place so deep, it seemed to come from the very center of her heart. Or what was left of her heart.

Looking at the bailey as it was now, she could almost believe that the castle had never been touched by war. That she and her father had not been captured by the enemy, had never spent a month as prisoners in their own palace.

That no lives had been lost here.

She rubbed at her eyes, letting her garnet-studded crown slip from her fingers. She had no tears left to cry. The grounds below looked so peaceful now, every stone restored to the way it had once been. Every drop of blood scoured clean.

But there was no way to change what had happened. No denying the truth of what her father had shouted at her when told of his only son's death: she *was* in part to blame for what had happened.

And she had no escape from the destiny that had been decided for her.

A knock sounded at the door. Startled, she glanced toward the thick oak portal that separated the spacious meeting chamber from the great hall. Then she turned her back and remained silent, deciding to ignore the summons. No one could know she was here. She had not lit the torches that flanked the door, or the fire in the hearth. And she had locked the door behind her, wanting to be alone this night.

For this was the last night she would spend here, in the only home she had ever known.

"Princess?" a soft feminine voice called. The knock sounded again, as insistent as the woman's tone. "Princess? Are you in there?"

Ciara sighed, recognizing that voice. Normally, she would not respond to an intrusion by a servant, but she knew that any hope of solitude was finished now that her lady's maid had set out to find her. Miriam knew all her favorite hiding places. And she would be as relentless as a mother hen rounding up a lost chick.

Setting her book down beside the flickering candle, leaving her crown in the rushes, Ciara rose and crossed the vast chamber. She threw the bolt and pulled on the heavy iron ring, opening the door just a crack. Just enough to admit a slice of light and music and mingled spicy aromas that poured in from the great hall—gingered rabbit and steamed cinnamon custard and pheasant roasted with violets. The sounds and scents of a grand feast.

Of her betrothal party.

"Good eventide, Miriam." Ciara blinked in the brightness.

Miriam dropped into a deep curtsy. "I should have known this was where you would be." Rising, she smiled, her expression, like her voice, gentle and concerned. Her generous height put her eye to eye with Ciara, and though she was eight years older, she could pass for the same age.

But the similarities between them ended there, for Miriam was blond and strikingly beautiful. "Nose-deep in a book, no doubt?"

Nodding, Ciara stepped back from the entrance to admit the serving woman. "Did my father send you to find me?"

Miriam hesitated for a telltale moment. "Well, he…that is—"

"Nay, do not lie to save my feelings," Ciara said tonelessly, turning away. The less her father saw her of late, the happier he was.

His shouted accusations still rang out in her memory. *If you had not been so stubborn, if you had heeded my wishes, if you had listened to Christophe, if…*

If. The word had been like a dagger in her heart for four months.

"Your Highness…" Closing the door, Miriam followed her into the chamber. "It is his majesty's many concerns of state that have kept him from you these past weeks. The negotiations with Thuringia, the signing of the peace accord, the repairs to the palace…"

And he has not forgiven me, Ciara thought, reclaiming her place beside the solar's huge stained-glass window. *He will never forgive me.*

Nodding, saying naught, she ran one hand over the worn stone of the window seat. It seemed much smaller than it had when she was a child.

When she was four, after her mother had died in childbirth, her father used to spend hours with her here. Sometimes cuddling her in his lap. Sometimes telling her stories or performing magic tricks.

Sometimes simply holding her while she cried.

A single tear formed on her lashes. She and her father had gradually grown distant over the years, as she had grown from child to young woman.

And now it was clear that Christophe's death had built a wall between them that could not be crossed.

"I am sure you are right, Miriam," she whispered,

blinking the dampness away. "He has many concerns that require his attention. Especially the plans for my departure on the morrow. My wedding to Prince Daemon."

Her gaze fell to her gold coronet gleaming on the floor. Daemon had demanded her hand as part of the terms of surrender. Royal advisors on both sides of the border had agreed that their marriage would be the best way to seal the fragile new peace agreement. Ciara had not been consulted.

But she had offered no resistance.

"Your Highness…" Miriam started to say something more, then held her tongue and turned away, moving to the unlit hearth. "Do you not find it rather cold in here, Princess Ciara?" she asked lightly. "You must take care not to fall ill. We've a long journey ahead of us."

"Aye, we have," Ciara replied numbly. Miriam was being prudent, remembering her place, as a proper servant should.

Staring at her discarded crown, Ciara thought of how often the royal tutors had scolded *her* for forgetting her place. A princess, they had lectured endlessly, must be regal and dignified and proper at all times. A shining example for her subjects to follow.

But she had never felt particularly shiny. And tonight more than ever, she longed to be a woman like any other, free of royal rules and restrictions.

Free to confess how frightened and inadequate and alone she felt.

Glancing up, she realized that Miriam had returned to her side. The older woman was waiting to speak until spoken to. As was proper.

"Miriam?"

"Your Highness…" Miriam reached out as if to place a comforting hand on Ciara's shoulder, then stopped herself.

Ciara swallowed hard, reminded again that her place set her apart and above, isolated from everyone around her. Even Miriam.

By law, commoners were forbidden to touch her royal person.

Miriam clasped her hands in front of her and glanced toward the door, as if to make sure it was still closed, that they were still alone. Then her voice dropped to a whisper. "Your Highness, I have served you for six years now, and I care a great deal about your happiness. I wish you to know that you do not have to do this."

"Take part in the betrothal celebration?" Ciara looked at the door with a sigh. She could still hear the merry music of harps and drums and viols on the other side. "Nay, I should return to the festivities. I have been gone more than an hour."

"Princess, I do not speak of the betrothal celebration. I speak of your marriage to Prince Daemon."

Ciara's head snapped around. "What?"

"Everyone has been talking of the peace accord. There are…rumors."

"What sort of rumors?"

"Of loyal subjects who wish to fight on," Miriam whispered quickly. "Of men who are making plans even now."

God's breath, it could not be true! Ciara sat up sharply. "Nay, Daemon would crush them. He would kill every last man at the first sign of rebellion. And punish their women and children in the bargain. What could they hope to…" Her racing thoughts calmed just as quickly. "Miriam, you *know* there are always rumors in the palace. They fly about and then evaporate like mountain mist in a strong wind."

"Aye, Your Highness. And I have no evidence that this is aught more than male bluster. But if it is true…" She cast another nervous look at the door. "I could spirit you out of the castle. Now. This night. You need not marry Prince Daemon. You need not leave Châlons at all."

Ciara gaped at her in shock. *Escape?* The possibility dangled before her like a sparkling gem on a golden chain, urging her to reach out and take it.

But after a moment, she slowly shook her head, her decision unchanged. "It is for the good of Châlons and my subjects that I go. Our people have been strained to their limits. Our supplies are low. Our knights are exhausted"—her voice dropped to a whisper—"and the king is undone with grief." She shut her eyes tightly. "We *cannot* fight on. Under the circumstances, we should be grateful that Prince Daemon's terms were lenient."

"But, Your Highness, have you not heard the tales of Daemon's greed? His ruthlessness? It is said that he had his own mistress stripped and beaten to death in front of his men when she pilfered but a few coins from him."

"Aye, I have heard." Ciara shuddered at the frightening image, one of many that had haunted both her waking hours and her nightmares. A year ago, when she had heard of that particular bit of cruelty, she had pitied Daemon's poor victim, pitied any woman who fell into his clutches.

Never realizing that she would soon be one of them. His bride. Bound to him for the rest of her life.

She stood abruptly. Miriam rose with her, dipping into a curtsy.

Ciara paced into the darkness of the room and back again, rubbing her hands up and down her arms. It was not the lack of a fire on the hearth that caused a deep chill to settle over her.

She returned to the window, looking out into the night, searching for something solid to hold on to. Something to strengthen her resolve.

Her gaze fell on the newly repaired curtain wall. The bronze cross gleaming in the moonlight. And she remembered her brother's last words to her.

I swear that Châlons will know peace and freedom once more.

It was up to her to make his final wish come true. She pressed her hand against the glass as if she could reach up to Heaven and touch his face.

For you, Christophe. For you.

"My brother," she said at last, fighting to keep her voice steady, "gave his life for his country, Miriam. Compared to that, is my sacrifice so great?" She stared down at the single candle she had lit. "After seven years of war, peace has come at last to our kingdom…and this marriage is mayhap the only way to secure it. To end all the suffering and death, to forge a lasting bond between Châlons and Thuringia. As my father pointed out, our children—"

Her and Daemon's children, she thought with a sickening lurch of her stomach.

"—will one day rule both countries as one." She could feel the darkness of the chamber closing in around her, like the black embrace of an unseen demon. "I have no choice."

Both of them fell into a long silence.

Miriam broke it first, in a shameless breach of etiquette, her voice choked with emotion. "You are very brave, Princess Ciara."

Ciara closed her eyes, knowing she did not deserve the praise. She was not brave. Not at all. At the moment, she was thankful Miriam stood no nearer—else she would surely hear Ciara's heart pounding.

But she must not think of herself, of her own fears…or her own happiness. She must fulfill her duty. Her responsibility.

For the first time in her life, she must live up to the title of princess.

"At least the journey will be enjoyable," Ciara said, turning to face her lady's maid, trying to muster some of her usual optimism. "When the wedding procession leaves at dawn, it will be the first time I have been allowed to venture beyond the palace since the war began. I will at last have the chance to *see* the world that I have only been able to read about since I was twelve." She gestured toward her book.

"Indeed, Your Highness," Miriam said warmly. "And mayhap we will find that Prince Daemon has changed. Thus far, he *has* been true to his word. You and the king were well treated during your imprisonment. And his mercenaries have been withdrawn from our lands."

"Mayhap victory has made him chivalrous." Ciara nodded, trying to believe it. "But as you said, Miriam, we've a long journey ahead of us on the morrow. I must have some sleep this night, if I am to look my best." *To please my father*, she added to herself. "Go and tell Alcina to prepare my chamber. I would say my farewells to the guests and seek my bed anon."

Miriam dipped into a low curtsy. "All will be well, Princess Ciara. I am certain of it." With her blond head bowed, Ciara could not make out her expression in the darkness, but as she rose, Ciara caught the glimmer of tears in those blue eyes. "I will remember you in my prayers tonight, milady. Good eventide."

She left to carry out Ciara's instructions, thoughtfully closing the door behind her.

Ciara remained where she was a moment, touched by Miriam's concern. Then she bent down to pick up the slim volume she had left in the corner. It fell open to a well-worn page, a favorite poem by Marie de France called "The Nightingale." The gilt letters glistened eerily in the moonlight.

Drops of blood ran down and spread
Over the bodice of her dress.
He left her alone in her distress.
Weeping, she held the bird and thought
With bitter rage of those who brought
The nightingale to death, betrayed
By all the hidden traps they laid…

Straightening, Ciara paused a moment, running her fingers over the familiar lines, words that spoke of intrigue and betrayal. She wondered whether she should tell someone of the rumor Miriam had mentioned. Of the rebels who might be plotting some sort of mad counterattack against Daemon. The tale might be mere rumor. False. Harmless.

Or it might be true.

Closing the book, she decided to mention it to Sir Braden, one of her father's most trusted advisers, on the morrow before she left. He would know what to make of it. Leaning down, she blew out the candle she had lit.

She was halfway to the door when she realized she had left her coronet behind. Turning with a whispered oath, she went back to the window, knelt down, and started fishing through the rushes for it.

When her fingers finally encountered the slim, jewel-studded circlet, she realized it had gotten dented when she dropped it. "By all the saints," she muttered under her breath, trying to bend the rim back into shape. "Now Father will think me careless as well as—"

A sound on the far side of the chamber startled her and she froze.

Turning only her head, she peered into the blackness, almost certain she had heard the door open. But the chamber remained utterly dark, silent. It must have been a mouse scrabbling through the ancient walls. Surely no one would dare enter the king's solar without knocking. "Is someone there?"

No one answered. And she could see no movement in the darkness.

But even as she rose, even as she told herself she was being foolish, she heard the sound again—and 'twas no mouse.

"Who are you?" she cried, backing away until her spine came up against the hard stone of the wall. "I demand that you answer me!"

"Do not fear, milady."

It was a male voice. Quiet. Rasping. The accent was that of an uneducated peasant. Her heart slowed. It must be some servant from the feast. Mayhap the knave was inebriated and looking for a garderobe. "Do you realize where you are, sirrah? You have wandered into the king's solar."

He did not reply.

And she heard him moving closer.

Her heart started to pound again. Faster. He stood

between her and the door. The only exit. And she could still hear music being played in the great hall.

So loud that no one would hear her if she screamed.

"Heed me well, whoever you may be," she snapped, forcing any hint of fear from her voice, "do you have *any* idea who I am?"

"Aye, Princess."

Icy claws of fear sank into her middle. Her thoughts started to race. She slid along the wall, away from the window, into the shadows. *What should she do?*

"I am sorry for the intrusion, Your Highness," he murmured in that gravel-rough voice, only a few paces from her now, close enough that she could make out his burly shape.

"What do you want?" She felt behind her for a truncheon, a weapon. Something. Anything.

All she had was the slender book in one hand and the dented crown in her other.

He was almost upon her. "I am not going to hurt you. I give you my word."

Ciara darted past him, drawing breath to scream. But he was faster.

He caught her and pinned her to the wall, covering her mouth with one beefy hand.

"I am sorry, Princess." His breath felt hot on her cheek. "But trying to make peace with Daemon is like trying to make peace with the plague. If we give him the chance, he will kill us all anon. We cannot allow this marriage to take place. And there can be no wedding…if there is no bride."

Ciara's lungs burned for air. Her mind screamed in denial. *He meant to kill her.*

She struggled against him, fighting with all her strength.

He raised his other hand, revealing a long knife that shone silver-bright in the moonlight. "Your Highness—"

Some instinct burst through her confusion. With a quick twist of her hand, she turned the spiky top of her coronet toward him—and jabbed it into his side.

He cried out in surprise and pain, releasing her mouth for one crucial instant.

"Help me!" Ciara shouted, pushing him off with a furious shove, lunging toward the door. "Someone help—"

He was upon her before she could run two paces. One powerful hand caught her by the shoulder and spun her around. Screaming, she struck out at him, then saw the blade in his other hand. She flung up her arm to ward it off.

And felt the knife bite into her, sharp and shocking, felt it slice through skin and muscle. Felt her own blood, hot as fire as it flowed down her arm.

Then her legs crumpled beneath her and she was falling, blinded and deafened by terror as the rush-strewn floor raced up to meet her. Some part of her mind was distantly aware of the door opening, light spilling into the room, someone shouting her name…the sound strangely faint, as if it came from far away.

And then blackness darkened the world and she knew no more.

Chapter 2

Only a monk or a mountain goat would willingly climb a peak such as this, Royce Saint-Michel thought, reining his destrier to a halt at the foot of the icy trail. Squinting in the glaring sunlight, he glanced upward and grimaced. Despite the fact that he had been born and raised in these Alpine slopes, he was no mountain goat.

And he was certainly no monk.

He pushed back the hood of his sable-lined mantle, lifting one gloved hand to shade his eyes as he studied the narrow path that twisted through the rocks. It rose at an impossibly steep angle and vanished into the clouds. He muttered an oath, his breath white in the bitterly cold air.

Somewhere above, his destination awaited. An ancient abbey. A place of peace, refuge, charity, absolution.

He knew that none of those blessings awaited him here. Had known it long before he crossed the border into Châlons this morning.

And as he assessed the treacherous climb with an expert eye, the knot in his gut—the one that had been there since he left France a se'nnight ago—tightened another notch. For a moment, he almost gave in to the impulse to turn his stallion and leave. Forget this madness. Ignore the urgent summons he had received.

But he had come too far to turn back now.

His horse shifted beneath him, whickering softly, more accustomed to action and battle than patience and caution. Like his master.

"Easy, Anteros," Royce murmured, patting the animal's dark flank. "It would appear you are staying behind, unless you sprout wings." He swung one leg over the destrier's broad back, adding under his breath, "This is one skirmish I must face alone."

He dismounted into the ankle-deep snow, every tired, sore muscle in his body protesting painfully. His movements slowed by the bone-chilling cold, he began unfastening the saddle and the supplies he had brought along, cursing himself for coming here. For having too little restraint and too much curiosity.

For responding to a missive that, by all rights, he should have torn into bits and burned into cinders.

He still carried it in his tunic—badly wrinkled from having been crumpled into a ball and smoothed out several times. *Your country has need of you*, it said.

That was all. No explanation, naught but those six words, followed by directions to this place. He would have thought it a jest, if not for the wax seal affixed to the parchment scroll.

He had thought never to see that mark again. Not as long as he lived.

It was the mark of a man who had once, long ago, been his commander and his liege lord. A man who had been like a father to him after he lost his own.

The man who had later turned on him and taken from him all he held dear.

Royce spat on the ground, but the taste of bitterness had been with him too long. It would not be chased from his tongue. Or from his soul.

Jaw clenched, he focused his attention on his task, his fingers nearly numb, his motions quick, angry. He removed Anteros's saddle, then opened the pack of supplies he had hastily assembled in France, withdrawing the items he would need for the climb: ropes; a special pair of boots he had designed, old and worn but still useful; a pickax; and a flask of wine—for warmth, he told himself, not for courage.

He also took out a pair of slender, curved Persian knives to accompany the Spanish sword at his waist. He never went anywhere without a concealed weapon or two. Especially when walking into a situation that held so many unknowns.

What could his former liege lord want with him? Why meet in this isolated place, in such a remote corner of Châlons?

And why the urgency? The note, though terse and mysterious, had been explicit on one point: if he was coming, he was to hasten with all speed and arrive within a se'nnight. An impossible task, to complete such a journey in so short a time.

But Royce had done it.

And now he faced an equally impossible climb.

Still exactly the same, the old cur, Royce thought, his mouth curving downward as he glanced up at the steep path. *Demanding, unreasonable.*

After a second, his memory added a third word: *unforgiving.*

Some men never changed.

Tying the pack of supplies closed, Royce straightened and led Anteros to a sheltered place behind an outcropping of rock, away from the wind. He scattered a small sackful of oats across the snow and dropped the reins to the ground. The well-trained destrier would need no other urging to stay here until his master returned.

As he changed into his old climbing boots, Royce tried not to notice how the air seemed clearer in these familiar mountains, the sky above a brighter blue, the scent of pine sweeter. All day, he had tried to ignore how right it felt to be here. To be *home.*

He swallowed past the lump that filled his throat. It would do no good to torment himself with hopes of returning. His homeland had become forbidden ground to him.

On the day he was banished in disgrace.

And if Aldric had meant to offer pardon or reprieve, he would have said as much in his missive. Instead, he had issued orders. Demands. And cunningly used six simple words he knew Royce could not ignore.

Your country has need of you.

Slinging the rope over his shoulder, Royce set off toward the path that led upward into the clouds, rubbing one gloved hand over his stubbled jaw. After seven days of travel, with little sleep and less attention to his appearance, he was hardly fit for an audience with royalty.

But that pleased him. 'Twould do well for Aldric to know from the start that he was not the same brash youth who had left four years ago, at the age of three-and-twenty. Being forced to make his way as a commoner, to live by his wits and his blade, to eke out a living as a mercenary or guardsman had a way of changing a man.

Slowly, Royce's frown curved upward into an unrepentant grin. In truth, some part of him was eager for this meeting, had longed for it during the years of exile. He had a few things to say to his former king.

And he looked forward to something else as well.

Mayhap, if the prince had accompanied his father to this isolated abbey, Royce would have the chance to see his old friend Christophe again.

His boots made no sound on the worn stone of the abbey's courtyard, since he wore no spurs; 'twas an honor reserved for knights alone. Even after all these years, Royce had not grown used to the absence of that sound, the familiar *ting* that had once accompanied his every step.

The monks awaited him, appearing out of the mist like a gaggle of small brown geese. They had no doubt seen him battling his way up the ice-slick mountain. He had made the ascent in a little less than three hours, despite his fatigue, earning a few bruises and a cut in his palm along the way.

The brothers gathered around him, one of them taking his climbing gear while the others ushered him through a battered oak door. He had to duck to follow them, straightening to his full height inside a cramped entry hall that smelled of incense and dampness and age. The door slowly creaked shut behind them, cutting off the sunlight. And the rest of the world.

It took a moment for his eyes to adjust. A clutch of candles flickered on a table to one side, huddled beneath a statue of some saint or other, offering little light and less warmth. From a distant chamber, the sound of monotone male voices filled the frosty air with ethereal music.

The entire place seemed steeped in holiness, purity, virtue. He felt as out of place as a fire-breathing dragon among soft, fluffy sheep.

One of the brothers came forward with a pitcher of water and a strip of cloth to tend his injured hand, but Royce waved him away impatiently. "Where is the king?"

None of the half-dozen men around him answered. Apparently this was an order devoted to silence, for they used gestures rather than words to indicate that he must first remove his weapons before they would allow him farther into their sanctuary.

He complied without argument. In a matter of minutes, his sword and knife, used in countless battles against faceless enemies, nestled on the table amid the neatly arranged candles, as if seeking some sort of benediction from the holy relics. He also surrendered his flask, though a bit more grudgingly.

He saw no reason to mention the second Persian dagger hidden in his boot.

Satisfied, the placid-looking men nodded among themselves, then led him through a door at the far end of the entry hall. He trailed them down one dark, cool corridor after another, the low music of the chants following everywhere, mingling on the air with the scent of bread baking for the evening meal.

Finally, they brought him to what appeared to be a large chamber, motioning him to enter, nodding pleasantly before they slipped away to go about their silent business.

Royce paused a moment, assaulted by memories of the last time he had seen Aldric. And by the sudden twisting of the knot in his stomach.

But he was not a man to give in to second thoughts. He gripped the iron ring, drew a deep breath, and pushed the door open.

It was the monks' vast dining hall, dark but for a single torch by the door and a scattering of candles that glimmered on tables here and there, empty but for a solitary figure standing on the far side of the chamber. A man half concealed by shadows. Tall, imposing. Familiar.

Royce took a single step forward. It occurred to him that he should bow. The old training, instilled from childhood, was so much a part of him that he nearly did. But he stopped himself, quelled the impulse.

He owed no man homage and fealty. Not anymore.

Especially not this one.

"Your Majesty." His voice echoed strangely across the stark, undecorated chamber. "Against my better judgment, I have come in answer to your summons." He kicked the door closed with his heel.

Aldric remained in the shadows. "So I see." The deep, regal voice held an edge of affront. Or anger. "And I see also that your time away has made you forget your manners."

Your time away. The pretty phrasing made Royce's jaw clench. "In many of the places I have been, a man has little use for manners."

"You are in Châlons now. Men here know the proper way to address a king."

"You are no longer my king," Royce shot back. "And if you think I will fall to my knees and kiss the hem of your robes and beg forgiveness, you are mistaken."

"If your anger has cooled so little in four years, why did you come at all, Ferrano?"

Royce fell silent, the name and Aldric's attitude striking a sharp double blow. How could the old cur expect years of exile to *cool* his resentment? And how could Aldric, of all people, address him by the old title? "Saint-Michel," he corrected. "That other name is old and forgotten. And I almost did *not* come. Your missive said little."

"Yet in spite of that"—a familiar, cunning tone crept into Aldric's voice—"here you are."

"What have I to lose?" Royce demanded hotly. "A man who possesses naught risks naught. I could turn and walk out that door anytime. Mayhap now." He clenched his fists, ignoring the pain in his slashed palm. "But first I would know what purpose you had in asking me here."

Aldric came forward, slowly, closing the distance between them one measured step at a time. Royce saw no welcome in the old man's eyes. No sign of relief, no thank-God-you-are-here expression.

And certainly no hint of forgiveness.

By nails and blood, had he truly hoped he *might* see any of that? Was he that much a fool? How could he have expected aught but this: disapproval.

Yet the old wound opened. And old questions struck like a hail of arrows. What right did Aldric have to judge him so harshly? To hold him to impossibly high standards and then find him lacking? Royce was merely a man like other men. Flawed and imperfect—

All thought of himself abruptly stilled as the king came fully into the light. Royce could see him clearly at last.

And what he saw hit him like a war hammer.

Old was the word that leaped to his mind. Old and haggard and spent. Too many years of war had taken a horrible toll. Aldric's frame looked almost gaunt beneath his royal robes. His face, once as craggy and solid as the mountains he ruled, and tanned by Châlons' bright sunlight, had become pale, deeply lined, his skin sagging loosely from his cheekbones. Naught remained of the man Royce remembered—except the regal bearing and the fierce blue eyes.

It was almost enough to make him bow, grant the courtesy that he had denied. Saints' blood, it was almost enough to send him to his knees.

But he instantly quelled that impulse as well. Aldric

would loathe pity even more than he loathed defiance. Any gesture of respect now would be met with scorn.

Besides, he reminded himself, any respect they had felt for each other had been demolished four years ago.

So he fought to keep his face impassive and merely dropped his gaze, unable to bear looking at this man he had once so admired.

Aldric stopped a few paces away. "You ask my purpose in summoning you here. Does that mean you have not heard that our war with Thuringia ended?"

Royce shrugged. "I have heard that it ended, naught more. I have not made it my habit to seek out news of Châlons." That was an understatement. "And it is not *my* war." He lifted his head, shot an accusing glare into those blue eyes. "I have no family left here. No lands. No position. No connection at all. Châlons and its battles are no longer any concern of mine."

"If that were true, you would not be standing before me. You endured a brutal journey and an ascent up this peak that would have killed many men. Even men of Châlons." A certain satisfied gleam came into Aldric's eyes. "And I said naught of reward or pardon, only that your country has need of you." He glanced at Royce's injured hand. "It would appear you are still willing to spill your blood in service to your homeland, Saint-Michel. You cannot pretend that you do not care."

Royce turned away, hating that he had no skill at hiding his feelings, despising the twinge of hope that went through him upon hearing the word *pardon*.

He picked up a battered wooden goblet from a nearby trestle table and turned it round in his fingers, wishing—not for the first time—that he possessed Aldric's stoicism. He usually found it impossible to tell what the king was thinking or feeling. He himself, on the other hand, tended to be as transparent as glass.

That was one of the last remaining legacies of his clan. No one had ever accused a Ferrano of being reserved or subdued. He had grown up surrounded by unruly brothers, giggling sisters, parents deeply in love and unafraid to show it.

And he was still too blasted emotional.

"I am curious, Your Majesty," he said, struggling to keep his tone neutral, "to know how *you* managed the ascent up this peak."

"I did not have to. There is another way into the abbey, a secret tunnel through the mountain."

Royce set the cup down a bit too sharply. "You might have mentioned that to me."

"I could not risk revealing such information in my letter. The missive could have fallen into the wrong hands." The king paused. "And I needed to make certain you were equal to the task I have in mind. I needed you to—"

"Prove myself." He spun to face his former liege lord. "Of course. I am relieved that I did not disappoint you. *This* time. And now that you have tested both my loyalty and my stamina, mayhap you would tell me what this 'task' is. The situation must indeed be desperate for you to stoop so low as to call upon me."

"It concerns the peace agreement with Thuringia."

Royce choked out a strangled laugh, his mind and memory reeling with disbelief. "Surely you do not intend to involve me in the peace negotiations—"

"Nay, the agreement was reached soon after the war ended. The arrangements have all been made."

He said it with such finality that Royce fell silent for a moment, a seed of foreboding planted in his heart. "And how *did* the war end?" He searched the older man's face, seeking some hint of the truth. "Did Daemon finally decide it was too costly, and retreat to spend his gold elsewhere?"

"Nay, he did not." Aldric's voice deepened, as if weighted down by the words he spoke. "He succeeded. It is we who have been forced to negotiate our surrender."

Royce flinched and took a step backward, an icy rain of shock washing through him. He tried to steel himself against it, to tell himself this was none of his concern. Tried to convince himself he felt naught for Châlons and its troubles.

But the pain was undeniable. The word *surrender* and the images of defeat it brought pierced the wall he had built around his heart.

"Sweet Christ," he choked out at last. "That cannot…how…"

"Mercenaries," Aldric explained tonelessly. "Daemon must have all but emptied his treasury. He assembled a force of ruthless barbarians hired from every dank hole on the continent. They breached the palace walls—"

Royce uttered a particularly vivid oath.

"And there is more. During the battle for the palace—" Aldric halted abruptly, a shadow passing over his face. He shook his head, then finally went on. "I thought you knew of this, Saint-Michel. I would have informed you in my missive, had I known that you were unaware." His voice deepened even more. "Prince Christophe is dead."

Royce felt as if the mountain had just shifted beneath his feet. "Mercy of God, *nay!*" he shouted in horror and denial. Unable to draw breath, he shut his eyes, images of his old friend—his best friend—careening through his head, only to be cut suddenly short.

Christophe was dead. The palace had fallen. Daemon was victorious.

Royce felt behind him for the trestle table and leaned on it with one hand, realizing he was shaking. He raked his other hand through his hair. If he had been here, if he had been able to do his usual reconnaissance, plot strategy with Christophe…

Aldric continued speaking, his voice quiet. "His death was not in vain. He was killed escorting his sister to safety."

"And where is Daemon now?" Royce asked through clenched teeth, murder brewing in his soul.

"In Thuringia."

Royce glanced up, confused. "He did not claim the palace for his own?"

"Nay. He insists he has no interest in it. He demanded only two-thirds of my holdings, our homage and fealty…and my daughter's hand in marriage." The king drew his ermine-lined robes more closely around him and turned away. "He awaits the arrival of his betrothed even now."

Royce straightened, stunned by this piece of news. How could Aldric hand over his daughter to a man like Daemon? Especially when Christophe had died trying to *save* her from the enemy?

But he held his tongue and did not ask the question. For he knew the answer.

Duty, crown, and country were everything to Aldric.

Everything.

But the older man seemed to sense what Royce was thinking. "She agreed to the match," he said, answering the question that had not been asked, as he studied a crucifix on the far wall. "And we had no choice. Daemon could have killed every last one of our subjects. He still may."

"But you said that a peace agreement had been reached."

"Aye, but it is yet fragile. There have been skirmishes between our people and his. The wounds of the past seven years are deep. They will not be quickly forgotten. Tempers are dangerously short."

Royce exhaled a harsh breath. "And Daemon's is no doubt the shortest of all."

Aldric nodded. "The wedding must take place soon, to seal the accord between our two countries. To cool the fires of war and make everyone see that"—he halted again—"that Châlons and Thuringia are now…one. In peace."

The king fell silent. Royce leaned back against the trestle table, his gaze on the floor as he absorbed all he had been told. *Peace.* What had seemed impossible for so long now appeared to be within reach.

But at a price that must be pure torment for the king.

Royce glanced up from beneath the dark hair that had fallen over his forehead, observing the man on the far side of the chamber: the very picture of a king, so silent and solemn beneath those purple robes that now all but hung on his war-weary frame.

Aldric always put his subjects' needs before his own. It was the quality Royce used to find most admirable about him.

And the most maddening. Because to Aldric, the needs of crown and country also came before the needs of his family. Of those he loved.

And that, Royce would never comprehend.

Crossing his arms over his chest, he cleared his throat. "Your Majesty, I still do not understand."

Aldric glanced over his shoulder, silent.

"It sounds as if all the arrangements have been made, as you said yourself. What is it you want of me?"

Aldric sighed, the sound barely noticeable even in the empty dining hall. But when he turned, his eyes glittered with a look of determination. "There are those who do not want this wedding to take place nor the peace accord between Châlons and Thuringia to succeed. Rebels." The silkiness of his voice as he said the word was more potent than venom. "They apparently believe that instead of bringing peace, the agreement will only make Daemon more powerful. Their fear and hatred of him is so great that they will risk anything to thwart his plans."

Royce found himself instantly sympathizing with these men, but he kept his opinion to himself.

"The fools do not understand what they risk in stirring his wrath," Aldric continued. "This agreement is the last hope I have to save my people from further suffering and death—but these heedless lackwits would destroy it. They have already tried. A fortnight ago, the night before the wedding procession was to leave for Thuringia, my daughter was attacked. In the palace." His voice remained calm, but the blaze in his eyes bespoke fury. "In my own solar."

Royce's gaze narrowed. "An assassination attempt?" Any sympathy he might have felt for the rebels evaporated.

"That is how it appeared to Princess Ciara, and to me,

though she escaped with only a wound to her arm. Some of my advisers think it may have been a failed abduction. Neither possibility endears these rebels to me in the least. They must be insane to even *consider* such treachery."

"And did you question this man who attacked the princess? Do you know who their leaders are?"

"Nay, we could not capture him. The incident occurred during the betrothal feast. A man appeared at the door of the solar, calling out that the princess had been hurt. A throng of people rushed to her aid, and the man blended into the crowd and escaped before we even knew what had happened."

"Clever," Royce murmured.

"Aye," the king agreed darkly. "He was gone before anyone could identify him, and the princess did not see his face. All she remembers is what he said—that he meant to stop the wedding."

Royce began to see why Aldric had summoned him here. "Are there any other clues as to who these traitors might be?" He started to pace, thinking.

"Only one. We had guards posted throughout the palace that night, and no one but our invited guests attended the betrothal feast. Which means it was either someone who pretends to be my loyal subject—"

"Or some of your own guardsmen are lending aid to the rebels." Royce swore under his breath. Now he understood why the king needed the services of someone from outside Châlons, someone far removed from the palace and its intrigues.

Someone who gave no pretense of being a loyal subject.

He stopped pacing, absently rubbing a hand over his stubbled jaw. "I assume you have the princess under protection?"

"The only protection I trust at the moment—my own." Aldric moved to one of the trestle tables, where he picked up an empty cup and reached for another. "She is here, in the abbey. That is why I chose this place for our meeting. Until she is wed, I fear for her life. I want her kept safe," he said adamantly.

Royce watched the king, thinking that only someone who knew Aldric well would detect the concern, the love behind his words. "So you want me to hunt down this assassin. Ferret out these rebels as quickly as possible."

Aldric glanced up at him, genuine surprise lightening his somber expression for a moment. "Nay." He shook his head. "Nay, I have other men pursuing them even now. I have a more vital task in mind for you, Saint-Michel. Come." He picked up a third cup and motioned for Royce to join him at the table.

Royce stepped closer, feeling strangely uneasy, wondering what could possibly be more vital than capturing those who had tried to kill a member of the royal family.

He came to stand on the opposite side of the table, watching in puzzlement as Aldric turned the three wooden goblets upside down and lined them up in a row. The sound of the torch crackling beside the door seemed unnaturally loud in the silence, competing with the monks' ethereal chants in a way that gave Royce a fleeting impression of hovering between Hell and Heaven.

The king reached into his velvet tunic and withdrew a gleaming jewel—one of the garnets found only in the mountains of Châlons, renowned for their bloodred color that was almost black. The rare gems were sought after by traders from all four corners of the globe.

He slipped the gem under one of the cups, then began moving them back and forth and around each other, his pale, gnarled hands surprisingly quick. "You have seen this game played at fairs, have you not?"

"Aye." Royce leaned down, bracing his arms against the tabletop. "It is used by tricksters to part fools from their coin."

"Indeed." A smile lifted one corner of the king's mouth. "With sleight of hand, the wily conjurer hides his precious prize. He confuses his opponents by keeping them guessing." He paused, and Royce pointed to one of the cups. Aldric lifted it to reveal that the jewel was not beneath it. "I dare not wait for the rebels' next attack. This time, they might succeed." He started shuffling the goblets again. "So I have devised a plan to get my daughter to Thuringia, as quickly and safely as possible. A decoy, her lady's maid, has already taken Princess Ciara's place in the wedding procession that left the palace five days ago, surrounded by guards."

Again he paused, and again Royce pointed to one of the cups, certain he had the right one this time. Aldric lifted it.

And again the garnet was not there.

The older man began shifting the cups again, a familiar, cunning tone in his voice. "We have explained that the princess is in delicate condition, still recovering from her injury, and must have privacy. I have also dispatched a band of courtiers to travel to Thuringia by the northern route. But the rebels will not find their quarry among that group, either. Because the *real* princess..."

He paused once more, and this time Royce concentrated before making his choice.

And when the king lifted the goblet, the jewel sparkled beneath it.

"The real princess," he repeated softly, picking up the garnet as if it might break, "will journey to Thuringia in disguise and in secret, traveling to the south." He held the gem out to Royce. "Through the mountains."

Royce stared at the garnet, then met Aldric's piercing blue gaze, suddenly understanding the importance of what the king was asking. If not for the table holding him up, he might have fallen to the floor. "You want *me* to serve as her escort?"

"Her escort and her guardian. I need a man who is willing to risk his life in this cause, a man with enough strength, daring, and intelligence to keep her safe. And I cannot trust those in my own court." When Royce did not take the jewel, Aldric set it on the table halfway between them. "Saint-Michel, the princess survived the first encounter with only a wound to her arm. Those plotting against us—whoever they may be—might take more ruthless measures next time."

Royce straightened, then backed away from the table. "They would have to be *mad* to follow anyone into those passes. Especially at this time of year."

"That is why no one will guess that she would journey in that direction. And that is why her escort must be someone who knows those mountains as well as he knows his own—"

Their gazes clashed, Royce daring him to say "name" when they both knew his had been taken from him.

"—identity," Aldric finished.

Shaking his head, Royce turned his back. "Surely you have other men you would prefer to entrust with this." A hint of his earlier sarcasm returned. "*Noble* men. Knights."

"None who know those mountains as well as you do. None who would be willing to use whatever means necessary to see her to safety."

When Royce turned around, he found the king casting a meaningful glance over the garments he wore: his black, sable-lined cloak, his embroidered gauntlets, the fine belt that cinched his tunic, the gold hilt of his sword. Commoners were forbidden to wear such finery. There were laws about such matters.

But Royce cared little for rules that made no sense to him.

He grimaced. 'Twas his lack of respect for the code of chivalry that had landed him in trouble and gotten him exiled four years ago. Ironic that the king now found such audacity admirable.

Nay, not admirable, he corrected. *Useful.*

He exhaled a harsh, bitter laugh. "So now that you have need of my services, you are suddenly willing to forget the past, and you expect me to forget as well. You expect me to simply lay down my life—and mayhap lose it—in the name of this noble cause you place before me." His voice rose as his anger deepened. "By God's breath! Do you think it is so easy to forget that I have been an outcast? Condemned to live without a country? Without even my family name? Do you think I can forget the way you ripped my life to pieces?"

Though the king stood only a few paces away, he showed not even a flicker of response. "Nay, I do not expect you to forget what happened four years ago," he said coolly, "because I assure you, I have not. Your exile was entirely of your own making. The discipline you received was naught more than you deserved."

"Deserved?" Royce almost choked on the word. "The negotiations were falling apart long before I unsheathed my blade. *You* were the one who set us an impossible task. Then you refused to tolerate failure. You were looking for someone to blame. I was convenient, so you had me all but spitted and roasted." His voice dropped to a harsh tone filled with pain. "Without so much as blinking an eye. I had been like a *son* to you, and you did not care half a *damn* what happened to me."

Aldric faced the accusations without flinching. He stood there, his gaze, his face impassive. And said naught.

Royce spun on his heel, paced away. Had he actually expected a reply? *Arrogant, demanding, unreasonable, unforgiving.* Aldric would never explain himself. Never admit that he had been wrong. It was far more important to him to be right than to be fair.

Some men never changed.

"I do not ask you to do this for me," Aldric said quietly. "What I am offering you is a chance to serve your homeland once more. A chance to redeem yourself for a mistake that cost Châlons a great deal—"

Royce shot him a seething glare.

"—and to secure a peaceful future for your countrymen. I once depended upon your military skill, your courage, and your loyalty, Royce. And it would seem to me that all of those qualities are still present in the man before me."

Royce ignored the accolades, too angry to hear them.

"And what will be my payment, if I survive? You will excuse me for asking, Your Majesty, but I have grown accustomed to receiving something more than gratitude in exchange for my blood and my blade. Lords from Paris to Navarre have plied me with riches. What have you to offer?"

"Something of far more value to you than coin. The moment the princess is safely in Thuringia and wed, I will restore to you all that you lost."

Royce's heart skipped a beat. He fought the astonishment—and the hope—that he knew must be written on his face. "You mean all that you *took* from me," he corrected sharply.

"Your spurs, your title, your name and position." Aldric could have been reading from a list of foodstuffs, for all the feeling he revealed. "Along with whatever lands you wish that are mine to give. And a generous reward."

Eyes narrowed, Royce slowly walked back toward the king, toward the table that held the cups and the glittering garnet, drawn by Aldric's words like a greedy man toward gold. Until this day, he had expected to spend the rest of his life as an outcast, as a man without a country. For four years, his best hope had been that someday, when Christophe took the throne…

But his best friend was dead.

And if Royce wanted to restore his family name and honor, erase the stain of disgrace and banishment, if he wanted to return *home*…

This might be his best chance. His only chance.

He reached down and picked up the garnet gingerly, as if it might burn him. "And what is she like, this daughter of yours?" he asked evenly. "What makes you think she could endure such a journey?"

"Though she is delicate of form and face, the princess is not so fragile as she may appear. And she will do what she must to carry out the duty that accompanies her crown. She understands the seriousness of her responsibility, and she has great strength of will."

Royce lifted his gaze to Aldric's. The princess sounded much like her father. Dutiful, responsible, strong-willed.

Which meant she could prove to be a royal handful, he thought sourly. *If* he agreed to serve as her guardian.

He glanced down at the gem in his hand. Try as he might, he could remember little about Christophe's sister. When he had been exiled from Châlons, she had been only…twelve? Fourteen? His only memory was of a plain, mousy child, always going about with her nose in a book. She had all but blended into the furniture.

And after growing up in the royal palace, with servants to see to her every wish and whim, she had no doubt blossomed into a spoiled, demanding, genuine princess. Not the sort of female he favored. Not in the least.

Still, he asked the question anyway. Bluntly. "Tell me, Your Majesty, how is it that you trust me with her virtue?"

Aldric blinked. Once. Slowly. "I have never questioned your honor"—he held up a hand, closing that argument before Royce could open it again—"in regards to women. It was your quick temper that I objected to four years ago. I ask only that you give me your word. Swear to me that you will deliver her untouched to her betrothed, and I will believe you—"

"How refreshing."

"—and if you break your vow, I will take much more than your spurs, your title, and your lands this time."

Their gazes locked. Aldric's meaning was unmistakable: if Royce dared touch one royal hair on the princess's royal head, the king would cut out his heart.

Not to mention other vital portions of his anatomy.

And he would do it. Even if it meant hunting Royce down in the darkest corner of the continent. Aldric did not make idle threats.

The king's voice was deep, forceful. "Do we understand one another?"

"Perfectly."

"Excellent. Then you may retire for the night. The

brothers have prepared a chamber for you, and you look as if you need the rest. Weigh the merits of what I have offered." He turned to leave, walking back across the dining hall the way he had come, into the shadows. "I will expect your answer at first light."

Chapter 3

Ciara's vision swam dizzily as she stepped into the chapel where her father had said to meet him after breakfast. Bright morning sunlight drenched the room and dazzled her eyes as the door closed softly behind her.

She reached for the back of a stone pew to steady herself, blinking hard, taking a deep breath. Neither her father nor the black-haired man beside him seemed to notice that she had entered the chapel. They both stood at the altar, bent over a map, engaged in a tense discussion about ice in the mountains at this time of year, and the chances that the rebels would find her before she reached the border, and—

Sweet holy Mary. She shut her eyes, wanted to cover her ears. For a moment, it was all she could do not to turn and run. Her stomach lurched.

Her heart and mind had been in turmoil for a fortnight now. Not even two weeks in this quiet, remote abbey had been able to heal the shock and pain of being attacked by one of her own subjects in the palace.

One of her own subjects. Not the enemy, but someone who was supposed to hold her in the highest honor and respect.

Opening her eyes, she clung to the cool, solid stone of the pew and tried to stop trembling. Tried to remember that Miriam had called her brave.

Good, kind Miriam, who had volunteered to take her place in the wedding procession—making herself a target for the rebels' arrows.

That was bravery, Ciara thought, a lump in her throat. Exactly the kind of bravery a princess should have. But she herself possessed no courage at all. Fear had wrapped its cold, black fingers tightly around her.

Fear of the traitors who wanted to kill her.

Of the cruel prince who would be her husband.

And of the journey ahead. She was about to venture into treacherous mountain passes, through small villages where assassins might be waiting for her around every corner.

With a man who looked like he was more accustomed to trampling enemies and plundering castles than to guiding and guarding a princess.

In that moment, before she could summon enough daring to interrupt her father's discussion, her newly appointed protector glanced her way…and the darkest, boldest gaze she had ever encountered captured hers.

Ciara felt as if the air all around her had suddenly become too hot, burning her lips, her mouth, her throat. She opened her mouth to speak, but no words would come. Scarlet warmth rose in her cheeks as she realized she was gaping at him, like a bedazzled child beholding a king for the first time. She was powerless to move. That potent stare held her fast.

He offered no greeting. Did not even bow. His eyes slowly widening with surprise, he remained silent.

They simply stared at each other across the chapel, through the beams of silvery mountain sunlight that poured in from the tall, arched widows to dance between them.

By all the saints, what was wrong with her? Mayhap it was disbelief that held her fast.

For this could not be Sir Royce Saint-Michel, the man her father had described as the best knight he had ever known, noble and honorable and chivalrous. The man her brother used to speak of with such high regard. Mayhap Sir Royce had not answered the summons, and her father had been forced to find another to serve as her escort.

Because this man looked like no knight she had ever seen. She could find naught in his regard that suggested either nobility or chivalry.

He was far too…too…*rough*-looking. From the dark stubble that bearded his cheeks, to the tangled black hair that hung loosely about his shoulders, to the impressive sword at his waist. She was not sure which stunned her more: the richness of the weapon with its golden hilt or the fact that he was wearing it here, in a chapel, in the house of the Lord. This was clearly a man who cared little for custom and less for the law.

If that were not enough to give one pause, his sheer physical size was even more alarming. The dark tunic he wore strained across a broad chest, outlining the heavy muscles beneath, and his sable-lined cloak, flung casually back over one shoulder, revealed thick-hewn arms.

But it was his face that held her attention most of all, with its hard angles, sharp cheekbones, and square-cut jaw. She had seen *stone* that looked softer.

Blinking at last, she struggled to right her thoughts, to tell if this was the man she remembered as Christophe's best friend. But the last time she had seen Sir Royce, before he had vanished from Châlons so suddenly and unexpectedly, she had been but fifteen. She could summon no image, except of an overloud, swaggering young lord who had never so much as spared her a glance.

If she could hear his voice, she would know. But before she could think of something—anything—to say, the man's piercing gaze left hers, sweeping to the toes of her slippers and back again. His brow furrowed. He flicked a look at the door behind her, as if he expected someone else to step in.

After a moment, his stare returned to her, his expression of surprise now joined by a dismay that he did not even attempt to conceal.

Twin sparks of indignation and annoyance ignited in Ciara. Did the man have no manners at all? Did he find her lacking in some way?

Or did he doubt that a woman as plain as she could possibly be the princess?

All three possibilities stung her royal pride. She might be wearing simple, homespun garments instead of her coronet and robes, but she was still Princess Ciara of Châlons. And she deserved better than this rude treatment. Lifting her chin, she bestowed upon him a look she usually reserved for misbehaving servant boys.

Instead of being chastened, the knave only lifted one raven brow. The hard line of his mouth curved into an expression that might have been a grimace or a grin.

Just then, her father finally noticed that he no longer had his companion's attention. Straightening, he turned to face the chapel door. "Daughter."

Startled, Ciara forced her fingers to release their death grip on the pew. His cool greeting stole all the warmth from the air around her. "I…I am here, Father."

He extended a hand toward her. "Come."

Swallowing hard, summoning her most regal smile, Ciara managed to command one foot to step in front of the other. She walked slowly down the aisle toward them, through the shimmering rays of sunlight, and a startling image struck her: of a wedding. *Her* wedding. Here, in her homeland, in a chapel like this. With her father waiting at the altar, beside her groom…

She blinked and the strange illusion vanished. How odd. It must have been a trick of the light and her frayed nerves. This man was not her groom; this land no longer her home. Her wedding would take place in Thuringia. In a grand cathedral.

And she was to be Prince Daemon's bride.

When she reached the altar, her father turned her toward the towering swordsman.

"Daughter, this is the man I told you of, Royce Saint-Michel."

She stared with unconcealed surprise. "You are…but you do not...or rather, what I mean to say…" Why on earth was she tripping over her own tongue? *By all the suffering saints, say something intelligible.* "Good morn to you."

Mortified that she had delivered such an ungraceful greeting—and in front of her father, no less—Ciara wished a nice large hole would open up in the floor beneath her feet.

She was close enough to Sir Royce now to make out the

color of those eyes: a deep earth brown that was almost black. Again she noticed the strange heat that seemed to sizzle in the air around her, warming her every breath.

This time, without the benefit of distance between them, she felt something more…a melting warmth *inside* her.

"And good morn to you, Princess Ciara." Sir Royce inclined his head, that odd grimace-grin still playing about his mouth. "I do not blame you for not recognizing me, for you are also much…changed from what I remember."

Ciara barely heard his words, for she was transfixed by his voice. It was softer than she remembered. Soft and deep and dark as a Châlons valley at sunset. The mellow richness seemed at odds with the hard angles of his features—and only intensified the hypnotic effect of his eyes.

Whichever part of her brain was still capable of reason noticed that he *still* did not bow or offer her a deferential greeting. Apparently he lacked respect for royalty. And common courtesy.

Yet to respond in kind would have been unforgivably rude. So she summoned a smile and one of the courtly phrases she had been taught by rote. "So pleasant to meet you again."

Her father rolled up the map he and Sir Royce had been studying. "Have you gathered your things, Daughter?"

"Aye, Father," she said, amazed that she managed to speak calmly. Her pounding heart had not slowed a whit. "Brother Evrard took my belongings down to the tunnel entrance while I ate my morning meal. All is ready." *Except me.* She wanted to shout those two words. Wanted to fall into his arms and sob out all her fears.

But she kept all those ignoble, childish feelings hidden, kept her smile in place.

"Excellent. We have agreed upon the route you will follow." Her father tucked the scroll into his royal robes. "None will know of it but the three of us. If you are to travel in safety, secrecy is vital. You must take care." His eyes darkened as he gazed at her intently. "Tell no one your true identity, Daughter. No one. The people and places you will encounter beyond these walls may not be as friendly as they seem. We cannot know who may be in league with the rebels."

"I will remember, Father."

He turned to Sir Royce. "The wedding procession left the palace several days ago, but it will take them more than a fortnight to reach Thuringia."

"I will do my best to travel quickly," Sir Royce said, "so that we arrive before they do. Before the rebels find out they have been tricked."

Her father nodded. "For now, the rebels are distracted. By the time they chase after the procession and the other group of courtiers and realize the princess is not among them, you should be safely in Thuringia." He glanced at Ciara again. "And my daughter safely wed."

She held his gaze. "By God's grace, it will be so, Father." *I will not disappoint you again. I will earn your forgiveness for what happened to Christophe. I will make you proud of me. I promise.*

If he sensed any of her feelings or fears, he said naught.

Though she thought for a moment that his blue eyes did soften, almost imperceptibly. "All will be well, Daughter. Saint-Michel will see to it. I know that he may seem unlike the knights you have met, but I assure you he is the right man for this task. He will keep you safe. In those mountains, he will have no equal. You may place your trust in him." He turned that gaze on the black-haired swordsman. "As I do."

Sir Royce swallowed so hard that his Adam's apple bobbed visibly. "I vow, Your Majesty," he intoned solemnly, "that no harm will befall your daughter while she is in my care. I will carry out my duty, exactly as we have discussed." He extended his hand. "You have my word of honor."

Her father took Sir Royce's hand in what looked like a bruising grasp. Their gazes locked. Ciara barely had time to wonder about it, or about what Sir Royce meant by "exactly as we have discussed."

Because her father released him and took her hand,

squeezing it gently.

She was pitifully grateful for even that tiny show of affection. 'Twas more than he had shown her in weeks.

"Be well, Daughter."

Her throat tightened. She longed to fold herself into his arms, to feel as safe and beloved as she had when she was a child. The sunlit chapel shimmered around her as tears veiled her eyes.

She blinked away the dampness, held herself regally straight and proud, knowing he would disapprove of any such display. "And you, Father."

He led her forward a step, placed her hand in Sir Royce's, and let her go. The warrior's strong, warm fingers closed tightly around her own as those dark eyes met and held hers.

"Guard her well, Royce," her father commanded quietly. "Guard her with your life."

Royce trailed Aldric's daughter through the darkness, his footsteps loud in the stone tunnel that spiraled downward to the foot of the mountain. Daylight marked the exit far below, but his mind was not on the journey ahead or the dangers it might hold.

His gaze lingered on Princess Ciara's back, his mind on a single thought—one that made his mouth dry and his palms sweat.

A girl who had started life as a plain, mousy child had no right growing up to look like this.

His heart and his stomach had performed a somersault the moment he first saw her in the chapel. In truth, he had not even *heard* her entrance, but rather…sensed it. She had appeared so suddenly, so silently, as if she had floated in on one of the beams of sunlight, deposited there by angels.

And then he had been struck speechless—by eyes a shade lighter than topaz, hair the color of exotic spice, beauty as subtle and natural as the simple, cream-colored gown she wore. Delicate. Soft. She even *moved* with a quiet grace that made him swear her footsteps caused no sound.

Snowfall. She made him think of snowfall, drifting down from the clouds to cloak the mountainside in pale innocence.

Even now, in the shadowed tunnel, when he could see only the outline of her shoulders and back ahead of him, his heart and his stomach kept repeating that irritating tumble. He tried to remind himself that this was the same dull, bookish girl he had barely noticed in the past.

But no man could possibly mistake her for a piece of the furniture now.

The gown and matching cloak she wore concealed her tall, slender body from neck to toes, but every curve of fabric promised matching curves beneath. And though her face and voice bespoke sweetness and charm, one feature did not fit that image.

Her exceptional, ravishing mouth.

Never had he seen lips more perfectly made for long, slow kisses. Full and lush they were, the lower one softly rounded, the color a liquid red that reminded him of the rich shade of a Châlons garnet.

Had she ever *been* kissed? he wondered. Properly, thoroughly kissed?

A familiar hunger sank its claws into him, so swift and strong it made him inhale as if he had been wounded. Angry at his own weakness, he shoved the thoughts away. Brutally reminded himself that those lips and this lady were forbidden fruit. She was Prince Daemon's betrothed.

Aldric's daughter.

But the thoughts of innocence and snowfall only made him remember how much he used to enjoy turning his face up to the sky to capture that pure, cool white essence on his tongue, to feel it melt in the heat of his mouth…

He clenched his jaw, forcing himself to remember every word of the warning Aldric had given him last night: *If you break your vow, I will take much more than your spurs, your title, and your lands this time.*

If he wanted to keep his head attached to his shoulders, he had better find a way to control himself. Keep in mind who and what she was.

Remember the vow he had made this morn.

He was still trying to subdue the heat simmering in him when they reached the end of the passage. Princess Ciara located the hidden lever that released a secret door, and sunlight flooded the tunnel. She raised a hand to shade her eyes, glancing toward him. "Do you—"

He cut her off with a sharp gesture, stepping in front of her to look around outside. He saw no one on the snowy slope that curved away into a deep valley, no intruders or travelers anywhere on the white, sun-blazed foothills surrounding them. No danger in sight.

Only his horse Anteros awaited, tossing his head impatiently, looking well rested after his night in the abbey's stable. A half-dozen bulky sacks lay on the ground next to him, along with his saddle and bridle.

Princess Ciara stepped out from the tunnel. "Why did you—"

"I did not yet tell you it was safe to come out," Royce said, his tone curt.

She froze. "Of course," she replied after a moment. "You are right to be cautious. I suppose I will have to grow accustomed to your…ways."

"Not *ways*, Your Highness. Rules." He turned to face her. "And you had best become acquainted with them right now. To begin with, I go through every door first, and you stay behind until summoned. I will not be trailing at your heels like one of your royal servants—"

"I do not—"

"And I want you in my sight at all times. There will be no wandering off. You will stay within reach, you will do your best to avoid attracting attention, and you will follow my orders without hesitation. Understood?"

Blinking at him in shock, she set down the brocade

satchel she had carried from the abbey. "I am *not* accustomed to being addressed in this tone, sirrah. Or to being interrupted when I am speaking. Or to—"

"Then I would say the next two weeks should be full of surprises for you, Princess. Your father has appointed me your guardian—and you will find I care little for royal protocol when it comes to carrying out my duty. Have you any questions?"

A storm was brewing in those jewel-bright eyes. "Only one."

"Aye?"

She crossed her arms over her chest. "Is it safe for me to come outside yet?"

The sarcasm in her tone made him frown. "Indeed, Your Royal Highness," he replied with exaggerated politeness, gesturing her forward with a sweep of his arm. "Please join me." He turned and led the way toward his destrier.

Picking up her satchel, she followed him onto the snowy hillside. "Where is my mare?"

"I told the brothers to keep her. Anteros is more than strong enough to carry us both."

"We are to share a horse? But why?"

"It is better this way." He picked up the bridle from the ground. "Safer."

He was no longer certain that was true. When he had made the decision this morning, he had not anticipated that the lady sharing the saddle with him would be so…enticing.

"But how will we carry my belongings?"

He slipped the bridle over the stallion's head, casting a glance at her satchel. "I wear chain mail, helm, and armaments when Anteros carries me into battle, Your Highness. I do not think one bag will overtax him."

"But what about the rest?" Setting down her satchel, she pointed at the sacks on the ground.

"All of these are yours?" he asked incredulously. He had thought they were foodstuffs being delivered to the abbey.

"Of course. I cannot travel for a fortnight without at least a few changes of clothes and—"

"We are *not* taking all of this with us, Your Highness. If you have belongings that you cannot live without in Thuringia, you should have sent them with the wedding procession."

A spark flared in her eyes, belying the courtly, polite smile that slid into place as she moved toward him. "But if we were to bring my mare, you see, there would be no problem."

"Aye, there would be. The mare would slow us down. Anteros has easily twice her speed." His fingers tightened on the reins, crushing the leather as she drew close. Too close. "And if you were seated alone on her back, you would make a fine target. The rebels could put a crossbow bolt through your heart and be gone before we knew they were there. You would be dead before you fell from your pretty little saddle."

She went pale and drew back from him, her right hand coming up to touch her left arm in an odd, protective gesture.

Smothering an oath, Royce turned and continued bridling the stallion. He had not meant to be so blunt in his explanation. She was not a squire or guardsman under his command; she was a princess. A sheltered, naive girl not used to the world's violent ways.

And it was not her fault that the merest blink of her lashes set his every nerve on edge. Being churlish with her would accomplish naught.

Sighing in frustration, he glanced over his shoulder and tried to make her understand. "If we ride together, with you seated in front of me, my body will block any arrows or other pointy objects that might come flying your way."

That delectable mouth of hers formed an O of comprehension and surprise. "You would do that? Risk getting wounded, risk your life…for me?"

He stared down at her, lost in those topaz eyes that were brighter than the sun that warmed the air all around them.

Then he cleared his throat, finally found his voice. "I should think a princess would be used to that—to having guardsmen and retainers risk themselves to protect her."

She shook her head. "Nay. There has been little cause to—" She stopped herself abruptly, leaving the explanation unfinished. "Nay."

He wondered what she was leaving unsaid. And why. "You need not concern yourself, Your Highness. No blood will be shed. If I carry out my duty with any skill at all, we will be in Thuringia before the rebels suspect that aught is amiss."

And he fully intended to carry out his duty. To keep his vow.

Every word of it.

"I see," she said quietly.

They stood there an instant longer, scarcely two paces apart, and he noticed for the first time that she wore some kind of scent. The breeze carried it toward him, teasing his senses. Jasmine, he thought. Or was it rose?

Refusing to give himself time to puzzle it out, he turned on his heel and reached for the saddle on the ground.

She moved past him. "I concede that we must share a horse, but I will not leave these bags behind." She picked up one of the sacks and held it out toward him. "You will have to think of a way to take them."

Royce straightened, the saddle in his arms. "I will?"

She blinked, apparently unaccustomed to having her orders questioned. "Of course." That polite, courtly smile of hers reappeared. "It is what I wish."

"It is what you…wish," he echoed, one brow rising. Evidently, Her Royal Highness was used to getting *whatever* Her Royal Highness wished. No matter how unreasonable. She was a spoiled, demanding little female, just as he had expected. A girl who had been indulged by too many people for much too long.

And he was having none of it.

"Very well, Princess." Imitating her smile, he placed the

saddle on Anteros's back, then came back and reached out for the bag in her hands. "Allow me to see what I can do."

She looked relieved as she handed it over.

Until he opened the sack and started pawing through it.

"What do we have here?" He held up a pair of blue silk slippers embroidered in gold. "Pretty." He tossed them over his shoulder into the snow.

She uttered a squeak of surprise.

"And so are these." He discarded a lavender pair. "And this is quite lovely."

"What are you—"

A plumed hat sailed over his shoulder. "And these…and oh, this must have cost a great deal."

"W-What…" She sounded as if she could not breathe as hats, hose, veils, and feminine frippery quickly accumulated at his feet. "What…what…"

The pile was nearly knee-deep when he reached the bottom of the sack. "And this, Your Royal Highness, I am certain you could live without."

A small mandolin hit the snow with a discordant *twang*.

The princess had been paralyzed—until the instrument fell. She lunged forward to rescue it, sputtering. "How dare you…how *could* you…I will not tolerate—you will stop that this instant!"

He ignored her, draping the now empty bag over one shoulder and picking up another. "I am merely complying with your wishes." He shrugged. "I am taking the bags."

He found the next sack filled with—of all things—books.

She gasped as he started discarding them. "I said you will cease at once!" She scrambled to scoop them up before they could hit the snow. "At once, I say! Cease!"

He paused, a slender volume of verse dangling from his fingertips, and lifted one brow. "Is there a problem, Your Highness?"

She straightened, struggling to balance the mandolin with an armful of books, clutching them all to her bosom.

For the first time in his life, Royce wished he were a mandolin or a book.

She stalked toward him and snatched the slim volume of poetry from his fingers. "You…you…" She seemed incapable of speech for a moment, as if she could not find words vile enough to describe him.

Then she found them. "You are a barbarian! Some sort of Mongol beast! How *dare* you come charging into my life, unasked, unwanted—"

"Hardly unasked, Your Highness," he said calmly. "Your father—"

"Appointed you to serve as my protector. The important word being *serve*. Your position does not give you the right to flout all law and custom and even simple courtesy!" Her voice shifted to an icy, regal tone, her gaze glittering. "You and I, *sirrah*"— she emphasized the term, addressing him as if he were a servant—"need to come to an understanding. If we are to…enjoy—"

He suspected she had wanted to say *endure*.

"—each other's company for the next two weeks, I must ask you to remember your place."

He dropped the heavy sack on the ground, barely missing her dainty royal foot. "My place?"

"Aye. Though you have been gone from Châlons for some time, you are, in fact, one of my subjects. I must insist that you treat me with proper deference."

His own pride ignited his temper. "You can insist all you like, Your Highness, but my *place* is wherever I want it to be. I am not your servant and I am not *anyone's* subject. I have been a free man for four years. Your father saw to that." He rudely turned his back and went to finish with Anteros's saddle. The point about her useless belongings had been made. He would argue about it no more.

"My father? What do you mean?"

He choked out a humorless laugh, tightening the cinch. "There is no need to pretend you do not know."

"Know of what? All I know is that four years ago, you

disappeared from Châlons quite suddenly. Without saying farewell to anyone."

Royce went still. His fingers clenched around the reins. "Your father never told you why I left?"

"Nay, he said naught to me. Or to anyone." She paused. "Did my father have something to do with your disappearance?"

Royce could not move, could not even turn to study her face, to see if she was lying. He knew she was not. The way she waited so expectantly for an answer told him that.

By nails and blood, Aldric had said naught? To anyone?

Shock and disbelief slammed through him. All this time, he had believed that Aldric told *everyone* of his banishment and disgrace. That he had been made an example. Why would the old warhorse keep it secret?

He could think of no reason, except that the king did not wish to shame him publicly.

Struggling for breath, he finished buckling the saddle, trying to sort out his confusion. It was unnerving to learn that he had been mistaken all this time. Disconcerting that he could not puzzle out the motive behind Aldric's silence.

But if the king had seen fit to keep the matter quiet, Royce saw no reason to drag his family name and honor through the mud. "I had…reasons for leaving."

"And I would like to understand them. I wish you to explain."

She did not phrase it as a question. Evidently, she had inherited not only her father's tendency to be demanding and impossible, but his arrogance as well.

He turned and pierced her with a glare. "And what makes you think that your every *wish* matters so much?" he asked hotly. "Up in your palace on a mountaintop, milady, all of your wishes may have come true, but you are out in the world now—and those of us who live down here do *not* exist merely to satisfy your every whim! We have lives and minds and wishes of our own. You cannot simply hand down demands from on high and expect everyone to gleefully dance to your tune. You cannot treat people like puppets. You cannot ask the impossible and then destroy them when they fail to—"

He cut himself off abruptly, chagrined that he had almost given her the answer she had demanded. He was *not* going to discuss the intimate, painful details of his past with her.

Clenching his jaw, he held her gaze, daring her to press him further. "I left. Now I am back. My reasons are my own. Have you any other questions?"

She held his stare, then turned aside and set her books and mandolin atop the sack he had discarded. "Only one," she bit out. "If you hold some sort of grudge against my father, why did you agree to serve as my escort to Thuringia? Why risk your life to protect me?"

"I should think that would be obvious," he snapped, his temper making him less than careful in his choice of words. "You mean a great deal to me, Princess—a great deal of land, a castle, and coin. I have been promised a generous reward. *That* is what I am risking my life for."

She picked up one of the hats he had tossed to the ground, brushing snow from the delicate fabric. "Thank you for explaining," she said frostily. "So kind of you to make clear exactly what sort of man you are."

He spat a curse. "I would not expect you to understand. You, who have never had to worry about a place to sleep for the night or where your next meal is coming from. Your whole life has been"— he cast a scornful glance at the costly belongings piled around her—"books of verse and blue silk slippers."

She lifted her gaze to his, her eyes still glittering. "Tell me, Sir Royce, are you this offensive to everyone you meet, or are your ill manners strictly reserved for royalty?"

"I have not been hired for my charming personality, Princess. I do not have to be pleasant to you. I do not even have to like you. And I certainly do not have to bow and scrape like one of your palace lackeys. All I have to do is get you to Thuringia in one piece and deliver you into the waiting arms of Prince Daemon."

"Aye," she said slowly. "That is what you are being *paid* to do."

"Excellent, Princess. I am glad we agree on one thing." Turning his back again, he finished tightening the saddle and securing his own belongings. "Because this is not going to be a pleasure trip or a summer cruise down the river in your royal barge. There are people out there"—he jerked his head toward the distant mountains—"who may want to kill you. I intend to prevent that from happening. Whether *you* like it or not, your father has placed me in charge, for your own safety. And if I am to protect you, I must insist that you obey my orders. Without question."

"I will try to be…accommodating."

It sounded as if the words had been pried from between her teeth. He had the distinct impression that she liked him even less than he liked her.

Which suited him fine, he decided. Let her despise him. It would be better that way. Safer. He *needed* barriers between them. A boundary that he would not allow himself to cross.

Not even for the sweet temptation of tasting those ravishing lips.

"Good." He glanced up at the sun, high overhead. "Then gather up whatever you can fit in *one* of those bags of yours, and let us be on our way."

Chapter 4

The sun dipped low behind them, gilding the fields of winter wheat that passed in a blur as Sir Royce's stallion carried them swiftly across the plain. The light struck bright sparks from the lakes that dotted the countryside and danced over the distant, snowcapped peaks.

Ciara had removed her fur-lined gloves and almost wished she could take off her cloak as well. The air here felt mild, rich with the earthy promise of spring. As they cantered through the broad, flat lowland that separated Châlons's western mountains from those in the east, a steady breeze warmed her cheeks and mischievously plucked strands from her neatly braided hair.

The sun's heat, the destrier's smooth gait, and the rhythm of his hoofbeats might have lulled her to sleep, but she held herself stiff and straight, trying to keep as much space as possible between herself and Sir Royce, uncomfortably aware of the solid wall of muscle at her back, of the musky scent that enveloped her. Both so unfamiliar. So foreign. So…

Male.

Even after an entire day of riding, she still felt shocked by the feel of his hard-sinewed legs pressed against hers, his heavy arm around her waist.

And by an unforgivable thought that kept bothering her conscience. A desire. What Sir Royce might call a wish.

A wish to push the black-haired lout off the first and tallest cliff that presented itself.

The idea held such appeal, she found herself fighting a smile. From the moment Sir Royce first looked at her, she had guessed that he lacked manners, but she had not suspected that he possessed a knave's heart to match his black eyes. Until he proved it to her.

Thus far, she had managed to endure his behavior. She had even obeyed his order to sacrifice most of her possessions, taking only what he called "practical necessities."

Which included a few of her beloved books. And her mandolin.

She had refused to compromise on that. The instrument now hung from Sir Royce's saddle, bouncing between his metal shield and a battle-ax.

That small victory almost made up for having to share a horse with him.

Almost.

She realized that riding this way was necessary so that he could protect her. But she was not accustomed to such…such…*intimacy*. Especially not with a man.

She did not like the way she fit so perfectly against him, the top of her head neatly tucked beneath his chin. 'Twas why she had refused to remove her cloak, despite the sun's warmth.

For some reason the idea of his bare, stubbled jaw brushing against her hair tied her insides into knots. She grasped the front of the saddle and tried to pull herself forward, to gain even an inch more space between them.

"Stop squirming, Your Highness." Sir Royce's arm tightened around her, tugging her back against him.

Her breath caught in her throat as their bodies came together. "Princesses do not *squirm*, sirrah," she informed him loftily, hoping he could not tell she was trembling.

"You have done nothing *but* squirm and wriggle all day, Princess. You are lucky that Anteros has not tried to throw you from the saddle."

"Fortunately for me, Anteros seems to have better manners than his master," Ciara muttered.

"What?"

"I was just wondering how your destrier came to have his unusual name," she lied, seeking a neutral subject.

Sir Royce did not reply. She was not even certain he was listening to her. His mood had grown more tense and taciturn with each passing hour.

Reining Anteros to a halt, he paused to study the horizon behind them—as he had done frequently all day—to make sure no one was following them.

"He had the name when I bought him," he said at last as he urged the stallion into a smooth canter once more. "I understood it was after some Greek god or other. What makes it unusual?"

"Anteros was one of the lesser-known deities in the Greek pantheon, a son of Aphrodite. He was one of the gods of love. It seems an odd name for a warhorse."

Sir Royce laughed mockingly. "I apologize for what I said earlier, Princess. You *do* know about more than poetry and pretty shoes. You know useless ancient myths as well."

"Useless?" She wished she could turn and face him. Since he held her tight, her glare was wasted on the lovely scenery. "My education has been quite extensive, sirrah. Mythology happens to be one of my favorite pursuits, but I have also studied astronomy, philosophy, the sciences, music, languages—"

"Tell me, Your Highness, how much do you know about your own country?"

"A great deal. For example, I know that Châlons has existed peacefully for almost three hundred years, one of many small kingdoms scattered across the Alps between France and the Holy Roman Empire—"

"I mean current information. There used to be a large keep near the town of Aganor, southeast of here. Do you know how it fared in the war?"

"Nay, I do not."

"Do you at least know how the *town* fared in the war?"

"Nay," she repeated, "I do not know."

He did not speak for a moment, as if he had been stunned into silence. "How is it possible that a member of the royal family could know so little about her own realm?

Have you been so busy with your *philosophy* and your *music* that you have no room in your head for practical matters? Do you not care—"

"Nay, that is not true at all! It is because of the war that I am unfamiliar with my realm. I have never even *seen* most of it."

"You were born and raised in Châlons. You have lived in this kingdom for nineteen years—"

"Aye, but despite your taunts this morn about pleasure trips and cruises down the river in the royal barge, I have experienced neither in my lifetime. Since childhood, I have lived in the palace, surrounded by courtiers and—"

"Shh."

"I will not be interrupted, sirrah! Never in my life have I been so—mmmph."

"When we are not alone," he whispered tightly, one gloved hand clamped over her mouth, "you will at least refrain from discussing your grand life at the royal palace." He nodded toward a muddy pasture on their right where dozens of serfs were at work. "If you recall, we are trying to keep your identity a secret."

When he removed his hand, Ciara lifted trembling fingers to her lips, so shocked at being thusly...*manhandled* that she could not speak.

The peasants straightened to watch them pass. Several called out greetings, but Sir Royce remained tense and nudged Anteros into a gallop.

Even after they had left the serfs far behind, he did not relax. "How great a risk is there that people might recognize you?" He tugged the hood of her cloak forward to better conceal her face.

"None." She pushed his hand away. "Châlons has been at war for seven years. As I was *trying* to explain, I have been cloistered in the palace since the age of twelve for my own safety. My subjects are no more familiar with my face than I am with theirs."

"Good."

With that terse comment, he fell silent. Ciara muttered an oath in ancient Greek and gave up trying to hold a civil conversation with the knave. As they rode on, she sought distraction in the passing scenery.

Fortunately, there was much to see, all of it new to her. They traveled through vast, green meadows. Fallow fields studded with rocks. Tall grasses that flowed like waves in the wind. Now and then a flock of birds would explode from beneath Anteros's hooves to fill the air with color and noise.

In the distance, she could see pine trees clustered around the hills as if on sentry duty, emerald lances aimed toward the sky. And icy lakes that flashed like silver coins in the sunlight.

It touched her deeply, in a way she could not explain, to finally see for herself the legendary beauty of her country. This sensation of the horse galloping beneath her, the wind in her face, the ground flying past felt so fresh, so *free*. Under other circumstances, she might have found it exciting. Exhilarating.

But she could not forget that every mile they traveled carried her away from her homeland, toward Thuringia.

Fighting the wave of sadness that washed over her, she made a decision: she would *not* allow her ill-tempered guardian to ruin what could be a pleasant journey. During the next fortnight—for the first time, and the last—she *was* free.

Free of her crown and her robes and all the rules that went with them. Free to fulfill her heart's most secret dream: to experience *real* life, to be like any other woman. For the next two weeks, she could steal a brief taste of the world, the adventures, the fun that had always been forbidden to her.

The plan made her smile, but as the afternoon wore on, the strain of the past days took its toll, and her eyes began to drift closed….

She came awake sometime later to find the evening sky darkened to violet, the horse's gait slowed to walk—and a hard, muscular arm locked around her ribs.

Just beneath her breasts.

She hardly dared inhale. "You may let me go now," she said sharply. "I am awake."

Sir Royce relaxed his hold slightly, just enough so that his arm now rested around her hips.

She was not sure if that was better or worse.

"My apologies, Princess," he said with cool sarcasm. "But you almost tumbled from the saddle when you fell asleep. I had to choose between holding your royal person upright or allowing you to get trampled beneath Anteros's hooves. And I would be a rather poor guardian if you ended up crushed into a pulp on the first day of our journey."

Ciara winced. Must the man be so vivid in his descriptions? "I see."

She knew his real reason had naught to do with concern for her well-being. He did not want to risk losing the rich reward she represented.

How had he put it? *Land, a castle, and coin. That is what I am risking my life for.*

"Are you still tired, Princess?"

"I am fine." She fought a yawn, refusing to show any weakness, to give him any further reason to taunt her.

"Good. I would prefer to cross the lowlands before we stop for the night." With a slight tensing of his thighs—which she felt along every inch of her own—he nudged Anteros into a trot. "We should be able to find lodging in Edessa."

She nodded wearily. She had never been to Edessa, knew naught of what it might be like. But at this point, she would not quibble with any place that offered her a hot meal and a warm bed. Anything softer than a saddle would do. After so many hours of riding, even with the thick padding of her cloak and gown, her backside and thighs felt sore, bruised.

And much too sensitive, she thought, scarlet warmth rising in her face.

The movements Sir Royce used to control and guide the

spirited horse kept making her flinch. Just as every time he moved one of his hands, her breath caught in her throat.

Thankfully, he seemed oblivious, as he had all day, to the strange effect his touch and his nearness had on her. He handled her with no more attention than he had shown her silk slippers or her mandolin.

If he could endure another hour or two of riding, she decided stubbornly, so could she. She would not complain, would not give him any more cause to find fault with her.

Stifling another yawn, she slid her right hand from beneath her cloak to rub at her sore left arm. The cut she had received in the attack a fortnight ago had healed, but the muscle still ached, especially when the air turned cool in the evening.

"Is that where you were wounded in the attack at the palace?" Sir Royce asked.

She felt surprised to hear what sounded like concern in his voice. "Aye."

"And it pains you still? I was told it was but a scratch."

Ciara's ire simmered. It had not been concern she heard in his tone; he had simply found another opportunity to belittle her. "Being attacked with a blade may be a common occurrence to you, Sir Royce, but this was the first time I ever had a weapon aimed in my direction. Most of the knives in my experience have been associated with supper tables—"

She cut herself off. If she wanted to enjoy her journey, she could not allow this mercenary to keep provoking her. She would not respond to his barbs anymore. She would *not.*

"But you are right," she amended mildly. "It is but a scratch, Sir Royce."

"Stop calling me Sir Royce."

"As you like, milord—"

"I am no one's lord," he corrected. "I am not *Sir* Royce. My name is Saint-Michel. Or Royce. I am just another commoner to you, Princess." He added under his breath, "At least until our journey is done and you are wed and I can claim my reward."

Ciara resisted the tart reply that sprang to mind. He did not have to keep reminding her that he was doing this out of greed rather than any sense of honor or duty.

Then her brow furrowed in confusion. "But I seem to recall that you *did* once have a title. And a castle. Or mayhap I am thinking of someone else?"

"So good to know I left a lasting impression."

"I meant no insult. I simply cannot remember the details."

"Indeed, Your Highness? All I remember about *you* is that you barely spoke two words to me the entire time I was in your father's service. A pity you are no longer so quiet."

Ciara held her tongue and glared off into the horizon, refusing to speak despite her curiosity about his past and his mysterious disappearance four years ago.

The stallion's hoofbeats made the only sound in the gathering darkness as they rode on.

An hour later, she was ready to slide from the saddle and form a small puddle of exhaustion on the ground. She very nearly swallowed her royal pride and asked Royce to stop for the night, but just then, the glint of a church spire appeared in the distance, poking up above the horizon.

"Edessa," he announced, a heavy sigh declaring his own fatigue. "I know of an inn on the south side of the village. A fairly pleasant little place."

She was too tired to comment, but the words *a fairly pleasant little place* filled her head with comforting images of a hot bath, a fluffy, down-filled mattress, a roaring hearth to chase away the chill. She almost groaned in longing.

As they neared the town, Royce slowed the stallion to a walk. His arm slipped from around her waist for a moment, and she could feel him fumbling with something at the neck of his tunic. She heard a muted snap, like a leather thong breaking.

"Here." He pressed a small object into her hand. "Put this on."

Ciara closed her fingers around the object. Though she

could not see in the darkness, she could tell what it was.

A ring.

"Why?"

"Since we will be sharing a room, we had best make it look as if we are husband and wife."

Startled, she whipped her head around—and collided with his jaw.

He cursed. "Princess, do you think you might warn me before you try to knock me from the saddle?" He rubbed at his injured chin.

Dizzying stars swam through her vision. She did not know if they came from the impact or his unexpected announcement. "We…we…w-we will be—"

"Sharing a room. Stop stuttering. And do not look at me that way." Placing his fingertips atop her head, he turned her forward again.

Her heart was beating so fast she could not breathe, and his touch only made matters worse. "B-but…"

"You have naught to fear from me, Your Highness. You have my word of honor that my behavior will be perfectly chivalrous."

"I…y-you—"

"Aye. You. Me. Together. In one room." He sounded exasperated. "I explained this morn that you must stay within reach at all times. That means day and night. I doubt the rebels will be so polite as to inform us of their plans, and they could strike after dark as easily as during the day. If they have half a brain between them, they would prefer the cover of night."

The idea of sharing a bedchamber…sharing it with a man…with *him*…"Could we not pretend to be brother and sister and take two rooms?"

"What an excellent idea. That way, when the rebels carry you off, my sleep will not be disturbed."

Ciara shivered. "I…I see your point."

Her mind and vision finally cleared long enough for her to see the logic in what he was saying. He could hardly guard her from a distance.

His voice gentled a bit. "The ring will help ward off any questions or unwanted attention you might attract. The rebels may be seeking information on your whereabouts, but no one will think to mention a young wife traveling in the company of her husband. If anyone asks, we will say that I am a tradesman from France who has come here to buy garnets."

She frowned, still holding the ring in her palm. "Will they not wonder why you would bring your wife along on a trading journey?"

She felt his shoulders lift in a shrug. "I suppose they will think that you are so irresistible, I could not live without you."

"In other words, we will lie."

He started to say something, then did not.

Ciara peered down at the ring, still hesitant. The moon was not yet bright enough for her to see it, but her fingertips told her it was a wide, heavy band, with some sort of raised pattern. The metal had been warm when he placed it in her hand. He must have been wearing it against his skin.

"Princess, I am merely trying to protect you."

"Aye," she said softly, "that is what you are being paid to do." Giving in at last, she slipped the ring onto the correct finger of her left hand.

And noticed that it fit. It was a woman's ring.

Why would he be wearing a woman's ring around his neck?

She banished the question, told herself it was no affair of hers. "If we are to keep my identity secret, I suppose you had better stop calling me Princess."

He chuckled ruefully. "Aye. Mayhap we should choose a new name for you." His laugh deepened. "How do you like—"

"Ciara will do," she said flatly, stopping him before he could suggest something awful. "It is common in Châlons. Many parents consider it lucky to name their daughters after the princess."

"Very well…Ciara."

A warm tingle chased down her body. She could not remember any man ever calling her by name, with no title before it. All her life, she had been Princess Ciara, or Princess, or Your Highness. Never just…Ciara.

Somehow it was more intimate than even the physical closeness between them.

Especially spoken in that deep, soft voice.

It struck her that *all* the outward signs of her rank had now been stripped away. But instead of feeling happy about that, she was beginning to feel terribly…

Exposed.

"Just remember, Ciara, you are supposed to be a commoner," he warned as they neared the town gate. "Try to act accordingly."

She would prefer to sleep outdoors on the grass, Ciara thought, standing in the doorway of the chamber where she would spend the night. Or mayhap she could persuade Anteros to make room for her in his stall.

Either would be more appealing than this…this…she could not even think of a word for it. *Room* was far too complimentary.

Mouth open, she followed Royce inside, setting down her satchel. When she failed to shut the door, he frowned and closed it securely behind them before he inspected the chamber.

Pushing back the hood of her cloak, Ciara watched, lifting the stubby candle the innkeeper had grudgingly provided. The light illuminated a single pallet in one corner, covered with a threadbare blanket, its mattress stuffed with a scant handful of straw. A four-legged stool with one leg missing sat beside it.

Glancing down, she realized that the floor beneath her soft leather boots was not made of stone or wood, but hard-packed dirt. And there were no rushes to lend the chamber warmth, no hearth, no torches. An oily goatskin served as a rug. Her nose wrinkled at the unpleasant smell. There was not even a window to provide fresh air.

Her shoulders slumped as exhaustion and dismay pressed down on her. She had hoped for soft pillows and a warm bed at the very least. How could Sir Royce—or rather, Royce, she corrected—have called this a pleasant place?

No wonder the innkeeper had laughed at her when she had inquired about a hot bath.

"This will do," Royce said tiredly, sitting on the bed, raising a cloud of dust.

Ciara sneezed. "Please tell me you are jesting." She spied a ewer of water on the floor in one corner. Picking it up, she warily peered inside.

"So sorry if the lodging does not meet your lofty expectations, milady." He gave her an annoyed look. "It is the best that a town as small as Edessa can offer. I have stayed in worse places." Under his breath, he added, "I have *lived* in worse places."

She wanted to ask him to explain that comment, but knew he would not comply. "I suppose if we will only be here one night..." There seemed to be a film of ice on the water. Trying to dislodge it, she turned the ewer sideways, hoping to find enough liquid to wash her face and hands.

Instead she was rewarded with a solid block of ice, which slid out and shattered on the floor.

Royce started to chuckle.

Ciara wanted to cry. The crystalline shards and Royce's laughter were more than she could endure after this long and trying day. She had always wanted to experience the life of an ordinary woman, but *this* was not at all what she had imagined.

Still, she would not give in to tears, she thought fiercely. Nor would she give in to the urge to throw the empty pitcher at her amused guardian's head.

Keeping her expression neutral and her hand steady, she

held the ewer out toward him. "If you would be so kind as to fetch some water. And find a way to make a fire so that we may have a bit of heat." With her other hand, she pointed at her satchel, which was still in the doorway. "And you may place my things on the—"

"I may?" He leaned forward, his gaze as hard as his chiseled features. "I am not your servant, Ciara. How long will it take to disabuse you of that notion? I will not be treated like a lackey or a lady-in-waiting, and I have *no* interest in playing nursemaid to a spoiled, demanding child who cannot do the least little thing for herself."

Startled, Ciara withdrew the pitcher, holding it against her as if the metal might provide armor against his barbs. Dampness burned in her eyes. She felt worn out, frustrated, and sick of being mocked and insulted. She had phrased her request politely. What more could he want? Could he not be the least bit kind?

She bit her tongue to hold the questions back, knowing there was no point in asking for the impossible.

"Very well." Still holding the pitcher, she walked over to the door, picked up her satchel, and carried it inside. "I will manage on my own. If you would send in a serving woman—"

"There are no serving women here. Only the innkeeper and his wife." Royce got to his feet, brushing dust from his clothes. "If you want your skirt mended, your hair brushed, or your royal feet rubbed, you will have to use your own two hands."

Ciara turned her back on him, fighting a hot retort. She mentally recited the first ten letters of the Greek alphabet before she trusted herself to speak. "I suppose there are no laundresses about, either?"

"None. You will have to grow accustomed to a bit of dirt here and there. Like the rest of us commoners." He moved past her, toward the door. "But your toilette can wait. Supper is being served in the keeping-room, and I for one am starving."

"Keeping-room?"

"The group of tables near the entrance. Surely you noticed when we paid for our chamber. There was a hearth? With a soup cauldron? And platters on the tables?"

"Aye, but I do not think I should—"

"We will be perfectly safe, Ciara. There is no one staying at the inn tonight but an elderly man and woman and two small children. I asked the innkeeper's wife while you were busy pestering the poor innkeeper about a bath."

"But I do not wish to—"

"This is not the palace, milady." He turned on his heel, his voice sharp. "If you want food, you will eat like everyone else. In the keeping-room."

She did not flinch, regarding him with her most regal cool. "I am perfectly willing to eat with everyone else." She pronounced each word distinctly, enjoying his expression of surprise. "What I was about to say—before you interrupted—was that I do not wish to eat until *after* I have washed and changed."

"There is no need for that."

"I have never worn muddied garments to supper and I see no reason to start now." After a pause, she added, "You have my permission to await me in the keeping-room."

She purposely said it like a royal dismissal.

His jaw tightened and a muscle flexed in his tanned cheek—and he did not obey her.

He leaned back against the door, crossing his boots at the ankle and his arms over his chest.

"What are you…" She blinked at him in confusion. "Not even you could be so bold as to—you are *not* staying in this chamber while I change!"

"Rules, Your Highness. Remember?"

"Nay, this I will not endure! I must have at least *some* privacy. Can I not have ten *minutes* to myself?"

"Ten minutes is long enough for someone to abduct you or—"

"But you just told me there is no one but an elderly

couple with two small children staying here tonight. Our chamber has no window. And the keeping-room is next to the inn's entrance. The only entrance, if I recall. No one could possibly reach me without going past you."

He still made no move to leave. Ciara was grateful she no longer held the pitcher—else she surely would have hurled it at his stubborn head.

Which would have dented a perfectly good pitcher.

They glared at each other, neither budging.

"Ten minutes," he grated at last. "No more. If you are not in the keeping-room in ten minutes, I am coming back to collect you." Without another word, he grabbed for the door and left, closing it sharply behind him.

Ciara stood there shaking, unable to move for a moment, surprised—and relieved—that he had given in.

Then she walked over to the bed and let herself go limp, sinking down onto the mattress. The straw stabbed at places that already felt sore and bruised, and the dust made her sneeze. She stared down at her skirt in numb silence. Anteros's flying hooves had left her cream-colored gown speckled with mud, the wind had sculpted her hair into spiky disarray, and though she could not be certain, she was fairly sure she smelled like a horse.

Propping her elbows on her knees, she rested her face in her hands and gave in to a soft sound of pure misery. Thus far, the world beyond the palace walls—the world that had intrigued her for so long, that *looked* so beautiful—was proving to be dirty, rough, and thoroughly unpleasant.

Much like her guardian.

Vexing, perverse man. She did not understand him at all. The more pleasant she tried to be, the more surly he became.

Sighing, she reached behind her, feeling for the laces at the back of her gown, tugging at them. She had best hurry and join him in the tavern, lest he come back and bark at her some more.

Chapter 5

He was doomed.

Royce sat alone in the keeping-room, oblivious to the barley soup the innkeeper had placed on the table in front of him. The fragrant steam rising from the bowl made his stomach growl, but he barely noticed. He sat with his back to the roaring fire, a single thought circling round and round through his mind.

He was doomed.

And the weapon of his destruction would not be a rebel arrow or an icy mountain pass.

It would be the scent that had permeated his tunic and his cloak—a delicate blend of rare roses and costly myrrh. *Her* scent.

After riding with Ciara all day, he could not even take a breath without being reminded of her. Of how soft she was, how light she had felt in his arms. When he had lifted her into the saddle, she had seemed no heavier than one of her veils, as if she were made of the same gossamer silk.

And when she had fallen asleep, she had fit against him so perfectly, her body curving into his as if she had been made to be there, close to him, encircled by his arms.

By nails and blood, he never should have left the abbey with her this morn. The moment he saw her in that chapel, he should have turned to Aldric, declared that he had changed his mind about this mission, and walked out a free and sane man.

Instead, he had confidently—foolishly—decided that he could deal with her. After all, she was merely a woman. A beautiful woman, true, but he had known more than his share of beautiful women. He had never been a man to deny himself life's pleasures, and lovely female companionship had long been one of his favorites. Even during his mercenary days, he had rarely spent more than a few weeks without a pretty lady by his side to amuse him, enchant him, brighten his days, warm his nights.

They usually floated through his life like soft petals on a spring breeze, each one delightful and different, each much appreciated and cherished while she was with him, and soon forgotten after she left.

Never, in all his experience, had any female taken such quick possession of his senses. Even now, when she was not in the room, he could not push her from his mind, could not subdue the desire searing through him.

He dropped his gaze to the bowl of soup, seeing his own pained expression reflected back. It made no *sense*, this intense attraction. He usually preferred women who were sweet, warm, witty, charming.

Not spoiled, willful, and quarrelsome. And a *scholar*, of all things.

Yet Ciara had him so on edge, he could not keep from snapping at her like a starving hound. In a single day, she had robbed him of his reason.

And of his appetite. He could summon no enthusiasm for the hot soup or stew or fresh bread on the table before him, though he had not eaten since this morn.

Whispering an annoyed curse, he snatched up the goblet of wine the innkeeper had provided, and drank a long draught. Ciara only tempted him because she was *forbidden* to him, he decided. 'Twas the only possible explanation.

And it was too late now to change his mind about this mission. Not simply because he wanted to return home and restore his family name—but because if he walked away, the people of Châlons would pay the price.

His gentle countrymen were far better at tending their flocks and fields than they were at warfare, and he wanted to give them back the life they cherished. To secure the peace that he had not secured four years ago.

Even if it meant having Ciara within arm's reach at all

times, spending the night in her bedchamber. Every night.

For more than a dozen nights.

He shut his eyes, wondering whether it was possible for a man to die from unrelieved arousal. He had heard stories, some of them gruesome.

A low groan escaped his throat. He was doomed.

"Are you unwell?"

He opened his eyes to find Ciara standing at the end of the corridor that led to the inn's chambers, her head tilted to one side, puzzlement in her eyes. He could not respond to her question for a moment, his attention arrested by the dark blue gown she now wore. The color only made her skin look more pale and flawless, and without her cloak, he could see the slim, fluid curves of her body much more clearly.

He forced himself to lift his gaze, only to notice that the bodice dipped a bit too low in the front, revealing the smooth skin at the hollow of her throat. And though she had tamed her long braid, a few stray tendrils still caressed her cheeks…as if awaiting someone's hand to tuck them back into place.

God's blood, if he did not know better, he would swear she was tormenting him apurpose. He suddenly, urgently wanted to know what her spice-colored hair would look like unbound, tumbling to her hips. Whether it would be smooth and silky or tickle her back in curly waves. How it would feel in his hands if he—

"I am quite well," he lied. His voice sounded dry and strained even to his own ears. "Finished with your toilette so soon?"

"I dared not take too long," she replied coolly, "for I did not think you would have the courtesy to knock if you came back to *collect* me, as you put it."

Royce could not form a reply as she crossed toward him. He felt grateful no one else was present—because there could be no mistaking her regal walk and royal bearing. Despite the badly wrinkled gown and the lack of jewels or crown or robes, she was every inch a princess.

He would have to mention that to her. Later. He did not trust himself to discuss the way she moved at the moment. Fortunately, they had the keeping-room to themselves.

"Had you taken much longer," he said, picking up his spoon, "I would have eaten all this myself."

"It looks as though you have hardly touched your food."

"I was waiting for you." Another lie. He refused to feel a whit of guilt.

She came to stand on the opposite side of the long trestle table, looking at the bench he was sitting on, which was closer to the hearth.

He paused, the spoon halfway to his mouth, wondering whether she would sit beside him. Praying she would not. He had endured enough torment for one day.

After a moment, she sat down where she was, arranging herself elegantly on the bench across from him.

He gulped down the hot broth, not caring that it seared his throat. It could not match the heat that burned lower in his body.

Especially when her scent drifted across the table to tease his senses. She must have refreshed her perfume. God's teeth, had he known she carried a vial of the stuff in her belongings, he would have tossed it into the snow with her books and her hats. 'Twas more dangerous than a rebel blade, that fragrance.

It could make him lose his head.

"What is this?" Ciara bent over the bowl that the innkeeper had left on her side of the table.

"Barley soup," he informed her between mouthfuls, trying to keep his gaze and his thoughts on the food. "It may not be roast pheasant served on golden plates, but you will find it filling."

She sniffed at the broth while the innkeeper came in carrying a flask and a tray.

"Good eventide, madame." He poured wine into her goblet. "Do you find your chamber to your liking?"

"Aye." She bestowed one of those courtly smiles upon

him. "It will do quite well."

"And what of the meal?"

"The food looks most tempting," she said cheerfully.

"My thanks, madame." He set a platter of dried mutton between them and headed back to the kitchen. "Call for me if I can be of further service."

"Thank you, good sir."

Royce observed her over the rim of his goblet. "So you *can* be courteous to the common folk," he murmured, "provided they are waiting on you."

"Most people are deserving of courtesy." She daintily picked up one of the shriveled bits of meat from the tray and took a cautious nibble. "Only a rare Mongol beast here and there is not."

"You must forgive my surprise. It is merely that the innkeeper managed to bring out a Ciara I have not yet seen. Kind, sweet-tempered—"

"Could you mayhap find some way to entertain yourself that does not involve provoking me?" Setting the mutton aside, she lifted a spoonful of broth. "I would greatly appreciate it if you would allow me to eat in peace."

"My apologies, *madame.* I shall take the innkeeper as an example and try to remember my *place.*"

She let that remark pass without comment, without reaction. Pursing her lips, she blew on the soup.

Which was a far better revenge than any caustic retort she could have uttered. Royce felt a shudder pass through his body, as if her breath had touched his skin.

He could not tear his gaze away from her mouth. Time seemed to slow as he watched those lips parting to taste the steaming liquid…her tongue, small and pink and satiny, rising to cradle the hot spoon so tentatively. Something deep inside him wrenched painfully tight.

He must have made some sound, because she glanced up at him after she had swallowed. "Are you certain you are well?"

"I am fine." He reached for the bread and ripped out a

large chunk, using his bare hands instead of the knife that had been provided.

She observed his violence against the innocent loaf with a perplexed look. "Must you always be such pleasant company, even at mealtime?"

"If I were you, milady," he warned, chomping down on the bread and biting off a mouthful, "I would choose another topic of conversation."

"I merely wish to understand *why* you have been in such ill humor all day. Are you concerned about our journey? Is there something I should know?"

Aye, there is a great deal you should know. Starting with a few creative uses for that mouth of yours, all of which you would find more pleasurable than blowing on soup.

"The only thing I am concerned about at the moment," he growled, "is that you hurry up and finish your meal." He wolfed down the bread in three bites. "I need to get some sleep."

She opened her mouth as if to argue, then apparently thought better of it. "As you wish." She returned her attention to her food. "Mayhap the morn will find you in better spirits."

"I would not wager on it."

She glanced up at him from beneath her lashes. "Do you take *pleasure* in being disagreeable?"

"I must take my pleasure where I can," he said with a meaningful smile that was completely lost on her.

"You seem to take a great deal of it in being rude and contemptuous to me." She set her spoon down with a clatter. "You would try the patience of a saint."

"'Tis a gift."

"'Tis a most perverse trait. Never have I met a man so wholeheartedly devoted to boorishness."

"Ciara, eat your—"

"Nay, I will not eat my soup and I will not be quiet. All day, I have followed your orders while you have ignored mine. I will have no more of it. I would know what I have done to merit this churlish treatment."

"The fault is not yours," he snapped. "I will say no more."

"Indeed? That would be a great relief. But I doubt you will keep your word. You seem unable to keep your opinions to yourself for longer than ten minutes at a time."

"Take care, Ciara. If you insist on pointing out my faults, I might be tempted to name a few of yours."

"Do you mean I have *more* faults than the ones you have already thrown in my face this day? Saints' blood—"

"Watch your language, milady. One might begin to mistake you for a *normal* woman instead of a pampered little girl more concerned with her belongings, her comfort, and her appearance than with—"

"How *dare* you!" she gasped. "You ill-mannered, overgrown oaf—"

"Good eventide," a voice called from the opposite side of the room. "May we join you for supper?"

The sudden interruption made them both turn toward the corridor that led to the inn's chambers. Royce realized only then that he was breathing hard and gripping his crust of bread so forcefully that he had reduced it to crumbs. He had gotten so caught up in his verbal duel with Ciara, he had forgotten to keep an eye on their surroundings.

Forgotten that he was supposed to be protecting her.

But by God's mercy, the four strangers filing in were clearly the inn's other guests: an elderly man and woman and two small children, all dressed in the rough, fawn-colored broadcloth favored by lowland peasants.

"Indeed you may," he said, sitting up straight and giving Ciara a warning glance. "We would welcome the company."

The look in her eyes told him she would welcome any company but his. She silently picked up her spoon again.

The newcomers smiled and walked over to share their table. "I am Nevin," the man said, holding out his hand, "and this is my wife, Oriel, and our grandchildren."

Royce shook the man's hand. "I am Royce. This is my

wife, Ciara."

Oriel went to fill four bowls with soup from the cauldron on the hearth while Nevin sat beside Royce. One of the children, a boy, clambered over the bench to sit next to Ciara. When the lad looked up at her, Royce half expected her to recoil—the child's face was badly scarred, as if he had been burned in a fire.

But instead of flinching away, she remained quite still, then smiled down at him.

Royce watched in stunned silence. It was not the false, polite smile she usually relied upon, but a look of genuine warmth and concern.

"And what is your name?" she asked gently.

"I am Warran." He pointed toward his sibling. "This is my sister, Vallis. You are a pretty lady."

"Thank you. What a chivalrous young gentleman you are to say so."

"Vallis says people are afraid of me now. But you are not afraid, are you?" he asked in wonderment.

"Nay, Warran. I have always believed that what a person is like on the inside is what is truly important." She lowered her voice to a whisper. "Some people can appear handsome, but on the inside they are quite mean and black of heart."

Royce might have replied to that last comment, but he could not stop staring in amazement as she conversed with the young boy. Gone was the regal, remote princess who had held herself so straight and proud in the saddle, who flinched away from his every touch. This Ciara was relaxed, caring.

Warm.

The grandfather, Nevin, accepted a bowl of soup from his wife and reached for the bread. "And where do you come from, sir?" Frowning at the ravaged loaf, he picked up the knife and cut a slice from the opposite end.

Royce reminded himself of the story he had settled on earlier. Being secretive and mysterious would only raise suspicions. "France," he said easily. "I am a trader, come to buy garnets."

He still could not tear his gaze from Ciara, who was now doing—of all things—a magic trick for the child. Reaching behind Warran's ear, she produced a silver coin.

"How did this come to be there?" she asked with a smile. Placing the coin in her other hand, she closed her fingers around it, holding out her fist toward the boy. "Can you make it disappear again, Warran? Wave your hand over mine three times and say 'Be gone!' "

The boy complied enthusiastically. "Be gone!"

Ciara opened her fist—which was now empty. "Behold!"

Warran laughed with delight.

Royce blinked at her in disbelief and realized Nevin was still speaking to him. "I am sorry, sir. You were saying?"

"I said it will be a difficult task to find any garnets." The white-haired man handed some mutton to the little girl who sat next to him. "I fear that Prince Daemon's men left little of value behind when they passed this way."

"May his soul rot in hell," his wife whispered fiercely.

Ciara glanced at the woman beside her with a look of surprise, "Prince Daemon's men were here? In the lowlands?"

"Aye," Nevin answered. "The brutes sacked every town. Edessa is the only one that escaped unscathed. After hearing of what took place to the east, the villagers here surrendered without lifting a blade."

"What happened in the east?" Royce asked, fearing he already knew the answer.

"A carnage that Satan himself could not match," Oriel told him, her wrinkled face quivering as her voice grew forceful. "The Thuringians burned and pillaged every castle and cottage. They rode through the streets cutting down people like blades of grass. Noble or peasant, armed or helpless, it mattered not."

"We are from Vasau," Nevin explained, "where some of the worst fighting took place. Only the church was left untouched. Daemon instructed his men to spare no one—"

"Please, grandfather." The little girl stopped him, clutching his arm. "Do not speak of the bad man anymore."

The elderly man's face gentled as he looked down at her. "I am sorry, my sweet."

Oriel looked over at the boy, her voice a fragile whisper. "Their parents—our son and his wife—were killed when the Thuringians sacked our town."

"My brother died, too," Warran said softly. "I tried to pull him from the flames, but I…"

Ciara reached down to cover the boy's small, scarred hand with her own. "I am sorry, Warran," she said softly. "I also lost my brother in the war."

Royce felt something in the center of his body clench tight. Her expression held both deep sadness and genuine empathy as she comforted the child.

And it melted him. Saints' breath, had he thought she cared for naught but her books and her silk slippers?

"Grandfather is taking us to the west," the boy said tremulously. "He says we will be safe there."

"I am sure he is right," Ciara assured him. "My father—"

Royce lightly tapped her shin with the toe of his boot. She dropped her spoon into her soup, splashing her face with bits of barley.

Her smile never wavered, but as she fished the spoon out of the bowl, her eyes told him she wanted to throw it at him. Along with whatever else might be within reach. "My father is from the west," she continued smoothly, "and he tells me that the towns there fared much better than those in the east."

Royce smiled his approval at her lie. "You are wearing your supper on your chin, wife," he said lightly.

"Thank you, husband," she replied in the same tone, though her eyes still glittered. She wiped her jaw.

"Nay, not there. Higher." Without thinking, he reached across the table to brush a speck of barley from her chin.

His thumb brushed her lower lip and both of them

froze.

The room, the people around them, the fire on the hearth all seemed to vanish from his vision. All he could see was her. All he could feel was the satin of her skin, the soft pressure of her lip giving way beneath his thumb, the warm dampness of her mouth.

And he suddenly wanted—*needed*—to slide his hand to the nape of her neck, bury his fingers in her hair, and draw her to him for a kiss. Needed it more than he needed air.

Nevin cleared his throat. "I would guess that you two are newly wed." He chuckled knowingly.

When Royce did not respond, the old man followed his comment with a bawdy joke. Royce barely heard it.

But Ciara seemed to catch it, for she abruptly sat back and turned her face away, cheeks crimson.

"Oh, now look what you have done," Oriel scolded, though she too was smiling. She reached across the table and swatted her husband. "You have embarrassed the poor dear."

The tension broken, Royce sat back, struggling to take a breath. The room seemed to be spinning and his pulse pounded in his ears like a drum demanding a military charge.

Nevin laughed, unrepentant. "Only thought I might give the lad a bit of helpful advice." He winked at Royce. "You will find there is naught in marriage that cannot be cured with a bit of the old dive in the dark." When Royce only looked at him blankly, he made a circle with his thumb and forefinger and proceeded to give a quick visual demonstration.

"Nevin!" Oriel gave her husband a quelling look.

Ciara, who had just picked up her goblet to take a sip of wine, started to choke.

The older woman thumped Ciara helpfully on the back. "Pay them no mind, my dear. Men can be such beasts."

"You have not *always* found that to be such a bad trait," Nevin said slyly.

"There are children present, you old beefwit," his wife

reminded him.

Royce glanced toward the little ones, but they were too occupied with their food to care about what the adults were discussing.

Apparently, however, Ciara was not used to being pounded upon by anyone. She looked as if she might faint from shock.

He thought it a good time for a rescue. "If you will excuse us," he said politely, standing, "I believe we had best retire for the evening."

That only made Nevin waggle his eyebrows.

His wife swatted him again. "Good morrow to you, young sir."

"And to you. And Godspeed for your journey to the west." He held out a hand to Ciara, who had not yet recovered her voice. "Come, wife."

A blazing torch beside the door competed with the warm glow from a small brazier next to the bed, the opposing fires casting long shadows that entwined on the earthen floor. Sitting on the pallet, her arms wrapped around her knees, Ciara watched the dancing light.

She should be fast asleep by now, but a fluttery, ticklish discomfort in her stomach made it impossible to relax. Mayhap it was the fault of that disagreeable barley soup.

Or the fault of her disagreeable companion, who was making far too much noise. Royce had prepared himself a place to sleep on the floor, using an extra blanket wheedled from the innkeeper, and he now sat with his back against the door, sharpening his sword with a whetstone.

The rock grating against the metal grated just as sharply on her ragged nerves.

"Must you do that?" she asked coolly.

"Aye."

The curt, irritable reply told her he still was not

interested in conversation. He had uttered no more than ten words to her since they had returned from supper an hour ago—and his surly attitude only made her feel more restless. She doubted she would get much sleep this night.

Especially since she had to sleep fully clothed.

She ran her fingers over one of the deep wrinkles in her blue skirt. As she had unplaited her hair until it hung loose about her hips, she had realized her nightshift was missing, left behind at the abbey with the rest of her belongings. Which meant she either had to sleep in her gown, or…

Nay, the alternative was unthinkable.

She lifted her gaze to study him again, mystified by the tension in his face, the unnecessary force of his movements. The way he was handling that sword made her flinch. She supposed she should be grateful he had found a way to vent his ire that did not involve snapping at her.

Mayhap, she thought, absently curling a long, wavy lock of her hair around one finger, he was still upset by the horrors that Nevin had described. Mayhap that was the true cause of her own unease as well.

Until tonight, the reports of casualties in the east had been but frightening tales and vast numbers to her. Now those accounts had faces and names.

Nevin and Oriel and Vallis…and Warran.

Her subjects. Innocent people who had suffered unspeakably at the hands of Prince Daemon. Who might suffer further if the peace accord did not succeed. She alone could prevent that from happening.

Strange, she thought; she had never viewed herself as a protector before. She was not sure she was brave enough, or strong enough, to live up to such a title.

But she would have to be. For that sweet little boy. And his sister and his grandparents and all the rest.

Yet even as she felt a renewed determination to carry out her duty, she found herself confused by the peasant folk she had met tonight. By the way they could shift so easily from discussing the war to making ribald jests. Their quicksilver moods made no more sense to her than her guardian's stubborn ill humor.

Or her own restlessness.

Suppressing a sigh, she lay down on the pallet. How could she hope to make sense of anyone else's feelings when she could not understand her own?

Curling up on her side, she covered herself with the blanket, then her cream-colored mantle, and still shivered. The cold night air easily overpowered the small brazier beside her pallet.

Royce finished with the blade and slid it back into its sheath. *Finally.* Grateful that silence had descended, Ciara let her lashes drift closed.

"Tell me, Ciara," Royce said quietly, "why were you so kind to the boy?"

She opened her eyes and glared at the wall. Why, after being taciturn all night, did he have to begin a conversation now? "What do you mean?" She kept her tone cool, unruffled.

"It was most unlike you."

She shot him a look over her shoulder. "Kindness is unlike me?"

"You were more than kind, you were…" His dusky gaze held hers for a moment, then he glanced away. "Were you trying to prove a point? To show me I was wrong when I said you care about naught but your belongings and your own comfort? Was it all an act?"

"An *act?*" Ciara tried mentally reciting the first ten letters of the Greek alphabet, but only made it through *alpha, beta, gamma* before her temper slipped its leash. "I have no need to prove anything to you, sirrah. I happen to love children. Is that so odd?"

That struck him dumb for a moment. "For most women, nay. For a woman like you, aye."

"A woman like me?" she echoed, remembering his earlier comment about her not being normal. She sat up, turning to face him. "You will tell me what you mean by that."

"I mean you are *not* like other women. You grew up in a palace, doted on by courtiers, your every wish and whim granted. You have enjoyed a life of luxury and ease, giving no thought to the war or your people—"

"How dare you judge me, you insufferable knave! *You* think *me* selfish and uncaring? You, a mercenary who cares for naught but…but *land, a castle, and coin?*" Ciara felt something snap inside her. She tossed the blanket and her cloak aside. "What makes you believe you know the first *thing* about what my life has been like?"

Before he could interrupt, she thrust herself from the bed, the words pouring forth like a flood through a dam.

"I have lived behind the palace walls the last seven years because my father wanted me kept *safe*. That makes me unfamiliar with my realm and my people, but it does *not* make me a spoiled child and it does *not* make me selfish and uncaring! You do not know me at all! I have been taught that I must always be a proper example for my subjects. And I have done my best to follow all the rules and *shoulds* and *musts* and *must nots*. You do not know how many times I stood atop the parapets, wishing it could be different. Wishing I were like any other girl in Châlons. An ordinary girl with choices and freedom and dreams and…and a family and friends and…saints' breath, wishing I had never been *born* a princess—"

Ciara halted abruptly, utterly mortified that she had said the words aloud. She had just revealed her deepest secret.

To *him*.

Chapter 6

Taken aback, Royce lurched to his feet. Her stunning declaration hit him like a slap. "Ciara—"

"Nay, you…you cannot understand." Drawing an unsteady breath, she shook her head, backing away. "No one can understand."

He stepped toward her, unwilling to allow her to retreat behind her regal defenses. "Understand what, Ciara?"

"What it was like to grow up in the palace." Her voice was trembling. She was trembling. "Alone."

He stopped a few paces away from her, unable to speak. That single, unexpected word cut into his heart.

But she needed no urging to continue. The palisade of *shoulds* and *musts* that had held her emotions prisoner for so long seemed shattered beyond repair. "My mother died when I was four…and my father had to tend to the demands of his kingdom and his subjects, especially after the war began. The only people in my life were…"

Again she stopped, but he could fill in the rest. *Servants. Courtiers.* A new and different picture of Ciara struck him: she had indeed grown to womanhood in that luxurious palace, showered with wealth and privilege—but she had been denied the one thing she needed most.

The warmth of a loving family.

Suddenly it made sense to him that she would have an affinity for children, especially those who had lost their parents. "But what of your brother?" he asked gently. "What of Christophe?"

She turned her back, wrapped her arms around herself. "He was the only one who understood…what it was like. Who understood…me," she whispered. "The only one who…"

Loved me.

She could not say the words, but he felt them, felt the pain in his heart deepen, so strong that he wanted to push it, push her, away. But he could not.

All her life, she had known only one person who loved her. Her brother. His best friend.

Who was now gone forever.

"Christophe was my one companion," she continued in a whisper. "But as we grew older, the obligation of preparing to rule took even him from my side." When she turned to face him again, she looked dangerously close to tears. "You say that I know naught that is useful." Her eyes were shimmering, her lower lip quivering. "It is true that all I know of the world I have learned from books, so mayhap you are right. Sometimes I have *felt* useless and…helpless. That night when Daemon's mercenaries attacked the palace, I foolishly went into the bailey, and Christophe…" She paused, gulped a mouthful of air, said the rest in a rush. "If I had not been so useless, if I had known what to do, he would still be alive."

"Nay, Ciara, you cannot blame yourself."

"I should have known what to do. I should not have run to him. He died trying to save me!"

Royce felt an almost overpowering urge to take her in his arms, to comfort her, soothe her.

He fought it by turning his back and pacing away. "Daemon and his mercenaries killed him, Ciara. Not you. Your brother gave his life for a cause he believed in, for the country and the people he loved." When he reached a safe distance, he turned, locking his gaze onto hers. "I knew him well, milady. And I know he would not have wanted it any other way."

She did not reply, did not argue, simply sank down onto the pallet, as if exhausted. Emptied.

He stared at her in silence, sensing that this was the first time she had ever admitted her true feelings to anyone. Mayhap even to herself.

And for reasons he did not understand, did not want to examine, he felt a need to ease her sorrow. Her loneliness. He knew from experience that such a deep loss could never truly heal.

But a bit of gentleness might help.

"I am sorry about your brother," he said softly. "I should have expressed my sympathies earlier, Ciara. Christophe was a good man. And a good friend."

She nodded, her gaze still downcast. "He would have made a good king one day."

"Aye." Royce's own grief made his throat tighten. "One of the finest Châlons ever knew."

She closed her eyes, as if lost in some memory. "There is something I should have told you earlier as well." She took a deep breath, dabbed at her eyes with trembling fingers. "I…I am not sure why I did not."

"No doubt because you were ready to push me off the nearest cliff."

The barest hint of a smile tugged at her mouth, as if he had guessed correctly. "Mayhap." She folded her hands in her lap. "It is something my father told me, at the abbey before you arrived. He said that if my brother were still alive…" Her voice faltered, but only for a moment. "He said that Christophe would have been the one to escort me to Thuringia. But with Christophe gone, you were the only other man he would ask to be my guardian. The only one he could trust." She lifted her gaze to his. "The only man he would want to take Christophe's place."

Royce swallowed hard, moved that Aldric still felt such esteem for him, in spite of everything. Moved and astonished—for when they had talked at the abbey, the king had hidden his feelings completely.

By nails and blood, mayhap Ciara was not the only member of the royal family he had judged too harshly. "Thank you for telling me."

"You were my brother's best friend," she said simply. "Christophe thought very highly of you. My father does as well. I…I thought you should know."

Nodding, he reclaimed his seat before the door, watching her, feeling as if he were truly meeting her for the first time. Feeling guilty that he had been so quick to condemn her today. He had accused her of being spoiled and childish, but in truth she was merely sheltered, inexperienced. He had thought her uncaring when in fact she possessed more warmth and kindness than many of noble birth.

Mayhap, he thought with chagrin, it was *his* attitude, not hers, that needed changing. "Tell me, Ciara…where did you learn to perform magic?"

"From my father, when I was small." Her lips curved in a wistful smile. "The trick with the disappearing coin was always my favorite. While young Warran was observing my left hand, I slipped the silver into his pocket with my right. I think he will be pleased when he discovers it there later."

She picked up the cloak and blanket she had tossed aside earlier in her heated burst of fury, and her smile faded. A hint of color darkened her cheeks. "I am sorry that I—"

"Nay, do not apologize for your anger, Ciara. You are not at the palace anymore. No one will think ill of you for acting like—"

"A normal woman?"

He winced, regretting the heedless insult he had flung at her earlier. "For being yourself," he corrected. "You are wearing no crown at the moment, milady. You need not fear that people will judge you."

"That is all you have done since we met," she pointed out quietly. "Judge me."

Guilt made him want to look away, but he forced himself to hold her gaze. "You are right. I have." He made no attempt to defend himself, calmly accepting her censure. "I am sorry, Ciara. It was wrong of me."

She stared at him in disbelief, as if an apology was the last thing she had expected. The silence stretched between them, filled only by the crackle of the torch and the brazier.

She finally broke it, blinking as if she were coming out of a trance. "And *I* am sorry if I have treated you like a servant today. I am so accustomed to dealing with royal retainers that I…it is not easy for me to adjust to taking orders rather than giving them, but I…"

"We will both try to be more accommodating," he finished gently. "And since we will press on at first light, milady, I suggest you get some sleep."

She nodded, drawing her feet under her and curling up on the bed. "I only hope we do not freeze tonight." She wrapped herself in the cloak and blanket, shivering. "I do not suppose there is any way to make it warmer in here."

"Not unless you care to share your pallet."

He regretted the words the instant he said them, not only because the suggestion made her gasp instead of laugh—but because it made him think of how very pleasant it would be to share a bed with her.

"I am teasing," he amended quickly.

"Oh." She looked relieved, but still a little wary. Apparently being teased was a foreign notion to her.

"I gave you my word, Ciara. You may trust me."

"Aye, you did." The reminder seemed to satisfy her, for she lay down at last, drew the covers close, and shut her eyes. "Good night to you, Royce."

It was the first time she had called him by name—at least without disdain or ire in her tone—and for some ridiculous reason, it made him smile.

Standing to snuff the torch, he fought the foolish grin, told himself he should not be happy. It would be far easier to keep his distance from those exquisite lips and tempting curves if he and Ciara were at each other's throats.

Mayhap that was what he had been doing all day: *looking* for reasons to dislike her. Building a barricade of hostility and derision bristling with sharp points of sarcasm.

But she had just struck a gaping hole in his defenses.

And he had allowed her to slip inside and make a tentative truce between them.

Gray smoke from the doused torch circled around him as he tried to make himself comfortable in front of the door, feeling uneasy. He did not like the fact that her pain struck so readily at his heart, made him want to reach out to her with more than words. Or the fact that he was already thinking of how he might make up for the insults he had hurled all day, to show her that she was not helpless or useless.

He had been far more comfortable thinking of her as a haughty and pampered princess than as a woman—a complex and vulnerable woman.

Gazing at her across the room, he realized she was already asleep, her breathing deep and even. It made his heart thud in his chest that she trusted him so easily.

He wished he could trust himself so well.

Unsheathing his sword, he placed it close at hand—not because he feared the rebels might attack this night, but because the gleaming length of newly sharpened steel reminded him of his duty. His promise to protect her, to keep his behavior perfectly chivalrous. To deliver her to her betrothed untouched.

He had given his word of honor to her father. And to her.

But even as he remembered the vow, repeated it in his mind word by word, he could not take his eyes from the graceful curve of her cheek. Her long, black lashes were like smudges of night against her moon-pale skin.

The handfuls of cinnamon curls spilling over the edge of the bed made his fingers tingle with longing.

Had anyone ever told her that she was a beauty? He doubted it. Aldric was not the sort to offer compliments, even to his loved ones. And by the time she had blossomed from child to woman, Christophe had been occupied elsewhere, learning to become ruler of the realm. And no courtier or commoner would have dared speak to her about a matter so personal as her appearance.

She was as innocent as a woman could be, he thought.

No man had ever kissed her, or touched her, or even told her that her lips were perfection, her scent beguiling, her hair like copper and gold spun together…

And he would not be the first. Clenching his jaw, he forced himself to look away. God's blood, if he was going to survive the next fortnight, he would have to stop tormenting himself. From now on, he resolved, he would not think of her as a woman at all, but as a precious object placed in his care. A package to be delivered to Thuringia.

He whispered a curse, realizing only now why Aldric had chosen him to be Ciara's protector—not only because of his loyalty to Châlons, or the sense of honor and chivalry that had been bred into him. Or even because the king trusted him and held him in high esteem.

But because Aldric had known that he would not break his word. Not this time. Not after what had happened during the peace negotiations four years ago.

Not even if it meant death by slow torture.

The midday sun felt warm on Ciara's shoulders as she sat in the grass, her back against a tree. A few feet away, Anteros grazed placidly, and a few feet beyond the destrier, Royce leaned one shoulder against a towering pine, his attention on the slopes that stretched above them. After riding all morning, they had stopped to rest in the trees that fringed the foothills of the eastern range.

Despite the fact that Royce had allowed her to sleep well past dawn, Ciara still felt restless and unsettled by what had happened last night. She was not sure which bothered her more: her outburst or his unexpected reaction. He had not shouted back at her or mocked her. Had not chastised her as her father or one of her tutors would have done. He had been understanding. Even more surprising, he had been…

Kind.

She tilted her head to one side, studying him while he

stood there, as rigid and silent as the trees around him, the sun glinting off his thick black hair. He was truly a puzzle, this knight who was not a knight. When she had awakened this morn, she had found herself covered with his sable-lined cloak. Touched, she had thanked him for sacrificing his own comfort so that she might be warm. But he had insisted he was merely doing his duty.

The possibility that he had been kind seemed to trouble him, almost as much as it troubled her. It was humbling to realize she had been hasty in her judgment of him. That she had been mistaken to think Royce Saint-Michel a black-hearted and mannerless barbarian.

She dropped her gaze to the ring on her left hand, turning the gold band on her finger. By daylight, she had finally been able to make out the raised lettering. It consisted of four words in French, followed by three in Latin: VOUS ET NUL AUTRE, COR VINCIT OMNIA.

You and no other, the heart conquers all. She glanced from the band of gold to the dark swordsman who had given it to her, wondering how he had come by the ring. It looked quite old, and 'twas clearly made to fit a woman's slender finger. And he had been wearing it around his neck. Over his heart.

Was it a family heirloom?

Or a token of love from some fair maiden he had left behind in France? Some lady who eagerly awaited his return?

Ciara could not understand why that possibility irritated her. Frowning, she folded her hands in her lap and looked back over the lowland plain they had crossed this morn, reminding herself that his life in France was none of her affair. He had been clear that he did not wish to discuss his past.

Besides, it should not matter to her where the ring had come from or what it meant to him. Prince Daemon would soon replace it with a real wedding band.

One that would bind her to him unto death.

She shut her eyes, bleak images of her future settling over her like dark clouds filled with bone-chilling rain…

"Ciara?"

Startled, she opened her eyes to find Royce standing before her. "I am sorry, did you say something?"

"I asked whether you were all right. You looked as if you were in pain." He reached down to help her to her feet.

When he clasped her hand, she felt again that strange warmth that seemed to heat the air around her. It chased away the thoughts of Daemon—and made it difficult to think at all.

Confused, she withdrew her hand quickly. "I am fine. Is it time to ride on so soon?"

He regarded her with a curious expression, but allowed her to change the subject. "Soon. I thought I might first show you something. Or rather, teach you something."

"Teach me something?" She furrowed her brow.

"A skill you cannot learn from books. One I doubt your tutors ever thought necessary for you to learn."

She was intrigued. "What sort of skill?"

"How to defend yourself."

She blinked, waiting for him to laugh, but he appeared completely serious. She looked at him askance. "You are teasing me again."

"Nay, I am not."

"But I cannot possibly learn to *fight*." She pointed to his sword, which hung from Anteros's saddle. "I could not even lift a blade. I am not strong enough."

"You do not need a weapon. And you are stronger than you know, milady. That is what I mean to show you." He took off his cloak and cast it aside. "Even if you are faced with an opponent much larger and heavier than you, you need not feel helpless."

She shook her head. "You cannot mean that I could fend off someone like…like you, a man easily twice my size."

"It is not a matter of power or size, but of balance." He hunted around on the ground, then picked up a stick. "I want you to be able to defend yourself, in case anything should happen to me."

"Do not say that."

He straightened abruptly at her vehement command, looking at her with a curious light in his dark eyes.

She stared back at him, feeling equally surprised by what she had said. And how she had said it. "I…what I meant was, you are my escort," she concluded at last. "I would be lost if anything happened to you. I…I need you to guide me."

That did not begin to explain it, not to him, not to herself. The thoughts and feelings whirling in her head were all new to her, and so strong and confusing she could not make sense of them.

"Fear not, milady." He grinned, a flash of white that revealed a dimple in his tanned cheek. "I have no intention of getting myself killed. I am told that in Heaven there is no wine, no sin, and no—well, never mind, but I assure you, I am not eager to go there just yet." He walked toward her, tossing the stick in the air with a nimble flick of his fingers. "The tricks I can teach you will not avail you much against a sword or an arrow. But if someone tries to carry you off, or comes at you with a knife again, at least you will be able to put up a fight."

"I will?"

"Aye. Although I must warn you," he said with mock seriousness, waggling the stick like a tutor's pointer, his expression dour, "some would consider it most *improper* for a princess to learn to fight…."

"Say no more." She relented, laughing. "The idea has just gone beyond intriguing to irresistible. You may begin your lesson."

An hour later, as she sidestepped his stabbing attack and tripped him to the ground for the third time, her reluctance had changed to enthusiasm and her doubt to confidence.

"I think I rather like this," she said with a smile, bending over her instructor, who lay stretched out facedown.

"You are a quick pupil." He groaned into the grass, not moving.

"You make a most excellent tutor." She felt warm, glowing from the exercise. "Shall we try it again?"

He mumbled something incoherent, pushed himself up. "I think you have mastered that particular tactic. Let me show you another."

Ciara stepped back, braced for whatever might come. It usually took several tries, but she had mastered each skill, one after another. He had shown her how to use an onrushing attacker's speed against him, stopping him cold by driving her elbow into his windpipe or sending him off balance with a sharp kick to his knee.

He had taught her that she could even defend herself at dose quarters by striking a quick upward blow with the heel of her palm, delivered to nose or chin, or gouging at her attacker's vulnerable eyes.

It was all very strange, almost frightening in a way, yet at the same time, it felt oddly…exciting. All her life she had been coddled, pampered, protected. This was the first time she had ever engaged in a purely *physical* activity.

And she was thoroughly enjoying herself.

She waited for Royce to make his next move, but he stood still, probing at a bruise on his jaw.

"I am sorry about that," she said meekly. "Does it hurt much?"

"No more than all the others," he told her with a pained grin.

She felt bad that he was suffering in order to help her. "We do not have to continue. I have learned a great deal."

He glanced up at the sun overhead. "One more practice and then we will ride on." Heading into the trees, he gestured for her to follow. "This is mayhap the most important skill, milady. It is simple enough to defend yourself when you can *see* your opponent coming for you. But if he attacks by surprise, you will need to think quickly and clearly if you are to escape."

He led her a short way into the forest until they were surrounded by towering pines and broad oaks, the thatch of branches overhead obscuring much of the sunlight. 'Twas cooler here. And darker.

"Now, then." He stopped, turning to face her. "Do you remember what I have taught you? Your two best weapons?"

"Elbow and heel," she said quickly. He had made her repeat the phrase until it was engraved in her mind. *Elbow and heel, elbow and heel.*

"Excellent. And how do you use them?"

"Elbow first, then heel, then run."

"Exactly. Do not forget the running part. Even if you strike as hard as you can, you will not disable an attacker for long. You must get away as quickly as possible."

She nodded. "I remember."

"Very well. Let us see how you manage when we add an element of surprise. Stay there."

She remained in place as he disappeared into the trees. As instructed, she waited a few minutes. Then a few minutes more. She peered into the shadows all around her. Watched. Listened. Heard naught but the breeze and a few birds.

She grew more tense as each minute passed, kept repeating the phrase in her mind. *Elbow and heel, elbow and heel, elbow and—*

Suddenly he sprang out of the shadows behind her. She let out a shriek of surprise but instantly responded as she had been taught. Even as he grabbed her from behind, one arm closing around her, she jabbed backward with her elbow—and was rewarded with his *oof* as she connected with his ribs. In the same second, she kicked back with her heel, caught him in the knee, and broke away.

She ran a few paces and turned, smiling, uncommonly pleased with herself. "Victory is mine." She kept moving, backward now, and almost felt like laughing. "Do you yield?"

"I yield," he conceded, one hand splayed over his ribs, a pained grin on his face. "You have won the day, mil—Ciara, watch out!"

His warning came too late. She never saw the low-hanging branch, but she felt the stunning blow to the back of her head. The impact knocked her senseless.

The next thing she knew, she was lying on the ground, Royce kneeling beside her, a stream of curses tumbling from his lips.

"God's blood, woman, are you hurt? Say something. Speak to me."

She blinked up at him, tried to focus, but the world seemed to be spinning. And she could not make her tongue form words.

"Ciara?" He lifted her, cradling her against him, touching her bruised head with gentle fingers. "Burn me, I never should have—"

"I am all right," she managed to say at last, resting her cheek against his shoulder. The trees stopped dancing in her vision.

"There is no blood." He did not release her, still examining the spot where she had struck the branch. "Only a lump. By all the saints, woman, you should have been more careful."

"It is only a bruise," she responded dazedly, distracted from the pain by the far more interesting sensation of his fingers moving through her hair. "And it is…only fair. Now we are even."

"Nay, it is not fair," he replied hotly. "You could have been badly hurt. If anything happened to you, I would…"

His voice trailed off. And she could not reply, suddenly aware of how close he was holding her…how solid and rather nice his shoulder felt beneath her cheek…how muscular and strong his arm felt around her back…how her breasts were pressed against him, flattened by his chest.

An icy-hot tingle danced down her spine. Neither of them spoke. Or moved. She could not even breathe. Again she felt that strange fluttering in her stomach, the odd feeling she could only call *restlessness*. But for the first time, like a bolt from the sky above, the real cause flashed into her mind: the sensation had naught to do with fear or nervousness or any strange peasant food she had eaten.

It had to do with him. His nearness. His voice. His touch.

Him.

She lifted her head, met his gaze. Those potent brown eyes pierced hers, filled with feelings she could not sort out. Longing. Concern. Something more. Something that frightened her. Yet she did not pull away. *Did not want to pull away.*

A breeze rustled the leaves over their heads. He moved his hand to her cheek, the leather of his glove surprisingly soft against her skin. His fingers tilted her chin higher and her heart missed a beat, then began to pound.

He angled his head, his mouth dropping toward hers. The air heated all around her, within her, and she felt herself melting like honey in the sun, her lips parting, her lashes drifting closed.

Then he suddenly froze.

She could feel his breath, warm against her mouth, but he did not kiss her. She felt a shudder go through him, so strong that it wrenched a groan from deep in his throat.

He abruptly released her. His hands came to rest on her shoulders and he pushed her away.

Before she knew what was happening, he had thrust himself to his feet and turned his back.

She sat there shivering with sudden cold, stunned, bewildered. "Royce—"

"Your injury is not serious, milady." His voice sounded hoarse. "And it is time to leave."

"But—"

"Our lessons are done," he said flatly, walking back the way they had come. "There is naught more that I care to teach you this day."

"But what happened just now—"

"Forget it," he snapped. "Naught happened. Do not speak of it. Do not think of it. *Forget.*"

He stalked away from her, toward his destrier, but she

remained where she was, unable to follow. She was trembling too hard even to stand.

She felt as if she had just been swept up into the air, like a fledgling bird on a warm wind, only to be suddenly thrown to the ground. Shivering, she lifted one hand to her lips, not sure whether she should feel embarrassed or angry or hurt or all three. There were too many new feelings crowding in on her at the same time.

All she knew was that she could not forget what had happened between them. She had *wanted* him to kiss her.

And wanted it still.

Chapter 7

They endured the rest of the afternoon in tense silence as Anteros carried them high into the rocky hills. The air grew cooler but Royce barely noticed, aware only of the heat pulsing through his veins, so scalding he was surprised that steam did not rise from his body. Heat from unleashed desire—and from fury.

Fury at himself.

He tried to keep a space between himself and Ciara as they rode. Fastened his attention on their surroundings. Checked frequently to make sure no one was following them. Tried to remember his *duty* and his *vow*, damn him to Hell's deepest pit. He had forgotten both far too quickly in that insane moment in the woods. Had been but a hairsbreadth from tasting the sweetness he was forbidden to taste.

Even now, he was not sure how he had stopped himself. Wished to God that she had slapped him, fought, protested with outrage that he would even *think* of holding her that way, kissing her.

But she had not resisted.

Saints' breath, she had wanted him.

Tentatively, shyly wanted him to touch her, kiss her. And as her innocent longing stirred to life, he had felt a fierce shot of desire that would not be quenched.

But he must *never* satisfy the hunger that had been unleashed within him. She had been ready to accept his kiss, aye, but she did not begin to understand where it could lead. She was as naive about passion as she was about everything else here in the world beyond her palace. She had no idea what it meant for a man to want a woman the way he wanted her.

But *he* knew. Knew that one kiss would never be enough. Feared that if he dared take that much, he could not resist claiming more.

So he would not touch her that way again. Would not allow himself to steal even a single kiss. The matter was closed. She was a valuable package, not a woman.

Unfortunately, the image no longer held any power to help, for it only made him think of how much he would enjoy unwrapping the package to discover the surprises hidden within.

Stifling a curse, he lifted his gaze to the clouds that had been gathering all afternoon. *Christophe, old friend,* he prayed silently, desperately, *if you are up there somewhere, if you could put in a good word, this would be an excellent time for some help from above.*

Mayhap an act of God could help him forget what it had felt like to have Ciara so warm and yielding in his arms.

The afternoon sun hung low in the sky by the time they reached the mountain summit. Snow had been sifting down for an hour now, surrounding them with a glittering veil of white. As they topped the rise, Ciara made a soft sound of wonder. Royce, captivated by the sight that greeted them, reined Anteros to a halt.

Alpine peaks studded the landscape as far as the eye could see, like massive diamonds scattered over the earth, wreathed in mist and snow. The sun gleamed on soaring ridges and sheer cliffs sculpted of stone and ice. Only a hint of sky could be seen here and there, between the towering giants that rose up to pierce the clouds.

His chest tightened. His throat burned. He glanced to the right, to the southeast—where the Ferrano lands were just visible in the distance.

He was home. For the first time in more than four years, he was home.

"It is beautiful," Ciara whispered.

"Aye," he agreed hoarsely. "There is no other place in the world like this."

They both drank it in for another moment, in silence, before he nudged the stallion forward.

"What is that mountain, there?" She pointed to the tallest peak, directly ahead of them, which dominated the horizon. "Has it a name?"

Her innocent question made his gut clench. "Mount Ravensbruk," he said gruffly. "It will be your new home anon, milady. That is where Daemon has his palace."

She flinched at the news.

Noticing her reaction, he could not keep from asking a question that had been simmering at the back of his mind. "I gather you are not looking forward to your marriage?"

"Looking forward to it?"

"Your father said you agreed to the match, yet the mention of Daemon's name upsets you."

"I am not upset." She accompanied the claim with a shrug. "It matters not what I feel for Prince Daemon."

"Of course it matters."

"Nay, it does not," she insisted. "Like him or loathe him, I have no choice in the matter."

"But your father would not have forced you, had you refused Daemon's proposal."

She shook her head. "Prince Daemon won the war and demanded my hand as part of the terms of peace, and Châlons was in no position to bargain. Had I refused…" She did not finish the sentence. "I will not risk unleashing Daemon's wrath on my people again. The wedding will unite the royal houses of Châlons and Thuringia, and forge a lasting bond that will ensure peace."

Those sounded like her father's words, not hers, but Royce did not think she would appreciate him pointing that out. "So you are marrying him because you must."

"I am marrying him for my subjects, for…" Her voice faltered, then strengthened. "For that little boy we met in the keeping-room last night. I do not want any other children to lose their parents. Or…" She finished in a whisper. "Or any other sisters to lose their brothers."

Royce remained silent, fighting his emotions. Not only did Ciara have a heart. She had courage. She might not see it in herself, but he had known hardened warriors who were unable to face challenges so bravely.

"The responsibility is mine," she continued, looking at Mount Ravensbruk. "As for my future…I shall simply hope for the best and depend upon Daemon's Christian mercy."

"Then you are in a predicament, milady, because there is precious little of that to spare." Royce clenched his jaw. "Of King Stefan's three sons, it is said that Prince Mathias inherited his spirit, Prince Telford his strength, and Prince Daemon his ambition. Unfortunately, Daemon was the one chosen as regent when his father fell ill. And he does not know the meaning of the word *mercy*. The whoreson once killed a servant for being late with his breakfast—"

"Save the vivid descriptions, if you please. I have heard most of the tales already." She shivered. "Daemon's character or lack of it does not change my duty."

Royce cursed himself for speaking so bluntly. For reminding her of what was to come. She had been trying to make polite conversation.

But he could not help himself. He did not want to make *polite* conversation or *polite* anything else with her.

Watching the snow fall around them, he listened to the creak of saddle leather and the muffled sound of his destrier's hoofbeats—wishing he could turn the horse and carry her away from Mount Ravensbruk. Away from Daemon.

"Your duty," he finally echoed, thinking he had never hated the word before. "Of course."

"I would really prefer not to discuss it further," she said softly, shifting her attention away from the massive peak. "Whether or not Daemon will make a suitable husband changes naught. My feelings on the matter are unimportant. The fact is, I am his betrothed. And I must honor my agreement."

Royce resisted the urge to argue. He had never in his life

believed that feelings were unimportant, and never would. But the rest of what she had said was true. And inescapable.

As they rode on, he brooded about words like *duty* and *honor.*

And *agreement.*

It took another hour for them to reach their destination for the day: the town of Aganor, at the bottom of the broad slope they had crossed.

It looked every bit as bad as Royce had feared.

"Sweet holy Mary," Ciara breathed.

He reined in before the town gate. Or what was left of it. The thick oak portal had been reduced to splinters by a battering ram. Beyond it lay the skeletal remains of buildings blackened from fire, their thatched roofs burned away, many of the dwellings no more than piles of ashes. Only the church had been spared.

Ciara shook her head in denial. "What—"

"Daemon." He spat the name like a curse. "Prince Daemon and his mercenaries."

She lifted a hand to cover her mouth, not quite fast enough to hold in a small sound of pain. Royce resisted the urge to touch her shoulder and draw her close.

Despite the fact that he had seen carnage of this sort before, his stomach turned. He saw no survivors in the streets but noticed bits of ivory scattered about, barely discernible amid the blanket of white. Not wanting Ciara to guess that they were bones, he touched his heels to Anteros's flanks, turning to circle the city wall.

As they left the town behind, Ciara glanced over her shoulder. "If we cannot stay here, where will we stop for the night?" She looked up at the thickly falling snow.

"At the keep I mentioned yesterday, there." He pointed, seeing it through the swirling flakes, perched high upon a nearby hill—its drawbridge smashed, portions of its curtain wall in ruins, one of its towers half crumbled. "A friend of mine and his wife live there. Or used to." His heart beat painfully hard against his ribs. "Let us hope they are still safe and well."

The great hall overflowed with light from two dozen torches, the scents of spicy rabbit stew and the dried herbs that had been sprinkled in the rushes on the floor—and the noise of more than fifty happy, well-fed women and children.

Seated at a trestle table before the blazing hearth, Royce sopped up one last bite of stew with a corner of bread, smiling at the brawny, fair-haired knight across from him. "I must say, Bayard." He had to speak loudly to be heard over the din. "Never did I think it would be possible to have too *many* women underfoot."

Bayard shrugged, his smile broad, his blue eyes sparkling with amusement. "What was I to do? They had nowhere else to go."

Royce washed down the last of his supper with a long drink of wine, then pushed aside his empty bowl and trencher. He grinned at his friend, still relieved to have found him not only alive but in good spirits.

And good company. Shaking his head in bemused disbelief, he glanced about the hall as he wiped his hands on the tablecloth. It looked as if Bayard had taken in every female refugee in the mountains. Some were orphans, others widows, many in peasant garb, others dressed in finery that marked them as members of the nobility. A few were still recovering from injuries suffered in the war.

"It began with the handful of local women who survived when the town fell," Bayard explained, "and the families of my men who were killed defending the keep. Then word spread to their relatives, and more arrived. This is the only castle left standing in this part of Châlons."

"You are a generous man, my friend, to take them all in, feed them, care for them."

Bayard waved a hand, dismissing the compliment. "It is

no more than any other lord would do. And they have insisted on doing their part, cleaning the keep, working in the kitchens. Still, I had thought the situation would be only temporary." He sighed, the sound of a man who had been outnumbered by females for a little too long. "Almost three score of them wintered here. Now it looks as if they will *spring* here as well."

Royce laughed. "It is a harem that many a Saracen would envy."

"Do not let my wife hear you say that."

The two of them glanced at a pair of ladies seated together in a far corner, surrounded by children. The din in the hall quieted a bit as music began to fill the air.

Mandolin music.

Royce lifted his goblet and drank another draught of wine, his gaze on Ciara as she strummed her cherished instrument. When Bayard and his wife, Lady Elinor, had met them outside, Elinor had immediately noticed Ciara's mandolin hanging from his saddle and begged her to play for them after supper. It had no doubt been a long time since anyone in the keep had enjoyed such entertainment. There were few traveling minstrels or troubadours in Châlons these days.

Ciara had said she was not accustomed to playing for an audience—but eagerly agreed once she met the children.

Now she sat with her head bowed, her attention on her mandolin. Her fingers moved lightly over the strings, bringing forth the notes of a merry tune. One unfamiliar to him.

He felt like one of the children at her feet, gazing up at her as if they had never heard anyone play so beautifully before. As if the lady seated before them were an angel descended from Heaven with a magical harp. The music became livelier and a small boy began clapping in time, then the others joined in. A little girl, no more than two or three years old, began to dance, waving her chubby hands, gurgling with laughter.

Ciara glanced up, as if surprised that her playing could bring them such joy. Then she smiled, her own happiness lighting her entire face.

Royce's heart seemed to stop. Everything around him seemed to stop—the sounds of the children, the heat and crackle of the fire at his back, even the music she played. All sense of time, of place, seemed to fade from his awareness, and there was only this lady, her sparkling amber eyes. And her smile.

He blinked, unnerved by the sensation. Never in his life had he experienced such a feeling—other than in the keeping-room last night. Never could he remember desire rendering him deaf, dumb, and paralyzed.

But this desire he felt for Ciara was far different from any he had known before. Not only stronger but…different.

He realized Bayard was speaking to him and finally wrenched his gaze back to his friend. "I am what?"

"I said," the blond knight repeated, his smile filled with understanding, "that your wife's talent is surpassed only by her beauty. You are a fortunate man."

"Aye. Fortunate," Royce croaked. He reached for a nearby jug of wine, refilled his cup, and quickly changed the subject. "Which of these did you say are yours?" Picking up his goblet, he gestured to the children scattered about the hall.

Bayard pointed them out with obvious pride. "That is my daughter, Ilsa, who will soon be two." The dark-haired girl had climbed into her mother's lap to snuggle. "And that"—he indicated a boy who scampered past them chasing a shaggy hound much larger than he was—"is my son, Brandis, who is five."

Royce watched as the lad caught up with the dog and fearlessly wrestled him to the ground. "He seems to take after his father."

"Aye." Bayard grinned broadly. "Hard to believe we were his age when first we met."

Royce nodded. "We had some good times in those

years."

"That we did. Do you remember when we were ten and thought it would be an excellent idea to spend an afternoon exploring the caves in Mount Kaladar—"

"Until we got lost. For three days." Royce chuckled. "I thought your father would flay us alive when he finally found us."

"That was *almost* as bad as the winter when we decided to use our fathers' shields to go sledding."

"It seemed such a sensible idea at the time."

"It was *your* idea." Bayard's laughter was deep and rich. "And they *were* much faster on the ice than our wooden sleds."

"Right up to the moment we crashed into the trees and mangled them. Not to mention ourselves."

"And our dignity. How old were we then?"

"Twelve." Royce smiled warmly at the memory. "When winter was naught but skating and sleds—"

"And fighting with snowballs. God's breath, I remember it like yesterday, how we loved battling with your little brothers and pelting your sisters…" Bayard's voice trailed off. His expression turned somber.

Royce felt his throat tighten, dropped his gaze to his goblet. An awkward silence fell, filled with other, more recent memories.

Bayard cleared his throat. "Royce, I am sorry. I did not mean to remind you of them—"

"It was seven years ago."

"Even so, to suffer such a loss—"

"It was seven years ago," Royce repeated, unwilling to reopen old wounds. For a time, he had tried to purge himself of the fury and pain, spilled a great deal of Thuringian blood, and too much of his own, before he realized that no amount of death and vengeance would help.

Grief, he had learned, was a wound that never fully healed. After all these years, he had simply become accustomed to it, lived with the pain until he did not notice it overmuch. Most of the time.

He lifted his gaze to Bayard's, seeing his own anguish mirrored there. Everyone in Châlons had suffered losses in the war, Bayard included. Their carefree youth had come to an abrupt end on that day seven years ago when Thuringia had suddenly changed from peaceful ally to vicious enemy.

That day when the Ferrano lands, which lay directly on the border, had been taken by surprise—and been the first to fall.

But Royce had vowed long ago that he would not drown himself in bitterness over what might have been. What would never be again.

Because God and King Aldric together could not restore all that this war had cost him.

Bayard pushed his empty trencher around on the tabletop. "So how long has it been since we last saw each other? Five years, is it not?"

Royce felt grateful for the way his friend shifted so easily to a less painful topic. "Aye."

"I take it King Aldric has been keeping you busy. Have you any news from court?"

Royce took another long swallow of wine while he considered his response. Thus far, he had explained only that he and his "new bride" were passing through on their way to see his old home, now that peace had come. Bayard had been happy to offer shelter, food, and drink without asking many questions.

Royce would prefer to keep it that way. For the safety of everyone involved.

"Nay, I have no news," he said as the mandolin music ended and the chamber erupted in applause. "I have not been at court for some time. And I am sorry that it has been five years, Bayard. The war—"

"Aye, the accursed war. It did more damage than merely separating old friends. You do not need to apologize." He took a drink, wiped his mouth with the back of his hand. "We could have used your skill, here in the mountains. But we all understood that you were needed elsewhere."

Royce looked away, assailed by a pain, a guilt, that was old and deep. His flair for battle tactics had first attracted royal notice when he had been but seventeen and newly knighted. A year later, Aldric had brought him to court to serve as one of his military advisers.

That was where he had been, on that day. That black day when his entire family perished.

He shut his eyes. "I have often wondered, Bayard, whether I could have made a difference, if I had…if—"

"If you had been there when they attacked? There is no point tormenting yourself, Royce. You would have been killed with everyone else." His tone softened. "It would seem that God had other plans in mind for you, my friend." Sighing heavily, he clicked his goblet against Royce's. "But let us talk no more of the war. We should be drinking a *salut*, to peace at last."

The bitter note in his friend's voice made Royce pause before he raised his cup. "You do not sound entirely happy about that."

"About peace with the Thuringians? Only months ago they were laying waste to our homes, murdering our families, and raping our women. Now we are expected to lay down our arms and embrace them like brothers. You will forgive me if I find it difficult to be happy."

A prickle of unease chased down Royce's spine. He looked down into his cup, posed his reply carefully. "Those sound like the sentiments of a rebel, old friend." He glanced cautiously, protectively toward Ciara, who was now performing magic tricks for the children, enchanting them, looking enchanted herself.

"Hardly," Bayard scoffed. "I want peace as much as anyone. More so. I do not want my children to grow up in Châlons as it has been these seven years. Nor do I want my son to have to fight the same battles I have fought, against the same foe." He looked around the crowded great hall. "And if my serfs cannot plant new crops this spring, how will I feed all of those who depend on me? I *need* peace."

Royce probed a bit deeper, casually. "Still, there are those who believe that the peace agreement will only make Daemon more powerful. That it is worth any sacrifice to thwart his plans."

"Sacrifice? Is that what they call it?" Bayard looked disgusted. "I may sympathize with the rebels' desire to keep our country out of Daemon's hands, but I cannot agree with their methods. Have you heard that they made an attempt on the princess's life? In the palace, no less?"

"Aye." Royce kept his tone light. "I heard about it."

"Any traitor who would stoop to that deserves to be drawn and quartered." Bayard's eyes blazed with outrage. "Before he is fed to the royal hounds in small pieces."

Royce nodded in agreement, relieved that his friend seemed as loyal to the crown as ever.

"If these rebels were from the east," Bayard continued hotly, "they would realize that there has been *enough* death and *enough* killing " He looked again at the refugees crowding his hall. "King Aldric has made peace, and it is for the best. I may not like the idea of laying aside my sword, but I see no other solution."

"Nor I," Royce said hollowly, glancing toward Ciara again.

She was now sitting on the floor—actually sitting on the *floor*—with baby Ilsa in her lap, toddlers clambering all over her royal person, and a shaggy gray-and-brown puppy attempting to make a meal of her skirt. All while she tried to show one of the older girls how to pick out notes on her mandolin.

She looked blissfully happy.

"Nor I," Royce repeated, his heart thudding painfully hard against his ribs.

Bayard signaled for servants to bring more food and wine, but Royce found that his stomach had turned sour. Their conversation had left him tense, reminded him that he dare not trust anyone, even his childhood friend. Thus far, the journey with Ciara had gone as planned, so mayhap Aldric had indeed managed to fool the rebels and they were far from here, on the other side of the kingdom, chasing decoys….

Or mayhap they were much closer, lying in wait and planning an attack.

"So tell me more about this bride of yours, my friend," Bayard said, grinning. "Where did you manage to find a lady so talented, lovely, and seemingly intelligent who was willing to marry you?"

Royce did not want to lie to his friend, but he was not about to reveal any secrets. So he told the truth.

"In a monastery."

"Very funny."

Royce looked up to see Ciara, Elinor, and Ilsa crossing the hall to join them. "She comes from the north," he elaborated. That was true enough.

"Beautiful women they have there in the north."

Elinor came up behind her husband just in time to hear this comment. "Is this what the two of you have been talking about?" She gave her husband a playful poke with one finger. "We leave you alone for a short while and already you are discussing other women."

"Ah, curses, we are caught." Laughing, Bayard tilted his head back as his wife bent over to give him a kiss.

Royce smiled as he watched his friends. Bayard had eyes for only one woman, had been besotted since the age of fourteen, when he had vowed to make the spirited Elinor his wife—after she bested him in an archery match at a local fair. The two of them had lived here, on Elinor's dower lands, ever since Bayard's family holdings were lost in the war.

Straightening, Elinor lifted her daughter to her hip. "It is time to put this little one to bed, milord."

"Aye, you are right." The child had lost a shoe, and Bayard reached up to tickle his daughter's bare foot, making her giggle.

Elinor smiled warmly at Ciara. "Thank you again, milady. I do not believe I have ever heard anyone play so beautifully."

The praise brought a dusting of pink to Ciara's cheeks. Her smile was bright, her eyes sparkling as she cradled her mandolin. "I am glad the children enjoyed it."

"They loved it. And you." Elinor turned her attention to Royce. "This charming bride of yours will make a wonderful mother. She has such a way with children."

Royce could not reply, his gaze on Ciara, his mind filled with a sudden, unbidden image of her round and heavy with child.

His child.

He blinked and the vision vanished, but it left behind a strange, tingling warmth in the region of his heart. A longing he had never felt before.

Elinor was still speaking to him. "And did you know that she composes her own music?"

It took a moment for Royce to find his tongue. "Aye," he lied. No wonder he had never heard the tunes before.

Chuckling, Bayard clapped him on the shoulder. "Let us go collect our son, Elinor. I think these two would enjoy some time alone." He pushed back from the table and stood. "They may even wish to retire early." He winked.

Royce forced himself to smile, trying not to think of the comfortable bedchamber his friends had prepared for him and Ciara. "Good eventide to you both."

Elinor handed her daughter to Bayard as he rose, then gave Ciara a quick hug. "Thank you again. I hope we will have time to get to know one another better on the morrow. And in the years to come."

Ciara looked startled by the display of affection, as if no one had ever dared hug her before. Then she set her instrument aside and returned the gesture, a tremulous smile on her lips. "I…hope so, Lady Elinor."

Royce lowered his gaze, busied himself by refilling his trencher with food he had no appetite for. His gut wrenched into a knot. Ciara would never have the chance to get to know Elinor better. They would be leaving in the morn. He would be taking her on toward Mount Ravensbruk. To her new home. To her betrothed.

And when she grew heavy with child one day, it would be Daemon's seed that made her so.

The possessive fury that shot through him made him drop the platter he had just picked up. For a moment, he was blinded by the red haze that gripped him. The feeling was savage, primitive. Utterly beyond the realm of his experience.

"Royce?" Ciara's voice was full of concern.

He shook his head to clear it. His friends had left. Ciara had taken Bayard's place across from him.

"I am merely tired," he bit out. "It has been a long day."

"Aye, that it has."

They said naught more for a moment, gazing at each other across the table, listening to the laughter and conversations that filled the great hall. The gray-and-brown puppy that had munched on Ciara before danced around her feet, yapping for attention, but she did not seem to hear.

Royce broke the stare, wanting anything *but* to spend the rest of the evening sitting here, alone with her.

However, his only other choice was to spend the rest of the evening alone with her in the bedchamber upstairs.

He glanced down at his full trencher and pushed it aside, reaching for the jug of wine on his left—at the same instant Ciara reached for it.

Their fingers met and heat sizzled through him. They each flinched as if burned. After a moment, he started to reach for it again, then hesitated as she did the same. They both thrust forward and their fingers collided once more.

Ciara withdrew, dropping her hands to her lap with a sound of unease. They avoided meeting each other's gaze. He realized she was breathing fast and shallow, as he was.

He muttered an oath. How were they to endure the rest of the journey if they could not even bear to have their fingers brush in the most innocent way? This was intolerable.

And entirely his fault, he thought angrily. He was the one who had overstepped his bounds this morn, created this constant tension between them. But he could control himself. He *would* control himself. The responsibility was his.

He picked up the accursed jug of wine and filled her cup for her.

"Thank you," she said softly, still not looking at him.

He grabbed an almond tart, ate it though he was not hungry. "The music was nice."

"It is kind of you to say so."

Silence descended.

"Your friends seem…nice," Ciara ventured.

"They are good people."

"And their children are very sweet."

"Aye."

That seemed to exhaust their supply of safe, polite conversation.

Which left Royce's thoughts free to dwell upon subjects that were not safe or polite. Such as her scent. That dangerous perfume drifted across the table to tantalize him. Why, in the name of all that was holy, was she wearing such a fragrance in the first place? 'Twas not at all suitable for a scholarly, innocent princess. It was much too vivid, too dramatic.

Too sensual.

He turned to look at her, found her regarding him with that curious, slightly bewildered expression. As if she could not understand what was happening between them.

But *he* understood it. God help him, he understood.

Even as their gazes met and held, her face flushed with color and her lips—those luscious, garnet-dark lips—parted slightly. All he had to do was lean across the table, close the scant space between them….

He wrenched his gaze from hers, in the grip of a hunger he could not vanquish. He could hear his heart beating too fast, wondered if she could hear it as well. Wanted naught more in that moment than to thrust himself from the table and walk away.

But he could not leave her alone. Not for an hour, not even for a minute. He was her guardian. Sworn to protect her.

Condemned to serve his duty in Hell—always in her company yet forbidden to touch her. Satan himself could not have designed a more painful torture for him. He gulped for air, only to inhale more of her scent. More of her.

He glanced around the room, seeking some focus for his wayward thoughts, some topic they might discuss, some…

His gaze landed on one of Bayard's refugees, a buxom brunette who had been smiling at him frequently through the evening. He had not given her any attention before, but now he offered her a wide grin, grateful for whatever distraction he could get. She responded with an openly hungry expression and a seductive toss of her long hair.

"Can we take her with us?"

"What?" Royce's gaze snapped to Ciara.

She was looking at the floor, her attention on the wriggling, yapping puppy. "This little one will not leave me alone." She scooped the dog into her lap. "Elinor said I could have her if I wished."

Royce shut his eyes and drew a deep breath, willing his heart to slow down. "Ciara…"

"She will be almost as tall as my hip when fully grown. At least that is what Elinor told me." The little beast licked Ciara's face, eliciting a giggle. "I think I shall name her after Hera, queen of all Greek goddesses and protectress of the home."

"Nay, you will not. We cannot possibly—"

"How can you resist this face?" She extended the squirming mongrel toward him with a hopeful smile.

"Easily." The little blur of fur did have rather endearing features—a long nose, floppy ears, and bright black eyes almost hidden by tangles of grizzled hair. "We have difficult terrain to cross and the last thing I need is one more unruly creature to watch over."

"*I* will watch over her." She frowned at his surly reply, withdrawing the dog. "I never had a pet before—"

"And you do not have one now." He was starting to lose patience. "She will make too much noise. Draw too much attention. Run away at every opportunity—and we will waste valuable time searching for her. We are not taking that animal with us."

"But—"

"Do not argue with me, Ciara," he snapped, unable to control both his desire and his temper. "You can either give her up now or give her up twelve days from now. I suggest giving her up now. Before you form any sort of emotional attachment." He leaned across the table, the rest spilling out in a harsh whisper. "Because your *husband* will never allow you to keep such a mongrel. You may wish to play at being an ordinary woman, milady, but he is *not* the sort to indulge you."

Ciara flinched, her expression stricken. She cradled the puppy close, her eyes suddenly glistening with dampness.

Blinking hard, she turned and put the dog down and let it scamper away.

Royce cursed himself under his breath. "Ciara, I am sorry. I did not mean to—"

"Nay, you are right to remind me of my duty," she said quietly, still looking at the floor. "The prince would never approve. I was enjoying myself so much this evening that…for a moment I almost forgot—"

The buxom brunette arrived out of nowhere before she could finish. "Milord?" The woman leaned over the table, sliding a tray of sugared nuts in front of him. "Can I tempt you with one of these?"

Royce wrenched his gaze from Ciara, only to find himself faced with an eyeful of bosom, artfully displayed by an indecently low-cut bodice. "Nay," he said curtly, "I am not—"

"Then at least allow me to refill your cup for you." She set down the tray and reached across the table to pick up the wine, her breasts brushing against his shoulder.

Instead of feeling aroused, as she so obviously intended, he was annoyed. He had had more than enough feminine attention and companionship for one day. "Thank you for the *offer*, but my wife and I—"

"Your wife?" She feigned surprise, lifting a hand to cover her bosom, only to stroke her fingers across the curving expanse of skin. "I did not realize. Someone said she was another refugee brought here for shelter. And from her garments…" She eyed Ciara's muddied gown with disdain.

For once, Ciara did not respond with a polite smile or courtly phrases.

She looked as if she wanted to spear the woman on a stick.

Which only made the brunette smile as she turned back to him. Evidently she enjoyed a challenge. "If you have finished your supper, I would be happy to offer you a tour of the keep."

For a second—just one second—Royce wanted to accept. God knew he *needed* release from the ravenous desire that held him in its talons. And the woman was obviously eager for a tumble. A half hour with her might clear his mind, enable him to focus on his duty.

But duty had naught to do with his decision. To his astonishment, he found that her offer did not, in truth, interest him. She was willing to serve herself up like one of the sweetmeats on the platter, but her wiles left him cold. He no more wanted her than he wanted the food forgotten on his trencher.

'Twas a stunning moment. Never in the past would he have refused such a brazen invitation.

"Thank you," he said unsteadily, "but I have no need of a tour. I am quite familiar with the castle."

"Ah, then you know of the east tower." Undaunted, she caught a lock of her long hair, twirled it around her finger, and brought it to her lips. "You can see the entire valley from its roof. And the view is especially beautiful at night."

With one last smile, she turned and walked away, hips swaying with obvious entreaty. Heading for the east tower.

He watched her go, then turned to find Ciara glaring at him.

"Do not let me keep you."

"Ciara—"

"Nay, go with her. You have my full permission. Why should *you* let any sense of duty stop you from enjoying your evening?" She rose from the table.

Royce reached out to grab her wrist. "You forget, milady, that I take my duty as seriously as you take yours."

She yanked her arm free. "Well, I hardly think one of the orphans means to carry me off this night. I will be perfectly safe in our chamber. The only window is an arrow slit, and any intruder would have to be rather thin to slip in that way. And I promise to bolt the door behind me."

"Ciara, I cannot allow you to—"

"I would *prefer* to be alone, if you do not mind. Surely you can grant me one evening's privacy. You can see our chamber from here, at the top of the stairs." Her voice became brittle as she glanced toward the spot where the brunette had disappeared. "Though I doubt you can see it from the east tower."

She turned and fled the hall, leaving him alone with his frustration, his hunger, and a table full of cold food that he did not want.

And her mandolin. Only after she was gone did he notice that she had forgotten her precious mandolin.

Chapter 8

Ciara slammed the bedchamber door behind her and fell back against it, covering her face with her hands, breathless from her dash up the stairs. Mortified that she had just run from the hall. From him.

She tried to inhale a calming breath, only to release all the air in her lungs with a sharp sound of hurt. She shook her head in denial, confused by her behavior, by feelings that made no sense to her. The way Royce and that woman had looked at each other, the idea that they might…that they would…

She pressed her palms flat against the door to steady herself, keeping her eyes squeezed tightly shut. She would *not* cry. Did not even understand why she *wanted* to cry. It was absurd to feel so upset by the actions of that…that…

Wench. That was a good word for her.

Ciara lifted her lashes, her vision swimming with tears. Fie, how she had wanted to snatch up the jug of wine and dump it over the shameless bawd's head!

Blinking hard, she wiped the moisture from her eyes with trembling fingers, perplexed by the intensity of her feelings. Never in her life had she experienced such animosity toward another woman. Toward anyone. What in Heaven's name was wrong with her? Mayhap she was ill, mayhap she had…

Her thoughts stilled as she beheld the contents of the room clearly for the first time since shutting the door.

A fire glowed merrily on the hearth. Someone had also left candles burning on low tables that flanked the bed, along with a silver flask and two exquisite goblets. The mattress had been covered with fresh sheets, folded back to reveal a scattering of rose petals, the four posts draped with white silk to form a canopy and bed curtains. Sniffing the air, she caught a musky scent—from sandalwood shavings added to the fire.

"Oh, Lady Elinor, *nay*." Ciara went to the foot of the bed, where Elinor had left a white cotton kirtle for her to sleep in. She picked up the garment, filled with dismay at its delicate beauty. The material was as sheer as mountain mist, the long, loose sleeves and full skirt edged with embroidery.

Her kind, thoughtful hostess had prepared the chamber for a romantic tryst! But Elinor did not understand. Did not know that Royce was not her husband.

That he would not be spending the night here, but in the east tower.

Biting her bottom lip, she set the garment aside and bent to blow out the candles.

But she paused.

Royce would be enjoying *his* evening. Why should she not enjoy hers?

She had the chamber to herself for the night. Why *not* savor the luxuries her hostess had provided? She had vowed to seek out pleasant experiences during her journey. And she did not know when she would have another evening alone.

Straightening, she exhaled slowly and left the candles burning. She would not sit about and sulk like some pitiful, lovesick damsel in a troubadour's tale. She was not pitiful. And she certainly was *not* lovesick. It was no business of hers where Royce chose to spend his evening. Or with whom. She did not care.

Did not care about him in the least.

Pleased with her decision, Ciara went to the corner where a servant had placed her satchel earlier. She dug through the contents and pulled out one of the books she had brought with her. Then she walked back to the bed and began to disrobe, her gaze on the kirtle, her spirits already lifting.

If she had been upset in the great hall, it was merely because she was tired. Overwrought. Exhausted by a day filled with new adventures and dizzying emotions—excitement at learning to defend herself, dread upon catching her first sight of Mount Ravensbruk, delight when she had played with the children, happiness upon discovering what it could feel like to have a friend.

And this other feeling. The one that was all tangled up with the way Royce looked at her, and touched her…

Shivering, she lifted the flowing kirtle over her head, making a soft sound as it drifted down her body like a cloud. Then she leaned against the bedpost, gazing into the fire as she began unplaiting her hair, trying at the same time to unravel this feeling Royce stirred in her.

It had been building since the moment they met—and it had taken a sharp, unexpected turn when she had noticed the other women in the hall noticing him. The brunette had been only the most obvious in a roomful of sighing damsels, all enchanted by his rugged features and windswept dark hair, his brown eyes, the way he moved with such confidence, the disarming smile that flashed at the most unexpected moments…

Gritting her teeth, resolved not to think of him anymore, she grabbed her book and climbed into the bed. She reached for the decanter on the table beside her and poured a draught of wine, taking a small sip. Her royal tutors had always insisted that a princess must take care with strong drink, must only partake in the most restrained, ladylike way…

She emptied the cup in one swallow and poured herself another. Tonight, she decided with a wicked smile, she would find out what it felt like to get well and truly drunk.

"A toast," she declared, raising the goblet, "to freedom."

Piling up pillows against the headboard to cushion her back, she sank into them with a sigh and picked up her book, enjoying the sweet taste of the wine and the heady scent of the crushed rose petals.

Only to find herself remembering how very different and strangely pleasant it had felt to rest against Royce's hard, muscled chest today, how his musky scent had enveloped her…

She dropped the book into her lap, disgusted with herself. Angry at him. How was it that the man could dominate her thoughts when he was not even in the room? Did he make such an impact on *every* woman who looked at him?

She swallowed hard, setting her cup aside, knowing that was the real question that had been bothering her all evening.

Did those other women feel this same tingly-hot sensation when they thought of him? Did their hearts beat faster whenever he glanced their way? Did they, too, wonder what his kiss would be like?

And did he care naught more for her than he did for them?

She sat up, pushed the covers aside, plucked a rose petal from the sheets, and tore it into shreds. This morn, in the woods, he had *seemed* kind, concerned for her…even tender. But it had not lasted long.

Hanging her head, she buried her face in her palms. Why, by all the saints, why was she doing this to herself? Why should it matter *what* Royce Saint-Michel felt for her, or she for him? He was her guardian, the man appointed to take her to her betrothed. To Daemon. She was not supposed to *have* any feelings for him.

All her life, she had been taught that her duty, her responsibilities, her crown must come first. Her *people* were what mattered. Her feelings were unimportant.

Had she not said as much to Royce, only hours ago?

Raking her fingers through her tangled hair, she lifted her head and reached for her wine, refilling the cup. She had to calm herself. Had to subdue all these feelings that were so new, so perplexing.

So forbidden.

♦ ♦ ♦

The candles had flickered out, and the fire had burned low, leaving the room in almost complete darkness. That was the first thing Ciara noticed when she opened her eyes. The second was a heavy, thick feeling that clouded her senses, an unnatural drowsiness that made her thoughts…and everything around her…seem muffled…slow.

The third was a footstep. Near the door.

There was someone in her room. Ciara's eyes opened wider and her heart struck hard against her ribs. But even the jolt of panic felt oddly sluggish. She could not seem to wake up fully, could not stir. Befuddled as much as frightened, she lay on her side beneath a jumble of covers, facing the wall, her cheek pressed against her book, her empty goblet still clutched in her hand.

Then she heard another footstep, closer this time. Quiet. Stealthy.

Into her foggy mind came a memory of the night she had been attacked in the palace.

Followed by a single desperate thought, a name. *Royce. Help me!* But he was not here. He had left her. Why had he left her? She could not remember. She opened her mouth to call out, but her tongue seemed too thick to form words. The only sound she uttered was a moan.

The intruder crept closer to the bed. Still did not speak. And who would be sneaking into her chamber so late except someone who meant her harm? Someone who had waited to attack until she was alone, helpless.

But…nay, she was not helpless. A new thought broke through the lethargy that dulled her mind, with surprising clarity.

Elbow and heel. Elbow and heel.

Closing her eyes, she pretended to be asleep. Prayed she had the strength. Waited until the intruder drew close…leaned over her.

Then she summoned every ounce of will she possessed and jammed her elbow upward, catching him by surprise, connecting with something hard.

Only to hear a familiar *oof* and a string of curses.

And the discordant *twang* of her mandolin hitting the floor.

The shock that rushed through her veins gave her enough energy to sit up, only to find herself tangled in the rumpled covers. She gave up trying to push them aside, blinking through the strands of hair that fell in front of her eyes, recognizing the brawny person sitting on her floor, even in the shadowy darkness. "Royce?"

He sputtered another oath, one hand pressed to his forehead. "Excellent aim, milady," he said with a muffled groan. "Right between the eyes."

"Oh, my…by all…the saints." Her words felt too slow, her head still muddled. She could not seem to focus either her thoughts or her vision. She tried squinting. "I did not hurt you, did I?"

"Nay." He remained on the floor, rubbing at his injured head, his voice full of annoyance. "I suppose I should be grateful you remember your lessons."

She tilted her head to one side, still confused by what he was doing here. "Why did you sneak up on me?"

"I was not sneaking. I only came to bring you this." He thumped her mandolin, which lay in the rushes beside him. "The accursed thing is so precious to you, I did not think you would want it left in the hall. I meant to leave it by the door, but then you made that…sound, and I…" He dropped his hand, resting both arms across his upturned knees, and looked away. "I also wanted to make sure you remembered to bolt the door—which apparently you did not."

"I must have…um…forgotten."

She could not explain why she had forgotten. Locking the door had been important, and it was most unlike her to forget something important. But at the time, she had been thinking about…What had she been thinking about? Fie, but her brain did not seem to be working at all well.

Royce pushed to his feet, sniffing the air. "What is that smell? Was something burning in here?" He walked over to the hearth.

"Lady Elinor…um…left us a few surprises. She seems to have thought…that you and I…"

"Sandalwood. Why would Elinor put sandalwood in the hearth?" He bent to stoke the fire. The glow brightened the chamber. "God's blood, but the woman is a fanciful sort. Reads too much."

The comment made Ciara frown at him indignantly. Which helped her recall what she had been thinking about when she had forgotten to lock the door: she had been cross with him.

"And what is wrong with reading?" She untangled herself from the covers and got out of bed, fists clenched, swaying on her feet.

"I did not mean to say that there is—" As he turned to face her, his voice choked out. His gaze slowly dropped from her face to her toes. "Ciara," he said hoarsely, "where did you get that gown?"

"Elinor. I told you." The room tilted crazily and Ciara reached out to steady herself on the table beside the bed. It seemed awfully hard to keep her balance. "She left it for me, along with this very lovely wine, and—"

"Wine? What wine?" He stalked over and picked up the silver decanter, looking alarmed. "Where did this come from?"

"Elinor," she said in exasperation. Honestly, men could be such buffleheads. "I found it here in the room, with all the rest."

"Do you mean you just went ahead and drank this without asking anyone? God's breath, woman, it could have been poisoned." He took the stopper from the decanter, sniffed at the contents.

"Why would Elinor do that?"

"Not Elinor, you silly fool. Anyone in this keep could have left this here."

"I am not a silly fool. And you are a very suspicious person."

"I am *supposed* to be suspicious," he said angrily, setting the wine aside. "It is my duty to keep you safe—a duty you make damnably difficult. If this had been tainted, you would be dead right now!"

She flinched, stepping back from the fury in his eyes. "Well, I do not seem to be dead."

"And you do not seem entirely well, either." He caught her arm as she began to sway on her feet.

Ciara shook her head, trying to clear it. "I cannot understand it." She was still cross with him, but she felt grateful for his strong, steadying hand. "I felt quite pleasant after the first two or three glasses, but now—"

"The *first* two or three? How much did you drink?"

"Five glasses…I think." She opened her eyes, but her mind still seemed fuzzy.

All she could think about was the way the firelight and shadows cast his features in harsh angles.

Handsome angles.

A ridiculous smile came unbidden to her lips. "It was a very mild, sweet wine."

"Ciara…it is not wine at all." A reluctant grin eased the harshness from his face, and his voice softened. "No wonder you can hardly stand up straight. What you have been pickling yourself in is called cassis, milady. It is a drink made from the blackberries that grow in these mountains—and only meant to be enjoyed in very small quantities. Bayard's family has been brewing it for generations."

"Ah. Now I see." She blinked drowsily. "It is a very pleasant drink."

He chuckled. "And very potent. Legend has it that it enhances…" His smile faded and he suddenly released her, stepping back a pace. "Never mind the legend. But I should warn you, little one, that you are going to awaken with the devil's own headache in the morn."

She kept smiling at him, deliriously pleased to hear him call her *little one*. What a pleasant title. Much nicer than princess. "It matters not to me if I wake up with a headache on the morrow. I do not want to…think about the morrow."

All she could remember was that they would be leaving. And she did not want to leave here. This place that was so full of kind people and sweet children and merry laughter.

This place where the rest of the world seemed so far away.

The fire on the hearth sounded unnaturally loud in the darkness as she stood there. His gaze lingered over her face, her hair, and she felt warm all over, suspected that it had naught to do with the cassis.

Then a painful memory intruded through the pleasant fog enveloping her: the reason she had left him in the hall earlier. She dropped her gaze to her bare toes. "Was the view from the east tower very pretty tonight?"

"I would not know," he said distractedly. "I did not go to the east tower."

"Oh." It took a moment for the significance of what he said to penetrate her muddled brain. "Oh!" She glanced up, happiness bubbling through her.

As their gazes held, that strange look came into his eyes again, the one she had seen earlier today in the woods—filled with longing.

But then he shook his head as if to clear it. As if he, too, had overindulged in some intoxicating drink. He turned abruptly and walked away from her, toward the hearth. "Why were you so certain I would go to the tower?"

"Because that woman was very persuasive, and very pretty," she said honestly. "But if you were not in the east tower…where have you been?"

"Sitting downstairs." He braced one arm against the mantel. "Keeping an eye on your door, waiting until I thought it would be sa—until I thought you were asleep."

She moved toward him, quietly, drawn to him in a way she could not explain, her earlier vexation replaced by an urge to ease the tension outlined so sharply in his shoulders. "I am sorry that I implied you do not care about your duty. You are obviously devoted to protecting me."

"My duty," he said roughly, "had precious little to do with it, Ciara."

"Are you angry with me again?"

"Nay, I am not angry." He sounded frustrated. "I was not angry before. I was merely…" He paused, as if he could not find the right word, and exhaled a harsh breath. "Concerned. About your safety. It is my duty to…" Hanging his head, he rested his cheek against his outstretched arm, his voice dropping to a deep, gruff whisper. "I do not want anything to happen to you, Ciara. I do not want to…lose you."

Her heart flickered like the fire that brightened the room, his words filling her with an unfamiliar, extravagant emotion that made her feel as dizzy as the cassis. Oh, how very nice it was to hear him say that to her. To know that she had *not* been mistaken about his kindness and concern. "But…but why are we always snapping at one another?" she asked in soft puzzlement. "Why are we always fighting?"

He muttered something under his breath that she could not make out. "Little one, there is so much that you do not understand. Much that is…better left unsaid."

"But I *want* to understand." She reached up to touch his back.

He choked out a curse, his muscles as taut as a string on her mandolin. He turned quickly to face her, his features chiseled into harsh lines.

She moved closer to him without hesitation, leaning forward to rest her head on his shoulder, knowing only that she wanted to be near him. His tunic beneath her cheek smelled not of the brunette's overpowering perfume but of woodsmoke from the fire in the great hall. She smiled, sighing. "Help me to understand, Royce…please."

A tremor went through him. She heard his heartbeat like wild thunder beneath her ear. "Ciara…" He lifted his hands—and she feared he would push her away again.

But then his fingers slid into her hair.

He tilted her head up, his broad hands cupping her

cheeks. "Innocent angel…do you know what you are doing to me?" He looked and sounded as if he were in pain. "I gave my word." His eyes closed, opened again, his gaze piercing. "I gave my word."

She found it impossible to make sense of what he was saying. To concentrate on anything but his dark, potent eyes, the sound of his voice, the feel of his callused fingers against her skin.

And the way her heart had started to beat in time with his.

She reached up to soothe a muscle that flexed in his jaw, and he whispered something profane. His breathing became ragged.

And then slowly…sweet Heaven, so very slowly…one of his hands wound through her hair while the other slid down her back. "Fight me, Ciara," he begged in a fierce whisper, even as his arm encircled her waist. "Refuse me. Push me away."

"Nay, I will not," she breathed, her pulse jumping as her body molded to his, her lashes drifting closed as her chin tilted upward. "I cannot fight what I feel anymore."

With a wordless sound of defeat and impatience, he captured her mouth with his.

And cascades of fire swept through her.

The sensation was shocking, his mouth unbearably hot and sweet against hers. Silky and hard. Gentle and savage. His arm pulled her in tight, and she could feel his heat and hunger burning through the flimsy material of her kirtle. She trembled, drowning in ribbons of flame, moaning, the sound but a faint echo of the groan that tore through him.

All of her senses came alive, opening her heart and mind and soul to him, and he poured into her. Ravished and claimed. Filled her with his musky, male scent, the rough texture of his stubbled jaw against her skin, the steely strength of his arm around her.

He lifted her right off the ground, staggered backward a step, came up hard against the stone wall of the hearth. But his mouth remained joined to hers, the sound he made not of pain but of a feeling that wracked her just as powerfully. 'Twas a wanting, a need that went beyond any physical hunger or thirst or torment she had ever known. A feeling that she would die without this. Without him.

His fingers were buried in her hair, and he angled his head, his lips ravenous, giving more, demanding more. Her toes touched the floor but she sagged against him, unable to stand, her legs melting beneath her, her body melting into his. Her breasts felt wildly sensitive, aching from the friction of the soft fabric she wore, the roughness of his tunic, the hardness and heat of his muscled chest. Her nipples rose to hard pearls, the unfamiliar sensation drawing a soft cry from deep in her throat.

And it stopped him. He tore his mouth from hers, staring at her with dark, glittering, savage eyes. Their harsh breathing sounded like a storm in the night.

Then her fingers curled into his tunic, her grasp fierce, as surprising to her as it must be to him. It was as if her body refused to be parted from his. His gaze dropped to her swollen, tingling lips.

And then their mouths came together again, their breath, hunger, need mingling, tangling. She clung to him recklessly and his fingers wrapped through her hair, drew her head back, the pressure of his mouth shifting, urging her to do something she could not understand…

And then suddenly she knew, parted her lips, opened to welcome him inside.

A groan shuddered through his chest. She felt as well as heard it, made the same sound as he deepened the kiss. His tongue glided over hers, exploring, plundering with silky thrusts that left her shivering. Never had she *imagined* anything like this.

She became lost in him, in the liquid heat of this scorching, infinite joining. Aware of no hesitation, no fear, no shame. Only these sensations, like snowflakes tingling over her skin, melting into a fire in her heart that burned for him.

Snowflakes and flame. *Fire and ice.*

His tongue lingered over hers, stealing the sweetness of the potent drink she had consumed, and she *tasted* him. Foreign and yet familiar. Spicy and hot and…male. A velvety, volatile heat pooled low in her belly, demanding that she find some way to be even closer to him.

And when he dragged his mouth from hers once more, the cry she made was one of protest. With a ravenous growl, he trailed sharp, wet kisses down her throat, his hand shifting to cup her breast. She gasped at such a bold caress, stunned by the intimacy of it. And by her own excited response.

Then he lowered his head and lifted the taut peak for a kiss that shocked her breathless.

With lips and tongue, he drew her deep into the hot wetness of his mouth. A low, violent sound tore from her throat. Her head tipped back, her hair trailing down her spine as unbearably intense sensations spilled through her. His arm locked tighter around her, holding her fast as his tongue touched the hard pearl of her nipple through the thin cloth she wore, brushing over it again and again. The ribbons of fire whirled around her, through her, until she thought she would go mad. She cried out, a plea, his name.

He lifted his head, but his hand covered her possessively, his fingers kneading her softness through the sheer, damp fabric. She fell forward, collapsing against his chest, heart pounding, head spinning, and his arms shifted to cradle her tenderly.

"Ciara…my God…" His voice was so deep and so rough she barely recognized it. He swore, dropping his head to press his cheek against hers, the stubble of his beard abrading her skin, his lips close to her ear. "If you were mine…" A bitter sound of longing, of frustration, issued from his chest. "If you were mine…"

He held her tight for a long moment that would never be long enough.

Then he choked out another curse and untangled her from his embrace. And let her go.

She sagged against the hearth, feeling as if she would never have the strength to stand again.

He backed away from her a step. Then another. "I want you to bolt the door behind me," he commanded.

She watched him through heavy-lidded eyes, her lips still tingling and warm from his kisses. "Royce…" She felt astonished by the husky depth of her own voice.

He turned and crossed the room in three strides. *"Bolt the door,"* he repeated forcefully.

And then he was gone, closing the portal with sharp finality.

It seemed to take forever to cross the same distance, to do as he had bidden, for she understood what he was asking of her: she was not locking the door to keep out her enemies, but to keep out her guardian.

She slid the bolt into place, then went limp against the wood, knowing that he was there on the other side, leaning back against the cold, hard oak even as she leaned into it. She could hear him breathing, shallow and fast, swore she could *feel* him, his heart pounding as hard as her own. And she closed her eyes, not understanding the hot tears that welled there.

And wondered what they would do on the morrow, when there would be no door and no lock to separate them.

Chapter 9

"I am dying."

"You are not dying, Princess." Royce held her long hair out of the way, kneeling beside her while she crouched in the snow and lost what little she had been able to eat this morn.

He had been forced to halt Anteros in the middle of a mountain pass when she could ride no further. Steep, icy slopes surrounded them with walls of white, and clouds dulled the midday sunlight to gray, but a mild breeze made the air unseasonably warm.

"I am," she insisted weakly, her face a sickly shade of green as she huddled on his cloak, which he had spread across the ground for her. "I hate cassis. I hate it. I…I intend to order every drop of that foul drink banned from the realm!"

Royce fought a pained smile, remembering the first time he had gotten drunk on cassis. "The feeling will wear off anon," he assured her.

"How soon?"

"A day or so."

She groaned, hunching over again, retching. He remained by her side, offering what comfort be could. Her features drawn and strained, eyes bleary, Ciara was the very picture of misery and regret—the same two emotions that wracked him.

He had delayed their departure from Bayard's keep as long as possible, allowing her to sleep late, telling himself it was for her benefit. In truth, he had dreaded facing her.

Had not wanted to remember her body so warm and pliant in his hands, her lips and tongue like hot velvet against his, her sighs like silk. Because this longing he felt for her, this possessiveness, was something more than desire. Much more. He could no longer deny it.

He shut his eyes, secretly grateful for Ciara's wretched condition. Thus far, he had been spared any discussion of what had happened in her bedchamber. When she joined him in the bailey this morn, she had shaded her eyes against the bright sun and mumbled only a few words about a pounding headache.

"How can a drink that makes one feel so pleasant," she asked in a feeble whisper, "make one feel so *vile* only a few hours later?"

Royce was not about to tell her she should have known better than to indulge so freely in something so intoxicating. He removed his hand from her long tresses as she sat up, trying not to remember how it had felt to wantonly tangle his fingers in the thick curls last night. "Why did you not braid your hair this morn?"

"Must you speak so loudly?" she protested, pressing one hand to her head.

He was already speaking softly but lowered his voice even more. "You usually braid your hair. But today you did not."

"I could not. It hurts."

"Your hair hurts?"

"Everything hurts," she said miserably, looking forlorn. "My head feels as if an entire legion of drummers is marching through it. And the sun is much too bright. Even the breeze is too loud. And I do not think I can ride anymore…" She grimaced as if the very idea made her queasy.

Royce nodded in sympathy, knowing that Anteros's smooth gait must feel to her like riding a ship on a storm-tossed sea. But he needed to get her fit for travel; sitting outside in the snow all afternoon would do her no good.

He pushed to his feet and walked over to where Anteros stood a few paces away. The stallion tossed his head impatiently while a shaggy gray nose poked out from a basket tied next to Ciara's mandolin. Hera growled.

Royce frowned at the puppy. "Ungrateful little beast," he muttered under his breath, closing the basket's lid. His hand still stung from the bite he had received while fitting her with a collar and leash. "Stay in your nice padded basket and do not make me regret bringing you along."

After searching through one of the packs lashed to his saddle, he tossed a handful of oats into the snow for Anteros, then withdrew three other items.

He returned to Ciara's side, crouching down. "Can you manage a sip of this?"

She had covered her eyes with her hands once more, and parted her fingers just enough to peek at the flask he held out. "Nay," she croaked.

"It is only water, Princess. I filled a flask from the well before we left Bayard's keep. I thought you might have need of it."

Still looking dubious, she took it, then sat back on her heels. She just stared at the flask accusingly for a moment. It seemed she did not want to drink *any* liquid ever again. Then she uncorked it and bravely lifted it to her lips.

"Just a sip at first," he instructed. "Rinse your mouth and then spit." Almost to himself, he added, "But not at me."

Her mouth full of water, she lifted an eyebrow, as if the thought had not occurred to her. Then she turned her head and spat into the snow.

He handed her a cloth, along with a small pouch. "Chew some of these. They are peppermint leaves. Elinor said they will ease the sour taste and calm your stomach."

Ciara's eyes widened. "You told Lady Elinor that I—"

"Nay," he explained quickly. "I said that you have been feeling ill in the mornings."

Ciara shut her eyes, twin spots of pink replacing the greenish hue in her cheeks. "So *that* is why she hugged me so tightly when I left. She thinks I am…" She started to shake her head, then stopped and quickly covered her mouth with the cloth, groaning, her voice muffled. "I believe this has been the most embarrassing morning of my entire life."

"Princess, there is no shame in drinking too much cassis. You are not the first to make that mistake."

"But I feel like a featherwit," she confessed. Wiping her mouth, she set the cloth aside. "I thought I was being bold and adventurous, but all I did was make myself sick. I must…I must look like a fool."

Royce had, to fight the urge to smooth the frown from her lips. "Nay, milady, do not trouble yourself. No one will know but the two of us. I vow that I shall carry the secret to my grave. In fact," he added lightly, "I may even make it my epitaph: 'Here lies Royce Saint-Michel, who was once thrown up upon by royalty.' "

He succeeded in chasing away her frown. "You are teasing me again." She opened the pouch of mint leaves.

"Nay," he insisted with a straight face. "I rather like it. Though it is not poetic enough. Mayhap, 'Here lies Royce Saint-Michel, who forsooth attended the spewing of a princess's breakfast.' "

Her grin widened. "Stop that."

"Or mayhap, 'Here lies Royce Saint-Michel, who had the honor of being present when a member of the royal family blew beets.' "

She laughed so hard that she winced. "One more and you will be in *need* of an epitaph!" She rubbed at her temples.

He grinned. "Now you are teasing me, milady."

She met his gaze with an expression of surprise, as if making a jest were a new experience for her. "Only because you are being a featherwit." Still smiling, she took another sip of water and chewed on a leaf, looking as if she already felt better. "You are also being kind. Just as you were when you presented me with Hera this morning. It was a very pleasant surprise." Her voice was warm, soft. "Thank you."

He shrugged, glad that he had been able to ease both her suffering and her somber mood. "There is no need to thank me for seeing to your comfort, milady. The fault is mine that you are ill. If I had been with you last night…"

He left the sentence unfinished, cursed himself for opening the topic he would have preferred to leave closed.

She glanced up at him from beneath her lashes, her smile fading. "You *were* with me last night," she whispered.

Unable to hold her gaze, Royce stood and turned his back, wishing the wind that raked through his hair and tunic could pass through his heart as well—and erase all memory of that reckless kiss. He could not lie and claim that it had not affected him. He had no skill at concealing his emotions.

"I apologize for my behavior last night," he said with cool formality, hoping to end the matter quickly, painlessly. "I took advantage of you when you were impaired, Princess. It will not happen again."

For a moment, the wind whirling through the snowy pass made the only sound.

"I cannot allow you to take all the blame," she said quietly. "I was quite within my senses. At least as much as it is possible for me to be within my senses when I am near you."

He suddenly could not breathe. God's blood, what was she saying?

"Royce? I—I only meant there is no need for you to apologize. I felt the same as…I wanted you to—"

"The fault was mine, Your Highness," he said harshly. "What happened last night was a mistake."

"Oh." She sounded hurt. "I see."

He clenched his fists, damned himself to whatever black pit of Hell would have him. Now he was making her feel rejected, unwanted. Was there no way to untangle himself from the mess he had created? "Nay, milady, I do not think you see at—"

"There is no need to explain. I am the one who should apologize." Her voice had become thin. "It seems I made more than one error last night."

"Ciara—"

"I thought when you said that…" Her words were almost lost on the wind. "I thought you felt the same as I do.

I thought that you—"

"By nails and blood, woman." He spun toward her, unable to stand any more, unwilling to hear the word *cared.* "I had no right! Can you not understand that? I have no right to touch you or kiss you or"—he swore vividly—"or *want* you the way I do."

Her lips parted on a gasp, her eyes widening in astonishment.

"What happened last night cannot happen again," he said roughly. "It cannot. It *will* not. Your father has promised you to Prince Daemon. Thousands of lives depend on you carrying out your duty. On *both* of us carrying out our duty."

She turned her face into the wind. "Of course, you are right."

The pain in her expression contradicted the mildness of her tone—and both were like blades in his heart. "God's breath, Ciara." He refused to let himself go to her, forced himself to remain standing where he was. "Do you know how much I have come to hate this damnable duty I agreed to? Your father has betrothed you to that foul whoreson, but *I* am the one delivering you into his hands." His voice became sharp. "Do you know how that makes me feel? Do you know what it *does* to me to think of you as Daemon's wife, in his bed?"

She shivered visibly, wrapped her arms around her waist.

And he felt as if he were being crushed between the walls of ice that surrounded them. "Do you think I *want* to give you to him, Ciara? Do you know how much that bastard has already taken from me?"

She turned to look at him, her gaze searching. "Nay, I do not understand. What did he take from you?"

As their eyes met, he could not keep the words from spilling out. "Everything. Everyone I loved. My parents, my younger brothers. My little sisters. They were not yet ten years old when one of his commanders slit their throats."

"Oh, dear God." Her eyes filled with pain. "Your entire *family*. But how…when…"

"On the day the war began. My family's lands are—were in these mountains." He looked at the horizon. "Just to the south. On the border." His voice choked out.

"And when the Thuringians came…" she whispered. "Oh, Royce, thank God you survived—"

"I only survived because I was not there to help them," he said bitterly. "I was at the palace, in your father's service."

He turned away, struggling to hold his emotions in check, failing. The rest of the painful details poured out. "But the Thuringian bastard who killed them paid with his life. Four years ago, during the first peace negotiations. Your father sent me as one of his emissaries—and the man who had shown no mercy to my family was there, as one of Daemon's military advisers. And he had the audacity to *taunt* me about it, about how easy it was, how much he enjoyed…" A haze of fury and anguish stole his breath. "I ran him through right there at the table during the negotiations."

Ciara gasped a wordless exclamation of shock.

"If I had it to do over again, I would," he said. "Without a second's hesitation."

To his astonishment, her voice remained gentle, filled not with accusations but with sorrow. "And that was when you left Châlons—"

"I did not leave voluntarily. Your father exiled me because I had broken my word. I had sworn to him that I would put the cause of peace before my own desire for vengeance." He turned to face her. "Do you understand, Ciara? I vowed that I would put my *duty* before my *feelings*."

Their gazes held for a long moment, burning across the distance that separated them.

Until he looked away, to Mount Ravensbruk, looming in the distance. "Daemon's men murdered my family, and your father took the rest. He stripped me of my spurs, my title and position—"

"So you *are* a nobleman."

"Was," he corrected. "After my father was killed, I

became baron of Ferrano, and Aldric allowed me to keep the title even though the Ferrano holdings had been lost to Thuringia. He knew it was the only legacy I had left of my family. The only thing that still mattered to me." His voice hardened. "Then he took even that away."

"Oh, Royce." She exhaled a low sound of pain. "How furious you must have been with him."

"We were furious with each other." He looked toward her, remembering, knowing that some of the fault had been his own. "Too furious to listen, or forgive." He shook his head. "I spent a long time hating him while I tried to survive as a commoner with no money and no name. I wandered through Milan, Castile, Navarre—wherever a mercenary could earn a little coin. Then I was fortunate to meet Sir Gaston de Varennes, a Frenchman who offered me a position as captain of his guards. It was hardly the high rank I was born to, but it meant a comfortable place to live, among friends." The memory made him smile. "Some of the best I have ever known."

A light of understanding dawned in Ciara's eyes. "And now my father has given you the chance to reclaim all you once had. All that you *are*." Her gaze traced over his face, searching. "You said that you cared about naught but the reward, but that is not true. You did not agree to serve as my escort out of greed, but out of honor. You want to make up for what happened four years ago." Her voice dropped to a whisper. "You want peace to succeed this time. And you want to come *home*."

He clenched his jaw, unable to speak, both pained and more touched than he dared say that she could know his heart so well. "Aye. But there is one problem, milady," he said hotly. "I also want *you*."

His declaration brought a rush of color to her cheeks. Longing shone in her eyes. "Royce—"

"But if I act on that wish," he continued quickly, "your father and your betrothed will be drawing lots to see which one wins the privilege of cutting my heart out."

She flinched, shut her eyes, "*Nay*, I would never allow anyone to—"

"You would have precious little say in the matter, Ciara."

There was no point in discussing it further, in trying to deny the inevitable. Unable to bear looking at her any longer, he turned his back, glancing up at the clouds—and a flash of silver on the slope high above them caught his eye. Made him freeze.

"Royce—"

He held up a hand to cut her off, a chill skidding down his spine. The flash might have been sunlight glinting off the ice.

Or the polished steel of a sword.

He searched the cliffs around them, suddenly aware of how vulnerable their position was, directly in the middle of the pass. If riders came at them from either end, they would be trapped.

His heart pounded against his ribs. In seeing to Ciara's comfort, he had neglected her safety. "It is time to ride on, milady." He kept his voice even, trying not to alarm her.

She made a sound of frustration. "Why must you always—"

He closed the distance between them and scooped her into his arms, giving her no further chance to protest. "My apologies, Princess, but there is no time to explain." He carried her toward his destrier, still studying the peak above them, certain he had seen something. Someone.

Ciara pushed at his chest. "You are the most maddening person I have ever met in my life."

Royce ignored her, swiftly reaching Anteros's side and lifting her into the saddle. Hera was growling in her basket and yapping nervously.

Only then did he hear the rumble.

Distant. Oddly familiar. Like thunder, or the hoofbeats of a hundred horses charging into battle.

Some instinct, some memory made him look up. Not at the open ends of the pass, but up. Just in time to see a sight that made him freeze where he stood for one second of paralyzed horror.

Ciara followed his gaze, and her voice was hollow with terror. "Holy Mary, Mother of God."

The entire top of the mountain seemed to be sliding toward them, lethal tons of snow raining down.

Avalanche.

He had no time to think, to save himself—only to strike Anteros's flank, hard.

And send Ciara out of harm's way.

Chapter 10

Some instinct made him drop to the ground instead of vainly trying to run. He could hear the avalanche thundering down toward him, drew his arms and legs close, protected his head with both hands—and felt the snow hit him like an explosion.

It swallowed him whole. But instead of crushing him into the ground, it shot him forward as if he were a ball in a child's game. Swept him helplessly toward the open end of the pass.

It was then he tasted the fear. Black, raw fear that made him strike out and fight wildly for his life. He battled against the snow as he would a drowning current, but the river of white was too strong, smashing everything in its path, filling the air with an unearthly roar as if the mountain had come to enraged life.

The force of it pushed him through the opening of the pass and down the slope beyond, carrying him like a leaf caught in a rushing waterfall. He struggled for breath, for consciousness, battered by chunks of ice, rocks, branches. The world tumbled insanely around him until sky and sun disappeared, until earth and mountain vanished, swallowed by the cold, smothering sea of white.

And then it all stopped. As suddenly as it had begun, the pounding flood slowed, then calmed. He slid to a halt, hovering on the edge of consciousness, aware only that he was no longer moving.

With an immense effort, he managed to pry his eyelids open, found himself surrounded by darkness. He could not see or hear. Or breathe. His limbs were weighed down. Pinned beneath a killing weight of snow.

He had been buried alive.

Fear slithered through him, followed hard and fast by a vicious shot of fury. He would not die. Not like this. Murdered by traitors. Spineless cowards who sought to bury him on a mountainside, to kill—

Ciara. He had to get to Ciara. If she had escaped the avalanche, they would be after her. He had to get free, help her. Protect her. Twisting his head, he found a small pocket of air, just enough to allow him to draw breath.

He began to move. First his hands, then his feet. Arching his body, clawing, kicking, he pushed and fought to clear a tunnel through his freezing tomb. Using all his strength, he struggled upward. At least he hoped it was upward. He had been tumbled and turned so much he could not tell.

Desperate for more air, he shoved aside handfuls, then armfuls of snow. It clung to him, heavy, wet, like cold armor, holding him down. But he filled his mind with an image of Ciara's face, her eyes, her smile.

Lungs burning, he broke into daylight at last, stuck his head through the opening, and gasped a mouthful of frosty air. It seared his throat, leaving him coughing as he pushed himself up and out, like a moth emerging from a cocoon. Shuddering, weak, he collapsed atop the snow, sprawled on his stomach, unable to move.

Only now did he feel the pain—from cuts across his chest, his ribs, his back. From dozens of bruises. His tunic and leggings had been shredded by sharp edges of ice and rocks. He felt the cold against his bare skin, felt his blood seeping into the snow. And agony in his left leg. The muscles hurt as if his limb had almost been twisted off. And his sword was gone, the belt and sheath ripped from his waist.

Choking out a curse, he opened his eyes, aware of the silence surrounding him, strange and eerie after the avalanche's deafening thunder.

Gentle flakes of fresh white drifted down from the clouds. The craggy peaks soaring above appeared the same, the sky unchanged. It was as if nature had failed to notice the chaos on the mountainside.

Failed to care whether the human beings below survived.

Ciara. He lifted his head, thought to call out for her—then stopped himself. Looking up the slope, he sought any trace of the rebel he suspected had caused the avalanche, or accomplices the bastard might have had. He saw no one.

No doubt they had fled to a place of safety after starting it, confident that the snow would do their lethal work for them. He dared not call out and alert them that their treacherous plan had failed.

His lips twisted in a snarl as the desire for retribution heated his blood. From some deep reserve, he found the strength to push to his feet.

Half dazed, he turned fully around, trying to orient himself. He had been carried out the western end of the pass and halfway down the slope. He was standing on ground that he and Ciara had covered earlier, little more than an hour ago, as they rode up the mountainside.

Except that now, the easily followed path had been transformed into an expanse of deep drifts.

And Ciara would be on the opposite side of the mountain. When the avalanche struck, Anteros had been carrying her away from him, toward the east.

He started moving upward, as fast as he could, whispering a prayer that his swift destrier had had time to get her out of the pass before the torrent of snow reached them. If not—

Nay, he would not think of the possibilities. His heart filled his throat at the idea of Ciara—slender, delicate Ciara, who weighed no more than one of her silk veils—buried as he had been. She would not have the strength to get free.

He kept his eyes on the summit, forcing his way through the drifts, ignoring his wounds, the blood, the pain. Hampered by the shifting snows beneath him, he made frustratingly slow progress back to the top.

It took what felt like an hour to reach the place where he

had seen her last, in the middle of the silent, empty pass between the towering cliffs—the very spot where he had joked with her about his epitaph.

Despite the fact that he was already chilled to the bone, the memory sent a fresh shudder through him.

Finally he reached the opposite end of the gap, where the eastern opening spilled into a long, gentle slope.

But as he stood there, breathing hard, staring out across the smooth expanse of white, he saw no sign of her.

Anywhere.

"Ciara!" Her name tore from him before he could hold it in, and echoed back from the cliffs, as if the empty valley below were mocking him.

She was gone.

He clenched his fists, shaking his head in denial, fury. Guilt. He never should have stopped in this place. Should have been thinking of her safety rather than her comfort. God's blood, he was her guardian, her protector, and he had failed her.

He staggered forward a step, then another, glaring out over the blinding field of smooth, unmarked snow—with no idea where to start looking for her. If she was trapped beneath the drifts, he would have only minutes to…only minutes…

Nay, she would already be dead. In the time it had taken him to get back to the top of the pass, she would have suffocated.

He sank to his knees, unprepared for the force of the anguish that hit him at the thought that Ciara was lost forever. He lifted his face to the heavens, furious that he had been spared while she…

"Nay!" he shouted, the word booming into the slate-gray sky.

Again the icy cliffs sent his own voice echoing back to him. But this time, he also heard another sound. Soft, distant. Familiar.

And not human.

Anteros!

He turned his head to see his horse limping up the south end of the slope toward him—with his saddle askew.

And empty.

Royce was on his feet and running headlong down the slope before he completed the thought. Paying no heed to the agony that shot through his left leg, he closed the distance in what felt like the span of a single pounding heartbeat. His stallion was lame, favoring his left foreleg. He caught Anteros's reins, examined the twisted saddle.

It appeared his destrier had escaped the worst of the avalanche, for their packs and weapons had received only minor damage, and Hera's basket was intact—though it was empty.

Only Ciara's delicate mandolin had been broken, snapped in two. And there was no clue of what had happened to Ciara.

If she had been swept from Anteros's back by the snow, she might not have been carried down the slope but into the mountainside.

Which was almost worse. She could have been slammed into the rock. Killed by the impact.

Curses tumbling from his lips, Royce left his stallion to rush down the hillside, retracing the horse's steps, following the hoofprints that led up from the valley. Hope twisted through him. Agonizing hope. "Ciara!"

Answer me. Please, God, she cannot be dead.

Royce quickly came to the end of the tracks, to a crushed place in the snow. It looked as if his destrier had fallen to the ground here rather than higher up the mountainside. But had Ciara still been on his back? Had she been swept from the saddle? Where…

He heard a sound, lifted his gaze, felt his heart stop. A few yards away, through a scattering of pine saplings, he could see the sharp, sheer edge of a cliff.

The tiny mongrel stood at its edge, whining softly.

Not breathing, not even blinking, Royce moved toward

the precipice and gazed down numbly, expecting to see Ciara's broken body at the bottom of the gorge.

Instead, the sight that greeted him made him shout a strangled exclamation of gratitude and terror. *"Sweet holy Jesus!"*

She was just a few yards beneath him, caught in a tangle of branches and roots that protruded from the rock. The boughs had broken her fall, caught her like a baby bird tumbled from its nest. She lay unmoving, unconscious, her loose hair and long cloak tangled around her.

He was not even sure she was still alive. The puppy dashed back and forth, barking and whining, as he flattened himself at the top of the cliff, leaning down, stretching out a hand toward Ciara. But he knew he could not reach her from here. The distance was too great.

And he could not tell whether she was breathing.

His mouth dry with fear, he pushed to his feet. She might weigh no more than a length of silk, but if she awoke, if she moved, if one of the branches broke…

He darted a glance at the bottom of the gorge far below—so distant he could make out naught but huge, sharp chunks of ice and boulders.

"Nay," he swore fiercely. "I will not lose you."

His heart thundering against his ribs, he scooped up the dog and turned from the edge of the cliff, running back toward Anteros, up the hillside, the ascent made easier by the path he had cut through the drifts in his mad rush down the slope.

His left leg burned and hurt. The wind cut mercilessly through his slashed tunic. But he paid no attention. When he reached Anteros, the stallion whickered in fear and in pain, but Royce had no time to soothe him.

He put the puppy in her basket and tied it securely shut. "Thank you for helping me find your mistress, Hera. You can best help her now by staying out of the way." Grabbing his pack, he tore it free from its fastenings and found his climbing gear—ropes, boots, pickax.

He quickly changed into the boots, then secured one of the ropes around his waist with expert knots. Studying the slender pines at the edge of the cliff, he cursed.

None of the saplings would be sturdy enough to support his weight and Ciara's together. His rescue was over before it had even begun.

Unless…

Jaw clenched, he turned to his destrier. Bent down and ran his hands over the stallion's injured foreleg. It was not broken.

The idea might work. It was insanely dangerous, but he had no other choice.

"I am sorry, old friend," he said tightly as the horse shied from his touch. "I know it hurts, but I have need of your help."

Refusing to think of the risk, of the horse's pain or his own, he grabbed the reins and led Anteros to the edge of the cliff.

He took just enough time to remove the saddle and its heavy load before fashioning a harness, using two ropes, looping both around Anteros's withers and broad chest and under his belly.

"Easy, my brave lad." He tried to keep his voice soothing, though his pulse and thoughts were racing. "Hold your ground and be steady. I need you to be our anchor."

He picked up the free end of the second rope, gathered the slack into a circle, and slung it over his shoulder.

Then he paused just long enough to stare into Anteros's dark eyes as he dropped the reins to the ground. He had never attempted anything like this in his life. But his stallion's strength and courage had saved his neck in battle more than once. He could only pray that those same qualities would keep him and Ciara alive now.

"Do not fail me, old friend," he commanded urgently. "Do not be afraid and do not move."

If Anteros panicked and lost his footing, or if his lame leg caused him to slip, all three of them would die at the bottom of the gorge.

The destrier neighed and tossed his head, still agitated. But there was no more time for reassurance.

Royce checked the knots one last time, then moved toward the cliff. "Steady, Anteros. Stay there, lad."

At the edge, he paused just long enough to make sure Anteros was holding his ground. Long enough to glance down and judge the distance to Ciara.

Then he pushed off and began his descent down the sheer wall of rock. The sharp iron nails that protruded through the soles of his climbing boots easily found purchase in the ice, helped him control his speed. He moved swiftly, letting his weight carry him downward, letting the rope slide through his gloved hands.

And he kept his gaze locked on Ciara, about fifteen feet below him—not on the gorge much farther below.

He was still about five feet above her when he heard her moan softly.

She was alive. "Ciara! Do not move."

Mayhap she could not understand his words over the wind.

Because she moaned again, eyes still closed, and reached up blindly to tug at her cloak. It was tangled around her neck, seemed to be choking her.

The branches that supported her moved, giving way.

"Ciara, stop!" He shouted the command past the lump of fear that clogged his throat. "Be still!"

She obeyed this time, opening her eyes at last—and when she spotted him dangling above her, saw where she was, all the color left her face. She opened her mouth as if to scream, but seemed incapable of making a sound.

Her terror struck at his heart. "I am almost there," he said hoarsely. "You will be all right, I promise."

He let more slack slip through his hands, moving closer to her, one cautious foot at a time. "Hold on, Ciara. And do not look down."

She remained frozen, wide-eyed, clearly too frightened

to even consider it. No doubt she could feel the open air beneath her—and the wind just below the interlaced boughs that held her in place. Only her fingers moved, grasping the branches in a death grip.

Three more feet…two…finally he was close enough to reach her.

But he did not dare put any of his weight on the tree limbs that supported her.

"Ciara, I need you to take my hand." Moving as close as he dared, he knotted the slack to hold himself in place and stretched one arm toward her.

Only inches separated them now.

But she would not budge. She remained as still as a terrified rabbit, her breathing fast and shallow, her eyes glassy.

"Ciara…" The wind whipped at his hair, yanked at his clothes.

The branches creaked.

This was no time for gentle persuasion.

"God's blood, woman," he swore, his voice rough with emotion. "I am not going to lose you now. Do as I tell you! Take my hand!"

His fury brought her out of her paralyzed stupor. She seemed to suddenly realize how near he was and reached up toward him.

And he caught her at last. Grasped her arm, pulled her to his side, wrapped one arm around her.

And held her so close that neither of them could take a breath.

She suddenly burst into tears. "Royce, I am so afraid. I am—"

"Nay, do not fear. I am with you now." He spoke in the same soothing tone he had used with Anteros as he slipped a rope around her waist. Releasing his grip on his own line, he tied hers in place, knotting it several times. "You will be safe, little one. I have you."

But when he tried to move, to start climbing upward, he

discovered he could not pull her free of the branches.

He bit out a particularly curt, vicious oath. Her long, loose hair and her cloak were caught, tangled in the boughs that had saved her life. She uttered a soft cry of alarm.

Not pausing to explain what he was about to do, he reached for the chain around her throat that held her mantle in place, released it, and let the cloak fall. Then he took the sharp-edged pickax from the waist of his leggings.

"I am sorry about this, milady." With one quick slice, he cut through her long tresses.

And set her free.

The two of them were dangling high above the gorge, held only by the ropes that bound them to Anteros.

Gasping out a terrified prayer, she clung to him, her arms fastened around his waist, her face buried against his shoulder.

Which, he decided, was awkward but better than having her look down.

"We are going to be all right, Ciara." He started climbing the sheer cliff face, one foot over the other, the soles of his boots digging into the ice. But it was too difficult to balance both her weight and his own.

He muttered a curse under his breath. If only Anteros would back up.

But his obedient, well-trained destrier remained firmly in place.

Royce grimaced as he stared upward. There were only a few short yards to the top of the cliff, but it might as well have been a hundred times that distance.

"You are going to have to help me, Ciara."

"Nay, I am afraid. I cannot—"

"You can," he said fiercely. "All you need do is walk beside me. One foot over the other. You have to let go of me and climb, Ciara. You can do it."

She shook her head, eyes wild.

"Fie on it, you are not a frightened child! You learned to defend yourself—you can learn this as well. You must. We have no choice."

Whether it was his words or the urgent tone, something brought a glimmer of courage to her expression.

She slowly, reluctantly unwound her arms from around him. "Tell me what I have to do."

Her willingness, her bravery made his mouth curve in a grim smile. By God's mercy, he did not think he had ever felt so proud of a woman as he did in that moment, as he watched her curl her small, pale hands around her rope and look to the top of the cliff.

"Pull yourself up, Ciara. One hand over the other, one foot in front of the other." He had to make her forget about the rocks far below, the wind that bit through their clothes, the distance to the top.

Had to keep her listening to his voice, only to his voice—not to the fear inside her.

"Good." He started to climb, showing her how, staying beside her "That is right. You can do it."

She grimaced with effort, lacking the advantage of his build and his boots, but she managed to stay right with him.

"Aye, milady, you are doing it. Only a little way now."

When they came within a few feet of the edge, he scrambled up first, then reached down to pull her up over the top. He carried her a safe distance away from the cliff before he sank to the ground.

She fell into his embrace, both of them trembling. He did not untie them, glancing up only long enough to see Anteros standing in place, tossing his head, unharmed by the exertion.

"Thank you." Royce did not know whether he was addressing the heavens above, his stallion, the woman in his arms, or all three.

He pulled her in tight against his chest. "God's breath, I thought I had lost you," he choked out. "When I could not find you, I thought—"

"Royce, please, just hold me." Shivering in his embrace, her voice trembling with fright and relief, she wrapped her arms around his neck and held on as if she would never let go.

He crushed her close, shutting his eyes, burying his face in her hair. And knew it was not duty that filled him with gratitude and protectiveness and concern. It was Ciara herself. Not *Princess* Ciara, but simply Ciara.

It was a long moment before he managed to lift his head, release her long enough to cut them both free of the ropes that had saved their lives. "You will freeze without your cloak. I have to get you to—"

A glint of silver at the top of the slope cut off his sentence and his breath.

For a second, he thought his mind was playing tricks. But then he saw it again. And this time there was no mistaking what it was: a shield.

Held in the hand of a mounted warrior who rode into view at the opening of the pass far above. Joined a moment later by three others.

They paused there only an instant before all four began galloping down the hillside.

"Dear God!" Ciara cried. "Who—"

"Rebels." Royce's first instinct was to stand and fight. Rip them apart with his bare hands.

But he had to save Ciara. Pulling her to her feet, he started toward his destrier.

And remembered only then that Anteros was lame.

They had no chance of escape.

Chapter 11

Ciara stared at the four horsemen pounding down the slope toward them, her mouth dry with fear, her head spinning. "But how do you know they are rebels? Mayhap they mean us no harm. They might merely wish to offer help—"

"They have already tried to kill us, milady." Royce threw down his pickax and the length of rope still looped over his shoulder. "There is no time to explain."

He grabbed his pack of supplies from the ground and his crossbow from the saddle that lay a few paces away, shoved both into her arms, then snatched up his shield.

"What are you doing?" she asked in confusion, struggling to balance the bulky pack and the crossbow. "How can we hope to fend them off—"

"I do not intend to fend them off." He took her by the arm, looked back once at Anteros with deep regret, then turned and ran toward the saplings that edged the cliff.

"I do not understand," she panted, breathless as she tried to keep up, his grip giving her no choice. "And what about Hera?" She could hear the puppy howling. "Where is—"

"Safely in her basket. She will have to stay behind." He raced through the trees, parallel to the cliff, until they reached a clear area beyond that dipped steeply down the mountainside, into an enormous valley.

"Royce, we cannot escape on foot!"

"Nay, we cannot." He threw his shield onto the snow. "But we can escape another way."

Realizing his intent, she almost dropped her armful of goods. "Are you *mad?*"

"Possibly."

She did not find that the least bit reassuring.

He grabbed the crossbow from her and slung it over his back by its leather strap. "But I have done this before and lived to tell the tale." Plucking the sack from her hands, he glanced back at the horsemen galloping toward them, adding under his breath, "Though I was somewhat smaller then. And I had no passenger."

She gaped at him. He ripped open the pack, seized a pair of knives and a pouch of coins, tossed the rest to the ground. Shoving the knives into his boots and the pouch into his ruined tunic, he gestured toward the shield. "Get on, Ciara. Now!"

She had no chance to protest. Heart hammering, she jumped on as he took a running start, pushing the scrap of metal before him like a sled. All she could do was trust him—and pray they did not break their necks.

After a few steps, he leaped on behind her, landing so hard he almost knocked them both off the shield. The speeding bit of metal whirled around in a circle.

And suddenly they went flying down the hillside, so fast the mountain became a blur around them.

She had to bite her bottom lip to hold in a scream. Royce's arms locked about her waist as the scrape of steel against ice filled her ears. The wind tearing at her hair and face felt like a thousand tiny needles. She grabbed Royce and hung on for dear life—or however many minutes might be left of her life.

They could not hope to guide their makeshift sled in a particular direction. They could only hold on to each other, at the mercy of whatever the mountain would do with them. Her stomach lurched upward as the earth fell away beneath them. They flew over the snow, picking up speed, falling at a sharper and sharper angle. Sailing straight toward the bottom of the valley as fast as an arrow shot from a bow.

A scream rose in her throat. She could not hold it in any longer. But even the echo of her voice was left behind as they sped toward whatever fate awaited them below.

♦ ♦ ♦

'Twas a scent that awakened her. A piquant, familiar scent. Sage. Rosemary. Sweet basil. Dried herbs, some part of her mind supplied.

Ciara lifted her lashes, groaning softly at the soreness that wracked her muscles. As she opened her eyes, she found herself surrounded by darkness, lying on her back in rushes that had been sprinkled with fragrant herbs. She was stretched out on a floor. In a chamber of some sort.

She blinked in confusion and her vision slowly adjusted, allowing her to make out interlaced ropes and a mattress just beyond the tip of her nose. She was lying under a bed. And she could hear the crackle of a fire not far away.

Where in the world was she?

And what was she doing under the bed?

Shivering, she tried to remember what had happened after her and Royce's wild ride had come to an abrupt end on the valley floor. Their landing had been cushioned by deep snowdrifts rather than trees or rocks. She recalled being grateful for that.

And she remembered thinking that she might have *preferred* a quick death to what had come next: they had been forced to trudge through the snow with no cloaks to protect them from the weather. They had walked for hours, up one hillside and down the next, struggling through drifts, climbing over boulders, even sloshing through an icy stream for a great distance to conceal their tracks.

Royce had insisted on changing direction several times, intent on confusing the rebels pursuing them. And she had followed him without a word of complaint—even after the sun had set and night made the air dangerously, numbingly frigid—until she had literally dropped, unable to take another step.

The last thing she remembered was Royce picking her up and carrying her, murmuring words of concern in a voice that had sounded deep, soft. She must have fallen asleep in his arms.

And now she was here.

But where, exactly, was here?

And where was Royce?

Teeth chattering, she reached out and cautiously lifted the sheet that hung all the way to the floor, peering out at her surroundings.

It was a small, neat chamber, no more than ten paces wide and ten paces long, dark but for a low fire that burned in a rough-hewn stone hearth, a few feet away. She could also make out a table, a stool.

But she was clearly alone. Worry gnawed at her.

Until she glanced the other way and saw Royce's crossbow and shield, propped in a corner—the metal dented and scratched from their harrowing flight down the hillside.

Exhaling slowly in relief, she pushed out from under the bed, biting back a moan. Every inch of her body ached, and the icy cold had penetrated to her very bones. Scooting away from the bed, she sat up, winced, and quickly lifted her hands from the rushes. Even her palms hurt, scraped raw by the rope she had had to climb.

Trembling at the memory, she stared down at her reddened hands, overwhelmed by emotions she had been battling to suppress all afternoon. Terror. Disbelief. Shock. A chaos of feelings that made beads of perspiration break out on her forehead.

She had come close to dying today.

More than once.

And she was not yet safe. The men they had left behind on the mountainside would be searching for them.

For her.

So they could try again to kill her.

She glanced at the door, wishing more than ever that Royce were here with her. But for some reason, for now, he had had to leave her alone. A reckless impulse made her want to go out and look for him, but she knew he would not want her to take such a risk.

She would have to wait for him here. And she did not wish to have him find her like this when he came back: a shaking, petrified heap on the floor. As she rose, she glanced down, realizing she was barefoot. Royce had taken off her sodden boots and hose. She noticed them drying in front of the fire.

Which seemed like an excellent idea. Moving to the small hearth, she crouched down. The heat barely seemed to penetrate her chilled skin. She started to rub her hands up and down her arms but instantly stopped, her stinging palms making her inhale a sharp breath.

Desperate, she turned to look back at the bed, wondering if it might offer even a threadbare blanket.

And she almost groaned in relief: the bed was not only piled with thick blankets, but with a *fur.*

She hurried over to pick it up, wrapping it around her body. It was a large coverlet made of silver-tipped white fur, and it felt as soft and warm as she imagined Heaven must feel on a summer day. Huddled within it, she sighed gratefully and studied her surroundings more closely. The room boasted not only comfortable furnishings of polished, light-colored pine but also a large window with shutters.

Unable to resist, she lifted the wooden bar that locked the shutters from the inside. Pulling one of them open just a crack, she peeked out to see where she was.

Moonlight illuminated the streets of a town, a fairly large town from the look of it. Thatch-roofed shops and homes crowded winding alleyways, many of their windows aglow with torchlight. Laughter and the music of a harp and pipes danced on the cold night air.

The door opened behind her.

She spun, gasping.

It was Royce who stepped inside. Bolting the door behind him, he set aside the armful of items he carried and strode forward to meet her even as she rushed toward him.

She melted into his embrace, a sob escaping her throat, the fur sliding from her shoulders.

"Shh." He held her close, his hand moving up and down her back, his voice a scant whisper. "I am sorry I had to leave you for a moment, Ciara. I chose an empty chamber and hid you here while I went to pay the innkeeper. I did not want anyone to see you." He led her over to the window, reached out to close the shutter she had opened, and dropped the bar into place to lock it. "It is better that they think I am traveling alone, in case anyone should come asking questions."

She nodded, clinging to his tunic, burying her face against his shoulder, her heart pounding at the thought of the danger they were in. "Royce, where are—"

"Shh." He tilted her head up, touched a finger to her lips. "We must be careful to keep our voices low."

She shifted to a barely audible whisper. "Where are we?"

"In Gavena. At an inn on the outskirts of the town marketplace." Releasing her, he bent down to pick up the fur and wrap it around her. "Gavena is one of three large towns in this part of the mountains. We have lost our pursuers for now. And they will not find us easily."

Ciara did not think that particularly reassuring.

She did not want the rebels to find them at all.

Shivering, clutching the fur with both hands, she followed him as he turned to walk back to the pile of goods he had brought in. "But who *were* those men chasing us?" she whispered. "How can you be sure they were rebels? Could they not have been"— she searched for an innocent explanation—"concerned fellow travelers who saw our distress and were coming to help us?"

"Mayhap, milady." He crouched over a long object concealed in a length of homespun cloth and began unwrapping it. "Mayhap it was merely an early spring thaw that started the avalanche. And a coincidence that we were right in the middle of the pass when it started."

She gulped, noticing that the object he was unwrapping was a sword. He did not look or sound as if he believed a word he was saying. "You think those men caused the avalanche."

He lifted the sword by the hilt, testing its edge with his thumb, hesitating. "Aye," he said at last. "Ciara, I saw something—some*one*—on the peak above us, just before it began. When you and I were…"

He paused again, leaving the sentence unfinished.

Setting the blade aside, he picked up another of the bundles. "But it could have been a coincidence. There is no way to be certain."

"Or it could have been another assassination attempt." She sank down on a nearby stool, feeling as if her legs would no longer support her. "An avalanche would have been a perfect way to kill me—to kill us both. Without leaving a trace."

Over his shoulder, he met her gaze. "Aye, milady," he said softly, a muscle tightening in his jaw, the expression in his dark eyes grim. "And the rebels have proven before that they are clever. I will not underestimate them again." He turned away, adding under his breath, "I have made too many mistakes already."

Ciara barely heard him, distracted by the cold knot of dread that had settled in her stomach. Over the last few days, she had given little thought to those who meant to harm her, had been too swept up in the new places and people and experiences she had encountered on their journey, the new feelings she had enjoyed.

Only now did she understand the peril of their situation. They were being hunted by men who were intelligent, ruthless…and mayhap as knowledgeable of these mountains as Royce was.

She shuddered, no longer finding warmth within the fur's soft folds. "I do not understand how the rebels could have found us so easily." Her voice was a thready whisper. "We have been traveling only a handful of days."

He rose with another blade in his hand, this one a short-sword, and carried it over to the fire to examine it more closely. "Either they have been following us undetected, or someone told them where to find us."

Ciara regarded him with wide eyes. Neither possibility was pleasant. "But you have been most careful to make sure we were *not* being followed. And who could have told them where to find us? Unless…"

He glanced at her. "What, Ciara?"

She almost could not voice the thought, had to force herself to say it aloud. "What if Sir Bayard is not so good a friend as you believe?"

Royce's eyes darkened. He straightened to his full height, shaking his head. "Nay," he whispered. "Nay, I will not believe that."

Ciara did not wish to believe it either, but Royce's troubled expression told her he had suspicions as well. "It is the only explanation that makes sense. Who else—"

"Bayard would not have tried to kill us."

"I do not mean to say that he would. But if he gave information to the rebels, did not know what they intended—"

"What information would he give them? And why? Bayard had no idea of your true identity."

"But who else could have given us away?" she asked desperately. "*No one* knows of my true identity. No one knows of our plan or the route we decided to travel, except you and me and my father. Every other person in Châlons believes I am traveling in the wedding procession—"

She paused as a new and even more distressing possibility flitted through her mind.

It seemed the same idea had just occurred to Royce. "Except for the one person who *knows* you are not in the procession," he finished for her. "The woman who took your place. The decoy."

"Miriam," Ciara whispered, already shaking her head in denial. "Nay, she is completely loyal to me. And she was so brave when she volunteered to take my place in the procession—"

"Volunteered?" Royce echoed darkly.

Ciara could not seem to catch her breath. Suddenly the fact that Miriam had stepped forward so quickly took on a different, more ominous meaning. And then another memory struck. "Oh, dear Lord," she whispered. "That night in the solar, the night I was attacked...Miriam was with me. She spoke of the rebels. Tried to coax me into running away. The man who injured me came in right after she left—"

"As if he had been signaled," Royce concluded. "Told that your maidservant had failed to persuade you to abandon your betrothal. Told that you were now alone."

Ciara dropped her gaze, the thought of such a betrayal almost too much to bear. "But for so many years Miriam has been...she was always..."

The closest I had to a friend.

Tears stung her eyes as she looked up at Royce. "I cannot believe she would be in league with traitors who wish to kill me."

His expression softened. "We may be wrong, milady. It could all be—"

"Coincidence?" she choked out. "Just as it was a coincidence that we were in the pass when the avalanche started? Nay, it all makes sense." Her throat tightened as the pieces fit together logically. "The rebels were able to locate us so quickly because they never *were* chasing the wedding procession in the first place. They *knew* I was not there...because she told them."

Awash in anguish, she fell silent.

"We cannot be certain, Princess," Royce said after a moment. "All we know is that either my friend or yours may be working with those who are trying to kill us." He started to walk back toward her. "And we do not know which one it is."

"But it would seem that one of us has been betrayed by someone we trusted," Ciara agreed in a pained whisper.

Royce sighed, sounding weary. "We will have to worry about bringing the traitor to justice later. For the moment, we have our hands full staying alive." Still carrying the short-sword, he returned to the array of goods he had deposited by the door. "There is no way to know how many men are looking for us. And they could already be searching the towns."

Trembling again, Ciara clutched the fur closer around her. "Royce, what are we going to do?"

"We do not have many choices, milady. Our pursuers have some idea where we might be, they know where we are going, and they also know what we both look like. They only saw us from afar, but it was close enough. The one advantage we had was surprise—and we have lost that."

If he was saying this to frighten her, he was succeeding.

He looked over at her, his mouth a harsh line, his eyes stormy. "I will take no more chances with your life, Ciara. Thuringia is only a few days distant, but the rebels will be expecting us to run straight for the border as fast as possible. They will be on the alert, searching all the trails and passes. I think it would be best to remain hidden for a time."

Ciara nodded gratefully in agreement. Rest and sleep sounded far more appealing at the moment than another trek through the snow. "I do not think I could travel another step if I had to."

"Then we will stay here for two days, mayhap three, and hope that the search will pass us by." He moved closer, reaching down to tilt her head up, barely touching her chin with his fingertips. "I have made too many mistakes, Ciara. I will not make any more."

"I trust you, Royce."

Her words made a muscle flex in his tanned, stubbled cheek. Withdrawing his hand, he turned away to finish sorting through the bundles of goods.

She watched him in silence for a moment. "I hope Hera will be all right. They would not hurt her, would they?"

"The rebels would have naught to gain by harming a defenseless puppy, milady. They no doubt confiscated our things—including our animals—in the hope of finding some clue to our whereabouts."

She sighed, trying to feel reassured. "It would seem only one good thing has come from our adventures this day."

"And what, pray tell, is that?"

"The effects of the cassis I drank have worn off," she said with forced cheerfulness.

She did not succeed in wringing so much as a smile from him.

Giving up her attempt to lighten the mood, she studied the items at his feet. In addition to the two swords, he had peasant garments made of rough homespun—tunics, leggings—and a pair of boots. "Where did you get all that?"

"In the stables. I helped myself to a few necessities."

"You *stole* them?"

"Milady, the shops are not open at this hour," he said dryly. "And when we leave here, I thought it would be best if we go in disguise. We might attract a bit of attention dressed as we are, at least by daylight." He indicated her ruined gown and his own tattered, bloodied tunic. "I left the stable boys a few coins in payment."

Picking up two of his "acquisitions"—a cake of soap and some lengths of clean linen—he crossed to the table in the far corner, which held a wooden ewer and washbasin. He poured water into the bowl, then motioned for her to join him. "Let me see your hands, Ciara."

She rose, still holding the fur close as she walked over to him, her bare feet tickled by the rushes. "I think you should see to your own injuries first," she protested. The condition of his clothes told her that he had been hurt far worse than she in the avalanche. The thought made her heart ache.

He glanced down at her with a strange expression. "*I* am supposed to be taking care of *you*, milady. And I have done a damnably poor job of it today."

Ciara tried to puzzle out the emotion in his midnight eyes, seeing warmth and concern there, and…

He dropped his gaze before she could make sense of the rest.

She had the distinct impression he was purposely trying to conceal his feelings from her.

She did not understand, knew only that the emotion she had glimpsed brought a flutter to her stomach, like a warm, flickering candle flame inside her.

"I suffered only a few scratches, Your Highness," he said briskly. "I can tend to them later." Gently taking one of her hands, he turned it palm upward.

And grated out an oath. "I am sorry, Princess," he whispered, frowning down at her raw skin.

"Do not apologize. You saved my life today, Royce. I am grateful." She realized that sounded too formal, that it did not begin to describe the feelings in her heart. "I should have told you earlier, should have told you that I—"

"There is no need to tell me anything," he said flatly. "And pray do not thank me. I almost got you killed today." Dampening a piece of linen, he began to cleanse her hand with a tenderness that belied his cool words.

"You did not almost get me killed," she insisted, struggling to keep her voice low, "You saved me. When I was trapped on the cliff, if it had not been for you—"

"If it had not been for me, you would not have been there in the first place," he said in a harsh whisper, the anger obviously directed at himself. "I should never have stopped in the middle of that pass. I should have been thinking of my *duty*, not my—"

He left the sentence unfinished. And completed his work in silence, bandaging both her hands with fresh lengths of cloth.

When he turned aside, his tone was once again mild. "I am finished with you, Princess."

Despite the softness of his voice, Ciara stepped back as if he had pushed her away. She told herself he was referring to her injured hands, but could not help wondering if his words held a different meaning.

She could not explain the hurt that twisted through her, but she kept it from her voice. "Then allow me to help you.

The cuts on your back—"

"I can manage alone. I have done so before."

"But you do not have to manage alone," she pointed out.

He faced the corner in stony silence for a long moment. Then he reached for the hem of his tunic and yanked the garment off over his head.

For a breathless instant, Ciara could not move or speak or take her eyes from him. She had seen men dressed only in leggings before—peasants, squires at practice in the bailey, stonecutters—but always from a distance. Never had she been this close to a man so…so…

Magnificent. The low firelight gleamed on his bare back, on the hard planes and corded muscles that flexed as he tossed the tunic aside and lowered his arms. He looked as if he had been sculpted from warm, dark stone. His many scars and cuts and bruises made her want to reach out, ease his pain.

Then he turned to face her, and she could not hold his gaze. But glancing down only made heat rise in her cheeks, for she could not keep from staring at his broad chest and thick-hewn arms, at the mat of black hair that covered his tanned skin, the way it narrowed over his ribs to vanish at the waist of his leggings….

Before she could recover her senses, someone knocked at the door. She almost jumped out of her skin.

"Nay, " Royce whispered. "That should be the innkeeper. Back under the bed. And do not make a sound."

She scrambled into her hiding place, as quickly and quietly as possible, her heart hammering.

Royce dropped the sheet in place to conceal her completely. Holding her breath, she heard him cross to the door, unlock it, open it…

"Good eventide to you, good sir," an unfamiliar, jovial male voice said. "We have the items you requested."

Ciara smelled the tantalizing aroma of roast meat and hot bread, heard the rattle of spoons and wooden trenchers.

Prayed that her stomach would not growl.

She also heard the sound of some large object being brought—rolled—in. Something so heavy it crunched the rushes on the floor. This was followed by the splashing of a great deal of liquid.

What on earth were they having for supper?

A few minutes later, the innkeeper bade Royce a pleasant stay, and she heard the door being closed and locked once more.

"You can come out now, Ciara."

She slid from beneath the bed—and had to bite back an exclamation of surprise and delight.

It was a wooden tub full of water. Hot, steaming water.

Smiling, she lifted her gaze to Royce's as she got to her feet. In the middle of all this madness, he had found a way to provide her with a hot bath.

He remained standing by the door, his chest still bare, his eyes piercing hers. "You were so cold earlier that I feared you might…I did not want you to catch your death, so I decided to…"

His strained expression made her smile waver, brought that strange, hot flutter back to her stomach.

She glanced from his face to the bolted door to the barred window and back again, realizing that they were locked in. Together.

That they would be spending the next several days alone in this small chamber.

With naught to occupy their attention but each other.

Chapter 12

He swore he could hear each drop of water as it glided down her body.

Seated on a stool in front of the hearth, his jaw clenched so hard that it hurt, Royce kept his back to Ciara and his gaze on the untouched trencher of food in his hands. And fought a desperate battle to ignore the liquid, sensual sounds just a few paces behind him.

He *should* have told the innkeeper and his assistants to take the hot bath away. The fire and the fur had clearly been enough to revive Ciara. She was in no danger.

But after all she had endured this day, he had found himself unable to deny her a few moments'…

Pleasure.

The word made his entire body go taut with strain. He realized he was sweating. The chamber that had seemed so cold just minutes ago now felt much too hot. Sultry. Confining.

Every splash of warm water caressing her naked skin made his heart beat harder. Each barely audible sigh that escaped her lips made his blood pound through his veins. He could not even draw a complete breath, longed to get up and pace—but that would mean turning around.

And seeing what he was hearing.

He grabbed a haunch of roast meat from his trencher and sank his teeth into it, struggling to remember that a great many lives depended on him doing what was right and honorable.

Including his own.

Wolfing down his meal, he resisted the urge to steal a glance over his shoulder…and tried to keep his mind off the large, soft bed in the corner.

At least the arrival of the tub had spared him one bit of torture: having Ciara tend his injuries. He had seen to his own cuts and bruises while she had prepared for her bath.

The thought of what her tender ministrations might have been like, of her fingers moving over his bare skin…

He gnawed the last bit of meat from the mutton bone, unable to forget the way she had looked at him when he had stripped off his tunic and turned to face her. The wonder in her gaze, and the unexpected, unmistakable arousal, had hit him like a punch to the gut, reminding him of the sweet, feminine passion he had tasted so briefly at Bayard's castle.

The passion that he had no right to taste or to take.

"Royce?"

He almost choked on his food. "Aye?"

"Could you…mayhap hand me something to…to dry off with? Please?"

His heart thudded. Her tremulous voice revealed that she was just as affected as he was by the heat sizzling through the room.

His gaze slid to the stack of linens on the table to his left. He wished fervently that she had thought of this before getting into the tub. "Of course."

He tried to say it casually, to act as if he had beautiful, naked women bathing within five paces of him every day.

Setting his trencher aside, he picked up some of the clean linens and moved as close to her as he dared, keeping his gaze averted. He placed them on the floor within her reach.

But he did not move away.

He heard her breath catch. For an instant, just one instant, he lingered there. Wishing…wanting…

Then he forced himself to reclaim his place before the hearth.

Water sloshed over the edge of the tub. "Thank you," she whispered.

"You are welcome." He glared into the flames, felt beads of sweat slide down his temple, his neck, into the matted hair of his bare chest.

Neither of the tunics he had pilfered from the stable boys fit him, both too tight to get past his shoulders. He could only hope one of the garments would fit Ciara.

The wish became a prayer a moment later as he heard her stand. He had to shut his eyes to banish the image painted by the sounds: water sluicing off her naked body. The little rush of breath between her teeth as the night air touched her wet skin.

He imagined her nipples tightened to hard pearls, imagined them a perfect, dusky pink.

Next he heard the crunch of the rushes beneath her feet as she stepped from the tub. And the quiet rustling of the linen as she rubbed the soft cloth over her smooth, wet curves.

Then silence.

Every muscle in his body tightened. He remained still, not trusting himself to move. Knowing that if he so much as dared draw breath, he would have her in his arms and on the bed before either of them could say a word.

He blinked once, slowly. Waited.

"Royce?" she whispered tentatively.

"What?" His voice sounded rough and hollow.

She hesitated a moment. "What am I to wear?"

The chamber seemed to grow smaller and even hotter around him. He waved a hand over his shoulder, motioning her toward the corner near the door. "See if any of those fit you."

He listened while she padded barefoot over to the pile of stolen garments. She could not put her ruined gown back on. The few bits of cloth left intact after their escape today had more or less shredded when she had disrobed for her bath. The task of getting undressed had apparently been difficult with her hands bandaged. And he had not dared to offer help.

Nor did he offer any now, as he listened to her wrestling with the homespun garments in an attempt to fit them over her curves.

She made a sound of frustration. "I do not think these will work. My hips are too…and my…my…"

He did not need an explanation. His imagination provided a complete, vivid picture.

Gritting his teeth, he whispered an oath and flicked a glance heavenward. Was it not enough that he had to spend the next few days alone with her in this room? Did she have to be as naked as Eve the entire time?

He stood, raking a hand through his hair. "I will have to risk a visit to the marketplace in the morn, to purchase us both some clothes," he told her, trying to think of what to do with her tonight.

Blankets were the only answer, he decided. Bundles and bundles of blankets. "For now, you will have to make do with the coverlets from the bed."

He felt relieved when he heard her cross the chamber quickly, heard the rustling of the blankets. But then silence fell again.

"Princess?" he asked warily. Mayhap she had decided to forgo her supper, to simply go to bed. It would be a relief to discover her fast asleep.

But when he heard her voice again, he realized he had not been born a fortunate man.

"I…I feel much better now," she said. "Thank you for ordering the bath for me. It was very kind. And thank you for being so…so chivalrous."

He would have laughed if he could breathe deeply enough. Aye, he had kept his back turned—but *chivalrous* was the last word he would use to describe how he felt at the moment.

"You are welcome, milady. Are you ready for…" As he turned to face her at last, the question died on his lips.

She had not covered herself with all the blankets; she had chosen only one.

The fur.

He felt every drop of blood in his veins surge into his

lower body like a flood of fire. The silky fur covered her from neck to toes, leaving only her oval face and damp hair exposed.

The thought of her pale nakedness hidden from him by only that soft robe…

He was suddenly aware of his arousal pressing painfully hard against his leggings. Of the overpowering desire to step toward her, slide that coverlet from her shoulders, reveal her body one slow inch at a time…

He forced his gaze back to her face, could not make himself look away fast enough to conceal his feelings. She saw it all in his eyes. How powerfully she affected him.

How much he wanted to make her his own.

He heard himself speaking, as if from far away. "Are you ready, Princess?"

She took a step toward him, even before he amended the question.

"For your supper," he said quickly. "Are you hungry, Princess?"

Mayhap if he kept calling her that, it would be enough to remind him of all the barriers between them. Of why he must not do what every fiber of his being urged him to do.

"Starving," she said with a tremulous curve of her mouth, drawing closer one hesitant step at a time. "But I…think I may have a problem."

She lifted her bandaged hands, still clutching the fur, and he understood: she was having a hard enough time keeping her makeshift robe in place. She could not eat and remain covered at the same time. Which meant she could either stay warm and go hungry…

Or eat her supper naked.

He shut his eyes, trying to banish that delectable image. And then he thought of a third possibility.

Opening his eyes, he gestured to the hearth, noticing that his voice sounded too deep, too husky when he made the suggestion. "Come and sit by the fire, and I will…see what I can do."

Turning away, he filled a trencher with food at the table in the corner while she settled herself before the fire. From outside their chamber, the delicate strains of a harp and pipes drifted on the night air.

"Where is that music coming from?" Ciara asked.

"The tavern down the street."

"The stringed instrument sounds like a tympanum. I have one of those at…"

Home.

She did not say the word, and Royce felt something inside him wrench tight, reminded that she had left her home behind. Forever.

'Twas a feeling he knew too well. His heart beating strangely, he felt somehow that he knew her thoughts as she gazed toward the window.

She had become an exile, as he had been. In a matter of days, she would be arriving at her new home, Mount Ravensbruk.

Where they would part, forever.

He stood there watching her, holding a trencher of food in his hands, racked by denial and frustration. And by another, new emotion. One that should have startled him. Alarmed him.

Instead, he could only yield to it, wonder when it had happened.

When it was that she had claimed his heart so completely, this lady with the topaz eyes and quiet grace, delicate as snowfall, rare and precious as a Châlons garnet. This princess who was both regal and ravishing, who had a soft spot in her heart for every child she met and courage enough to climb an icy cliff.

And willingness to sacrifice her own happiness to save her people.

Mayhap, he thought, swallowing hard past a lump in his throat, he had first realized it on the cliff today. Or later when she had walked for hours without telling him how badly she was suffering.

Or mayhap it had happened the moment he first saw her in the chapel, when she had appeared like an angel drifting into his life on a beam of morning sunlight.

He was in love with her.

His grip tightened on the carved wooden trencher, almost hard enough to break it, as everything inside him was breaking. *He was in love with her.* With this sweet innocent who looked so vulnerable huddled within the fur, her damp hair trailing down her back. Princess Ciara. Christophe's sister. Aldric's daughter. Daemon's betrothed.

A lady who belonged to everyone but him.

He looked away, had to set the platter down before he snapped it in two. Brutally reminded himself that she was never meant to be his. He could not change what had to be—and he could not make the same mistake he had made four years ago.

Peace depended on him carrying out the mission he had been entrusted with. This time, he had to do what duty and honor demanded. This time, he had to put his country's needs ahead of his own.

The music still drifted in through the shuttered window, and he knew he would never again hear the sound of harp and pipes without remembering this night, this moment.

This bitterness.

Steeling himself against the forbidden feelings, he picked up the trencher again, poured a cup of wine for her, and returned to the hearth. Sitting with his back against the warm stone wall, he tried to keep his voice casual.

"You say that instrument is called a tim-what?"

"Tympanum." Ciara was still looking toward the window. "It is a stringed instrument, like a harp, native to Scotland. I have rather a large collection of stringed instruments at…home."

She finished in a scant whisper, still holding the fur close with her bandaged hands.

Glancing from his face to the platter in his hands and back again, she regarded him with a bewildered expression.

"Have you given thought to how I might eat that, or are you teasing me?" She attempted a smile, lifted an eyebrow. "Nay, now I have guessed—you mean for me to gobble my supper like a hog at a trough."

He realized she had noticed his somber expression and was trying to lighten his mood. But he could not muster even the slightest grin. "Nay, I thought we would try something more civilized. Not to mention more tidy." He cut a bite-size chunk of meat for her and held it out toward her.

"Ah, I see. Instead of a hog, I shall be fed like a loyal hound." Still smiling, she leaned forward and nipped it from his fingers.

He tried to ignore the sensual impact of the brief contact, dropped his gaze to the trencher, and cut another piece for her. "Have you always liked music?"

"Aye," she said between bites. "It is hard to say whether I like reading or music best."

"A lady of many talents."

She shrugged at the compliment. "A lady with a great deal of time on her hands," she corrected. "And many costly tutors."

"You are being generous, milady. And modest."

She chewed and swallowed before speaking, shaking her head. "Nay, my musical skills are entirely the fault of my royal tutors." She laughed. "When I was young, you see, I used to sneak away from them whenever possible to spend time with the minstrels who visited the palace. The minstrels were the ones who taught me to play and compose."

Royce could not help grinning, picturing a mischievous little princess skipping her lessons. "And the musicians were no doubt more colorful and fun than your stuffy royal tutors."

"Much more fun." She nodded. "But in truth, I believe I have always favored intellectual pursuits like reading and music simply because I have never been particularly good at physical..." She had leaned toward his outstretched hand again, her eyes on his as she spoke, and it took her a moment to finish the sentence. "...activities."

He held her gaze, silently sharing her memories of the various physical activities they had engaged in together.

Not only today, but last night.

Her mouth hovered just above the meat in his fingertips. Then she took it quickly.

And sat back, drawing the fur closer around her, as if suddenly aware of the erotic aspect of what they had been doing—of the way the pads of his fingers just brushed against her lips each time...

Of the savory juices on his fingertips, and in her mouth...

Of the unintentional, wet touch of her tongue against his skin...

"B-but I-I should..." she stammered, "I should not be so critical of my tutors. They were most...most..."

"Most fortunate to have a pupil who is both intelligent and gifted," he whispered, "as well as beautiful."

Her eyes widened, shining. Her gaze searched his for a long moment before she replied, softly, "No one has ever said that to me before."

He knew he had no right to be the first. Knew he should stop.

And instead he heard himself telling her more. "Ciara, you are more beautiful than"—he searched for a comparison worthy of her—"than snow falling in the mountains at dawn. You are more beguiling and more lovely than any woman I have met."

Her cheeks colored. "I always thought that I...I did not compare well to other women. My eyes are too dark, and my mouth is...and my hair..." She reached up to touch the jagged ends of her damp tresses.

"Your eyes are much better than blue, and your hair is like copper and gold spun together. Not even my handiwork could mar its beauty." He lifted the cup of wine toward her. "And your mouth..."

She leaned forward and took a sip from the offered goblet, lifting her gaze to his.

He purposefully ran his thumb over her lower lip. "Your mouth is perfect, Ciara," he said huskily. "*You* are perfect. And you have become more precious to me than anything in my life."

If she had not looked at him that way, her eyes suddenly glistening with dampness, filling with warmth and longing and so many other, deeper emotions…

He might have been able to stop himself. But the need had become too strong, the feelings in his heart and in her gaze too powerful to resist. As if in a dream, he picked up another piece of meat and held it out to her, leaning closer. Groaned softly as she parted her lips to let his fingertips slip inside.

And then he was sharing the taste of it with her, kissing the succulent juices from her lips. Sliding his tongue along hers. Meeting her mouth as she sought his and devouring her with a hot, deep kiss.

One of her hands came up to rest in the center of his chest, over his heart, and he flinched. Thought for an instant that she might push him away. End this now. *Now, before it was too late.*

Instead, she made a low sound of need. Of wanting. Kept her mouth molded to his.

And then she released her grip on the fur, slid her palm up over his chest to the nape of his neck.

He dropped the trencher, undone by her touch. Lost in her silky heat and delicious sighs. Cupping her face, he deepened the mating of their mouths, reason gone, sanity slipping. All he knew was that he needed her, wanted her. *Loved her.*

Driven by the deafening, pounding demand of his heart, he lifted his mouth from hers to nip a hungry path along her jaw, her throat. Glancing down, he caught a breathtaking view of her ivory skin warmed to gold by the firelight. The fur had parted just enough to reveal the soft curves of her breasts, their rosy peaks taut.

He went still, stared in awe at the sheer perfection of her, exhaled a harsh gasp of air. And the touch of his breath made the tempting pearls tighten even more. Dusky pink, they were, just as he had imagined. He told himself he should not, must not…

But then his hand was there, cupping one exquisite globe, his thumb whisking over her nipple. Her skin was so satiny pale against his dark, callused palm; her voice so soft as she inhaled a small cry of pleasure, of discovery.

Of longing.

A single drop of wine had trickled from her lips to splash onto that soft curve of flesh, and he could not resist the urge to bend his head and kiss it away. She shuddered in response, making small, passionate sounds that touched him like hot brands and set him ablaze. His lips and tongue licked up the tiny dot of liquid…and then he lifted her to his mouth, tasted her, suckled her.

His boldness did not seem to make her afraid. Or even cautious. She had become as reckless as he, as lost in the flames that threatened to burn them both to ashes. Her fingers buried in his hair and she arched her back, allowing him to take her more deeply, allowing the fur to slide down her body. Revealing more of her, all of her. Her slender rib cage, her impossibly tiny waist, her flat stomach…

Driven to the edge of madness by her response, he lifted his head, slanted his mouth over hers once more, encircling her with his arms. The feel of her soft, naked body against his, the way she pressed herself closer to him, snapped the last threads of his control.

And before he knew what he was doing, he lowered her to the floor, pressing her down into the fur.

Ciara trembled in his arms, not from fear or even uncertainty, but from an unfamiliar excitement that left her gasping for breath between his deep, hot kisses. Royce's words and his touch and the steely strength of his arms had all woven a glittering tapestry of magic around her.

She surrendered to it, to him, to the tumult of emotions in her heart and the infinite gentleness of his hands, until naught existed outside of this small chamber and the firelight and the heat and longing that bound them together.

The bristly hair on his chest felt rough against her breasts, made the sensitive tips pinch tight. When he tore his mouth from hers, she heard a moan of protest issue from her throat, but then he was sliding down her body, his lips closing over one aching crest. He kissed and teased it with his tongue until her breath broke and she arched up off the soft fur beneath her, his name a whispered plea on her lips.

His arm slid around her back to hold her fast as he gave hungry attention to each tender peak in turn. The need that twisted through her, the shocking, indescribable sensations felt like tendrils of flame. Like lightning. Sharp, glittering. Her pulse pounding, she tossed her head helplessly, lost in the exquisite storm.

She knew she should stop him, knew that what they were doing was wrong. By all the laws of God and man, this was wrong. *Forbidden.* He was not her husband and never would be.

Her hands sought him, her fingers curling into the hard muscles of his arms. But she did not stop him, did not even try. To the depths of her soul, she felt—knew—that this was what she was meant for, what she had been born for, to be held in this man's arms. Caressed and cherished and claimed.

She heard his breathing, ragged and hoarse, as he lowered her back down onto the fur, balancing his weight on his forearms. She felt his body so hard and hot against hers, streaked with sweat, shuddering with his own need. Yet he nuzzled her gently, brushing his stubbled cheek over the wet, delicate skin he had kissed, making her shiver and writhe beneath him.

She buried her fingers in his hair, did not care if she was

condemned to spend eternity in Hell as punishment for this one sweet night of Heaven—for she had already been condemned to spend the rest of her life without him.

Nay, she could not think of that. Not while they were still together. Not tonight. Unable to deny him her body or her soul, she offered up both willingly, gladly. For he already possessed a part of her that Daemon never would.

Her heart.

And all that mattered was here, now, *him.*

She tried to draw him back to her, longing to wrap her arms around him, to be closer to him in a way she could not begin to understand. But he pulled away from her grasp, moving lower over her body. Tracing a damp path down her ribs, her belly.

Unable to reach him, she grasped handfuls of the fur beneath her, shock lashing through her when he kissed his way even lower. His fingers followed, brushed against her hip. Her thigh.

She went rigid, stunned breathless, unable to believe what he meant to do. Surely he could not…dear God, he could not…

He answered her unasked question with a touch. With a breath. His fingertips burning her like a brand, he gently nudged her thighs apart.

Heat ignited inside her, a liquid fire born deep within the core of her being. Sizzling through her until she could not even remember being cold only minutes ago. Could only surrender to him. Closing her eyes, catching her lower lip between her teeth, she parted her thighs, bared her most intimate, feminine secrets to his eyes, *to his touch.*

The deep, strained sound that came from his throat told her more vividly than words of his passion and desire for her. But instead of claiming her quickly, he went more slowly, drawing out the tension. Tracing a single fingertip along her thigh…higher…closer…one slow inch at a time. She held her breath, quivering. Trusting. Willing to go wherever he would take her.

She could not hold in a low cry when his fingers brushed over the soft, dark triangle between her thighs. Lightly, so very lightly. Stroking her, exploring. Tenderly seeking and finding the liquid fire that poured forth from deep within her.

And then she felt the touch of his lips there. And his tongue.

Her body jerked in a spasm of pleasure, arching into a bow, undulating in a dazzling storm of fire and lightning. If she had not been biting her lip, her cry of wonder and ecstasy would have filled the darkened chamber.

But it was only the beginning, for his hands came to rest on her hips, held her against him while he found a small bud, at the core of her being, touched it with just the tip of his tongue. Softly. Again and again. Until she was twisting on the fur, tossing her head wildly.

Dazed, mindless, she felt the storm building again, more powerfully this time. He held her fast and sampled her intimately, parting his lips to taste her. Bright stars whirled inside her. A tempest of stars and flame and lightning. Hotter. Faster. Spinning tight.

And then his tongue slipped *inside* her.

She shattered in his hands, felt all the lightning and stars explode in the same instant, and she was falling through the rain of heat and light, sailing downward through the storm, drenched with pleasure.

Her body went limp, spent. Shivering, she felt too weak to move, almost thought she had fainted. When she finally opened her eyes, it was to find Royce wrapping her in the fur, covering her nakedness as he gently gathered her in his arms.

Though he was still breathing harshly and shaking with his own need, he sat back against the hearth and cradled her against him, whispering soft, sweet words in her ear.

The unexpected end of their loving stunned her almost as much as the unexpected beginning. She closed her eyes and pressed her face against the strong column of his throat, trembling, filled with awe at what had just happened.

And she prayed that he could not tell she was crying. Knew she could not explain her tears. Could not put them into words. Not to him, not aloud.

He had taken no pleasure for himself, had left her maidenhead intact—for her future husband to claim.

And that made her want to sob. The idea of sharing such intimacy with Daemon, with *any* other man—nay, she could not! She wanted to give herself to only one man.

To *this* man.

And it endeared him to her more, that he would give to her without taking, when his own longing had been so fierce.

She bit her lip, fought back the tears, wanted to rail against God for bringing Royce Saint-Michel into her life when it was impossible for her to share a future with him.

She clung to him as he gently stroked her hair. It mattered not that he had refrained from taking her virginity, for he had already breached a far deeper and more important place within her.

And she would never be the same again.

Chapter 13

Morning light slipped through the shutters, a thin line of brightness that slanted over the bed and awakened her. Ciara lifted her lashes slowly, reluctantly. Curled on her side beneath the blankets and the fur coverlet, she saw Royce…stretched out in front of the door, one arm crooked behind his head. Asleep.

She did not stir for a moment, allowing herself simply to gaze at him, to feel her heart beat a fast, unsteady rhythm, as it now seemed to do every time she glanced his way.

For the second night in a row, he had insisted she take the bed, despite her protest that he needed a comfortable rest more than she did; she had slept almost all day yesterday while he had stood watch.

But last night, when she had offered to sleep on blankets in front of the fire, he had refused to hear of it. And she realized he was not merely being gallant.

He had avoided coming anywhere near the bed the entire time they had been here.

Just as he had avoided the subject of what had happened between them that first night. He had not spoken of it. Had not touched her again, even in the most innocent way. 'Twas as if he had built an invisible curtain wall around her.

And as much as that hurt, she had made no effort to close the distance he had created between them, for she knew this was how it must be. To touch him, kiss him, hold him in her arms would only make it more painful when they had to part. She had accepted that.

Or rather, she was trying to accept it.

Trying to be the dutiful, responsible princess she was supposed to be.

Her throat tightened as she gazed at him in the pale light

of dawn. He lay on his side, his chiseled features relaxed in sleep, his sword not far from his hand. The warrior at rest. Except for a stray lock of dark hair tangled over his forehead that ruined the image, adding a hint of boyish charm, making him look so sweet. Almost innocent. A wave of tenderness stole over her.

Tenderness and this other, stronger feeling that she had been resisting for some time now. The one she did not want to explore or even acknowledge.

Because it was destined to end, and soon.

Silently, she slipped from the bed, wrapping herself in a sheet, and crept over to him. They had been doomed to part even before they met, she and this dark swordsman. Their destinies had been decided by forces much larger and more important than the happiness of one woman and one man.

And now they had but a few days left together, a mere handful of hours.

Unable to resist a single stolen touch, she brushed the hair from his forehead with her fingertips. And felt her heart turn over as the gold ring on her hand glimmered in the dawn light.

She had almost forgotten she was wearing the wedding band, she had grown so accustomed to its weight on her finger. It had come to seem a natural part of her. So right. So real.

With her hands no longer bandaged, the engraved circle of metal caught and reflected the sun. Kneeling in the rushes, she remained there by his side, indulging in a brief, sweet fantasy….

How wonderful it would be if the ring were truly hers, if she were Royce's wife.

How it would feel to wake beside him each morn, to share his life, ease his pain, know his joy. To let him tease her. Let him love her. To be free to love him in return, in every way a woman could love a man.

To carry his children inside her, just beneath her heart.

She lifted her hand to her mouth to hold in a soft sound

of yearning, of anguish—and she saw, remembered, the ring's inscription for the first time in days.

You and no other. The heart conquers all.

Tears filled her eyes, blurring her vision. The words seemed to mock her, the first part true…the second impossible.

Impossible for her. For them.

She rose, forcing herself to turn away from him, from all the dreams she dared not dream. More than ever, she knew she had to carry out her duty and fulfill the betrothal agreement. Not only for her country, her people, and her father, not only to ensure peace and to honor the memory of her brother.

But for *him*, for Royce. Only when their journey ended safely and she was wed to Daemon could Royce reclaim his lands, his title, his family name and honor. She could not share his future, but she could give back to him what he had lost in the past.

She could help him return home.

With quiet steps, she moved to the ewer and basin on the corner table and dampened a cloth to wash the tears from her cheeks. She tried to set aside her melancholy thoughts and resolved that she would not waste the time she had left with him. She would cherish every moment, every memory the next few days might bring.

Quickly performing her morning ablutions, she donned the leggings and tunic Royce had purchased for her yesterday. Both garments were large and loose enough to conceal her feminine shape, the brown homespun material scratchy against her skin. It was the first time in her life she had ever worn masculine garb. A few days ago, she would have been shocked at the very suggestion, but now it did not seem outrageous to her at all.

Not compared to some of the other things she had done recently.

Blushing, and banishing that thought, she plaited her hair. It did not take long, for 'twas much shorter than it had been.

Royce had brought her a small looking glass from the market square yesterday, and she had squeaked in dismay upon viewing the damage to her formerly waist-length tresses. His pickax had not created a particularly becoming style.

He had apologized again and loaned her one of his small, sharp knives so that she could even the ends. Her hair barely touched her shoulders now.

Finished with her braid, she tiptoed back to the bed, putting the sheet back in place, straightening the blankets and the fur coverlet.

And wondered how she and Royce would pass the time today.

Sitting on the newly made bed, she drew her knees up under her chin, looking at him again. Feeling her heart beat too fast. Last evening, they had filled the awkward silences with talk of the weather, the kinds of shops he had seen in the marketplace, the fact that the innkeeper seemed a kindly sort.

And Anteros. Royce was as worried about his destrier as she was about her puppy. He hated that he would probably never know the brave stallion's fate.

Ciara felt a sad smile curve her lips. It was so like Royce to worry about his horse and to speak of his concern openly. He had to be the most softhearted, expressive man she had ever met.

Not traits one would expect to find in such a battle-hardened warrior.

Certainly not traits *she* had expected to find when she first saw him in the abbey's chapel.

Had it been only days ago?

She shut her eyes, remembering the scars she had seen on Royce's chest and arms and back. Marks that bespoke how many battles he had fought, how much pain he had been forced to endure in his lifetime. Yet instead of becoming cold or cynical, as some men did when surrounded by death and violence, he remained kind and honorable and…

Noble.

Despite all that had been taken from him, Royce Saint-Michel remained a true *noble*man. Far more so than the prince who would be her husband.

A noise outside the window distracted her. Sneaking over to unbar the shutters, she opened one just a crack to peek out. Daylight sliced in, blinding her for a second, but then her eyes adjusted and she could see that the narrow streets were crowded with peddlers and peasants and carts laden with goods.

It must be the weekly market day. She had read about such things: free farmers and serfs who had surplus to sell came to offer meat and cheese, grain and livestock to the townsfolk, while itinerant peddlers sold salt, tools, firewood, shoes, and other necessities. The town gates must have opened at dawn. At the moment, each vendor was scrambling to claim the best space to erect his stall.

The town's craftsmen were also opening their workshops to customers, folding down the hinged panels over their windows to form display tables, piling them with tempting arrays of goods meant to lure customers inside.

Ciara wished she could persuade Royce to take her outside for a quick visit to the shops. They could both do with some fresh air after being cooped up so long in this room. But she knew he would never allow it.

She was about to close the shutter when she spied an irresistible temptation, directly across from their window, only a few paces away: a silversmith's shop, its display table glittering with brooches and baubles…

And one item that she simply had to have for him.

She bit her lip, an idea forming in her mind. Nay, she could not. 'Twas too reckless. Outrageous…

Then again, those two words no longer deterred her as easily as they once might have.

It would only take a moment, she reasoned, peering out

at the silversmith's shop. And she was dressed as a boy. Concealed beneath the hooded cloak Royce had bought for her, she would be completely disguised. And she would be back before he even stirred from his sleep.

The decision made, she moved from the window to quickly don her boots and the cloak, pulling the hood close to hide her face. She paused only long enough to take a few marks from Royce's coin purse on the table.

Then she stole back to the window, opening both shutters, her heart thrumming with excitement and a little fear. Pulling herself up onto the wooden sill, she glanced back once, making sure Royce had not noticed.

And slipped out into the bustling street.

The flood of sunlight on his face woke Royce, made him groan and throw an arm across his eyes to block it out. He came to awareness slowly, resentfully, for he did not want to leave behind the dream that had enveloped him in a pleasant fog.

A dream of a keep, familiar and yet strange, of a great hall with a roaring fire and Ciara by his side, their children playing nearby. A young girl with her mother's golden eyes and bright smile, and a small boy, just learning to walk, with black hair like his.

It had been so vivid, it took Royce a moment to remember where he was. As reality seeped in with the sun, he remained still, eyes shut, wishing he could recapture the dream.

But it was gone.

And as it faded, he felt empty. Gradually opening his eyes, he let his arm drop to his side and remained on the floor. He could not bring himself to look toward the bed. To see her there, so close to him, yet so impossibly beyond his reach.

He had decided this would be their last day here.

Tonight they would continue their journey under the cover of darkness, at least until they were safely away from the town. After that, they would either have to risk traveling by daylight—or risk dying at the bottom of a crevasse or a cliff.

He rubbed his eyes with the heels of his palms, hating that he was being forced to choose between such deadly alternatives. But there was no other way out of here. None that would guarantee Ciara's safety.

Except for one. An insane idea that had occurred to him last night as he watched her sleeping. In truth, he *did* have one sure way to keep her safe from the rebels.

He could give them what they wanted: take her away from Thuringia, from Mount Ravensbruk. From Daemon and her wedding. She would be safe if he changed directions and took her far away with him.

He sat up, gritting his teeth, recognizing the true motives behind that mad plan. The impulse was selfish, impossible, unthinkable. He could not simply steal Aldric's daughter and disa—

As he glanced at the bed, his thoughts stilled abruptly.

Because Ciara was not in it.

The sight of the unoccupied covers, so unexpected, held him paralyzed for an instant. Just long enough for his heart to pound a single, horrified thud.

Then he sprang into motion, jumping to his feet, snatching up the sword. The rebels! How could he have slept through—

His looked at the window, noticed the wooden bar on the floor. Knew that his first guess had been wrong.

The shutters had not been smashed from outside but unlocked and opened from the inside. He realized, too, that the bedclothes had been neatly tucked in place—not left rumpled, as they would be if she had been snatched from her sleep.

And her boots and the garments he had bought her were missing.

He stalked to the window, already filled with dread.

It was market day, the streets jammed with peasants and peddlers shouting their wares, housewives and servants haggling over bargains, beggars pleading for alms. As he stared into the crowd, fear tore at his heart. Ciara could be anywhere.

What could have possessed her to venture out in such a throng? Had the woman lost her senses?

Did she not remember that there were men out there who sought to kill her?

Ice trickled down his spine. "By nails and blood, Ciara," he choked out under his breath, already turning to grab his homespun cloak and his weapons. "Where the devil are you?"

Muttering every curse he knew, he returned to the window, wondering whether any woman could possibly make it *more* difficult for a man to protect her. He pulled himself up onto the sill and leaped out.

An hour later, he was still searching the streets and alleyways, stopping at every stall and shop. He had begun his search in those establishments offering musical instruments and books for sale, but he had found no trace of her.

What else would Ciara have been tempted to buy? Stepping out of a perfumer's workshop, he squinted in the bright light and moved into the bustling street, his pulse unsteady.

She could have been found by those searching for her.

She might be dead already.

Shoving that possibility to the back of his mind, he pushed through the throng, heading back toward the inn, praying every step of the way. Mayhap she had merely gone out for a moment and returned. And he would find her waiting for him, sitting on the bed, smiling at her own audacity, eyes sparkling with delight over her adventure.

If so, she would be treated to the tongue-lashing of a lifetime.

Before he kissed her breathless.

Mayhap *after* he kissed her breathless.

He hurried past fishmongers offering the latest catch from mountain streams, women struggling to balance laden baskets on one hip and babies on the other, peddlers extolling the virtues of their spices, fabrics, dyes, candles, or meat pies. Rounding the last corner, he came to the street where the inn was located. He almost reached their room when he noticed a shop he had not seen earlier: a tiny place with no sign to advertise its wares—only a single mandolin displayed by the door.

Of course. If Ciara had peeked out their window and seen that, she would have found it impossible to resist. Royce headed straight for the shop and darted through the door.

Inside, he found the proprietor seated at his worktable amid a clutter of tools and wood, already engaged in a discussion with another customer, a well-dressed man who stood with his back to Royce.

"…and you would have marked her appearance," the customer was saying. "She is tall and most fair, her hair reddish brown, her eyes a pale gold like…"

Royce froze, his every muscle clenched taut just as the man turned to look at him while finishing his sentence.

"…topaz."

Their gazes locked across the scant paces that separated them. Royce's hand tightened on the hilt of his sword. *A rebel.* He did not recognize the blue-eyed, sandy-haired stranger—but did the man recognize him?

Was this one of the four who had been at the cliff? One of the traitors who had tried to kill him and Ciara in the avalanche?

"You are looking for someone?" he asked, trying to sound merely curious, helpful.

"I am," the fair-haired man replied with equal caution.

Royce saw no light of recognition in those eyes. And something else gave him hope: if the rebels were still searching the town, asking questions, it meant they did not have Ciara.

"Mayhap I can help you," he offered.

"Indeed, good sir?"

Royce managed a rakish smile. "I am well acquainted with the women of this town."

"The lady I seek is not from this part of Châlons."

"Oh?"

The man had a height and build similar to his own, Royce noted, but looked several years younger. Experience might give him the advantage in a fight.

"She is the daughter of my liege lord, and has run away from a marriage she does not wish." The sandy-haired rebel moved away from the table. Royce noted that he kept his hand on his sword. "We have been sent to bring her home."

"We?"

"My comrades and I."

Comrades. Royce wanted to spit in disgust. *Traitors. Assassins.* He kept his expression bland. "Mayhap you could describe her." *And mayhap you could tell me how many "comrades" you have and where they are.*

"Gentlemen, please." The mandolin maker rose from his seat, his eyes darting from one to the other, his fingers nervously turning the small hammer in his hands. "Would you prefer to discuss this matter outside? I have already told you, sir, that I have never seen this lady you seek."

That piece of information was most helpful, Royce thought, his gut tightening into a knot. Ciara had not been in this shop.

So where in the name of all that was holy was she? Safely in their room?

Or in the hands of one of this man's "comrades"?

The rebel never took his gaze from Royce's. "I thank you for your help, sirrah," he said to the proprietor. "So sorry to have interrupted your work." He nodded toward the door. "Mayhap this would be best discussed outside."

"Aye," Royce agreed, with a smile he hoped was more friendly than feral. He politely gestured for the stranger to precede him.

The younger man hesitated, just for an instant.

Then he stepped past him and out the exit.

Which allowed Royce to fall in close behind him. They had barely cleared the doorway when he pressed a small, sharp knife into the rebel's back.

"Do not call for help," he said with soft menace. "This blade will spill your guts in the street before you finish the first word."

The man froze. "What do you want?"

"I want you to keep your hands where I can see them. And keep walking." He nudged him with the point of the knife. "Toward that alley."

They reached the dark space between buildings in only a few steps. Once within the shadows, Royce disarmed his opponent and shoved him away. When the young fool spun to face him, he lifted the point of the man's own blade to his throat.

"I congratulate you on the excellent condition of your weapon." He pressed it closer, drew a bead of blood. "It is very sharp. Possibly sharp enough to take a man's head off in a single stroke."

The young rebel wisely remained absolutely still, hands raised, gaze on the sword. "Who are you?"

"I think you already know the answer to that. I am not going to waste time playing games."

"If it is money you want—"

"Do not pretend ignorance with me, you traitorous bastard. The only reason you are still alive is because you may be able to provide answers to a few questions. Starting with how many *comrades* are here in town with you."

"It seems there has been some misunderstanding. I do not know what you—"

He lost the rest of his sentence in a gasp of alarm as Royce backed him into the wall. Shifting the blade to press the long edge against the rebel's throat, Royce lifted the small knife he still held, positioning it beneath the young man's ear.

"How many?" he demanded through clenched teeth.

"And where might I find them?"

"Threatening me will avail you naught. I can reveal nothing. I took an oath."

"How unfortunate for you." He moved the knife upward.

"Wait! You are making a mistake, I tell you. It is all a misunderstanding. Our…our intentions are peaceful—"

"Truly? Mine are not." Royce smiled humorlessly. It was amazing how quickly a man could spout creative lies when his life teetered on the edge of a sharp blade. "Now tell me what I want to know before I carve you a new face."

"Karl!"

The shout came from the end of the alley. Royce glanced over his shoulder.

And found one of the rebel's comrades running toward them, sword in hand.

Royce turned on his heel and yanked Karl in front of him, keeping the sword at his throat. "Back away or this one dies!"

That stopped the other man—a strapping blond warrior with a longbow slung across his back.

"Back away," Royce repeated, moving toward the end of the alley, keeping Karl in front of him as a shield.

"Kill him and you will not leave here alive," the bowman replied coolly. "Your life is not particularly important to us."

"What a surprise. I am so deeply hurt."

"We only wish to speak with you." The man made no move that would get his friend killed. "That is all we wanted in the mountain pass."

"Before or after you started the avalanche?" Royce kept backing toward the street, toward freedom.

"Landers is telling you the truth," Karl said. "If you would listen—"

"And wait here for the rest of your 'comrades' to arrive? I think not." Royce was only a few paces from the crowds. He prepared to release Karl, planning to shove him forward into his friend and run. "Now, I hate to cut this pleasant rendezvous short, but I—"

He heard the sound behind him a second too late.

Recognized the *thunk* of a crossbow being fired at the same instant he felt the razor-sharp point of the steel-tipped bolt bury itself in his right arm.

He shouted in pain and rage as agony shot through his muscles. He lost his hold on the sword. And on Karl.

He stumbled backward, into the crowd, clutching at his blood-soaked arm, and turned to see his attacker rushing toward him, still holding the crossbow. With the snarl of a wounded, cornered animal, Royce drew his own sword with his left hand.

The throng around them erupted in screams and scattered in every direction.

Just as Ciara stuck her head out the window of their room a few yards away.

"Royce!" Her gaze on his wounded arm, she leaped from the window, heedless of her own danger.

"Nay!" he shouted at her. "Run!"

It was too late. The rebels had already seen her.

Karl and Landers rushed toward her. Royce whipped another knife from his boot, flung it with all his strength—and sent Landers tumbling into the dirt.

He turned to face his third opponent even as Karl reached Ciara. She screamed in fright.

But the third man was already on him, swinging the crossbow like a war hammer, aiming a blow to the head that Royce barely managed to dodge. He hit the ground and rolled clear of the next blow, shouting in agony as the crossbow bolt in his arm snapped off, the point driven deeper.

Burning in a haze of pain and fury, he kicked out savagely with one booted foot as his attacker closed in, landing a vicious strike to the man's groin, sending him to his knees. Ciara was shouting for him, mayhap fighting for her life.

With no time to spare, he lunged to his feet, grabbed the

crossbow, and smashed the rebel over the head with it, knocking him unconscious. He turned toward Ciara.

Karl was trying to subdue her, wrestling to keep his hold on her—until she jammed her elbow into his gullet and stomped sharply downward with her heel. Right onto the top of his foot.

Karl howled in pain, taken by surprise just long enough to let her go. Long enough for Ciara to remember the third part of her training.

She ran for all she was worth. Straight toward Royce.

He grabbed her hand and raced down the street, dodging through the crowds, not pausing to look back and see if Karl was following, if Landers or the other man had recovered enough to give chase.

They ran until she was struggling for breath, until he felt dizzy from loss of blood and the pain in his arm. Unable to go any further, he led her into a thatched-roof stable behind a small house and sank down in the hay, leaning back against the daub-and-wattle wall, gasping for air.

She dropped to her knees next to him, her voice tremulous. "Royce, you are hurt."

"I know that," he said dryly, grimacing as he glanced down at his blood-soaked sleeve. The broken wooden shaft of the thick crossbow bolt protruded from his upper arm, the point buried deep in the muscle.

"Oh, Royce." She touched his shoulder gingerly, tears in her eyes. "I am sorry! This is all my fault. I was gone only a few minutes, but when I returned you were not there, and I wanted to go and search for you, but I knew you would not want me to leave again and—"

"Ciara," he breathed, struggling to think clearly through the pain and dizziness. "You can explain later. We have to buy a horse and get out of here before they find us."

"But they know we are here and they know we are going toward Mount Ravensbruk. How can we hope to lose them?"

Royce stared hard at her. How indeed could he hope to

lose the rebels now?

How could he keep her safe—especially with his sword arm injured?

There was only one answer.

"They *think* we are going to Mount Ravensbruk, milady," he said, barely able to believe he was saying the words aloud even as he heard them. "Our destination has just changed."

Chapter 14

"Sweet Mary," Ciara whispered, gazing down at the destroyed castle in the valley far below, a light spring breeze tangling her hair. "Royce, this is your home, isn't it? This is Ferrano."

She did not know what made her guess, whether the vast size of the ruined stronghold or the fact that Royce's mood had grown increasingly somber with each passing hour as they had traveled south.

When they had left Gavena last night, he had said only that he intended to take her somewhere safe. After she had tended his wounded arm, they had used the last of their coin to purchase the best horse they could find—a finely boned, dappled gray mare, smaller than Anteros but swift and used to the mountain trails. She had carried them both all day without flagging.

Now they had halted at the top of a rise, Ciara still perched in the saddle, Royce dismounted beside her, holding the reins. They watched as the setting sun broke through the clouds overhead to bathe the deserted fortress below in fiery shades of red and gold.

"Aye," Royce replied at last, his voice strained. "This is—was my home."

He tugged on the reins and led the horse forward, down the gentle slope that flowed into a wide, shallow vale.

The castle dominated the broad expanse of land between two peaks, blocking what would have otherwise been an easy passage into Châlons for any force coming from the east. Ciara could make out an enormous keep surrounded by mural towers, in the center of a labyrinth of walls and gates, fortified bridges and outbuildings, all of it protected by a curtain wall and moat. The size and majesty of this place must have once rivaled the royal palace itself.

As they drew closer, she could name some of the structures—garrison quarters, stables, a chapel, a mill, falcons' mews—most blackened by fire, many reduced to rubble.

She gathered her rough homespun cloak around her, despite the fact that the weather had turned this morn. The air felt warm, heavy with the promise of rain, of spring and the new life it would bring to the mountains, but this place had known no season but winter for some time.

Her throat dry, she glanced down at Royce, remembering what he had told her about the surprise attack by Daemon's forces here, at the start of the war seven years ago. About how his family had died that day, murdered without mercy.

She could not see his expression, but his back was rigid, his fist clenched tight around the reins as he led the mare into the valley. He remained silent until they reached the edge of the stone causeway that spanned the moat.

He stopped at the foot of the drawbridge, gazing up at the towers that flanked the gatehouse. She could hear him breathing harshly, unevenly, as if every gulp of fresh air, every beat of his heart pained him.

She dismounted, sliding from the mare's back to stand beside him, reaching out to touch him. "Royce."

"We used to run footraces across this bridge," he said quietly. "Back and forth until we were breathless. And every spring, my sisters would sit in the sun, there at the top of that tower, and weave circlets of violets for their hair. And for our mother's hair."

Ciara's eyes burned with tears. She slid her fingers down his back, took his left hand in hers, and let him keep talking, reliving the memories of a sweeter, more innocent time.

"They even tried to put the flowers on the hounds once." The shadow of a smile tugged at his mouth. "Said that everyone at Ferrano should be pretty because it was spring."

She entwined her fingers through his, closing her eyes, feeling a tear fall.

"One summer, my younger brother and I were arguing and he pushed me off the bridge into the moat. I had to swim to shore, covered with muck. I swore I would never forgive him…."

She glanced up at Royce as his fingers tightened around hers, and wished she could find words to comfort him. Instead she rested her forehead on his shoulder, telling him without words that he was not alone. Not anymore.

He inhaled, then let the air out slowly, his breath soft against her cheek. "This is the first time I have been back, the first time…since…" His voice became a hoarse whisper. "After the war started, I could not get through the enemy lines, even to…"

She felt him tremble, did not know whether it was from the grief that wracked him or from weakness caused by his wound. The crossbow bolt had been buried deep in his arm—so deep that he had instructed her to push it through the rest of the way in order to get it out. He had endured the horrifying ordeal stoically and had refused to stop and rest even once today, though he had lost a great deal of blood.

Worried, she lifted her hand to his cheek and found his skin too warm, his eyes too bright. "Royce, you need to rest," she murmured gently. "You need sleep."

He nodded. "We should be safe from the rebels here," he said hollowly. "In truth, we are in Thuringia now. Daemon claimed all the lands here in the southern range, though he never spared the coin to repair the castles he had destroyed." He glanced up at the deserted remnants of the once grand fortress. "So it has been left as it was seven years ago."

Tugging on the horse's reins, he started forward, his gaze dropping to the lowered drawbridge at their feet. "Daemon's forces overran them so quickly, they never even had time to raise the drawbridge."

Ciara kept her fingers wrapped tightly through his as

they crossed the causeway, side by side. The mare's hooves clattered on wood, then on stone as they passed beneath the gatehouse.

On the other side of the moat, they moved through a second gatehouse, this one part of the curtain wall, and into the castle's outer bailey. Royce left her for a moment to enter one of the guard towers.

She heard what sounded like the creaking of a lever and pulleys and metal chains—and miraculously, the drawbridge rose, at the same time that an iron-reinforced portcullis slid downward in each of the two gatehouses, blocking anyone from following them over the bridge.

"A device of my father's invention," Royce explained when he rejoined her a moment later. "He was a brilliant military tactician."

Ciara looked up at him, not knowing if the dampness on her cheeks came from her tears or from the cold rain that had started to spatter down from the evening sky. "I am sure he was the best of men and the finest of knights." *Like his son.*

Royce did not reply, his attention claimed by a small grove of trees on the opposite side of the bailey.

Ciara followed his gaze, wondering how even a single tree could have survived untouched when the outbuildings on either side had been reduced to ashes. It seemed unaccountably strange to see an oasis of green, of life, here in this devastated place.

"Saints' breath," Royce murmured, his eyes narrowing, "where did those come from?" He started toward the grove.

Ciara almost called out to stop him, for she did not want him to stay outside in the rain when he was already unwell. But she knew that trying to stop Royce once he set his mind to something would be futile.

Leaving the mare at the gate, she hurried to follow him. When they reached the little orchard, she realized it was not an orchard at all, but a half-circle of evergreens, planted in a protected corner near the keep, in what had once been the castle's garden.

Six evergreens…encircling six flat, white headstones of the finest marble embedded in the earth. Someone had created a peaceful sanctuary, a tranquil resting place here amid the ivy and other greenery that had started to grow back. Violets dotted the ground beneath the trees, bright spots of purple pushing through the melting snow. And between the pines stood a statue of the Savior, hand raised as if in blessing over the markers.

Royce sank to his knees in the center of the stones. "My brothers…" he whispered brokenly, looking at the names chiseled into the pale squares of marble. "My sisters…my parents. But how…who…"

Ciara came to stand behind him, resting one hand gently on his shoulder. "This must have been done by someone who loved your family very much."

"But who?" he repeated in bewilderment. "It tore me apart that I was never able to return and give my family a proper burial. All those loyal to us were from Châlons—and no one from Châlons could have gotten through the enemy lines."

"Mayhap you had an unknown friend in Thuringia."

"What friend could *I* have in Thuringia? What Thuringian could care enough to do *this* and afford such fine marble…" Royce lifted his gaze to the statue. "Mathias," he said in a stunned whisper. "It must have been Prince Mathias."

"Daemon's brother?"

He nodded slowly. "We came to know one another during the first peace negotiations, four years ago." Shaking his head in wonder, he glanced up at her as she knelt beside him. "Mathias is a year older than Daemon, and by right he should have become regent when their father fell ill, but he refused in favor of his younger brother. He is a deeply spiritual man, and he was studying to join the priesthood…."

"He sounds very different from his brother."

"Aye. Two men could not *be* more different." Royce

glanced down at the white markers, rain soaking his hair and clothes. "It was Mathias who initiated the first peace negotiations. He wanted an end to all the violence and death. And he must also have seen to this, for me. For a man he had met only briefly. An enemy." His jaw tightened. "That is how different he is from Daemon. If it were Prince Mathias you had been betrothed to"—he paused, glancing at her, his mouth curving ruefully—"I still would not like it," he finished softly.

Ciara slid her arms around him. "I am sorry for all you lost, Royce." She rested her head on his shoulder, unable to hold back her tears any longer. "I am so sorry."

He buried his face in her hair and drew her close, and they knelt there together, holding one another in the small sanctuary his friend had created, while the rain pattered down around them.

"This helps, Ciara," he whispered after a long silence. "To know that they were cared for…and having you here. It…helps."

She looked into his eyes, grateful to this enemy prince she had never met for helping to ease Royce's pain. He had lived with it for so many years, mayhap he had not believed it could ever truly heal. "I am glad, Royce. I think your family would have wanted you to hold on to your memories and your love for them, but not the sorrow."

"Aye, little one." He caressed her cheek with his fingertips. "As Christophe would have wanted for you."

She nodded, warmed by his concern for her when his own grief was so great.

But as she lifted her hand to his face, worry lanced through her. Despite the cold rain, his skin was hot to the touch. "Royce, you have to go inside. You must rest."

"Are you watching over me now, milady?"

She brushed the wet hair from his forehead. "Aye."

His eyes darkening with emotion, he held her a moment longer. Then he rose, taking her hand to help her to her feet. And when he glanced down at the stones once more, the anguish in his expression had lessened.

Threading his fingers through hers, he led her back to the entrance of the keep, and together they went inside.

Ciara braced herself for the worst, but they found no bodies, no trace of human suffering; it seemed that Prince Mathias had seen to it that all who lost their lives here were given a decent Christian burial.

Which left naught but the empty, silent shell of what had once been a magnificent castle, torn asunder. Sections of the roof were open to the sky, which had allowed seven years of rain and snow to clean away some traces of the devastation that had taken place. But blackened piles of wood and stone and other debris remained, jumbled throughout the great hall and the towers she and Royce explored. Only the ground floor was still intact, water pooled here and there on the stone. The wooden beams supporting the floors above had given way.

They found odd bits and pieces that had escaped the Thuringians' savagery: a tapestry with its lower half burned away, metal plates and goblets, a wooden chandelier hanging from the ceiling of one chamber, its candles untouched, as if they had been replaced on the day of the attack.

That made Ciara's heart clench more than anything else they saw, for the fresh candles made it agonizingly clear that the people here had had no warning of what was to come. They had been calmly going about their daily lives when death had swept down upon them from the east.

She could not bear what it must be like for Royce, seeing this place he had loved brought to ruin. Only one thing they found eased the stark pain in his eyes: in the great hall, above the hearth, hung a shield and sword on display. They were blackened with soot but undamaged.

He climbed over some debris to reach them, took the sword in his hand, and wiped it clean with the edge of his damp tunic. She could see a bright blade beneath, a gold hilt.

"Royce, it looks just like the sword you carried."

"It is my father's sword," he said hoarsely, climbing

down to rejoin her. "A twin of the one that I…" He paused, glancing from her face to the hearth. He went still, staring as if he could see flames that were not there.

"Royce? Are you all right?"

"It was here that I saw you," he whispered.

She touched his arm, concerned that he was becoming fevered, delirious. "I do not understand."

"I had a dream of you, the night before last…and it was here. You were here. *We* were here…"

"Royce," she said softly, gently. "It was only a dream. We were not here when the fire happened. We are all right."

He looked down at her and shook his head, started to explain further—then stopped, apparently changing his mind.

"You are right, little one." His voice was heavy, sad. "It was only a dream. And will never be more."

She gazed up at him, perplexed. She wiped a black smudge from his stubbled cheek, wishing she could as easily soothe the frown from between his eyes. "You were telling me about the sword," she coaxed.

"Aye." He lifted the gleaming steel blade in his left hand. "It is the twin of the one I lost in the avalanche, the sword my father gave me on the day I was knighted. When I left here at eighteen and went to serve your father at court, I took two things: the sword my father had given me, and my mother's ring."

Ciara raised her left hand to her heart, touching the gold band she wore. "Then the ring *is* an heirloom."

"Aye. What did you think it was?"

"I thought…" She blushed, dropped her gaze. "I worried at first that it might be a token of love from some lady you left behind in France."

He reached out to tilt her head up, his brown eyes sparkling. "Nay, Ciara, I left no lady behind in France. My father gave that ring to my mother on the day they promised themselves to one another, when she was but fifteen. After they married, she wore it next to her wedding band, until the day I left for court. She gave it to me because she felt certain I would find some lady at the palace who would steal my heart, a lady I would want to make my bride."

Ciara felt her eyes burn as their gazes held, especially when he finished with three simple words.

"And I did."

She leaned into him, her fingers curling into his tunic. "But it happened all wrong, Royce. It was never meant to be this way."

Royce set the sword aside to wrap his arms around her. "But my mother was right. A lady at the palace did steal my heart—"

"The wrong lady."

"Nay, the right lady. The perfect lady. In all the years I have had that ring, I never met the woman I wanted to give it to. I thought I never would." He threaded his fingers through her hair, tilted her head up again. "But now I know the inscription is true, Ciara. *You and no other.*" He finished in a whisper, "I know what it means now."

She ached to give in to the feelings in his eyes. To forget everything and everyone outside this keep, to part her lips for his kiss, stay here in his arms forever.

Instead she withdrew, trembling from his touch and from the riot of emotions inside her. "Your arm needs to be tended. Let us see if we can…find a place where we can…draw some water and change the bandages."

She could not bear the look in his eyes, but he offered no protest when she pulled away from him. He clearly knew as she did that they dared not steal even a single kiss.

Their feelings for each other had become too strong, the pull of honor and duty too tenuous, like a rope that had frayed to a single thread. One more tug and it would snap.

And they would do something they could not undo.

Something Royce would not live long enough to regret.

"The kitchens," he suggested, his calm voice at odds with the hot tempest in his gaze. Picking up the sword, he turned to lead the way.

♦ ♦ ♦

Two hours later, Ciara stood before a blazing fire in the kitchen's main hearth, trying not to scald herself as she used a hook to pluck a small iron cauldron from the flames. She wrinkled her nose as she peered down into the pot, not sure whether the broth was fit to eat yet. It was her first attempt at cooking.

She glanced at Royce, who lay dozing a few paces away on a makeshift bed he had created from tablecloths. He had not been hungry at all, but she thought it would do him good to eat a hot meal. Determined, she hooked the little cauldron again and set it back in place to continue bubbling.

The kitchen had withstood the ravages of the Thuringian attack better than any other chamber in the keep, since it had been built with doubly thick stone floors and walls, designed to prevent the huge hearths and brick ovens from setting the adjoining rooms ablaze. The main hearth, the one she stood in front of, was so large she would be able to step into it without even ducking her head.

She and Royce had also discovered that the buttery, the large, cool underground storage chamber dug beneath the kitchens, had been spared the worst of the fire's damage. The food in it was no longer fit to eat, but a few useful casks and bags had offered up utensils, wine, and several clean cloths.

After re-bandaging Royce's wound and leaving him to sleep, Ciara had gone outside to see to their horse. One of the structures in the bailey had just enough of a roof left to protect the mare from the rain, and she did not seem to mind being covered with tablecloths rather than a blanket when Ciara removed her saddle.

Taking what little food they had brought with them from Gavena she had decided to try her hand at cooking. Which was not going quite as well as her other endeavors.

Reaching up for a dangling metal spoon to stir the soup, she burned her finger. Snatching it back, she stuck it in her mouth, whispering one of Royce's favorite oaths.

A low male chuckle made her glance to her left, where she found him lying on his side, observing her with a drowsy grin.

"You were not supposed to hear that," she mumbled around her stinging finger.

"A most unladylike word," he scolded lightly, his grin widening. "What on earth are you doing?"

"Cooking supper. And that word is one I never heard in my life before I met you," she lied, fighting to keep her own lips from curving. "I warned you once that I am a quick pupil."

That made him chuckle again. "Aye." He sat up, shifting his rumpled bed closer to the hearth so he could recline against the warm stone. "And you also enjoy proving me wrong."

"I do?"

He nodded. "When I met you, I thought you were a spoiled, helpless girl who could not do a single thing for herself, a haughty child who cared for naught but her silk slippers and her gilded books of verse. Yet here you are wearing peasant garb, working like a kitchen maid, taking care of me. You have taken charge of everything around you."

Ciara felt color rising in her cheeks, remembering how she used to feel inadequate. Helpless. Only now did she realize that she had not felt that way in some time.

It was as if she had left behind the regal, proper, uncertain Princess Ciara along with her royal coronet and robes. As if she had become someone new.

Someone she liked much better.

All because of this man who had come into her life so unexpectedly and changed everything so completely.

She looked down, toying with the edge of the rough homespun tunic she wore. "I have learned to take care of myself. You taught me that. You taught me"—she paused, listening to her rapid heartbeat—"a great many things."

When he spoke again, his voice had dropped to a deeper, softer tone. "I was also wrong about a great many things…such as thinking that you were selfish and uncaring. I do not think I have ever been so wrong."

Ciara did not reply, kept her gaze on the floor. She had promised herself that she would not reveal her true feelings for him. It made no sense to torment them both by discussing what was in her heart.

Turning away, she searched for another spoon to stir the soup.

"I have been wondering about something, Ciara."

"Hmm?" She tried to keep her attention on the rack of cooking implements hanging on the wall, not on the way his deep voice made her feel so tingly and warm inside.

"You never did mention where you went in the marketplace yesterday, when you disappeared from our room. What was so tempting that you would take such a risk to have it?"

She hesitated, not wanting to lie to him, yet not wanting to reveal what she had purchased. It was to be a surprise for him.

A gift when they parted for the last time.

"I…saw something in a shop across the street, but…" She shrugged, selecting a long spoon from the rack. "It did not look so nice when I examined it closely. It was a bauble at the silversmith's shop."

"Ah, the silversmith's. No wonder I could not find you. I was searching in the booths selling musical instruments and books and perfumes—"

"Perfumes?" She turned, blinking at him. "How did you know I like perfume?"

She saw the answer in his eyes before he expressed it with words. "Because the scent you wore when we were riding those first few days all but drove me mad with wanting you."

She turned the spoon she held in her hands, her fingers fluttering as her insides were fluttering. "Oh." Never before had she given thought to the effect her scent might have on a man. To the effect *she* might have on a man.

'Twas a heady, strangely powerful…not unpleasant sensation, the idea that she could somehow weave the same magic around Royce that he had woven around her.

As they gazed at each other across the kitchen, she was suddenly aware of just how clearly the masculine leggings and tunic she wore outlined the feminine shape of her hips, her legs. Though the garments fit loosely, they were much more revealing than any skirt.

And when he stood, she was vividly reminded that he had not put his own tunic back on after she had re-bandaged his arm.

"Royce…" She could not move as he walked toward her. Did not want to move.

"I have been going mad since the day we met," he said hoarsely, "and I think I may have finally lost my mind completely. I told you—I told myself—that I was bringing you here to keep you safe. But that was a lie."

Her heart pounded as he came to stand before her, towering over her. "A lie?" she whispered.

"I did not bring you here to keep you safe. I brought you here thinking that I could *keep* you. Steal you away. From Aldric, from everyone…"

"From Daemon."

"I thought we could stay here for a while, and then keep going, that we could just—"

"Disappear."

The thought made her tremble even as she said it. She clung to that idea as if it were a bright star that had fallen from the sky and into their hands.

She gazed up at him, possibilities spinning through her mind. "No one would know," she whispered. "We would simply vanish into the mountains."

"We could keep riding south—"

"To Provence or Granada, or some island no one has ever heard of—"

"Some place not found on any map. A land where no one fights wars."

She closed her eyes. "And we could make our home there."

"And stay," he said softly. "Forever."

"Together."

The spoon in her hand clattered to the floor as she stepped into his arms, holding on to him tightly as he crushed her against him. Holding on to that glorious vision.

Just for a moment.

She pressed her cheek against the hard muscles of his chest, imagining a small cottage in a faraway land, hidden, secret, where he could hold her this way every night. All the rest of her life.

She closed her eyes to savor the feeling of his arms around her, wanting to emblazon it on her memory forever. "If only we could take them all with us," she whispered.

"Who?"

"Nevin and Oriel, and Vallis and Warran, and Elinor and Bayard and all the children in their castle. Everyone in Châlons. Everyone who needs us."

"I need you," he said roughly. "*I need you.* In the name of all that is holy, why do our needs matter least?"

"Because of the war. If only it had never happened, if you had not been sent away, if we were still at the palace and you were Christophe's best friend and—"

Royce made a choked sound. "By now Christophe would have run me through with the nearest available blade."

She lifted her head, gazing up at him in surprise. "But he was your best friend."

"And your brother. Can you imagine how he would have reacted to seeing his swaggering friend pursuing his little sister?"

"I suppose you are right." She closed her eyes, resting her forehead in the middle of Royce's broad chest. "But I do not think he would have looked unfavorably on your asking for my hand. We might have—"

"Nay, Ciara, it never could have been. Even if the war had never happened, even if I had never been banished, if I were still a knight and one day baron of Ferrano." He wound his fingers through her hair, drew her head back until their gazes met. "Princesses do not marry mere barons. A princess must marry a prince, or a king. Or an emperor if one is available." His mouth curved in a sad, defeated expression. "I am not of royal blood. I would never have been allowed to ask for your hand."

Her eyes filled with frustrated tears. "If only I had never been *born* a princess, if only I had been born a mere noblewoman—"

"And I your lord."

"Or a shepherdess—"

"And I your shepherd." He lowered his head to hers.

"I would be anyone, anywhere," she whispered against his lips, "if only I could be with you."

His mouth covered hers, softly, gently. Briefly.

And with her next breath, she said the words she had promised herself she would never speak aloud.

"I love you, Royce."

She felt just how much she startled him, felt the shudder go through him, saw his eyes gleaming, almost black, when he lifted his head.

And felt hot tears slip past her lashes. "I have tried to deny it, even to myself, but I cannot keep it inside anymore. It is too big, so big sometimes that it feels as if my entire heart and soul are filled with you." His face shimmered in her vision. "I…I used to be better skilled at keeping my feelings hidden. I do not know how…" Her throat seemed to be closing off. "It is all your fault."

"That you love me?" he asked roughly, his thumbs whisking the tears from her cheeks. "Or that you cannot keep from saying it?"

"Both," she accused.

He was smiling that sad, bittersweet smile. "You are

certain that you cannot try to hate me, little one? Even a bit?"

"Nay. It is too late for that."

"You once called me blackhearted," he reminded her helpfully. "And an ill-mannered knave, and impossible, and—"

"That was before I learned that you are kind and brave and giving," She looked up at him stubbornly, defiantly. "And the most caring, most noble man I have ever known."

"You have not known very many men."

"I have no wish to know any others," she whispered. "I love this one."

He cupped her cheeks in his broad, callused palms, angled his head.

And when his lips covered hers this time, the kiss was neither soft nor brief. She twined her arms around his neck, welcoming him, wanting him in a way that went beyond all she had felt before. He sealed her mouth with his and they came together in a fierce, mutual claiming, a taking of breath and body and soul.

Heat arced between them, flashing inside her, a bolt of lightning that struck deep at the core of her being. His tongue parted her lips to thrust inside and sparks of longing glittered through her, cascading into a liquid heat. She drew him deeper, moaned at each velvety stroke, needing more. Needing to be closer to him, to give and to share and to know more of him. An unbearable, hollow ache had begun low in her belly, an emptiness that demanded to be filled.

And when his hand slid down her back, pressing her closer, fully against him, she responded eagerly, arching her hips to rub her softness against that hard, male part of him. Groaning deep in her throat at the torment of being separated from him by the rough fabric of their clothes.

He tore his mouth from hers, curses hot on his lips. "I want to be inside you." He nibbled at her jaw, her throat, her earlobe. "I want to become part of you and hear you make that sound when I take you. I want to feel you tight and hot and silky around me."

His words and his kisses sent shocks of need and excitement through her. "Now," she whispered, a single word of agreement, of consent, of demand.

But he was already lifting his hands to her shoulders, as if he meant to push her away, though he could not stop kissing her, nuzzling her neck, her chin. "Ciara…"

"I love you, Royce." She kept her hands linked around his neck, refusing to let go. "I love you. I need you—"

"And I love you. More than I love my own life."

That made her go still, as if she had been drenched with ice, suddenly reminded of the price he would pay if they dared give themselves to one another. "Dear God." Her hands were trembling when she slid them down to his chest, started to push away. She shook her head, tried to clear her passion-fogged senses. "We cannot. They will kill you if we—"

"I do not care if they kill me," he said hoarsely. "You are worth dying for." His hands closed around her wrists. "Ciara, it is *you* I am worried about."

She stared up at him mutinously. "If I cannot be with you, I do not *care* what happens to me."

His hold on her tightened. "But *I* care. And by all the saints, I cannot take the risk. I will not. If Daemon were to discover on your wedding night that you are a maiden no more, there is no way of knowing what he might do to you. I have to protect you, Ciara." He loosened his grip, slowly letting her go, his voice ragged. "I love you too much to break my vow."

When he released her hands, she slid them around his waist, holding on to him for one last, long moment, unable to stop the tears that slipped down her cheeks and into the mat of hair on his chest.

He remained rigid in her embrace for only an instant before he gave in, tucking her close, allowing himself to hold her. Only to hold her.

"When will we leave here?" she whispered when the

silence had stretched to its limits.

She knew he understood what she was asking: not when they would leave for Provence or Granada or some distant, secret island, but when they would leave for their final, inevitable destination.

Mount Ravensbruk.

"In the morning," he told her, the words edged with pain and regret.

Ciara nodded, silently accepting, telling herself that if she could just stay here with him a few more hours, could just rest here in his arms where she always felt so safe and cherished and loved, it would be enough.

Enough to last a lifetime.

Chapter 15

Darkness had claimed the room, but for a few banked coals still glowing on the hearth. As Royce opened his eyes, he wondered drowsily how much was left of the night, whether morning was an hour away or two. The kitchen's stone floor still held the heat, warming the soft cloth piled beneath him. His wounded right arm felt stiff and painful.

But he did not move for fear of waking Ciara.

His fingers gently curling into the silky strands of her hair, he gazed down at the lady nestled in his arms on the makeshift pallet, her breathing soft and even against his bare chest. The two of them lay entwined together, sharing a bed for the first and last time.

He had selfishly wanted a night with her. One night to hold her, to memorize the softness and scent and feel of her in his arms.

One night to remember during all the rest of the nights he would be spending alone.

She sighed in her sleep, as if she were enjoying a sweet dream, and snuggled closer. The small movement made him agonizingly aware of how his body had responded to having her beside him. But he would endure the discomfort willingly, would endure any pain if it meant keeping her near for even a short time longer.

She settled back into blissful slumber but a moment later made another soft sound, this one a whisper of his name. Her lashes lifted. She gazed up at him sleepily, blinking, as if unsure whether her dream had ended.

They both remained still for a moment, enveloped in the quiet, peaceful darkness, warmed by the glow from the hearth. Then her soft gasp told him she had just become aware of his arousal pressed against her hip.

She did not move away, did not say a word.

Instead she startled him for the second time this day, nestling closer and brushing a kiss over his cheek.

Then his jaw.

"Ciara…"

"I love you, Royce," she said in a scant whisper, her voice husky and sweet. "Let me love you. Let me please you—"

"Nay, sweet angel, we cannot—"

She pressed a fingertip against his mouth. "Not in that way," she murmured, tracing the outline of his lips before she nuzzled her cheek against his, whispering in his ear, "but can I not please you as you pleased me…with a special kiss?"

He felt as if he had been speared by a hot lance. Felt every drop of blood in his body suddenly set ablaze, sizzling straight to that hard part of him that so ached for her attentions. He struggled to answer her, could not find words. She sounded so innocently curious about whether it was possible, so passionately ready to give him pleasure, to ease his torment.

And the thought of what she wanted to do, what she was eager to do…the thought of that exquisite, ravishing mouth of hers…

"Ciara," he whispered roughly, unable to catch his breath, "there are…certain things a man does not ask of a lady—"

"You are not asking." She nibbled at his earlobe as he had done to her earlier. "I am."

The hot spear twisted, drawing everything inside him into a tight cord that threatened to snap. "But many…ladies find the idea—"

"I have found," she said, making a low, sensual sound in the back of her throat, "that I enjoy many things that some would consider unladylike."

Before he could gather up the scattered shards of his reason, before he could recover from his shock enough to resist the temptation, she was kissing her way down his chest, her gaze on his. Her soft lips and darting tongue tore a groan from his throat. And the love and desire in her eyes proved his undoing.

When she pressed her palm against his body, lightly urging him to lie back, he yielded, surrendered to the fire of her touch and the dark shadows that enveloped them, to the need that had been building in him through all the long days and longer nights. He rolled onto his back and her loose, silky tresses lashed him with fire as she moved lower, pausing to caress him, to learn the angles and planes of his body.

She outlined the muscles of his chest with her fingertips, her mouth. And every damp brush of her lips over him, every graceful stroke of her hands scorched him like a hot brand touching dry tinder. He grasped fistfuls of the fabric beneath him to hold himself still, breathing raggedly, watching her while she explored him.

Her nails grazed his nipple, as if testing to see what sort of response she might win, and when it drew tight, she made a small sound of wonder and discovery and soft, feminine hunger. As if she could not resist, she closed her eyes and covered the hard pebble with her mouth, lingering over him, licking and suckling as he had done to her. Tugging with her lips, her teeth.

Groaning wordless, hollow sounds of pleasure, he buried one hand in her hair, his body rigid. Never had a woman enjoyed him so. Never had a woman given such passionate, loving attention to every part of him.

When she lifted her head, glancing up to meet his gaze, her eyes had darkened to molten gold. She turned her face into his palm, kissing his hand, pausing to glide her tongue between his fingertips. Innocently teaching her teacher of the sensual pleasures to be found in the most unexpected places. He reached for her when she pulled away, but she evaded his grasp to continue her loving explorations.

Slowly…so slowly…she moved lower, sliding her hands along his rib cage, exhaling a soft expression of awe at its breadth. When she touched the ridges of muscle on his flat stomach, all the air left his lungs.

For the next thing he knew, her fingers were working at the laces that bound his leggings.

He shut his eyes, clenched his jaw, felt his lower body throbbing with heat until he was so hard he feared he would burst before she so much as touched him. It took her a moment to unfasten the garment, and he allowed her to do it alone, seared by anticipation, undone by the erotic experience of having Ciara undress him.

She moved more quickly now, pulling the snug garment down his body. With his eyes still closed, he was intensely aware of the warm air against his nakedness, of the sudden silence.

A second later, the sound of breathless excitement she made almost brought him to release, without so much as a single caress.

She moved over him as if she were made of liquid silk, stretching out beside him. He opened his eyes, lifted his head, just enough to see her regarding his rampant arousal with dark eyes…and parted lips.

"Ciara…" He could not gasp enough air to say more.

She stared without shock or shame, her expression one of fascination at the naked evidence of his desire for her. And she would not be swayed from her purpose. Lifting her gaze to his, she raised one hand to caress that rigid, male part of him, her touch gentle, almost reverent.

He fell back into the soft fabric beneath him, wrenched by a hoarse groan, cut to ribbons by sharp blades of pleasure. By talons that sank into him with every light, feather-soft brush of her fingertips as her hand glided down to the base and back to the rounded crest

His entire body went taut as her fingers circled him, clasping tight and then releasing and then clasping tighter again. The sound that escaped him was one of pure, animal hunger, the frustrated roar of a lion being tormented by his lioness.

She made a softer, answering growl, a feminine, feline sound. Unmistakably possessive. And pleased. As if she enjoyed the effect she had on him. Discovering the drop of silky liquid at the tip, she paused to explore it with her fingers.

Then leaned down to taste him.

His heart thundered in his ears as he felt the first touch of her lips. His body drenched with sweat, with strain, he dug his fingers into the pallet, wrestling for control, for sanity. The sensation of her tongue gliding over the most sensitive part of him rendered him senseless. A blinding, dazzling shower of flame shot through him, tearing away the last of his control.

Then he felt her lips close around him, felt her take him deep into the hot satin of her mouth.

Her exquisite, ravishing mouth.

"Ciara."

The strangled sound of her name was warning, plea, profanity, prayer. He could endure no more.

But she would not stop. Reckless, shameless, she abandoned herself to the glorious, unspeakably carnal kiss. He felt his hips lifting toward her, knew he was lost. Lost to her, to the feminine power she wielded over him as she worshiped every inch of him with her lush, wet lips and darting tongue.

An instant later the entire world exploded in hot shards of fire as a shattering release ripped through him. His hoarse shout thundered through the chamber as he felt his seed rushing forth. Felt the very essence of his self, of his soul pouring out of him and into her.

Collapsing back into the soft pallet, spent, drenched with sweat and ebbing rivulets of pleasure, he could not find the strength to open his eyes for several minutes. When he did, it was to find her curled up alongside him, her head pillowed on his flat belly, her eyes shining with love and tenderness—her lips curved in the most satisfied, wanton smile.

"My God," he choked out, repeating it in a whisper. *"My*

God."

"You taste very silky and sweet," she whispered, looking thoroughly pleased with herself, not even blushing. She glided upward along his body, and he caught her face between his hands and kissed her thoroughly, deeply. Kissed the taste of his own desire from her lips.

And wished the morning would never come.

The weather grew warmer with each passing day as they traveled north and east. The songs of birds and the damp, earthy scents of spring filled the air, together with the splash of water that could be heard at every turn of every trail—drops trickling together into streams that joined to form powerful rivers as the snow began its annual melt. Ciara found it bitterly ironic that spring, with all its brightness and beauty, should finally come to the mountains now.

Now, just when all the light and warmth were about to vanish from her life.

Royce had brought two useful mementos with him from his home: his father's sword and shield. But in three days of riding, they encountered few people on the roads, despite the pleasant weather. These were the borderlands, he explained, where occasional skirmishes had been erupting between the people of Châlons and Thuringia, no matter that peace had formally been declared. Few travelers wanted to risk getting caught in the middle of an outbreak of hostilities.

Ciara almost wished she and Royce *would* meet with some kind of trouble, some interference, some delay that would keep them from their destination. But no one paid them any particular attention. And the rebels had apparently lost their trail.

So it was that at midafternoon on the fourth day after they left the Ferrano lands, they entered the thick forests that ringed the foot of Mount Ravensbruk.

Ciara's insides wound into a knot as they rode through

the hushed shadows, amid dancing beams of sunlight that broke through the pine boughs as if to guide their way. Royce slowed the horse to a walk, his arm tightening around her waist. But they kept going forward, both silent.

She could find no words to express this feeling inside her, this awful rending asunder, as if something deep within her were being torn away. She looked up at the sky, blinking hard, not wanting his last memory of their time together to be of her tears.

High above, she could see the towers of Daemon's palace, just visible through the trees. Could see the red-and-gold royal pennants snapping in the wind above the parapets.

By nightfall, she would be confined within those walls, dressed in royal robes…separated from Royce Saint-Michel by an impassable chasm of law and custom and responsibility.

She would once again be what she had been: a princess. Dutiful and proper. Set apart and above, distant from everyone around her.

Everyone she loved.

With naught but memories of the places and freedom and feelings she had come to cherish. Of the man who had shown her a whole new world. Who had opened her eyes, and her heart.

"How long?" she whispered, still staring up at the towers.

He did not ask what she meant, did not look at the castle. "Another hour."

She dropped her gaze, looking down at his arm holding her so tight. They had not dared tempt fate by sharing any intimacy these past three days. She had barely allowed herself to touch him at all, except to change his bandages. "Is your arm feeling any better?"

"The wound is healing well enough, now that the fever has passed."

She knew he was in more pain than he would admit. "Royce, I…" She almost could not make herself say it. "I could go on from here alone. You do not have to—"

"I am your guardian, Ciara, bound by my oath and my honor to protect you until you are wed. I have no intention of abandoning you."

"You mean to stay until the wedding?"

"Until the last possible moment."

She closed her eyes, rested her hand over his. "I do not want to part either…my love…" Her voice became dangerously unsteady. "But we both know that we must, anon. And there could be danger for you here. When last you met with Daemon and his men four years ago, you did not leave on the best terms. I am afraid for you—"

"I can deal with Daemon's men."

"An entire castle full of them? Even with your sword arm injured?"

"Ciara, I am not sending you into that place alone."

"But Royce…once we pass through those gates, I *will* be alone. I can bear it only if I know that you are safe."

His voice became as soft and warm as his breath against her cheek. "I cannot leave you yet, little one. Not yet. Not while there is still even a moment left that we are—"

"Hold!"

The shout came from the trees on their right. Royce yanked hard on the reins, turning the mare as he drew his sword.

Ciara screamed, gripping the saddle as a half-dozen men came galloping toward them. She saw at a glance that these were not rebels. They were royal guardsmen, wearing red-and-gold silk surcoats over black hunting garb.

Any relief she might have felt vanished when she saw how they were brandishing their weapons.

Royce did not try to outrun them. Several were armed with bows and arrows. "You will need no blades. We will go with you peacefully. We are—"

"You are trespassing on royal lands," one of the guardsmen snarled as the riders came to a dirt-spraying halt only paces away.

"Poachers," another surmised as he stared at their homespun garments. He raised his lance, aiming the gleaming point directly at Ciara. A third man blew on a hunting horn, the sound rising above the trees like the howl of an unholy beast.

Ciara realized they had leaped to the wrong conclusion, did not even know she was a woman—and were ready to mete out swift punishment. "Nay, you do not understand!" She reached up to push back her hood.

Royce caught her hand, stopping her. "Do we look as if we were poaching?" he demanded hotly. "We have no bow or arrows—"

"Discarded, no doubt, when you saw us coming." One of the guards grabbed the mare's reins.

Another disarmed Royce. "On the ground, thieves."

"Before I run you both through," the man with the lance threatened.

Ciara shook off Royce's restraining hand, shoved back her hood. "You are making a mistake! I am Prince Daemon's betrothed!"

The guardsmen all froze, gaping. Royce swore.

Then one of the guards laughed. "And I am King Stefan," he scoffed.

A chill snaked down Ciara's spine. Too late she realized her error—she had no way to prove her identity. They thought she was a thieving peasant, lying to save herself. "B-but it is the truth! I am Princess Ciara of Châlons and this is—"

The tip of the lance pressing against her middle cut off her words. The man holding it leered at her. "Mayhap we shall enjoy a bit of sport before we hang this one."

One of the others dismounted, leaving his weapons as he came toward her. "Off the horse, my lovely."

Ciara's heart hammered in her chest. She and Royce were going to die. Here at the foot of Daemon's castle. After all they had survived, she was going to be raped and they were both going to be killed.

Royce slipped his arm from around her waist. "Do as he says, Ciara," he ordered in a low voice.

"But Royce—"

"Do as he says," he repeated, deadly calm.

His tone gave her no choice. She awkwardly swung her right leg forward, up over the mare's neck, and slid from the saddle. Felt all six pairs of eyes on her as she dropped to the ground.

Which was apparently what Royce had been counting on—for he suddenly burst into action. Lunging forward, he seized the lance with both hands and yanked hard, pulling the man who held it from his horse.

Jerking the weapon free, Royce swung it sideways with a grunt of pain, catching the guard on the ground a solid blow across the back of the head before the man could reach Ciara.

Grabbing his shield, Royce tossed the lance to her but she dropped it, utterly taken by surprise. She snatched it from the ground as he leaped from the saddle. He placed himself between her and the other four men, taking a sword from the one who lay groaning on the forest floor.

"The lady is telling the truth," he snarled, keeping the shield raised as he backed through the trees, away from the guardsmen who were spitting curses and drawing their swords. "We are from Châlons and she is Daemon's betrothed. In the spirit of peace, I would prefer to avoid killing any of you—but if you dare touch even the toe of her boot, you will answer for it with blood."

Trying to look brave instead of terrified, Ciara raised the lance to ward off the men who had dismounted and were advancing on them.

"Try the other end, Ciara," Royce advised calmly. "The pointy end is more effective."

With a squeak of dismay, she realized she had been holding it backward. So much for looking fearsome. She turned the heavy weapon around, her heart pounding a panicked race.

The guards spread out, preparing to come at them from several directions at once. And the two Royce had knocked to the ground were getting to their feet.

Royce backed her into a tree, positioning himself in front of her. "I suggest all of you think carefully before you make any more mistakes," he snapped. "Your prince is not known to be a forgiving sort."

The guards were too angry to pay him heed.

Ciara screamed in terror as all six closed in at once and Royce stepped forward to meet them with shield and sword raised.

But before more than two or three blows could be struck, the thunder of hoofbeats and the yelping of hounds echoed through the trees. The rest of the hunting party rode into view.

"What is this, Gilroy?" an angry voice called out as a score of riders surrounded the combatants. "Why have you interrupted the hunt?"

Ciara took him to be the falconer, for he carried a huge bird of prey on his arm—and he was apparently a person of some importance, for the guardsmen lowered their weapons and turned to face him.

She rushed to Royce's side, but he warned her away with his eyes. The look stopped her, made her keep her distance as if a tree had suddenly fallen between them. She understood his message as clearly as if he had said it aloud: she dared not touch him.

They could not allow any trace of their feelings for each other to show.

"Your Highness, we caught these two peasants…"

Ciara gasped, the rest of the guard's words dissolving in a strange buzz that filled her ears as she turned to stare up at the man holding the falcon. As if in a dream, a nightmare, time itself seemed to stop.

Your Highness.

She noticed only now that the guards were all dropping to one knee and bowing to him.

Holy Mary, Mother of God.

He was dressed like the others, in black hunting garb with heavy gauntlets and a fur-lined cape. Yet this was the man responsible for the seven years of killing and destruction that had been visited upon her country. For the murder of Royce's family.

For Christophe's death.

She felt as if she had turned entirely to ice. He did not look like a warrior—slender, his face youthful, almost handsome. He could not be much older than Royce, though his brown hair was streaked with gray.

But his silvery eyes were as cold as a mountain peak in midwinter. And the way his upper lip curled in a permanent sneer made him look as if he disdained everything and everyone around him.

When he spoke, there was no mistaking his identity.

"More mewling peasants trying to fill their bellies by poaching from my forests?" He looked at Royce, then at her. "Kill them."

Ciara felt all the blood drain from her face, stricken and outraged by the way he could so easily order the deaths of two people he thought were his own subjects. She stepped forward. "Prince Daemon, I am—"

Those colorless eyes fastened on her. "Who is this wench who dares approach me with a weapon?"

Ciara realized that she still gripped the lance in her hand. "I am not a wench. Nor am I a peasant or a poacher." She threw the spear aside but stood her ground. "I am Princess Ciara of Châlons."

If she had claimed to be the pope, he could not have looked more surprised.

"She speaks the truth, Your Highness," Royce said, throwing aside the sword he had stolen from the guard. "We have come from Châlons, sent by King Aldric himself." He lifted the shield he held. "Mayhap you remember me."

Daemon tore his gaze from her just long enough to study Royce's face—and the family crest on the shield.

"Ferrano," he bit out, his eyes widening in recognition. "How in the name of Christ did you come to be here? How is it even possible that Aldric let you live? If any of my emissaries had done what you did four years ago, I would have fed him to my royal hounds."

"Fortunately for me," Royce replied coolly, "my king is a more lenient man."

Daemon made a sound of derision and turned to stare at Ciara again. "And you…nay, you could not be my betrothed. She is to arrive on the morrow. My couriers told me only this morn that the wedding procession is yet a day's ride distant."

Ciara glanced at Royce, struggled to find words. What would happen to them if she could not convince Daemon?

The guards still stood eager to tear them both to pieces.

"My father feared for my life," she explained, turning back to face the sneering prince. "I was attacked in our palace. You must have received word of that—"

"Aye. The work of the rebels," he said with distaste.

She nodded. "My father thought it too dangerous for me to travel in the wedding procession, so he had another take my place, and sent me here in secret by a southern route. Through the mountains, with"—she remembered at the last second to speak impersonally—"this man to serve as my escort and protector."

Daemon lifted an eyebrow and stared down his long nose at her, studying her face, which was grimy from the day's travel, and her masculine garb, which was in little better condition. "You will forgive me, wench, if I find it difficult to believe you are a princess." He flicked a glance at Royce. "What sort of trick is your king playing this time, Ferrano?"

"It is no trick." Royce's jaw clenched. "The only ones who have been tricked are the rebels who sought to kill Her Highness before she could fulfill the agreement King Aldric made with you."

"Ah, the agreement." As if that had given Daemon an idea, he looked over his shoulder, flicking a hand to summon one of the other hunters forward. "If you are who you claim, *milady*," he said sarcastically, returning his attention to her, "you will no doubt recognize this man."

Ciara stared up at the bearded, grizzled, portly man who came to the front of the group of riders.

It was one of the emissaries Daemon had sent to settle the terms of peace with her father, more than three months ago. "Aye, of course I remember him. He is..." She desperately searched her memory for the name. "Sir William Cameron, minister of your treasury."

Daemon squinted at her in disbelief. "Cameron," he asked slowly, "is this indeed the princess?"

The older man dismounted from his horse, puffing from the exertion, and walked over to look at her more closely. His bushy eyebrows knitting together, he examined her face as he might examine a ledger of accounts.

Then he nodded emphatically. "Aye, Your Highness," he said in his distinctive Scottish accent, " 'tis indeed King Aldric's daughter."

Ciara managed a tremulous smile. "So good to see you again, Sir William."

Daemon recovered quickly from his shock. "You will forgive me, Your Highness," he said with smooth, courtly charm, "if I was taken by surprise by your unexpected and"—he glanced at Royce—"unorthodox arrival. It would seem you have endured a terrible ordeal. But I am pleased that you have arrived safely." He gestured for one of his knights. "Dalian, escort Her Royal Highness to the palace, and order the servants to see that she is made comfortable."

The knight rode forward, extending a hand to lift her onto his horse, but Ciara backed away a step. "Wait, I..."

Suddenly afraid, she turned to look at Royce.

His gaze met and held hers, but he made no move, no gesture. Gave no outward sign of what must remain, now and forever, secret.

Ciara felt as if the sunlight and the trees whirled in a dizzying blur around her. This was the end for them.

The end of all they would ever have, all they would ever

be.

Not yet. I am not ready yet. Had she thought herself prepared for this moment? It was all happening too fast. She had counted on having the chance to say her farewell to him in private. A chance to hold him one last time.

To tell him she loved him, just once more.

"I…" She tried to swallow and failed, her throat too tight. "I would be assured that my escort will be well treated."

Daemon exhaled a low, amused sound that was not at all reassuring. "In the spirit of our peace agreement, I shall personally guarantee his safety. He can stay in the quarters that have been prepared for members of the wedding procession."

Ciara tried to thank her betrothed politely, tried to say or do something appropriate, but could not even draw a breath. Could not tear her gaze from Royce's.

Then, as if to rescue her one last time, Royce stepped toward her—and did something he had never done in the entire time they had been together.

He bowed. Dropped to one knee and bowed before her.

"It has been my honor to serve as your protector, Your Highness."

His deep voice betrayed no emotion. Only one who knew him as well as she did would detect the soft huskiness.

And when he lifted his head, only she was close enough to notice that his eyes had become so dark they were almost black.

"I wish you every happiness, Princess Ciara," he said formally.

Only she could have marked the way he drew out her name ever so slightly, as if he could not bear to let it go.

Standing there above him, fighting to keep her expression impassive and her hands from shaking, she did not trust herself to speak.

The time had come to give him her gift. She might never have another chance. Using every ounce of will she possessed, she studied the guards who had accosted them earlier, then held out her hand toward the one who still held the sword he had claimed from Royce.

"Give me his sword, sirrah," she ordered in her most regal tone.

The man glanced toward his prince, then quickly did as she commanded.

Royce remained on one knee, his eyes filling with curiosity and a hint of uneasiness.

When she had the heavy weapon in her hands, she lifted it by its gold hilt, and stepped back from him a pace.

She fought to keep her voice steady as she touched the flat of the blade to his left shoulder.

"In the name of Saint Michael"—she lifted the sword to touch his right shoulder—"and Saint George, I dub thee Sir Royce Saint-Michel, knight of Châlons and baron of Ferrano. For your most loyal and noble service to the crown of Châlons, for fulfilling your oath and your duty, I restore to you your title and all the position and privileges attaining thereto."

His calm expression dissolved in a storm of emotions, his dark gaze shining with astonishment.

And love.

Quickly, before the burning in her eyes could become tears, she withdrew the small, cotton-wrapped package she had been carrying in her tunic since they left Gavena, slipped the ring from her finger, and pressed both into his hand.

Then she straightened, turning the sword around to offer it to him in the traditional way, holding it by the blade.

"Rise, Sir Royce."

He stood, one hand closing around the hilt of his father's sword. For a moment, they both clung to it, and she tried to say with her eyes what she was forbidden to say aloud, a silent message for him alone. *I love you, Royce. I will always love you.*

You and no other.

Then she let go and instead said what she was expected

to say. What duty and responsibility demanded she say.

"Farewell, milord."

Trembling, she turned from him and allowed Daemon's knight to lift her into his saddle.

And forbade herself from looking back even once as the royal hunting party carried her swiftly toward the palace.

Chapter 16

Spurs. She had bought him a pair of exquisitely made silver spurs. They gleamed in his hand as he stared down at them numbly, seated at a table in the palace's kitchen long after most of the servants had finished their supper and retired. Daemon's hospitality had allowed him a bath and a change of clothes but had not included an invitation to eat in the great hall with his knights and his lords and his betrothed.

Royce had not objected, had not trusted himself to remain impassive if he had to watch the two of them together.

Farewell, milord.

A muscle worked in his jaw and his fingers closed around the bits of silver in his palm. This was what she had risked herself for in Gavena. She had not been buying some bauble for herself but a gift for him. *I saw something at the silversmith's shop*, she had said.

His eyes burned, his throat hot and tight. She must have been planning her surprise ever since that day. The dubbing of knights and bestowing of titles was usually left to lords and kings, but both were within her power as a member of Châlons' ruling family.

She had fulfilled her father's promise to him, given him what he had wanted, hoped for, longed for during all his long years of exile: to reclaim his title and position, to return to the country he loved. To come home.

But if this was what it felt like to be rewarded for serving the crown nobly and honorably, it was damned hard to distinguish from the gut-wrenching pain he had experienced when he was banished in disgrace. He felt every bit as hollow, empty. Guilty.

Alone.

He glanced up at the kitchen's stone ceiling, blackened from years of soot. She was up there, somewhere, many floors above him. His Ciara, with her sweet smile and gentle grace and tender heart. Delivered into the hands of Prince Daemon.

His fist tightened until the spurs' sharp edges bit into his skin. Never had he been more inclined to murder than when he had seen Daemon looking at her with anticipation in his eyes.

Was the bastard with her even now? Talking to her?

Touching her?

Royce shoved away from the table and rose, ignoring the pain that stabbed up his wounded arm. His lips curled back from his teeth in a snarl. He wanted to hit something. Break something. *Kill.* If he did not find an outlet for the violence coursing through his veins, he was going to cause yet another incident that would jeopardize yet another peace agreement.

As he strode through the kitchen door, he was quickly flanked by his two shadows—the guards Daemon had assigned to him "for his own protection" during his stay at the palace.

One guard was an older man whose jowls and downturned mouth made him resemble a bullfrog. The other was a skinny twig of a lad who always seemed to have something to eat in his hands. Both had volunteered for the duty, apparently undaunted by the tales whispered among the guardsmen of how he had taken on six armed men in the forest.

They hastened to keep up with him. "Are you ready to retire, milord?" the younger one asked hopefully, biting into the wing of roast chicken he carried.

Milord. Royce's mouth curved. It seemed odd to be called that again after four years of being addressed as a commoner. Astonishing how much had changed in a single afternoon.

"Nay," he said curtly. "Do the two of you intend to keep nipping at my heels all night?"

"We have been assigned to protect you, milord."

Royce's frown deepened at the irony in that statement. He was beginning to appreciate how Ciara must have felt at first, when she had been forced to deal with an unwanted companion day and night.

The older man yawned wearily. "It is late, milord." His deep, resonant voice matched his bullfrog appearance. "We could show you to your quarters." They passed several servants on their way to bed.

"I do not feel tired. I wish to go"—*beat someone or something to a pulp*—"riding."

"But the gates are closed and the drawbridges raised by this hour," the younger one said around a mouthful of chicken. "No one can leave the palace."

Royce ground his teeth. "Then mayhap I shall spend some time on the practice ground in the bailey." Stabbing a few straw-filled training dummies would be satisfying.

"It is cloudy tonight, milord. There will not be enough moonlight for you to see. You could injure yourself—"

"And then we would have to explain it to Prince Daemon," the younger one said tremulously.

Royce stopped in the middle of a torchlit corridor, turning to regard them with a frustrated glower. Glancing from one to the other, he briefly considered starting a fight.

Then he thought better of it. He did not wish to bring down the wrath of their merciless prince upon them. And if he abused his throbbing right arm any further, the wound might start bleeding again. But he had to do *something*.

A fat cook ambled down the corridor and he stepped aside to let her pass, trying to think of a more peaceful way to ease his black mood. "Mayhap the two of you could tell me where I might find Prince Mathias. I wish to speak with him, but I have not yet seen him."

"Prince Mathias?" the two guards said in unison.

"Aye." By all the saints, what was wrong with them

now? He could not interpret the odd look that passed between them. "Mathias. Daemon's older brother, King Stefan's middle son. Mayhap you have heard of him?"

The older man cleared his throat, his jowls dancing. "Prince Mathias has been gone these four years, milord."

"What?" Royce stared at him in disbelief. "Gone where?"

"On pilgrimage," the younger one explained. "He was deeply saddened when the first peace negotiations ended, and blamed himself for their failure. He could not abide seeing his country at war, so he left to continue his search for spiritual peace, on a pilgrimage to Rome."

Royce absorbed all this in stunned silence. It was hard to believe that Mathias would leave his country at such a crucial time—but then, he had always been a sensitive man, sickened by the brutal business of war, better suited to serve as a priest than a prince. He had been about to take vows and join a holy order before the war interrupted.

Still, how could Mathias just walk away, abandon his people to his brother's cruel tyranny?

"Milord?" the older guard asked. "If you wish to speak with Prince Daemon about it—"

"Nay." Royce shook his head. The less he saw of Daemon, the better. "I believe I will retire after all."

"Very good, milord." The younger man smiled in relief, finishing his chicken and tossing the bone aside. He took a torch from the wall and set off down the corridor to lead the way. "The rooms that have been prepared are in one of the outbuildings."

"Fine." Raking a hand through his hair, Royce followed them out, knowing he would not sleep tonight, no matter how much he wished he could lose himself in unconsciousness.

Moonlight sprinkled across the bailey outside, offering just enough light for him to glance up at the towers above…to seek some hint of where she might be. To hope he might catch a glimpse of her at one of the windows.

But all the shutters were closed tight, and guards prowled the walls.

If she were on the other side of the world, the distance between them could not be greater.

Dropping his gaze, he tried to banish the memories that filled his mind and heart. His family ring, once more hanging from a leather thong around his neck, seemed to burn his chest.

He gradually realized he had been following his escorts across the darkened bailey for some distance—all the way to the rear of the castle. The younger man had lagged behind a pace. If not for his torch, they would be in utter blackness here.

"Where exactly has the prince decided I shall spend the night?" Royce asked sardonically. "In Spain?"

"Nay, milord."

Some instinct made Royce tense, the fine hairs on the back of his neck tingling. The torch suddenly went out. He whirled, drawing his sword.

Only to step directly into the blow aimed at his head. The world exploded in pain as the torch connected.

"I am sorry it must be this way, milord."

They were the last words he heard as he fell into a bottomless darkness.

Ciara paced the luxurious bedchamber, back and forth, until she wore a path through the rushes. It was a round room that occupied the entire upper floor of the castle's southern tower, so vast that she could not see the other side, despite the fire that blazed on the hearth. She had been in here all evening, had managed to avoid supper completely, claiming she was too tired from her journey to get better acquainted with her betrothed.

In truth, she would prefer to postpone their first meeting as long as possible.

Her stomach twisting with nausea, she headed toward the window, wanting a breath of air, wishing she could take off the heavy, ruby-colored velvet gown she wore, with its quilted, pearl-encrusted bodice and embroidered sleeves. Though she had worn such garments all her life, she had never before found them so…suffocating.

Reaching the window, she pulled open the shutters and leaned out, gulping the cool night air.

The bailey seemed to be a dizzying distance below, the tower so high that the sentries patrolling the walls looked as small as a child's puppets. In the scant moonlight that penetrated the clouds, she could see that the palace grounds were deserted.

Was Royce staying in one of the outbuildings she could see from here? Or somewhere within the keep itself? Was he being treated well?

She prayed that Daemon would keep his word and ensure Royce's safety. She had promised God that if only Royce were kept safe and allowed to return home to Châlons, she would accept whatever cruelties her marriage might bring.

A knock sounded at the door. Ciara froze, paralyzed by a sudden jolt of fear.

It was almost midnight. Who would be so bold as to intrude on her privacy at this hour…except her betrothed?

She had thought Daemon would wait until the morn to see her alone for the first time. Mayhap she had guessed wrong.

Steeling herself, she closed the shutters, clinging to the bar she dropped in place. "Come in." Her voice echoed loudly across the dark, empty chamber.

She heard the door open, then close.

Heard the bolt being thrown into place.

A trickle of fear seized her. He did not bother to announce himself. She turned, slowly.

Only to find herself facing the last person she had expected to see.

"Miriam!"

Chapter 17

Pain wrenched him to awareness. Pain and an urgent voice that seemed to come from a great distance, echoing strangely.

"Milord?"

Royce fought his way toward consciousness, only to be battered down by the savage, pounding ache between his temples. Cold water splashed his face. He groaned in protest, tried to raise his hands to defend himself—but his wrists were bound together behind his back.

Anger pushed him upward through the last layers of black fog. A second splash of water made him open his eyes.

A dark cave shimmered into his vision—uneven walls of rock, dank and damp, glistening in the light of torches. Shadowy figures crowded around him. Voices.

"I apologize for the ambush, milord, but we needed to speak with you and did not think you would accept a polite invitation," an unfamiliar voice said. "And our need for secrecy is of great importance."

Royce blinked to clear his eyes. Water and blood dripped down his face, dampening his tunic. He was sitting on the clammy floor of the cave, his back against a wall of rock.

A dark-haired man crouched before him, a metal ewer dangling from his fingers. "Welcome back, Baron Ferrano." He handed the empty water pitcher to one of the others. "For a moment, I was afraid we might have lost you. Sometimes young Hadwyn does not know his own strength." He smiled, a crooked grin that revealed white teeth in a tanned, angular face shadowed by a week's growth of beard. "How do you feel?"

Royce furrowed his brow, not sure he was seeing or hearing right with this ferocious pain in his head. Glancing left and right, he could make out five figures surrounding him. Two he recognized as his Thuringian guards, but the other three were—

The warriors he had fought in Gavena.

His eyes widened as he glanced from lanky, well-dressed Karl…to the strapping, sandy-haired bowman called Landers…to the dark-haired knave crouched before him, the one who had shot him in the arm.

He had been captured by the rebels.

But why now, after Ciara had been safely delivered to Daemon?

And why had they not killed him?

Royce wet his dry lips. "If you think to torture me for information, you are a little late."

The crooked grin widened. "Nay, milord. Tying you up merely seemed the safest way to make you sit still long enough to listen to what we have to say. It has become clear to us that you are a dangerous man, regardless of the odds against you."

Royce regarded him through narrowed eyes. The man had the look of a seasoned warrior and an air of confidence and command that marked him as the leader. "Where in the name of Hell am I?" He tested his bonds and found them more than secure—tight, but not painfully so.

"A cave several hundred feet beneath the palace. There is a vast labyrinth of caverns and passageways inside this mountain. The Thuringian branch of our forces has been using this particular one as their base for more than six months now."

"The Thuringian…what?" Royce echoed.

The skinny young guardsman who had struck him over the head—Hadwyn, the man had called him—knelt beside him. "The Thuringian arm of the rebel forces," he explained, setting aside an apple he had been eating. "We have been working together since before the war ended." He folded a damp cloth and pressed it against Royce's injury. "I am sorry, milord, for the blow to your head, but it was necessary for the benefit of the sentries. In case they are asked to verify that we did our duty."

Royce winced as the lad gingerly dabbed the blood from his forehead. "And what exactly *was* your duty?" He could not believe he was seeing Thuringian guards in their royal colors standing shoulder to shoulder with Châlons rebels.

Mayhap he was dead after all, and God had a sense of humor, and this was some particularly bizarre corner of Purgatory.

"Our orders came from Prince Daemon himself," the older Thuringian guard explained in that bullfrog voice as he came to stand behind Hadwyn. "He said that you were not to live to see sunrise."

"Some of the guards were less than eager to face your blade after the incident in the forest today, so no one objected when Jarek and I volunteered." Hadwyn set the cloth aside. "We were ordered to spirit you out of the palace and leave you at the bottom of a cliff, where your body would be found a few days from now. It would look as if you had been drinking, gone for a walk—"

"And met with a tragic accident," Royce concluded grimly. "Good to know that Daemon's word of honor is worth as much as it ever was."

"Landers and Karl arrived three days ago, and told us to keep watch for your arrival," Jarek said, jowls quivering as he nodded toward his comrades. "Thayne felt you could be valuable to us—though none of us knew your true identity until today, Baron Ferrano."

"So when did I become valuable?" Royce turned an assessing stare on the dark-haired warrior crouched before him. "I assume it was *after* you shot me in Gavena?"

The man exhaled a soft sound of amusement and ran his thumb along an old scar on his bearded jaw. "Sir Royce, I believe a formal introduction is long overdue. My name is Thayne. I am a huntsman by trade, but for the last few months, I have been the leader of more than fifty of King Aldric's loyal subjects, who have unfortunately been branded rebels. For now we are outlaws, but as Karl tried to explain to you in Gavena, our intentions are peaceful."

"For a peaceful man, you are rather quick with a crossbow," Royce replied dryly.

Thayne's lips tightened. "My intent was to disarm you, milord. I merely wished to prevent you from cutting my brother's throat."

Lifting an eyebrow, Royce glanced from him to Karl, seeing the resemblance between the two. Though their coloring was different, the features were similar.

As was the crooked grin, he discovered, when Karl spoke. "Thayne never misses, Sir Royce. He could have killed you had he aimed higher. And I *did* try to convince you that we meant no harm."

"Aye," Royce said slowly, still dubious.

"And you were not the only one who lost a bit of blood in Gavena's marketplace," Landers reminded him.

Royce turned to regard the sandy-haired rebel whose broad shoulders almost matched the length of the longbow he favored. "It was my duty to keep all of you away from the princess."

"Indeed, and you are damned fast with a blade," Landers complained with a glower, rubbing his right thigh, which was still bandaged. After a moment, his mouth curved in a grudging smile. "Had I been the one charged with protecting Her Highness's life, I only hope I would have been as fierce. It seems King Aldric chose well."

Before Royce could respond, footsteps echoed from a narrow passage at the end of the cave.

"That will be the ladies," Thayne said, rising.

"Finally," Landers muttered, his tone one of relief.

Royce looked toward the cave entrance as a tall, blond woman stepped inside.

Just ahead of Ciara.

"Your Highness," a chorus of voices said with hushed reverence. Every man in the cave dropped to one knee and bowed—except for Royce, who could not move despite the shock racing through his veins.

Ciara looked quite calm as she walked right into the rebels' lair. At least until she saw him. Gasping, her gaze on his bruised and bleeding forehead, she rushed past the others to kneel at his side. "Oh, Royce, are you all right?"

He could only choke out a small sound of confusion as she gingerly probed his sore head.

The rebels got to their feet, yet still made no move to harm her. Landers slipped one burly arm around the blond woman's waist. "Did you have any trouble?"

"None, my love." She stood on tiptoe to brush a quick kiss over his lips, but her smile faded as she saw Royce's injury and bound arms. "Thayne, was that necessary?" She turned a frown on the group's leader.

"Miriam, I told you we might have to—"

"You promised me that this time no blood would be shed. Instead, it would seem you have all been brawling again."

Royce finally recovered from his astonishment enough to speak. "By nails and blood, what is—"

He never got to finish because Ciara had remained still only long enough to make sure his injury was not serious before she threw her arms around him, without regard for their audience. "Royce, I was so worried, but everything is going to be all right. Miriam explained that the rebels never *were* trying to kill me—"

"And you simply believed her and left the palace?" Royce choked out. "Ciara..." He would have unwrapped her hands from around his neck if his were not tied behind him. Would have stepped away from her if he were standing.

Since he had no choice but to submit to her embrace, he closed his eyes and leaned into her, inhaling her scent, reveling in her closeness and the caress of her hair against his cheek.

He heard the sudden, astonished silence fall among the men gathered around them, realized that everyone in the cave had just guessed that his and Ciara's feelings for each other went deeper than what a princess and her protector were supposed to feel.

But he did not care at the moment. He was too grateful to have her here with him, beyond Daemon's reach. "Thank God you are all right." He finally managed to pull back from her. "But how did you get out of the palace? You could not have simply walked out without anyone seeing you—"

"A secret passage, Baron Ferrano." The blond woman crossed to stand before him and curtsied. "I am sorry we must meet under these trying circumstances, milord. I am Miriam, lady's maid to Princess Ciara."

"The decoy," he rumbled. "The one who told these others where to look for us?"

"Of that I am guilty, milord, but I never meant for *any* harm to befall milady. Or you."

Ciara sat back on her heels, heedless of her velvet gown being dampened by the cave floor. "I believe she is telling the truth, Royce. The incident in my father's solar was not an assassination attempt at all. It was an abduction gone awry."

"I am sorry you were injured, Your Highness," Landers said. "I would rather have plunged the blade into my own heart."

Ciara turned to look at him. "You were the one who…" Her eyes widened in recognition. "It *was* you!"

He knelt before her, his head bowed, his voice strained. "I offer my deepest apologies, Princess Ciara, and swear to you it was an accident. I only drew the knife hoping to frighten you so you would stay quiet while I tied you up. I beg your forgiveness."

"And I grant it, sir. I understand now that you had your country's best interests at heart. And you took a great risk to your own life."

"Everyone here has taken a great risk for their country, Princess Ciara. Yourself included," Thayne said, his eyes filled with respect and admiration for her.

"Wait a moment. Will someone please explain all of this to me?" Royce interrupted. "*After* you untie me."

Thayne motioned to young Hadwyn, who quickly slit the

ropes with a knife. Set free, Royce flexed his fingers and allowed Ciara to help him to his feet, his head still pounding. Touching his temple, he found he was no longer bleeding. He fixed Thayne with a hard stare. "What do you mean it was a failed abduction attempt?"

"We never intended to kill her, milord."

"As I explained to Her Highness," Miriam put in, "if that had been our purpose, I could have poisoned her food at any time and spared us all a great deal of danger."

"Our intent was simply to keep her from Prince Daemon," Landers said. "To prevent the wedding."

Royce glanced from one to the other as they spoke, still finding it hard to believe that the rebels were not the traitors and assassins he had believed them to be. "But what about the avalanche? How was *that* intended to prevent the wedding—except by killing us both?"

"We had naught to do with the avalanche," Karl said.

"It must have been caused by the weather," Landers added, "by a spring thaw."

Royce looked at Ciara, who nodded, as if to remind him that he himself had told her that was a possibility. Frowning, he lifted his gaze to Thayne's. "So it was purely a coincidence that your men were there when it happened?"

"Only one was there when it started," the rebel leader corrected. "I had scouts searching for you in all the southern passes. One of them spotted you and left at once to inform his companions that you had been located at last. But by the time the four of them returned to the pass, it was obvious a catastrophe had taken place."

"And before they could reach you, you escaped," Landers said. "They claimed you sledded down the hill on your shield. I accused them of making that part up."

"Nay, it is true." Ciara glanced at Royce, her eyes bright.

One corner of his mouth curved upward as he remembered that particular adventure…and what had followed that night at the inn.

He hoped he was the only one close enough to notice

her blush. She quickly turned to Thayne. "So Sir Bayard had naught to do with what happened?" she asked. "He did not tell you where we were?"

"Nay, Your Highness." Thayne shook his head, his brow furrowed. "I have heard of Sir Bayard, but he is not involved with our efforts."

Royce almost sighed in relief and shared a quick smile with Ciara, glad that he had been wrong in suspecting his friend.

"Milord, please tell me that we have convinced you," Miriam pleaded. "We mean neither of you any harm. What reason do we have to lie to you now?"

"The lady has an excellent point, Baron," the rebel leader added. "If we wanted either you or Her Highness dead, you would be dead already."

Royce held Thayne's steady, green-eyed gaze for a long moment, realizing he could no longer deny the obvious truth. "Very well, so you are not murderers or assassins. But that still leaves one question—what do you want with us?"

"Your help."

Now it was Royce's turn to respond with a soft sound of amusement. That was hardly the answer he had expected.

But he was willing to hear more. "How is it you think we can help you?"

"Aye," Ciara said curiously, her hand lingering on his arm as she turned to regard Thayne. "Miriam said that you would explain the rest. I still do not understand what good it would have done you to abduct me. If I do not marry Daemon, the peace agreement will fail and he might wreak havoc on Châlons again. We have already learned that we cannot defy him."

"We only wished to keep you from your wedding, Your Highness. To delay your marriage—"

"Long enough to give us time to locate Prince Mathias," Karl continued. "He is the rightful heir to the throne."

Royce began to understand their plan. "You intend to persuade Mathias to return and wrest power from his brother."

"Exactly."

Royce shook his head. "A fine idea, *if* he would agree. But Mathias has no interest in ruling."

"We believe he would change his mind," Jarek explained, "if he knew what has been happening in Thuringia these past four years. Prince Daemon has brought our country to the brink of ruin in his thirst for power. He has spent so much money on war that his own subjects are starving. The people despise him and long for his brother's return."

"We would rather have a priest for a king than a devil," Hadwyn said flatly.

"But where *is* Prince Mathias?" Ciara asked. "You said you have all been working together for months. Have you not spoken with him yet?"

Miriam sighed. "Nay, Your Highness. We must find him first."

"It should be simple enough to dispatch messengers to Rome." Royce turned toward Hadwyn. "Did you not tell me he went there on pilgrimage?"

"Aye, milord. That is what Prince Daemon told everyone. And Mathias did indeed disappear quite suddenly four years ago, not long after the first peace negotiations ended—"

"But we no longer believe he went on pilgrimage," Jarek explained. "Some of us in Thuringia have been trying to find him for more than a year, but there has been no trace of him. In Rome or anywhere else."

Royce felt a chill. "Mathias was the one who initiated those first peace efforts. If Daemon decided he did not want any further trouble from his brother—"

"We do not believe Daemon killed him."

"You sound certain of that."

"*Hopeful* would mayhap be a better term," Thayne said.

"There is a chance that Mathias is dead," Jarek admitted, "but even a man like Daemon has his limits. His fears."

Ciara blinked in amazement. "What does Daemon fear?"

"Death, Your Highness. Daemon fears for his immortal soul. After all he has done, he is afraid he will be condemned to spend eternity in Hell."

"You may have noticed that in every town of Châlons he conquered, the churches were spared," Thayne noted. "He does not want to provoke the wrath of God."

"And even for a prince, it is one thing to kill enemies, or even peasants, but quite another to kill your own brother—especially a holy man. A man who was about to take priestly vows," Jarek concluded.

"We believe it is more likely that Daemon let him live," Hadwyn said, "imprisoned where he would be no more trouble."

Royce grimaced. "But where? Have you any ideas?"

"Aye," Thayne said darkly. "We have narrowed our search to the Ruadhan Mountains. One of our Thuringian guards was able to secure that much information, after weeks of secretly eavesdropping on Daemon's meetings with his most trusted ministers. The man later paid with his life when Daemon came to suspect he was disloyal."

"And if you think the prince is harsh with his enemies," Hadwyn murmured, "you would not wish to imagine how he deals with traitors in his own ranks."

Ciara shivered visibly. Royce had to resist the urge to slip a comforting arm around her.

He glanced at Hadwyn and Jarek, realizing that the two of them were placing their lives in danger every time they set foot in the palace.

"This is madness." Shaking his head, he turned to Thayne. "The Ruadhans are the most treacherous range in all of Europe. Even if you knew on *which* mountain Mathias is imprisoned, you could be killed making the ascent when you try to rescue him."

"Exactly. Which makes it the ideal place to imprison someone, permanently."

"Which is why we will need the assistance of an expert climber if we are to free him," Karl added. "You left behind a most interesting array of equipment with your destrier."

Royce glanced at him. "I do not suppose you could tell me what *became* of my destrier?" he asked hopefully.

"We left him with one of our people in the town of Vasau," Landers said.

Royce smiled in relief at the news that Anteros was safe. Then he frowned. "I will want him back."

"Aye, milord." Thayne laughed. "That will not be a problem."

"And did you find a puppy as well?" Ciara asked eagerly. "She was in a basket—"

"She is safe in Vasau as well, Your Highness." Thayne's expression was hopeful as he looked at Royce. "Though we did take the liberty of having your other things sent here to us…just in case you agreed to help."

Royce hesitated, but only for a heartbeat. He had to do it. For his country's future, for Ciara's sake—and for Mathias.

He owed the kindhearted prince a great deal.

Glancing down at Ciara, he gave her a rueful grin. "Your Highness, I hope you will forgive me, but I believe I have just become a rebel."

She did not look particularly happy about his decision, but his announcement brought a hearty round of male cheers.

Which were interrupted by Miriam speaking softly to her mistress. "You, Your Highness, also have a difficult task. We need you to ask a few careful questions and find out *where* Mathias is, if you can. The men could spend weeks searching for him in the Ruadhans, and we do not have weeks—"

"Wait a moment," Royce protested hotly, his heart skidding to a halt. "You have been trying to abduct her all this time—and now you mean to send her back to Daemon? She should remain here, where she will be safe—"

"Milord, now that she has arrived at the palace, she must

stay there," Landers told him. "This is not how we wanted it to be, especially with the wedding planned for ten days hence. That is why we tried to stop you *before* you reached Mount Ravensbruk."

"We have little time left to find Mathias," Thayne said tightly. "If Her Highness disappears now, it will raise Daemon's suspicions. We can ill afford that at this critical point."

Miriam took Ciara's hands in hers. "Your Highness, you may be the only one who can get the information we need. It will not seem amiss that you are curious about Daemon's family. It makes sense that you would ask about his brother."

"I do not like her taking such a risk," Royce bit out.

"Royce, they are right." Ciara squeezed Miriam's hands, then turned to face him. "Daemon would never suspect that *I* of all people am in league with the rebels. I am the only one who can do it."

Royce felt as if the cavern walls were closing in on him. He looked at Thayne. "I do not want to send her in there alone," he insisted, jaw clenched. "I will—"

"Nay, milord, I cannot allow that." Thayne's adamant tone held a note of regret.

"You would be well advised to stay completely out of sight, since you are supposed to be dead," Hadwyn reminded him. "Daemon believes you are at the bottom of a cliff somewhere."

Royce muttered a frustrated oath, realizing they were right. He could not return to the palace.

"But she will not be alone," Miriam said firmly, standing beside her mistress. "I will be with her."

"And we will be near at all times," Jarek assured him.

"And I am not the same helpless princess I once was," Ciara whispered, her liquid gaze on his. "I have learned that I am stronger than I thought. I can do it, Royce."

Her courage, her willingness to place herself in danger, only made him want to draw her close and keep her safe. Keep her with him.

But once again, he had to let her go.

He clenched his fists, lifting his gaze to the rebel leader's. They stared hard at one another for a long moment, and he sensed that Thayne understood what he was feeling.

Understood that Royce was not merely protecting his princess, but the woman he loved.

He asked one last question, fearing he already knew the answer. "And if we do find Mathias, and he does agree to take the throne from Daemon, what happens to her then?"

"Our plan was that the wedding would go forward as planned," Thayne said quietly, "with a different prince as the groom, to fulfill the peace agreement and assure the future of both our countries."

Royce looked down at Ciara, seeing the hope in her eyes flicker and die. She had not understood until now, must have thought that being free of Daemon meant she would be truly *free*, that the two of them could…

Only now did she realize what he had always known: she would never be truly free. What he had said to her a few days ago was still true. *Princesses do not marry mere barons.*

His throat closed off at the anguish in her eyes.

"It would appear that neither of us has a choice." Her voice was hollow.

"Indeed, Your Highness." His mouth curved in a bitter half smile. "It would appear that some things never change."

At least, he thought, she would not have to wed Daemon. If he could never have her for his own, he could at least give her that.

And with Mathias and Ciara on the throne, Thuringia and Châlons would enjoy a bright future.

She dropped her gaze from his, blinking hard, then looked up at Thayne. "I will have to return to the palace at once, before anyone notices my absence."

"Aye, Your Highness. But first let me tell you how you might go about securing the information we will need."

Chapter 18

Ciara slipped into Daemon's bedchamber and closed the door behind her.

Barely daring to breathe, she remained frozen a moment, clinging to the latch. But the room was empty, as she had hoped. And there was no time to waste on being afraid. One of Daemon's ministers had come to her chamber early this morning to explain that the prince was busy with affairs of state and would be unable to see her until after noon.

Which gave her the perfect opportunity to do a bit of secret exploring before their first meeting.

Releasing the latch, she moved into the room. The wedding procession from Châlons had arrived soon after breakfast, and she and Miriam had enacted a joyous public reunion, as if they had not seen each other in a fortnight. Everyone in the castle now knew of King Aldric's clever plan to protect his daughter's life.

And all rejoiced that the rebels had been fooled.

Leaving Miriam upstairs to supervise the unpacking of her belongings, Ciara had wandered the palace for the past hour, and no one had questioned her. The servants and retainers seemed to think it entirely natural that their future mistress would wish to view her new home.

In fact, her gold coronet and ermine-lined robes had everyone bowing and curtsying and generally keeping their eyes downcast.

Which was most helpful to a princess who had just become a spy.

The hem of her amber velvet gown rustled in the rushes as she crossed the floor into the heart of Daemon's private lair. Sunlight streaked through a pair of large cathedral windows fitted with clear glass, illuminating a room more lavish than any she had ever seen.

Opposite the windows was a huge four-posted bed hung with gold brocade curtains and covers, positioned between two massive hearths that took up half the adjoining walls. The soaring, vaulted ceiling had been hung with red-and-gold silk banners, and there were tapestries everywhere—two of them depicting Daemon himself, one in battle and one on the hunt.

A bathing tub filled one corner, and a long, ornately carved chest stretched between the two windows, topped with an array of precious goods, including gleaming silver great helms and sparkling goblets made of glass. The rest of the room also burst with riches: gold plates displayed above each hearth, finely wrought silver stands crowded with candles, chairs cushioned with tasseled pillows, carved chests of every description, many crusted with jewels. It was clear he denied himself naught.

While his people had been forced to resort to poaching to feed their starving families.

Ciara choked down her anger and focused her attention on her task. She had to help the rebels find Prince Mathias. Everything depended on that.

Including her own plan.

The one she had devised late last night while unable to sleep.

'Twas as simple as it was outrageous, an idea based on emotion rather than cool reason. Her father would not like it. Royce might not even like it.

But she rather thought that Prince Mathias would agree.

That hope made her heart flutter as she opened one of the trunks, glancing at the door before examining the contents. Inside, she found blank sheaves of parchment, quill pens, horn inkwells. Checking another, she discovered silver chalices and drinking flasks. Other trunks overflowed with coins, embroidered silk gloves, jeweled daggers.

As she closed the last one, she sighed in frustration. There was naught here other than the riches one would expect to see in a greedy prince's private chamber. She was not even sure what she had hoped to find. Daemon had not attained his current power by being careless. He would hardly leave a map lying about, with a large X showing where his brother was being held. Or a key on a tasseled cord that would unlock Mathias's prison door.

But there must be *something* she could discover. Some bit of information. Some clue that would reveal where Mathias was. If she could do anything to make Royce's journey into the Ruadhan Mountains any less dangerous, she had to try.

With another quick glance at the door, she continued her search, crossing to the long chest between the windows. Here, too, she found more luxuries: the polished great helms and matching gauntlets, glass goblets, a reliquary box, gold candlesticks…

Pausing, she returned her gaze to the silver box, remembering what the rebels had said about Daemon's fear of God's wrath. Many wealthy nobles owned a reliquary, a small casket used to hold some priceless religious artifact believed to perform miracles, like a splinter from the True Cross, or the bones of a saint, or a strand of the Virgin's hair.

Curious to see what Daemon thought might be powerful enough to save him from the flames of Hell, she lifted the lid.

Inside, on a lining of red silk, lay a small black cross on a velvet cord.

Her brow furrowed, she picked it up. The necklace was lovely, but it did not appear particularly old, or even costly. She lifted it by the cord, letting it dangle in the light that streamed through the windows. The cross was not made of onyx, as she had guessed, but of a strange black stone with sparkling facets that glittered almost like glass in the sun. She could never remember seeing the like.

"What a pleasure to find you here, Princess."

Startled, she whirled, her heart thundering. "Your Highness!"

Daemon stood at the door, flanked by a pair of servants.

When he saw the open reliquary box and the necklace hanging from her fingers, his courtly smile vanished. "I had intended to change into more formal attire before going to see you," he said coolly, his voice revealing none of the displeasure in his expression. "But here you are. How kind of you to save me the trouble." He waved away the servants who had accompanied him inside.

They left with alacrity, closing the door behind them.

Ciara felt the thud echo through the chamber, heard her heart make the same sound.

Knew she could not hope to hide what she had been doing. "I was just admiring—"

"Something that means a great deal to me." He stalked across the room and took it from her hand. "It was a gift sent by my brother, from Rome. In the future, Princess, you will refrain from touching my things."

"I am sorry. I meant no offense." *But if the rebels were correct, Mathias had never been in Rome.* "It is a most beautiful and unusual stone. What is it called?"

Turning his back on her, he replaced the necklace in the reliquary box and closed the lid. "It has some Latin name I cannot recall. They are masters at glasswork, the Italians." With a flick of his hand, he indicated the sparkling goblets arrayed atop the chest as he turned. "My brother knows how much I admire their art."

When Daemon's pale gray eyes fastened on her, Ciara felt icy fear stab through her. She suddenly wanted to run, had to steel herself against the impulse. In the forest yesterday, she had thought the prince most unlike a warrior—but now, standing face-to-face with him on level ground, she realized he towered over her.

His black garments only added to the effect. This close to him, she also noticed the gray in his hair and deep lines around his eyes and mouth. 'Twas a harsh, cruel face. The face of a man who had spent a great deal of time in worry. Despite all his riches, all his power, he evidently knew no peace.

She wondered if that was what made him so brutal.

"Now, then." He smiled, but instead of softening his features, it only added a sharpness that reminded her of the white wolves common in the mountains. "It is time we got better acquainted, is it not?"

"Of course, Your Highness."

When he took her elbow, she forced herself not to flinch from his touch. He led her away from the windows. "Tell me how you like your new home thus far." He swept an arm around the ornate room. "Does my bedchamber meet with your approval?"

"It is most—" *Revolting.* "—pleasant, Your Highness."

"I am glad you find it so." Stopping a few paces from the bed, he raised his hand to toy with the chain that held her ermine-lined robe in place. "Once we are married, you will be spending a great deal of time here. In my bed."

Ciara felt as if a lead weight had just dropped through the pit of her stomach. She did not know if she should express her shock at his comment. She dared not slap him.

His smile widened as he looked down at her, clearly aware he was making her uncomfortable—and enjoying her distress.

She felt suddenly, horribly aware of the fact that they were alone together—and she doubted his servants would come to her aid if they heard any suspicious noises from this room.

Even a scream.

But nay, surely he would not…

As if reading her thoughts, he pushed both sides of her robe from her shoulders, the casual way he handled her making his intention clear.

He wanted her to know that he owned her, the same way he owned the candlesticks and the tapestries and everything else in this room, in his country. *And in hers.*

His gaze traveled over her body and settled on her breasts. "These garments are much more becoming than the rags you wore yesterday when first we met."

As she stood there, unable to speak, a now familiar instinct broke through the fear and disgust that held her frozen.

Elbow and heel, elbow and heel—

She cut the impulse short, tried instead to change the direction of his thoughts. "Your Highness, I was wondering—"

"Have you always worn your hair so short?" He caught the end of her braid in one hand, rubbing it between his fingers.

"Nay, Your Highness" She resisted the urge to jerk away from his grasp, forced herself to remain still. "My long hair became troublesome while traveling." *That was certainly true.* "I thought it best to trim it. It will grow back anon."

"I see." He released her braid, only to trace his fingers along her shoulder. "It was brave of you, Princess, to undertake such an arduous journey…especially with no servants to attend you. Only Ferrano." His fingers reached her throat, slid back to the nape of her neck. "I am told that he left the palace last night and has not been seen since."

"Aye, the servants mentioned it to me this morn."

"Do not be concerned, Princess. I assured you of his safety, and I promise he will be found. I have men out looking for him even now."

He is alive, you lying, murdering bastard. She kept her voice cool, disinterested. "I am certain he will turn up anon."

Daemon's thumb moved to the front of her throat, his hand neatly encircling her neck. "Tell me, did you have reason to regret traveling alone with Ferrano?"

She blinked, fought the icy nervousness that rained through her. "I do not understand."

"Princess…" His voice turned silky and his fingers tightened, just enough to indent her skin.

Ciara stiffened, resisted a spark of panic.

"I beg of you," he murmured, "do not pretend ignorance. I want to know whether you lost aught more than your hair." He leaned down until his eyes were level with hers. "I would know whether that ill-mannered knave dared tamper with *my* royal goods." His upper lip curled in that disdainful sneer.

She could not catch her breath. "You may be at ease, Your Highness. I am a maiden still."

"Are you, my lovely betrothed?" He did not relax his grip and did not appear convinced. "The guards who first came upon you in the forest yesterday told me that you and Ferrano appeared quite…close before they called out to you. And I well remember the baron from four years ago—as a hot-tempered sort not given to following rules."

She glared at him. "Baron Ferrano's behavior was completely honorable."

His fingers only tightened. "If you are lying to me…"

"It is the truth! You have my word."

That made him laugh. "The word of a woman is worth less than the empty purse of a peasant." Straightening, he released his hold on her. "Before I make you my bride, I would have better proof. I will send my royal physician to examine you."

Ciara stepped back from him, eyes wide with outrage, stomach churning with nausea. "There is no need. I have told you—"

"Have you something to hide, milady?"

"Nay!"

"Then my physician will visit you this afternoon. My heirs will one day rule, Princess, and I would be assured that they are indeed *my* heirs."

Ciara bit her tongue to hold in an oath, more angry than afraid. She knew she was telling him the truth.

She also had no intention of being around long enough to marry him, much less bear his children.

"Very well," she said flatly, seeing no way to avoid his order. She did not wish to make him any more suspicious of her than he already was.

Not when she had important work to do.

"Excellent." He smiled at her again. "I am glad we understand one another. Once I am assured that I have not been made a cuckold before our vows have even been spoken, all will be well." He turned away, changing the subject as casually as if they had been discussing the weather. "Have my retainers been treating you well?"

Ciara longed to turn on her heel and stalk out. "Indeed, Your Highness. Everyone has been most kind."

"If there is aught you have need of, simply ask and it shall be provided."

How about a map showing where you have your brother imprisoned? She watched as he opened a cabinet built into one wall and took out a flask, pouring himself a drink.

Mustering her courage, she eased into the subject she needed to discuss. "Actually, Your Highness, I was curious to know when I might be introduced to the rest of your family."

"My father the king is still indisposed. He has been ill for many years, and is almost bedridden now."

"I am sorry to hear of it," she said with genuine feeling. It was well known that King Stefan, a good man much loved by his people, had been afflicted in his later years with a terrible malady that slowly robbed him of his reason, rendering him unfit to rule.

Daemon waved a dismissive hand, lifting the goblet he held to admire its jeweled surface. "The royal physicians keep him comfortable. He no longer even recognizes me."

Ciara might have felt sorry for Daemon—except that his father's condition did not seem to bother him at all.

She suddenly wondered what could have happened to this prince to make him what he was. He had started life with every advantage, including a loving family—only to turn into a cruel tyrant who would kill heedlessly, tax his people to the point of starvation, and hire the most vicious mercenaries to make war on a former ally.

But she kept those questions to herself, turning away, pretending interest in a nearby tapestry.

"And what of Prince Mathias?" she asked lightly. "Everyone speaks so highly of your brother. Will he be returning to attend the wedding?"

"My brother"—Daemon took a long swallow from his cup—"has long preferred solitude, prayer, and reflection to life at court. That is why he refused the throne in my favor when our father first became ill seven years ago."

"But surely he will return home for your wedding." She glanced over her shoulder, secretly watching for his reaction.

The smallest hint of a smile curved Daemon's lips. "Nay, I do not think so."

Her heart beat faster as she tried to interpret that look. "But he is your only brother. Would you not send a—"

"Mathias is an odd man with odd ways, Princess. I assure you he would have no interest in our wedding. None at all." He changed the subject once again, setting his goblet aside. "I grow weary of this tiresome discussion. The only family I am interested in is the one I will create with you, my sweet bride."

She turned to face him, holding her ground as he moved closer.

His gaze passed over her in that cold leer again, and his voice dropped to a low, lustful tone. "You look well able to bear me sons."

"I hope to have many children, Your Highness." The words were true, the feeling behind them genuine.

Daemon closed in until he backed her against the tapestry. He leaned over her, bracing one hand against the wall. "I am glad to hear of it, Princess. Because I intend to plant my seed deeply and often until it bears fruit. And you may not find the experience especially pleasant. More than one lady has complained of feeling split asunder when breached by my fearsome sword."

Ciara refused to tremble before him, revealed no hint of the sick feeling that twisted her stomach. He sounded as if he looked forward to hurting her.

"I will do my duty," she whispered, meaning every word.

"Aye, you will." His wolflike smile reappeared.

Just as suddenly as he had boxed her in, he straightened and turned away. "I am so pleased we have become better acquainted, Princess. But at the moment, other matters require my attention." He moved toward the door, pausing there to glance back over his shoulder. "You may remain here if you wish, but remember what I said about touching my things. You will find that I do not tolerate disobedience."

With that, he left her alone, shutting the door behind him.

Ciara closed her eyes, took a deep, shuddering breath, and very nearly sank to the floor. Then she shook her head, refusing to succumb to her fear.

Daemon would never have the chance to make good his sickening threats. She would never be his bride. The rebels' plan would succeed.

It had to.

And she had to help. Straightening, pulling her royal robes more closely around her, she went to find Miriam, to report what little she had learned in her first day as a spy.

Ciara sat up in bed, groggy with sleep. The fire on the hearth had burned to embers. Blinking drowsily, she realized the hour must be well after midnight. She pushed her tangled hair out of her face, wondering what had awakened her.

Then she heard it again. A soft knock echoed across her chamber.

Rubbing her eyes, she got out of bed. It must be Miriam. After supper, she had gone to tell the others about Ciara's meeting with Daemon, though the two of them had agreed that there was no need for the men to know *everything* Daemon had said to her. Nor did they need to know that he had sent his royal physician to examine her this afternoon and was now satisfied that she was, indeed, a maiden.

Royce and the others already wanted Daemon's blood. It

would not help to make them so angry that they became reckless.

Barefoot, wearing only a thin cotton kirtle, she was halfway to the door when she realized that the knocking sound was not coming from there at all…but from the window.

Someone outside was tapping on her window.

She froze, turned, looking at the barred shutters with her head tilted to one side, thinking she must be dreaming, yet certain she was fully awake. And quite sane.

But her room was at the very top of the tower, more than two hundred feet above the ground. And there was no wall outside, not even a sill. Naught but a sheer, deadly drop to the courtyard below.

Who—what—could be rapping on her window, other than some crazed bird?

If it was a bird, it was quite a large and impatient creature, for the knock sounded again, more insistent this time.

She rushed over and lifted the bar.

Then jumped back with a gasp when a black-garbed figure kicked the shutters open and leaped into the room.

The bar almost slipped from her numb fingers, but he dived and caught it before it could clatter to the floor.

"Take care, my love," a familiar deep voice whispered. "I would hate to survive such a climb only to be run through by Daemon's guards."

Her heart performed a somersault. Royce turned back to the window, yanked hard on a pair of ropes that dangled outside, and quickly gathered both in, along with a heavy wooden device attached to them.

She gaped at him, shaking her head in shock. He was garbed from head to toe in black, including his gloves, his boots, and the raven-colored tunic and leggings worn by Daemon's guards—minus the bright red-and-gold silk surcoat. He had even blackened his face with soot.

Her questions finally sputtered out in a stunned whisper.

"Where…how…what in the name of all the saints are you *doing* here? How did you—"

"Shhh." He pushed the shutters closed, dropped the bar back in place. "It was no more difficult than a steep mountain slope," he claimed, setting down his equipment. "And with a new moon, a cloudy night, and a bit of sooty help from a torch, I am all but invisible—"

"Invisible? You could have been killed! What could have *possessed* you to take such a risk? Dangling out there from a rope when your arm cannot have healed yet from the fight in Gavena—"

"I would have asked you to let down your hair," he said, turning to regard her with a grin, his teeth a slash of white in his blackened face, "but it is not quite long enough anymore."

Ciara blinked at him. Not only was the reckless madman unrepentant, he was thoroughly pleased with himself! "I do not find this at all funny." She placed her hands on her hips. "Daemon thinks you are dead, and if he catches you in the palace, you will be."

"Then we will have to make sure he does not catch me." He leaned back against the wall and removed his metal-studded climbing boots. "I needed to test this new device I have been working on all day." He nodded toward the ropes on the floor, which were attached to what looked like a pulley and a crossbow bolt. "It makes a difficult ascent faster, but as I told Thayne, I needed some practice."

"And did you tell Thayne *where* you intended to practice?"

"Aye." The white grin flashed again. "He relented after only an hour or so of arguing with me." Straightening, he stripped off his gloves and tossed them aside. "Now, are you going to stand there chastising me all night, or are you going to come over here and give me a kiss?"

The only thing Ciara gave him was a glower. She wanted to throttle the man! Wanted to shake him! Wanted to…to…

He held out a hand in silent entreaty and she ran

forward into his embrace, whispering his name, and settled for kissing him senseless.

His arms caught her close, molding her body to his as their mouths met in a deep, hungry joining. She forgot her anger and fear, reveled in the feel of his strength and his tenderness enveloping her. Their lips and tongues caressed, stroked, plundered until she was trembling and dizzy. Her face became almost as sooty as his and she did not care.

Finally he lifted his head, breathing hard, still holding her tight. He nuzzled her cheek, his voice thick with emotion. "God, how I missed you."

She pressed her face against his chest, listening to the thunder of his heartbeat beneath his black tunic. She had missed him as well, more than she dared tell him. "It has been only a day, but it felt like a lifetime."

He tilted her head up, tracing his fingers over her cheek. "I never did have a chance to thank you for the gift you gave me yesterday."

She smiled. "It was no more than you deserve, Baron Ferrano."

He was silent for a long moment.

"I love you, Ciara."

He said it so solemnly, his eyes and his voice so dark and intense, that the words took her by surprise. "And I love you, Royce," she whispered.

She lifted her head, her mouth seeking his again.

But he evaded her this time, releasing her gently and stepping away. "And now that you have made me a knight again," he said lightly, "I will have to keep my mind on certain knightly virtues like…chastity."

Ciara could not recall that ever being a knightly virtue and would have told him so, if her head had not been spinning from his words and his kiss, if her attention were not fastened on the way he was looking at her.

Or rather, the way he was looking at the thin cotton kirtle she wore.

Her entire body still felt sensitive from the heat and

friction of being held against him, and as he gazed at her, she felt the flood of restlessness that she now knew was called *desire*. She caught her lower lip between her teeth as the tips of her breasts rose to hard, tight pearls.

He turned suddenly away, walking over to a table in one corner, where there was a basin and ewer and a neat stack of linens. He splashed his face with cold water. "In truth, Ciara, I came here for more than climbing practice. I came to tell you that your meeting with Daemon today yielded more helpful information than you thought."

"My meeting with…" The memory and the name cleared the fog of passion from her mind. "But all I found was a room full of riches and—"

"The black cross you described to Miriam, the one he said was a 'gift' Mathias sent from Rome." Scrubbing his face with a length of linen, he cleaned away the rest of the soot. "There is a mountain in the Ruadhans that spewed up molten earth centuries ago, and when the rock cooled, it hardened into a strange, glassy black stone such as you described."

Ciara gasped. "So *that* is what it was."

"Apparently Daemon had some of it made into that cross, which he keeps in a reliquary, mayhap to serve as some kind of talisman—"

"Thinking that sparing his brother will spare him an eternity in Hell," she whispered, seeing how it would make sense to Daemon's twisted way of thinking. She shook her head in disbelief…but then felt a rush of hope. "So now we know where Mathias might be!"

"Aye." Royce set the sooty towel aside, then seemed to think better of it and carried it to the hearth, tossing it in and stoking the flames. "On a peak they call the Gunlaug."

The somber tone of his voice as he said the name made Ciara shiver with apprehension. "What does that mean?"

"It is an ancient word from the language of the tribes that once lived in those mountains. It roughly means"—he hesitated—" 'the Maker of Widows.' "

Ciara felt her blood run cold. "And *that* is the mountain you are going to climb?"

"If I hope to rescue Mathias," he said quietly, gazing down into the flames, "aye, that is the mountain I am going to climb."

She shook her head in denial. "When?"

"We leave at dawn."

Terror gripped her, icy and overwhelming. She suddenly understood why he had taken the risk of coming here tonight: he had wanted to give her one last kiss, hold her one last time, tell her he loved her before he… *"Royce—"*

"I am to meet the others at first light." He turned to face her. "That is why Thayne finally relented and allowed me to see you. It seems he lost someone who mattered a great deal to him in the war…and he never had the chance to say farewell to her."

Her vision blurred with tears as he drew close. She could not lose him! Not again, not now. Sweet Mary, only hours ago, she had felt such hope. "But you cannot—"

"Ciara, I have no choice." He took her hand and led her to the basin in the corner, dampening a fresh cloth. Tilting her head up with his fingertips, he began to tenderly clean the dark smudges from her face.

She stood gazing up at him in mute anguish as cool drops of water and hot tears ran down her cheeks, down her neck, dampening her kirtle. Why did he have to be so honorable and loyal and brave? The very qualities she loved about him were taking him from her.

"The wedding is in nine days," he whispered as he worked, "and until then you must pretend as if naught has happened. I have every intention of returning before you walk down the aisle, little one. We would not be going if we did not believe we had a chance to succeed. A good chance. Every one of us was born and raised in these mountains, and my new device over there"—he nodded toward the window—"worked even better than I had hoped. We will be back, with Prince Mathias—"

"So that I may marry him instead of Daemon," she finished dully.

He paused, the wet cloth poised above her chin.

Then he continued washing away the marks that his kiss had left on her. "Aye." He turned away before she could interpret the clash of emotions in his eyes.

"Will Mathias make a good king?" she asked quietly.

"He is a gentle and kind man, but I think he is strong enough to rule." He rinsed out the rag. "And his subjects love him greatly, as they did his father."

"And will he be good to both his own people and those of Châlons? Will he deal fairly with all?"

"Aye."

"Then I will not marry him."

His head came around with a jerk and his eyes fastened on hers. "What?"

"I wish to marry you," she informed him softly.

"Ciara…"

"My duty is to assure that my people have a safe, peaceful future, and with Mathias on the throne, that is what they will have. You just said so yourself."

"But there is still the matter of the peace agreement between Châlons and Thuringia—which includes a betrothal." He set the cloth aside and moved away from her, toward the hearth.

"Aye, but everyone has said that Mathias prefers the life of a monk or a priest," she pointed out, following him. "Is it not rather presumptuous of us to be arranging his marriage? You do not even know if he would *want* me for his wife."

Royce spun to face her, about to utter some quick retort, but as he looked down at her, only a strangled groan escaped him.

Ciara followed the direction of his gaze, realizing that the water he had used to clean away all evidence of his kiss had created a different, and far more sensual, display: the damp front of her kirtle clung to the curves of her breasts, the cloth almost transparent in the low firelight.

"There is not a man alive who would not want you," Royce grated out, his voice hot and thick, his broad shoulders rising and falling rapidly as he struggled for breath. "And regardless of whether Mathias wants you or not, *I* am not of royal blood, and that fact will never change. Your father would never allow you—"

She stepped closer, lifted a finger to his lips. "But there is still Provence, or Granada, or an island somewhere. Some place that appears on no map, where no one will care who or what we are." Her lips curved gently as she revealed the plan she had been holding in her heart all day. "And I am still perfectly willing to live as a shepherdess."

His eyes met hers, those potent depths gleaming.

She let her fingers slide downward along his hard jaw, to his throat, to his chest, let her hand rest over his pounding heart. She could almost feel the battle being waged within him.

Knew they were both very close to surrender.

His hands came up to cup her cheeks, and he threaded his fingers through her hair. "What have I done?" he asked, his voice raw. "You used to be such a sane, sensible lady."

"You took me on a journey," she whispered, "into my own heart."

He closed his eyes, murmured an oath, bent to press his forehead to hers.

"On the day we met," she whispered, "you told me that the world does not exist to satisfy my wishes. And you were right. But sometimes, Royce…sometimes I believe that wishes really can come true." She slid her fingers into the thick silk of his hair. "I love you, and I want you. *You and no other.*"

With a groan, he captured her mouth in a searing, possessive kiss, pulling her hard against him. Branding her with his touch as his and his alone.

Her heart soared with love and joy, swept up on wings of new hope. His fierce embrace made her shiver with need, and when he finally allowed her a breath, her lips felt swollen and tingling as she asked the question. "How much time is there until first light?"

He whispered something profane, the rampant evidence of his arousal pressing against her belly, his teeth closing on her earlobe. "Ciara, we cannot—"

"But it is not yet dawn. You do not have to go. Not yet."

His voice had become so deep she hardly recognized it. "But if I do not return, on your wedding night Daemon would—"

"There will never *be* a wedding night," she insisted, "until the one I share with you."

And if all their dreams and plans ended on a mountain in the Ruadhans, if he never returned and she were forced to marry Daemon, if she were condemned to a lifetime without the man she loved…

She wanted one memory. One night to cherish forever.

His name was a hot, tremulous plea on her lips. "Royce."

She awaited his answer, saw it in his eyes before he said the words, low and urgent.

"Bolt the door."

Chapter 19

He released her just long enough to let her cross to the door, watched her kirtle flowing around her like a veil of mist, her slender curves washed in firelight and shadows. The only sounds in the night were the crackle of the flames behind him and the unsteady rhythm of his own breathing.

His entire body felt heavy with desire. For so long he had wanted her, his princess of fire and grace. Wanted her in every way a man could want a woman—to cherish and claim, to possess and protect. She had become a fire in his blood, a gentle rain in his soul.

And now he would finally make her his, tonight and forever. In that ancient way that bound a man and a woman more deeply than any vow.

As she came back toward him, she paused near the bed, looking puzzled when he remained by the hearth.

"Come here to me, Ciara," he said in soft, husky command, holding out a hand toward her.

She did as he asked, her eyes wide, curious. He did not explain his reasons, did not want to tell her that they dared not risk leaving the mark of her lost virginity on the sheets and the mattress.

Catching her hand, he pulled her close, lifting his other hand to her hair. He would take her here, before the fire, as he had always imagined her in his midnight dreams.

She looked up at him with complete trust, complete love…and the smallest hint of uncertainty, as if she realized only now, standing before him, that his body was large and muscled and heavy, while hers was soft and light and delicate.

The hint of maidenly shyness only endeared her to him more. There was time, he knew, lowering his head to brush a reassuring kiss over her lips. Two hours, mayhap more. Time enough to make it perfect for her.

Taking both her hands in his, he drew her with him as he backed toward the huge, thick pelt of ebony wolf fur that covered the floor before the fire. Then he gazed down at her for an instant, letting her anticipation build, letting the moment become a memory.

And when he glanced down, he once more saw her nipples draw tight through the damp, sheer fabric of her gown, merely because he was looking at her.

And this time he was the one who trembled. With awe at what she felt for him. With the need to touch and to taste. To feel her sweet passion igniting in his hands. To watch her innocent longings blossom into a woman's desire while he was inside her.

His hand moving down her back, he bent his head and tasted one sweet pearl through the sheer cotton, sliding his lips across it, then his tongue.

She uttered a soft cry, burying her fingers in his hair. He teased and nibbled, pulling her closer, bending her backward over his arm. Her hands clutched at his shoulders, her nails digging into his muscles through the rough material of his tunic. Her low moan was feminine music that ignited his blood and sent hot, sharp bursts of desire through his veins.

Impatient at being separated from her by the cloth, he slid the garment down over her shoulder, exposing her other breast before he captured its naked, rosy crown. With a sound of ravenous longing, he sipped at it, curling his tongue around her nipple, tugging and suckling until her breathing came shallow and fast and she was writhing in his embrace.

His free hand skimmed down her body from her wet bodice to the soft triangle between her thighs, seeking and finding a different sort of dampness. Sweeter. Hotter.

She was ready for him. Dear God, she was so ready, so wet. Groaning hungrily at her response, he sank to his knees before her, pulling her close, nuzzling her through the thin fabric. The spicy scent of her desire clouded his senses and he remained there a moment, closing his eyes, breathing hard. Shaken by how much he loved her, needed her—all of her, every soft inch of her.

She moved as if she would slide down beside him, but his hands held her still, kept her on her feet. And then he reached down to draw the hem of her gown upward, his fingers lifting the fabric, his palms gliding up past her knees, her thighs, exposing her one glorious inch at a time.

Until he could see those soft, dark curls glistening in the firelight.

He bent his head and blew softly, felt her quake in his grasp, heard the low, sharp cry of surprise and excitement that came from her throat. Ignoring the throbbing hardness of his own body, he inched forward and pleasured her with the lightest kiss. Then he drew her nearer, his hands sliding behind her to knead and caress as he brought her fully against his mouth.

He explored her softly with his lips, the tip of his tongue, until she was gasping, shivering with tremors, her hands braced on his shoulders. He sought and found the tender bud of her desire, licked at the small, hard pearl, urging it to fullness. Her breath broke, her hips beginning to move in small, insistent motions that brought a groan of approval from deep in his throat. He slipped one of his hands around to the front, stroking her with his fingers, gently, delicately.

She twisted in his hold, her nails digging into his shoulders hard enough to leave marks. Her body shook with spasms that came faster and stronger as he continued the dual torment, sampling her with his fingertips and his tongue. Suckling…tickling…nibbling.

"Royce." His name tore from her, deep and demanding.

But he would not stop, kept urging her onward, higher, wanted more, wanted to watch and to taste her fulfillment. He kept teasing that sensitive nub with his thumb, with his lips. And suddenly her whole body stiffened.

He felt the first vibration against his mouth, felt her

arching above him, curving away from him like a taut bow—and she shattered, caught in an explosion of pleasure that he could feel rippling through her as release took her violently.

Before it had even passed, she collapsed against him, sinking to the floor as if her legs would no longer hold her, sliding down into his arms.

He held her close as they knelt on the fur, caressing her, whispering in her ear. Assuring her that that had been but the first.

That the next would be even sweeter, with him inside her.

She uttered a husky sound that was half growl, half whimper and lifted her head, her eyes molten with desire, her body damp with perspiration that made the gown stick to her skin. His every muscle shuddering, taut with his own need, he removed the garment with quick, gentle hands, pulling it over her head, casting it aside.

Sighing, she wrapped herself around him, her mouth meeting his, the feel of her in his arms so slender and soft, her curves so pale against his black tunic.

Reaching for the discarded kirtle, he spread it on the fur behind her and gently lowered her onto it. Then he let go of her just long enough to tear off his own garments, kneeling beside her, reveling in the way her gaze traced over him—from his face, to his chest, to the rampant evidence of how much he wanted her.

He had never felt more aware of his own sensual, masculine power than he was in that moment. Her expression as she looked at him with such passion and possessiveness made him feel…

Like a king. Like a god.

Kicking free of his tunic and leggings, he moved over her, pressing her back into the furs, set ablaze by the long-awaited friction of his naked skin against hers. Her moan of welcome was a softer echo of the sound that poured from him. Her breasts felt so exquisitely soft against his chest, her nipples hard and tantalizing against the mat of black hair. As his body covered hers, she slid her arms around his back to hold him dose.

He feasted on her, kissing her lips, her cheek, her lashes, her shoulder. She tasted luscious and feminine, felt softer and silkier than the fur beneath them. He lingered over the hollow of her throat, pressing his mouth there to feel the throb of her pulse against his lips.

He wanted to go slowly this first time, to treat her with such care and tenderness, to sweep her to the brink of ecstasy before he entered her. But she moved restlessly beneath him, instinctively lifting her hips—and he almost lost his grip on his control. The contact of her naked, downy triangle against his rigid arousal wrenched a strangled exclamation from him.

"Royce, now," she pleaded, raining urgent, hot kisses along his throat, his jaw. "Please, my love, *now.*"

Her eagerness, her passionate demand unraveled the tether that held him in check. His lady was impatient to give him more, to give him everything, to share what they had waited so long to share.

His lady, his love, his Ciara. *His.*

Balancing his weight on one forearm, he reached down to stroke that silky center of her being, probing gently. With a throaty murmur of acceptance, of pleasure, she parted her thighs as he moved into position.

He tried to resist the rising storm within him. God's breath, she was so small, *so tight.* The urge to possess, to mate descended like a white-hot haze.

Struggling for sanity, he fitted himself to her.

Ciara's head tipped back and she inhaled a long, slow breath as she felt that rounded, hard part of him nudging open the entrance to her body.

She caught her lower lip between her teeth to keep from crying out—not because she felt any discomfort but because the sensation was more wildly exciting than anything she had ever known.

He pushed forward, so gently, so carefully, despite the fact that his own desire had reached the same feverish height as hers. She could feel his strong, muscled body shaking with barely leashed power, could hear his breathing lashing the darkness around them like a storm.

Her hands gripped his trembling, sweat-sheened arms, her fingers digging into his shoulders at the exquisite sensation of him becoming part of her. She felt stretched and filled and by all the heavens, he was so big, surely too big for the small, snug sheath that clasped him. He felt huge and hot and throbbing within her.

But he brought her no pain, even when he came to the delicate barrier that was her heart's gift to him. He made even that a gentle claiming. There was only a feeling of pressure, and then he arched his hips and she felt a single quick, sharp twinge, a giving way…

And then he was there, fully inside her, hard and silky, embedded within her most feminine depths. Filling her as she had never imagined possible.

"Open your eyes, Ciara."

She obeyed his tense, whispered command, not even realizing that she had shut her eyes as her mind spun out into bliss. She still held her lower lip between her teeth.

He was gazing down at her, his face etched with strain and concern, his body trembling, rigid, utterly still, his chest heaving with the effort.

She relaxed her grip on his shoulders and smiled up at him, beyond words, sighing in pleasure to reassure him he had not hurt her. Never had she known a sensation like this, this feeling of fullness, of sweet, intense completion that was so deeply satisfying.

Threading her fingers through his hair, she pulled his head down to hers. Groaning, he kissed her, his tongue parting her lips even as that male part of him parted her below.

And then he began to move, withdrawing and then thrusting forward. Silky, sliding, probing the depths of her body.

She trembled at this new sensation, moaning into his mouth, caressing his tongue with hers. Sharing his breath, his body, his soul. Wanting to feel this complete, this cherished all the rest of her life.

And then without conscious thought, she began to move beneath him, instinctively seeking and matching his rhythm in a passionate dance. Her hips rose to meet his long strokes, drawing a muffled growl from deep in his throat. Enjoying his response, she did it again, moving her hips in a slow, deliberate circle this time.

He lifted his mouth from hers, shutting his eyes, clenching his teeth. "Ciara, be care—"

"Mmmm…" Lost in the feeling, she repeated the interesting, provocative motion once more.

And felt his entire body convulse as if whipped by a lash. He choked out a curse, pressing his forehead against her shoulder as he exploded within her, throbbing, pumping deep inside her for a long, endless moment, his seed and a muted roar of release pouring from him.

Seized by spasms that she could feel rippling through his muscles, he collapsed atop her, pressing her back into the furs. She wrapped her arms around him with a smile, welcoming his weight, holding him tight, stroking his back, his hair. It was over rather sooner than she had expected, but that did not lessen her soul-deep joy and satisfaction.

After his breathing returned to normal a long moment later, a different sound rumbled in his throat. He lifted his head, looking down at her from beneath his tousled black hair, those dark eyes glazed with passion and an unexpected spark of amusement.

"There is simply no stopping you, is there, my little one?"

She blinked up at him. "Did I do some—"

"Nay," he assured her quickly, dropping kisses on her

nose, her lips, her chin. "Nay, you did naught wrong. God's breath, you are the most…I have never…" He gave up trying to express what he felt in words. "It is only that I had planned to take longer," he whispered in her ear, "and take you with me."

"Oh." With a relieved smile, she nuzzled her cheek against his, secretly pleased in a thoroughly female way that she had made him lose control. "My apologies, milord," she teased.

Chuckling, he kissed her, long and slowly, before he eased himself from her body, despite her moan of protest. The instant he was gone from her, she felt a loss, an emptiness. As if she had lost part of herself.

But he only moved to her side to take the soft kirtle from beneath her, and she saw the spots of scarlet, the stain of her lost maidenhood. He tenderly pressed the wisp of cotton against her, removing any mark from her, from him. When he moved away from her again, it was to place the garment in the fire.

She felt many emotions, none of them regret. The strongest was her love for him, her joy at what they had shared. And a sense of contentment and pride and pleasure that she was no longer a maiden, but a woman—his woman.

"Now, milady," he whispered huskily, returning to her side, kneeling on the fur. "This time I mean to make good on my promise."

Her heart pounded with excitement as she saw that he was already aroused again, as she realized that their night of loving had just begun. She smiled at him in surprise and wonder and anticipation. Reaching up, she thought to draw him down to her, her breath quickening at the thought of his muscled body covering and claiming hers once more.

But when he caught her hands, he instead pulled her up until she was kneeling before him. Sitting back on his heels, he gazed at her with sparkling eyes and a wicked smile, tugging her forward. She did not understand at first.

But then he showed her what he wanted, using his hands

and a few instructive whispers. With a little sound of curiosity and arousal, she moved until she was astride him, her knees parted wide, the silken core of her body hovering just above his hard length. She trembled, feeling very vulnerable and open.

Until he arched his hips and pressed her downward, and the blunt tip gently invaded her. The sound of her groan matched his as she lowered herself over him, astonished at how deeply she could take him in this position. How utterly he filled her.

His hands slid up and down her back, clasping her to him as he began to move, and they renewed their dance of ecstasy. It took only an instant for her to discover that she was perfectly positioned in another way—for him to lavish kisses on her lips, her neck, her breasts. He suckled and teased as she arched her body, as she sheathed that steely part of him within her softness.

The tension whirled tight within her, faster and stronger this time, a wildness she could feel building even more powerfully than before. Caught in its grasp, she surrendered, clinging to his shoulders and meeting every stroke as he thrust deeper, harder.

He drew her mouth down to his for a kiss, and when she lifted her head to gasp for breath, opening her eyes, she could *see* as well as feel what it meant to have him inside her. Staring down, she saw their bodies joined as one, bathed by the golden light of the fire.

She watched in fevered fascination as he withdrew from her, letting her see that hard male part of him glistening with her body's dew. He pulled out all the way, then rubbed against her, sleek and wet over the swollen bud of her own desire, pleasuring her while she watched.

Uttering soft, sharp cries, she shifted against him, recapturing him, feeling the storm so close to breaking. He slid inside her, deeply but slowly, so very slowly. She felt him shuddering as much as she was, every rock-hard muscle of his body beginning to tremble.

Moving urgently, rising and falling as one, they strained upward into the hot, bright, dazzling lightning. Faster now, they raced higher, soaring, reaching for it, wildly. Together.

And then in the span of a single heartbeat they found it, plunged to the heights of a scorching shower of ecstasy that burst inside them both at once, ripping through them in a rain and thunder of power and pleasure. He held her fiercely as she felt him inside her, around her, shattering at the same time she did, his seed pumping deeply into the core of her being.

Spent, moaning, collapsing together, they fell back onto the fur, Ciara tumbling atop him, and their lips met in long, slow, hungry kisses.

He caught handfuls of her hair, loving her mouth as he had just loved her body. Passionately, deeply. Tenderly. And this time he did not leave her, remained joined to her.

And a few minutes later, when she felt his body stir within her, when he rolled her onto her back and pressed her down into the fur once more, she welcomed him with whispers of love.

It was more than an hour later that she stood near the closed window, wrapped only in a sheet, watching him dress.

Watching as he donned the black leggings and tunic, the gloves, the boots. He had already blackened his face with soot from the hearth.

She blinked away the moisture in her eyes. Refused to think of the dangers he was facing. *Nine days*, she told herself stubbornly. She would see him again in nine days. Until then…

Dear God and all the heavens, she was not sure she could survive so long without him. Did not know how she was going to conceal her feelings for him during his absence.

How could anyone look at her and not know that she had spent this magical night being thoroughly ravished in the arms of the man she loved? Saints' breath, her body still burned from his touch. She felt certain she must glow like the sun.

She would spend as much of the time as possible in her chamber, she decided, fearing that someone would notice her passion-bruised lips, a certain lambent look in her eyes. Now that her mission as a rebel spy was ended, there was no need for her to spend her time elsewhere. She would stay here.

And pray for him.

Picking up his ropes and equipment, he turned toward her, and she felt tears pooling in her eyes. Once again, she had to say farewell to this man she loved like no other.

But she could not say it this time.

"Come back to me," she said lightly, smiling up at him. "And do try to be a bit cleaner next time, my sooty baron."

His grin shone white. "I shall do my best, milady." He reached out and cupped her cheek with one hand, the leather of his gauntlet soft against her skin. "I will return in time for the wedding," he whispered. "*Our* wedding."

"Do not be late."

"I promise" He brushed his thumb across her lower lip. "Farew—"

She stopped the word with her fingertips, not allowing him to say it. "Until I see you again," she corrected, her gaze burning into his. "Until I see you again."

Chapter 20

Ciara stood at the entrance to the cathedral, desperately wishing that someone would awaken her from this nightmare.

Dressed in her gold silk wedding gown, the long train trailing behind her, she stared down the aisle toward the priest.

And her groom.

Prince Daemon stared back at her, his gaze colder than usual, his sneering upper lip drawn into a tight smile—which was purely for the benefit of the scores of nobles assembled in the pews.

She had delayed as long as she dared. He was already furious with her for keeping everyone waiting all morn. Numb with fear and denial, she stepped forward, into the vast sanctuary made of gray stone and brilliantly colored glass, into the smell of incense and the chanting of the choir Daemon had brought in from Avignon.

And she prayed that she would awaken. Now. Before this nightmare could go any further. *Awaken...awaken...awaken...*

But she was not asleep. It was all horribly, inescapably real. As real as the heavy royal robes she wore, the jeweled crown on her head, the lords and ladies garbed in velvet and silk who had been awaiting her arrival for two hours.

As real as the nine days that had passed, and the tears she had cried last night and this morn.

Not blinking, not even breathing, she walked down the smooth, stone-paved aisle toward the altar. Toward her inescapable fate.

With each step, the horrifying images filled her mind, the ones that had torn at her heart for days: of a black mountain too difficult to climb, of ropes shredded by glassy stone, of Royce pushing himself too hard and losing his footing, falling to the bottom of a cliff…

She did not know what had happened to him. All she knew was that something had gone terribly wrong. Miriam had received no word from the men.

It was as if the rebels had gone into the Ruadhans and vanished. Swallowed up by the greedy maw of the Gunlaug. *The Maker of Widows.*

She blinked hard and the red-and-gold banners that swathed the cathedral danced in her vision. Even as she moved closer to the altar, conscious of all eyes upon her, she kept hoping. Waiting. Thinking that Royce would burst in through the church doors. Rescue her as he had so many times before. Carry her away from this place. This moment. This man.

But he did not come.

She was alone.

Not even Miriam had been allowed to attend the ceremony. There was no place at his wedding for servants, Daemon had scoffed.

She was within a few paces of the altar when she noticed Hadwyn and Jarek, standing at the front of the twin lines of guardsmen that streamed down either side of the church. The guards were all dressed in silks, each holding a halberd, a tall pole weapon with a curving, axlike blade at one end—their presence clearly intended to impress everyone with Daemon's power.

Jarek's eyes met hers, but she subtly shook her head. If they made any move against the prince, it would cost them their lives. Too much blood had already been spilled. She could not let them try to interfere.

She had but one choice now: to do her duty, fulfill the betrothal agreement, protect her people.

When she reached the altar at last, Daemon grabbed her hand. Though his wolfish smile was wide, even triumphant, his grip was bruising, as if to let her know he was displeased that she had kept him waiting.

No doubt he would show her just how displeased in less subtle ways, later when they were alone.

A numbing buzz filled her head as the choir ended its chanting and the priest began speaking in Latin. She was only remotely aware of the words. Could think of naught but a single phrase that kept repeating over and over in her mind until it became a certainty.

Royce is dead.

It hit her like a blow to the center of her body, but somehow she remained standing. Somehow her heart kept beating. But her strength, her breath, her soul all seemed to flow out of her, taking with them the last of her courage. And her hope.

The priest reached the place in the ceremony when she must make her vows, asking in somber tones whether she would take this man as her husband.

She looked up at Daemon, one last spark of spirit igniting within her. *Nay, not this man. Not him. Not Daemon. Nay, she could not.*

"I will."

Everything became a blur after that—the endless mass, the glaring sunlight outside when they left the cathedral, the blast of trumpets, the cheers of the crowd Daemon had ordered assembled along their route back to the palace, the din that arose in the great hall when they arrived for the wedding feast…

She remained only distantly aware of her surroundings until she found herself enthroned on a massive carved chair, sitting beside her new husband on the dais. Feeling as if she were suffocating, she stared down at the laden trencher before her, not eating a bite.

Once, just once, she allowed a last, lingering shred of hope to make her glance up at the massive, iron-hinged doors on the opposite side of the hall.

No one came charging through them. There was no sign of Royce. There would be no rescue.

He was dead.

Bleak despair settled over her. She sought a glimpse of Miriam, seated at one of the dozens of crowded trestle tables arranged in rows below the dais. The older woman shook her head, as if to say she had no answers, her expression distraught. Ciara knew that Miriam was just as afraid for Landers as she herself was for Royce.

Over the past few days, she had poured out her heart to her lady's maid, her friend. Had told her all she felt for the dark-haired swordsman she was forbidden to love, all that had happened since the two of them set out from the abbey on that cold day…

Sweet Mary, had it been only weeks ago? It was hard to imagine, to remember how much she had disliked him that day, how annoyed she had been when he—

The weight of a hand on her thigh made her jump, brought her head snapping around until her gaze met Daemon's.

"You have not touched your food, my lovely bride," he said in a cold, mocking tone, observing her over the edge of a gem-encrusted goblet. "Did the meal not please you? Or is it the company?"

His fingers tightened on her thigh, his grasp possessive and painful through the gold silk of her wedding gown. The cloth-draped table prevented the lords and ladies below the dais from seeing what he was doing.

"I…" She fought the bubble of panic that rose in her throat, noticing that he glanced toward the spiral stairs in the far corner, beyond the hearth.

The ones that led up to his bedchamber.

"I…I am feeling unwell, Your Highness," she choked out, trying to delay the inevitable, even for one more night. "Mayhap I should—"

"Be put to bed," he finished for her, eyes gleaming as his gaze slid back to hers. "So it is maidenly nervousness that has you ill at ease." He set his cup down. "I can remedy that, my sweet princess."

Her heart thudded a single stroke of pure terror. And not only because she was no longer a maiden. This morn, Miriam had instructed her on how she might deceive Daemon, on a way to leave traces of blood on the sheets. But even armed with that knowledge, Ciara knew that no ruse could protect her from her new husband's cruelty.

Even if she *were* a maiden, he meant to use her brutally.

"If you are not hungry," he continued, pushing his heavy chair back from the table, "let us retire to my chamber. I would be happy to dispense with the usual rituals. We will not need laughing courtiers throwing grain in our faces to ensure a fruitful union."

He stood, his hand encircling her arm, his fingers like talons, giving Ciara no chance to protest. She looked for Hadwyn and Jarek, found them standing with the other guards stationed along the walls—saw them watching her with frustration in their eyes, as if waiting for her signal.

But she dared not ask for help, could not endanger them to save herself.

Her stomach clenching, she barely had time for one quick, frightened glance at Miriam before her new husband led her from the hall.

Most of the guests were already too deeply in their cups to mind that the bride and groom were making an early departure. Only a few lords and ladies called out bawdy advice as Daemon strode to the rear of the enormous chamber, pulling her along beside him.

He headed straight for the spiral stairs, past the four sentries at the bottom who were part of his personal guard. The men bowed as they passed, dipping their halberds—but she saw them regarding her with knowing leers as their prince led her up the steps.

At the top, Daemon issued a single, sharp command to the two others posted there. "Do not allow anyone to disturb us until morning." He pushed open the door to his chamber and shoved her inside.

Then he slammed the heavy oak portal shut behind him

and threw the bolt in place.

Heart hammering, Ciara backed away from him, rubbing her arm, bruised from his ruthless grasp. The chamber glowed with light, despite the darkness that had descended outside the windows. The twin hearths blazed, making all his riches and jewels and glassware gleam.

Her gaze fell on the reliquary and she felt tears threaten. *God, please.*

"Disrobe, Princess."

She turned to face him, still moving away, no longer able to disguise her fear.

Which only made him smile. "I like to see my belongings displayed before I handle them," he said icily, taking off his crown and placing it on a velvet pillow beside the bed. "Disrobe."

She shook her head, mute, retreating until her waist collided with the long chest in front of the windows.

"There is nowhere to run, Princess." Smiling, he stalked closer. "And I warned you once, I do not tolerate disobedience. You should have remembered that before you kept me waiting this morn. You embarrassed me in front of my lords—and for that you will pay."

A panicked impulse made Ciara snatch up one of the goblets from the chest and smash its glass rim against the wood.

With a snarl, Daemon leaped toward her, grabbing her wrist, twisting hard until the makeshift weapon fell from her numb fingers.

It tumbled harmlessly into the rushes.

Then he yanked her against him, sending her crown clattering to the floor as well.

"It seems you have a difficult time understanding what I mean by the word *obey*." He glared down at her, his lips curling back from his teeth. "Allow me to give you a demonstration."

♦♦♦

"Your Highness, you cannot walk in without warning."

"Aye, I certainly can."

The group of ten riders reined in on a hill above the palace. They had approached from the rear, to avoid being noticed by the sentries as they came within sight of the keep.

Royce looked toward the slender, brown-haired prince who rode at the head of the band of wearied and wounded rebels. "Thayne is right, Your Highness." He shook his head in warning, despite the fact that his own impulse was to gallop down the slope and battle whatever odds they might face until he had Ciara safely in his arms.

If the wedding had taken place as scheduled this morn, she was now Daemon's bride. His only hope lay in the fact that darkness had just fallen, that the wedding feast should last several more hours—that the groom had not yet consummated the vows.

Because the rebels dared not risk Mathias's life.

"Daemon's men will try to protect him," Thayne pointed out.

"Aye," Royce agreed through clenched teeth, studying the moonlit keep below, wishing in vain for some sign, some evidence that she was all right. "There is a danger—"

"They are in truth *my* men," Mathias corrected, his voice quiet yet determined. "They will not raise arms against their own prince."

Royce shared a look with Thayne, not at all certain that was true. They had learned a hard lesson on the Gunlaug: the ascent had not proven half as deadly as the guardsmen Daemon had placed in charge of his brother's prison. The well-paid troops had kept the rebels pinned down on a treacherous slope for almost two days.

Their final assault on the stronghold had cost them a half-dozen lives. They had been forced to leave two more men behind in a village, both wounded and unable to travel—including Landers, who had taken an arrow in the chest.

"Your Highness," Thayne said firmly, "we have risked

much and lost much in the past weeks and months to come this far. If Daemon should order his men to move against you, before you have time to speak to your nobles—"

"Then surprise is our best chance, is it not?" Mathias asked calmly, looking back over his shoulder at them, his gray eyes fearless in the moonlight. "I have been awaiting this moment for four years. It is time to put right what I should have put right long ago."

Royce regarded him with a respect that had been growing steadily over the past two days as they had galloped back to the palace. Despite four years as his brother's captive, Mathias was still the noble, coolheaded man of deep faith he remembered.

But the prince also had a steely edge no one had suspected he possessed.

"Very well, Your Highness." Thayne gathered up his reins and glanced at Karl, who rode beside him. Their crooked grins flashed in the darkness as if they, too, were in truth eager for a bold ending to their months of danger and secrecy.

Mathias led the way down the slope and Royce needed no more convincing. He spurred his mount, charging forward. All ten of them descended at a gallop, straight toward the keep, swift as judgment raining down from above. They did not stop when the guards at the gate—mayhap lulled to inaction by the festivities taking place inside—called out to them. Nor were the sentries quick enough to raise the drawbridge.

The rebels thundered over it, their horses' hooves pounding on the wood like blows from a catapult. They sped into the bailey, dismounting even before they had pulled to a stop. Guards came scrambling from their posts in every direction, too late to block the unknown intruders from racing up the steps that led into the keep.

Taking the stairs two at a time, they encountered little opposition as they rushed inside, past the main entrance. It seemed that most of Daemon's forces were stationed elsewhere this night.

Royce's heart was pounding as they reached the great hall. Mathias led the way through the massive doors, shoving them open to find the wedding feast underway.

"My lords!" Mathias called above the din, throwing back the hood of the drab peasant cloak he wore. "My lords!"

Royce barely heard the rest of what Mathias said, only dimly aware of the commotion that erupted as the wedding guests recognized their beloved long-lost prince, as the sentries finally caught up with them, as Mathias began to explain that the Thuringian nobles had been deceived by Daemon's treachery.

Royce's own gaze had locked on the two chairs at the center of the dais.

The two *empty* chairs.

His mind roared with denial. *He was too late.* Then he saw Hadwyn and Jarek rushing forward, pushing their way through the crowd of nobles who were all surging to their feet in shock at what Mathias was saying. The rest of the silk-clad guards, many loyal to Daemon, began milling toward the entrance as well. A battle could ignite at any moment.

But his mind and heart had only one thought. When Hadwyn reached him, Royce shouted a single word over the tumult.

"Where?"

The young man pointed toward a spiral stair at the back of the hall. "The chamber on the second floor, mil—"

Royce was already running, leaving the others to protect Mathias, shoving aside wedding guests, vaulting over tables in his headlong race toward the stairs.

Only to find his way blocked at the bottom by four members of Daemon's personal guard armed with halberds—who were quickly joined by two others rushing down the steps.

One against six.

Then he heard Thayne at his heels. "Give way!" the

rebel leader demanded. "We would see our princess—"

"And *we* have orders that our prince is not to be disturbed!" The guardsmen brandished the lethally sharp halberds, holding them like axes, their eyes almost eager as they regarded Royce.

He exchanged a quick glance with Thayne—who agreed with a silent signal that two against six made acceptable odds.

Drawing their swords, they launched themselves up the steps, side by side.

The guards charged down to swarm over them, ready to cut them to pieces. Royce struck one man a glancing blow to the leg and sent him tumbling, dodged a slice from a halberd, and danced in to pierce its owner through the ribs.

A third guard tried to spear him with the halberd's sharp point and Royce barely stepped aside in time. The man pivoted instantly, slicing upward, almost taking Royce's head off before he could dive out of the way. When the guard attacked again, Royce stood his ground and used his opponent's momentum against him, leaping sideways at the last possible moment and slicing through his midsection.

He could hear Thayne's guttural curses behind him. Saw that the rebel had already dispatched two of the guards who had attacked him. Whirled to help.

Just in time to see the last guardsman catch Thayne with the side of his halberd, the steel edge slashing deeply and coming away red with blood.

Thayne shouted in surprise and agony and went down. Before the guardsman could deliver a death blow, Royce attacked, shoving him away. With two lightning-fast thrusts, he finished the last of Daemon's personal guard.

Then he turned and bent over his fallen comrade, swearing at the sight of the long gash through his side.

"Go." Thayne reached up a bloodied hand to push him away. "Save your lady."

Royce looked up to find Karl and the other rebels rushing toward them. Saw that Mathias had things well in hand at the entrance.

Without another second's hesitation, he turned and ran up the spiral staircase, his sword still gripped in his hand. He came to the door at the top, grabbed the latch.

Found the chamber locked from inside.

Spitting curses, he threw his whole weight against it. Once. Twice.

The second time, the door gave way with a splintering of wood and a snap of metal, sending him tumbling into the room. He rolled and came up with blade drawn.

"Royce!"

Ciara lay on the floor on the opposite side of the huge chamber, near the windows, dressed in a gold wedding gown—her lower lip split and bleeding, a red welt on her cheek from where Daemon's fist had struck her.

"Ferrano," Daemon spat, standing over her. "You are—"

"Not dead," Royce supplied with lethal silkiness, his eyes locking on Daemon's as he thrust himself to his feet. "But you are. I am going to carve your heart out, you whoreson."

Before he could reach them to make good his threat, Daemon grabbed Ciara by her hair, jerking her roughly to her feet. She screamed as he pulled her in front of him. He drew a knife from the jeweled sheath at his waist. "Guards!"

"Let her go, Daemon. Your guards are finished. And I am not here alone." Royce moved closer, his scarlet-stained blade held in front of him, his gaze on the prince to keep himself from being distracted by the fear in Ciara's eyes and the blood on her face. "Your brother is in the great hall even now, explaining to your lords and ministers that he has *not* been on pilgrimage the past four years."

Daemon paled. "You are lying! That is impossible—"

"We found him right where you left him. Imprisoned on the Gunlaug. The game is up, you lying bastard. Now let her go."

"Nay, I do not believe you! My brother never could have escaped, even with your help. And now that the war is won, it does not matter. I have more than enough lands and wealth to secure my position. All the power is in *my* hands now. The throne is mine. Châlons is mine. *She* is mine."

Royce heard someone enter the door behind him, heard a low, even voice fill the chamber.

"Wrong on all counts, my dear brother."

Daemon's eyes darted in that direction, widened in shock. "Nay…how could…this is not possible…"

Royce shifted his gaze to Ciara, conveying a quick, silent message while Daemon was distracted.

She understood him without words. Her lips curved as she jammed her elbow backward, straight into Daemon's stomach, and brought her heel down hard on top of his foot.

Daemon lost his hold on the knife and on her as he doubled over, cursing.

Ciara broke free and rushed across the room into Royce's arms. He caught her close, wrapping her in his embrace, taking a full, deep breath for the first time in nine days. "I have you now, my love. I have you now."

She pressed her unbruised cheek against his chest and a sob escaped her, muffled by his tunic.

"It is over, Daemon." Mathias came to stand between his brother and the two of them, as if to prevent Daemon from trying to reclaim his lost prize. "I have told our retainers everything."

Royce drew Ciara a safe distance from her furious groom and noticed that the Thuringian lords and ministers had followed Mathias upstairs. Many of them, along with members of the guards, crowded into the royal bedchamber.

"I told them where I have been," Mathias continued, "and who put me there."

Daemon straightened, his eyes filling with rage and the beginnings of panic as he saw the nobles, saw the looks on their faces.

"And I told them what happened on that night four years ago, after the peace negotiations failed. When I came to your chamber and told you that I had decided *not* to return to my studies at the monastery after all—because I had realized what a mistake I made when I stepped aside in your favor. A mistake I wished to correct by taking my rightful place on the throne. So that I might bring an end to the war." Mathias's voice grew heavy with sadness. "My one error that night was in trusting you."

"I let you live," Daemon spat, as if that should forgive everything else he had done. "You always wanted a monastic life. I merely gave you what you wished."

"There is a difference between a monastery," Mathias bit out, a flash of anger showing for the first time, "and a dungeon."

"And how in the name of Hell did Ferrano locate you?" Daemon demanded, slicing a murderous glance at Royce.

"With the help of the rebels," Royce told him. "They have been working for Prince Mathias's return all along. Members of your own guards supplied them with information, after a bit of careful eavesdropping."

"A certain piece of glass that did not come from Rome supplied the rest," Ciara finished, nodding toward the reliquary.

Daemon looked from Ciara to the silver box, his expression changing to one of disbelief and white-hot fury. "*You* were in league with the rebels? I was betrayed by my own bride?"

"Nay, by your own fear and greed," she shot back.

"And by your cruelty," Mathias added, "to our people and to those of Châlons. Accept your fate, Daemon. Your reign is ended."

Daemon backed away from him, from everyone, toward the windows, shaking his head. "Nay, you will not take my crown from me! All my life, I had to settle for my older brothers' leavings. I will not go back to existing on mere scraps—"

"You had everything," Mathias countered angrily, "but that was not enough for you. Everything you had only made you want more. More riches, more power, more prancing minions to surround you and shower you with praise. It would appear you have had all that since you stole the throne from me." He gestured at the luxuries piled around the room. "Tell me, Brother," he challenged, "has it made you happy?"

"I *had* to take the throne," Daemon sneered, not answering his question. "*You* were too soft to rule—wasting all your time on your books and your prayers. You are weak. You have always been weak."

"Am I truly, Daemon? If that is so, how did I survive the last four years in that pleasant little dwelling you built for me in the Gunlaug?" Mathias's voice took on a hard edge. "A man does not have to be a vicious killer to be a king. I am strong enough to rule."

"Then prove it." Daemon reached behind him to grab a sword displayed on the wall beside a tapestry. "I should have killed you four years ago. Step aside or I will remedy my mistake here and now."

Royce and the guards instinctively moved forward, but Mathias held up a hand to stop them. "I will deal with him," he insisted calmly. Without taking his eyes from Daemon, he backed toward Royce and extended his hand, palm up. "If you would be so kind as to lend me your blade, Ferrano."

"Prince Mathias," Ciara whispered in concern.

Mathias glanced down at her, his gaze meeting hers for the first time. "Fear not, Your Highness." He smiled warmly. "I thought this moment might come one day. I have no intention of being killed." The smile faded as he turned back toward Daemon. "I stepped aside once before—and my subjects paid the price. Innocent people lost their lives because I refused to accept the responsibilities I was born to." He shook his head, his voice resolved. "I will not step aside again."

Royce drew his sword—his father's sword—and silently handed it to him.

Mathias accepted it and moved toward the center of the huge bedchamber. He unfastened the homespun cloak he wore and threw it aside…and the muscled frame revealed beneath drew soft murmurs of surprise from those gathered in the room.

Including Daemon. "It would appear you did not suffer too terribly during your stay on the Gunlaug."

"There is little to occupy one's time in a cold mountain prison other than exercise to keep warm." Mathias lifted the heavy sword easily. "And as I said, I thought this day might come."

The two brothers faced each other, neither backing down.

"Then come," Daemon hissed, "and let us see how this day ends."

Bringing up his blade, he lunged forward. The two locked in battle with a clash of steel on steel.

Royce tensed but forced himself to stand fast. This was Mathias's fight. Every man in the room understood that. No one interfered. Royce's arms tightened around Ciara as she buried her face against his chest with a sob, apparently certain of the outcome.

But he was not so sure. Daemon had the advantage of experience, but he was also attacking at an emotional fever pitch. Mathias remained cooler as they parried back and forth, deflecting every blow, defending himself without drawing blood.

Royce understood his strategy. Mathias meant to wear his brother down. Tire him, mayhap wound him—force him to admit defeat without killing him.

"I am not so weak as you thought, little brother," Mathias gritted out, dodging a blow that might have cost him an arm.

"And I am not so little anymore!" Daemon shot back, hacking and slashing, driving Mathias toward the windows.

Royce clenched his jaw, half afraid that Daemon meant to send his brother crashing through the panes to his death in the courtyard below—but Mathias seemed to realize the danger at the same time, moving aside, following the length of the carved chest.

They were both sweating and breathing heavily now. For long, tense minutes the combat wore on, silent, grim, each man soon bleeding from numerous cuts.

Royce held his breath, for it seemed Mathias was the one who was becoming fatigued. *God, please, help him.* The elder prince had to understand that he was fighting for his life. He could not miss any chance to strike a mortal blow.

With Daemon's next thrust, the point of his blade sank into Mathias's shoulder. Mathias's cry of pain brought an exclamation of triumph from Daemon's lips—and shouts of alarm from everyone in the room. Daemon yanked the blade free, quickly whirling it upward as if he would take off his brother's head.

But Mathias caught him off guard by dropping to his knees.

And thrusting his sword forward, straight through Daemon's right side.

Daemon shouted in agony and looked down in shock. Mathias wrenched the sword backward and staggered to his feet, dripping with sweat, jaw clenched. He was shaking. Mayhap with fatigue or loss of blood—or horror at what he had been forced to do.

It was a mortal wound. His face going slack, Daemon stumbled aside, toward the chest in front of the windows, his own blade still gripped in one hand. Then he snarled a curse and raised the weapon again, his features contorted with fury. He hurled himself toward Mathias.

Only to trip on something in the rushes and fall headlong to the floor. He landed facedown—and there was a sound of something cracking as he hit. His face froze in a mask of shock.

Gasping a choked cry, he pushed himself up with one hand and fell again, rolling onto his back.

Royce could see the thick stem of a jeweled glass goblet protruding from the center of his chest at an awkward angle.

And near his feet—it was Ciara's crown that had tripped him.

With a sound of grief and regret, Mathias knelt beside his brother. "Daemon…"

Daemon lifted one trembling hand.

Instead of reaching for his brother, he grasped at the jeweled stem of the goblet that had delivered the final blow to his plans and his life.

His expression was still one of stunned disbelief.

"Mine…"

The word took the last breath from his body, and his eyes went sightless.

Mathias bent his head, made the sign of the cross, and gently closed his brother's eyes. He remained silent a moment, as if in prayer, and no one in the room moved or uttered a word

Then he stood, Royce's sword still gripped in one hand, his other palm coming up to staunch the bleeding at his shoulder. "My lords," he said hollowly. "Prince Daemon is dead."

"Long live Prince Mathias!" one of the nobles called as they all surged forward to surround and congratulate their new ruler. Two of the guards bent to cover Daemon's body with Mathias's discarded cloak.

Royce realized that Ciara was trembling in his arms, her cheeks wet with tears. "Shhh," he soothed as he gently tilted her head up. "It is over. You are safe now, and free. You have just become a widow."

She did not say anything for a moment as he tenderly examined her bruises. Then her words came out in a rush. "Royce, I was so afraid when you did not come back from the Ruadhans. I thought—"

"I made you a promise, remember?" Satisfied that her injuries were not serious, he let himself relax enough to smile. "We encountered some trouble on the mountain, but Thayne—"

He cut himself off abruptly, glancing around, seeing none of the rebels in the room.

"God's mercy, *Thayne*." Holding Ciara's hand, he turned

and ran for the door, pushing his way through the crowd, into the corridor, down the twisting staircase.

He found the rebels in the great hall gathered around their fallen leader. They had moved him to one of the trestle tables and bound his wound with strips of fabric torn from Daemon's expensive tablecloths. As Royce and Ciara approached, Karl looked up.

There were tears in his eyes.

With an oath, Royce released Ciara and leaned over the dark-haired man who lay bleeding from the deep gash in his side. He was deathly pale.

Despite the help of his comrades, his life was seeping from him.

Thayne's eyes fluttered open. When he saw Royce, a hint of a crooked grin curved his mouth. "Always was better with a crossbow…than a blade," he said weakly.

"Summon the royal surgeons," a voice commanded from behind them, forceful enough to send the servants in the hall scrambling to do as they were ordered.

Royce turned to find that Mathias, heedless of his own injury, had followed them down the stairs. His lords and ministers were close at his heels.

Thayne reached up to grip Royce's tunic, reclaiming his attention. "Did you…" His green eyes were glazed with pain. "…get to your lady…in time?"

"Aye." Royce glanced at Ciara, who stood back from the group, a hand over her mouth to hold in a sob. "She is safe. Princess Ciara is all right. She is here with me."

The crooked smile appeared again. "Then that is…all that matters."

He dropped back against the table beneath him, his eyes closing, his body suddenly limp.

"Nay!" Ciara cried.

With an anguished shout, Karl bent over his brother, pressed an ear to his chest.

But then the young man exhaled shakily. "He lives. Thanks be to God, he lives." He glanced up as the surgeons pushed their way through the crowd that had gathered around the table. "But his heartbeat is weak."

"Take him to one of the bedchambers above," Mathias ordered, shaking his head when one of the surgeons tried to examine his wounded shoulder, nodding toward Thayne. "This man is to have the best of care. I owe him a great deal. We all owe him a great deal." He turned to the servants. "Fetch bandages, hot water, whatever the surgeons may need. Quickly."

The hall became a flurry of activity as the servants hurried to do their prince's bidding, the rebels lifted the unconscious Thayne and carried him up the steps, and a score of ministers and lords surrounded Mathias again, all of them talking at once.

In the middle of the chaos, Ciara elbowed her way to Royce's side. He pulled her into his arms, burying his face in her hair as they comforted each other.

"He will be all right," she said fiercely. "He has to be."

"Aye. And what about you—are you sure you are all right?"

She nodded, her arms gripping him as if she would never let him go.

He lifted his head, gut clenched at the thought that he had almost been too late to save her. "When we first came into the great hall and I did not see you—"

"You were just in time," she reassured him, smiling tremulously.

"Daemon did not—"

"Nay, you were there to protect me, exactly when I needed you most. As you always are."

He threaded his fingers through her hair. God, how he wanted to kiss her. But he did not want to hurt her injured lip.

So he settled for dusting a kiss across the tip of her nose, just as he heard someone nearby clearing his throat.

Tearing his attention from Ciara for the first time in several long minutes, Royce saw that the hall had almost cleared. Mathias stood alone beside them.

"I persuaded my lords that their questions could wait until morn." He sighed in exhaustion, glancing down at the bandage someone had hastily wrapped around his injured shoulder, then nodded in the direction Thayne had been taken. "You have my word that your friend will be well cared for. Our surgeons in Thuringia are renowned as some of the best. We will fight for his life as he fought for mine."

"Thank you, Your Highness," Royce said gratefully.

"Nay, it is I who should be thanking you, Ferrano. You and Thayne and the others risked everything to save me from that prison. I owe you much more than my thanks. And so do the people…" He paused. "*My* people," he amended, pronouncing the words as if for the first time, his expression one of wonder as he adjusted to the idea. "My subjects."

Royce smiled. "Let me be one of the first to say welcome home, Your Highness."

Mathias returned his smile, then shifted his attention to the lady in Royce's arms. "Now then, do you not think an introduction to Her Highness is overdue?"

Ciara dipped into a curtsy. "I am very pleased to meet you, Prince Mathias."

Mathias bowed. "I have heard a great deal about you, Princess Ciara" He slanted a wry glance at Royce. "Though you neglected to mention that she was such a beauty, Ferrano."

"Did I?" Royce cleared his throat. "It must have slipped my mind."

Mathias chuckled, his gaze returning to Ciara. "I doubt this lady could slip any man's mind."

"Indeed, Your Highness." Royce tightened his arm possessively around Ciara's waist.

Still grinning, Mathias gestured for them to sit at a nearby table. "There are matters we need to discuss, milord, concerning the peace agreement. It occurs to me that if I am to be king one day," he said slowly, his eyes on Ciara as they claimed their seats, "I will be in need of a queen."

Chapter 21

The western mountains sparkled like massive diamonds in the midday sun as Ciara rode across the lowland plain, the wind in her hair, spring's warmth scenting the breeze with the fragrances of flowers and earth, her gray mare galloping through the fields.

As Châlons's royal palace came into view at last, its towers and walls little more than dots at this distance, she reined her horse to a walk, then to a halt. She could not seem to catch her breath, watching while the sun painted that familiar keep with streaks of gold. The sight of home filled her with longing, with love. And with uncertainty.

She prayed this would not be the last time she ever saw it.

Closing her eyes, she inhaled deeply of the sun-warmed air, of the beauty all around her, and held fast to her hope. *Her father had to agree to Mathias's offer. He had to.*

Surely he would sec that he had every reason to give his consent. Her country was free. Her people were free. Free from war, from the tyrant who had so abused them. As the news had spread, cheering crowds had turned out in every town and village on the way home from Thuringia.

But she herself was not entirely free.

Not yet.

She heard hoofbeats behind her and glanced over her shoulder as Royce came across the field at a gallop, catching up with her at last. He pulled Anteros to a rearing halt.

Laughing, Ciara tugged on the reins to control her skittish mare. "Keep that great black beast away from my little Merlin," she chided. All the commotion brought a growl from the basket tied to Merlin's saddle. Hera poked her head out from beneath the lid, barking excitedly.

Undaunted by the protective puppy, the stallion pranced nearer, towering over the mare, tossing his head and nickering impatiently.

"It is impossible to hold him in check, my love." Royce laughed. "I think he believes we bought that little beauty just for him. He does not like to let her out of his sight." His voice turned husky. "I know how he feels."

As Anteros nuzzled Merlin's neck, Royce bent down in the saddle and cupped Ciara's chin in his hand, lifting her mouth to his. With a soft moan, she reached up to grasp the edge of his cloak as their lips met in a kiss that was slow and soft and deep. The first kiss they had been able to steal in days.

The satiny invasion of his tongue sent desire shivering through her, but it was all too brief.

Groaning, he lifted his head, and they both glanced back at the entourage of riders not far behind them—Karl and the other rebels, the emissaries Mathias had sent to speak with her father, and the guards and serving maids and other retainers who had been in the wedding procession.

"Five minutes," Royce muttered. "What I would not give for even five minutes alone with you."

Ciara released her hold on his cloak, sighing in agreement. Since leaving Mathias's palace a fortnight ago, they had not been able to steal an hour alone together, much less a night. Though Miriam had stayed behind with the recuperating Landers, there were more than enough maidservants and courtiers with them this time to ensure that Ciara was well chaperoned on her journey home.

"It is even worse than before," Royce grumbled, letting her go before anyone could see them.

"Worse?" Ciara nudged her mare forward and they rode on, side by side, Hera content to rest her muzzle on the edge of her basket and yip at the scenery.

"During our first journey, all I could do was *imagine* what it would be like to touch you."

Ciara glanced sideways and their gazes met for a long,

heated moment.

"This time, I *know*," he told her in that low, husky tone.

"It will all be over soon," she said softly, turning to look up at the castle in the distance.

"Aye."

"And we will be together."

It took him a moment to respond, and when he did, his voice revealed his uncertainty. "Aye."

Ciara fell silent, not wanting to put her own fears into words. Behind them, shouts of happiness rose as their traveling companions caught their first sight of the palace.

Which only made the uneasy quiet between her and Royce more uncomfortable.

She shifted to a different topic. "I wish we could have stayed at Mathias's palace until Thayne was strong enough to come home with us."

"He will need at least another fortnight's rest in bed, even though the surgeons worked a miracle with their stitches and their herbal potions."

Ciara nodded. "I know, but I hated to leave anyone behind."

"He has Landers and Miriam for company. And I am not sure Thayne would have *let* us tear him away from his many admirers." Royce grinned. "Every pretty serving maid in that keep seemed to be thinking of some excuse to spend time in his bedchamber."

The Thuringian ladies had been quite taken with the brave, handsome rebel who helped save their beloved prince. "They were most attentive, weren't they? Changing his bandages, cooling his brow, feeding him tea and broth—"

"Seeing to his every need..." Royce chuckled dryly. "Giving him incentive to get his strength back..."

Ciara slanted him a quelling look. "I thought they were simply being kind."

"*Most* kind. I am not sure we will ever get him home, now that he has experienced Thuringian hospitality."

Ciara shook her head, unable to suppress a smile.

"Thayne does seem to possess a certain charm with the ladies."

"We men of Châlons are born with it." He reached out to ruffle her hair. "It is in the blood."

She caught his hand in hers, twining their fingers together as they rode on, not caring if anyone behind them noticed. Looking up at the sun glittering across the snowcapped mountains, she sighed. "Have you ever seen anything as beautiful as that?"

"Aye," he said quietly, glancing down at her. "Aye, I have"

They rode in silence for a while, both gazing up at the soaring ridges dotted with pines, the mists parting over the mountains, the almost unearthly blaze of color—blue and white and green and gold.

"Ciara…how can I take you away from all this?"

"You will not have to if my father agrees to Mathias's terms."

He did not reply.

She dropped her gaze to her horse's mane. "You do not think he will agree, do you?"

"I do not know," he said carefully. "Your father is not a man who forgives easily. In four years, he did not forgive me for my actions during the first peace negotiations."

"But I am sure he will forgive you now. You have done all he asked of you, at great risk to your life. You did your duty, and more."

"It is the *more* that worries me," he muttered with a pained expression.

"I meant that you not only escorted me safely to Mount Ravensbruk but you helped rescue Mathias."

"Aye, but I seem to recall your father mentioning something about drawing and quartering if I dared so much as look at you. And you do not want to know what he meant to do if I dared touch your royal person."

She lifted their twined hands, rubbing her cheek against his fingers. "I had no intention of mentioning any of the wonderful ways you have touched my royal person."

"Ciara, I am serious. He has at least a half-dozen reasons to refuse Mathias's offer—"

"He will agree, Royce. He has to."

"And if he does not?"

"Then this will be the last time I ever see my home."

For a moment, there was no sound but the wind in the long grass and the muted thudding of their horses' hooves. Little Hera had curled up in her basket to sleep.

"You would give up all of this?" He nodded toward the mountains, the palace, his voice soft, serious. "Leave Châlons forever?"

"For you, aye."

He glanced away from her, and she knew what he was thinking: he did not want to tear her from her homeland. Nor did he want to leave this realm he had fought for, risked everything for, loved all his life. She knew how much the four years of banishment had pained him.

The idea that they might have to leave forever…

"Well then, my love ..." Still holding her hand in his, he lightly tapped his silver spurs against Anteros's flanks. "Let us go and see what your father says."

They waited in the solar, the two of them alone, while her father and his ministers held an audience with the Thuringian emissaries in the great hall. Ciara paced, her stomach queasy.

This was the chamber where it had all begun, she thought as she moved restlessly from the door to the hearth and back again. This was where she had come to hide the night of her betrothal party, where Miriam had spoken to her about the rebels, where Landers had tried to kidnap her—though she had not known that at the time.

And this was where it would all end.

One way or another.

"You are making me dizzy, my love," Royce said lightly. "Which is not unusual, but this time I am not even kissing you." He was perched in the window seat, long legs stretched out in front of him, boots crossed.

When he patted the empty place beside him, she shook her head. She could not sit down. With a look of understanding, he returned his attention to the window, gazing down at the bailey below.

Earlier, he had gone out to spend some time alone at the small brass cross that marked the place where his best friend had fallen in defense of his realm, and his home…and her.

Ciara wondered whether her father had yet found it in his heart to forgive her for her part in Christophe's death. She remembered all too vividly his angry words to her.

And knew that what Royce had said was true. *Your father is not a man who forgives easily.*

She finally stopped pacing and turned to rest her back against the hearth, wishing she could have remained with Hera, happily ensconced on the bed in her room. "He has been out there a very long time," she said uneasily, her gaze on the door. "What if—"

"The emissaries have a great deal to explain." Royce's tone was calm, reassuring. He tallied the subjects on his fingers. "Prince Daemon's deceit. The fact that the rebels were never trying to kill you at all. How Mathias was rescued from his prison. The fact that he has reclaimed his proper place on the throne—"

"I know." She sighed. "But I am beginning to think that the rebels had the right idea in staying a safe distance from the palace until their fate was decided."

Royce chuckled. "This is the way we wanted it, Ciara—you and I and Mathias. We all agreed that the royal ministers would discuss the past…while you and I would be the ones to present the decisions that need to be made concerning the future."

"But what if—"

The door opened. Ciara turned, tensed. "Father."

The king's velvet robes swirled around him as he closed the door, his eyes on her, his expression…

As always, it was impossible to discern from his somber face what he felt or thought. She almost took a step toward him, then fiercely reminded herself how much he hated emotional displays.

Silent, he stared at her for a long moment, his gaze tracing over her face before he turned his attention to Royce…

Who slowly got to his feet, then dropped to one knee and bowed. "Your Majesty."

For the first time since coming into the solar, her father showed a hint of emotion, one silvered brow lifting in surprise. "Rise, Sir Royce." He turned toward Ciara. "And come here, Daughter."

She crossed the distance between them, so nervous and uncertain she held her breath.

But when she drew near, he opened his arms and reached out to her.

And enfolded her in a strong, silent embrace.

All the air left her lungs as she relaxed against him, closing her eyes, too overcome by emotion even to speak. Her arms went around him and she hugged him hard, shamelessly letting her tears fall against his velvet tunic, as she had not done since she was a little girl.

His usually cool, regal voice wavered when he finally spoke. "I am so grateful that you are safe and well, my Ciara. If aught had befallen you, it would have been the death of me."

Her only reply was a tearful sniff as she tried to blink away the moisture in her eyes. But he did not seem to mind.

After holding her a long while, he set her away from him, his hands gentle on her shoulders, and she saw the unmistakable love in his eyes before his attention shifted to Royce.

"I understand that I have you to thank for my daughter's life, Baron Ferrano. And for my kingdom's return to both peace and freedom."

"It is no more than any loyal subject would do," Royce said quietly, "in service to a worthy king."

The two men's gazes held for a long moment.

Ciara felt new hope bubbling up inside her. "Father, did the Thuringian emissaries explain all that has happened?"

"Aye, including the fact that there is a huntsman by the name of Thayne and a few of his friends who are in need of a royal pardon." He let go of her shoulders, glancing from her to Royce. "And they said you and your guardian would explain the rest. I understand that Prince Mathias has demands to make?"

"Requests, Father. He has asked us to present four requests."

Her father sighed heavily. "And what are they? What could I possibly give him that his brother did not already take?"

Ciara hesitated, glancing over at Royce, who nodded for her to go ahead.

"First," she began slowly, "Prince Mathias asks Your Majesty and the people of Châlons for forgiveness. For himself, and for his subjects. Seven years of war have cut deep wounds between our people and his, and he wishes to begin healing those wounds."

Her father made a grudging nod, still looking wary. "Since that is my wish as well, his first request is easy enough to grant."

Ciara did not allow herself to feel confident just yet. The other requests would be more difficult for him to accept. "Second, he wishes to restore to us the lands that Daemon took by force, and return our borders to the way they were seven years ago, before the war began. Mathias is willing to relinquish Thuringia's claim to all the conquered holdings"—she paused—"except for a band of neutral territory in the mountains between our two kingdoms. He wishes to set that aside for the present, for he has need of those lands."

Her father contemplated that for a moment but said

neither aye nor nay. "And what else?"

She took a deep breath. "Third, he asks that we move our capital to the keep at Ferrano. The castle that is in ruins there can be rebuilt and expanded—"

"Move our capital?" her father demanded, his brow furrowing until his silver hair almost touched his eyebrows. "Our palace has been here for more than two hundred years. It is the safest location in Châlons."

"But as Daemon's mercenaries and their new siege weapons proved, Father, it is not so safe as it once was. And it is isolated. Prince Mathias wishes for the royal family of Châlons and the royal family of Thuringia to become closer, in every way. The keep at Ferrano is only three days' ride from the Thuringian palace on Mount Ravensbruk. And as Prince Mathias says, it is much harder to make war on a beloved friend than on a stranger."

Her father seemed to understand, but still did not look pleased. "And what is his final request?"

Ciara took another deep breath. "He was quite adamant about the last one." Clasping her hands in front of her to keep them from shaking, she glanced down at her intertwined fingers. "Prince Mathias wishes to marry soon because he realizes that a king needs heirs. So the matter of the betrothal agreement that was made between Châlons and Thuringia must be resolved. He wishes to make a specific appeal that you grant my hand in marriage"—she lifted her gaze, not sure what her father's reaction would be—"to his friend Sir Royce."

Her father had no reaction at all for a second. He blinked down at her as if she had just declared she planned to marry Anteros.

And then he turned the same stunned look on Royce. "Prince Mathias wishes you to marry…Sir Royce?"

"Aye." She hastened to mention all the reasons Mathias had spelled out for her. "The prince realizes that I am the sole heir to Châlons's throne, that one day I will be queen of this realm. There are many unscrupulous princes and kings in Europe who might seek my hand for less than noble reasons. He wishes to see me wed to a man he can trust. A man strong enough to rebuild and to rule, brave enough to fight if he must"—she snuck a secret smile at Royce, who had not been present when she and Mathias made up their list of his good qualities—"and gentle and honorable enough to care for his people. And to keep the peace."

Her father said naught, still regarding Royce with an assessing gaze. The two men faced each other for a long, tense moment.

Ciara tried to think of something more to say. Some way to nudge them both past the stubbornness and hurt of the past, to persuade them to reconcile. "Father, if you can forgive the Thuringians for the war, if you can forgive me for what happened to Christophe—"

That brought the king's attention swiftly back to her. "Forgive you for what happened to Christophe?" he asked in confusion.

"I…I know you blamed me for his death. When you and I were hostages after the palace was taken, when you said—"

"Nay, Daughter. Saints above, nay." He shook his head. "Can it be that you have believed all this time that I…" A look of pain crossed his features. "I spoke to you in anger, Ciara. God in Heaven, I am sorry. The fault was Daemon's, *not* yours. You were innocent." He reached out to brush a tear from her cheek. "Can you forgive me for my harsh words?"

"Aye, Father." She looked up at him with a tremulous smile, her heart lightened. "I forgive you, gladly."

"This is, I think, a day for forgiveness," Royce said quietly. "Your Majesty, I spent four years in exile being angry at you. Hating you because I thought you had purposely disgraced me and my family name in order to make an example of me—"

"Nay, Ferrano, my intent was never to shame you, only to make you understand the seriousness of what you had done. I told no one that you had been banished." He paused, his voice becoming heavy. "Only Christophe knew. After you disappeared so suddenly, he pestered me for the truth about what had become of you until I told him. He always insisted I was wrong for punishing you so harshly…and mayhap he was right."

"Mayhap, Your Majesty." Royce shrugged one shoulder, as if it no longer mattered to him. "But I have come to understand that sometimes a king must do a thing he finds distasteful, for the greater good of his people."

"True." Her father shook his head with a rueful expression. "But I was trying to punish you for losing control of your anger—and yet I acted purely out of anger when I banished you."

"We were both angry that day."

"Aye." Her father glanced toward the window behind Royce, where the sun was setting. "But Christophe always knew it would not last. He intended to bring you home after the war."

"And you knew that?" Ciara asked.

"Your brother was as stubborn as his sire." Her father glanced at her before returning his attention to Royce. "And I never meant for the exile to last forever. That is one reason I never wished to shame you publicly, that and…" He stopped himself.

Royce regarded him with a puzzled expression.

Finally her father continued. "You said it yourself, when we met at the abbey." His majestic voice wavered with emotion as it had when he embraced her. "You have been like a son to me, Royce."

Royce swallowed hard, his look of confusion dissolving into one of gratitude and pride. He bowed his head. "I am honored, sire."

"The honor is mine." Her father reached out to clasp his shoulder with one hand. "Sometimes it is possible for even a king to forgive."

Ciara felt tears gather on her lashes again—of joy and hope. "Then will you give us your blessing to marry,

Father?"

Her father turned to her, his gaze searching. "I once promised you in marriage to a man you did not want. I will not do so again, regardless of Prince Mathias's request. Do you wish to have Royce for your husband?"

Did she wish to have him? Ciara dropped her gaze to the toes of her boots, furiously fighting a blush, realizing there was a great deal that was better left unsaid in front of her father. "I came to know him well during our travels, Father. I believe I could make the best of it." Lifting her head, she could not hold back a broad smile. "Aye, I wish to have him for my husband."

Her father nodded his acceptance of her answer, turned to Royce. "And you?"

"Your Majesty, earlier today, outside in the bailey, I made a vow to Christophe, and I give you the same promise." He looked at Ciara, his brown eyes darkening. "I vowed that I would protect her and care for her and love her all the rest of my life."

Ciara felt her heart soar, let her love for him shine through in her eyes.

"There is yet a problem," her father pointed out slowly, reluctantly. "In that Sir Royce is not of royal blood…"

"Nay, Prince Mathias has remedied that problem for us." She turned a beaming smile toward her father. "You recall that I mentioned the band of neutral territory he wishes to create between our countries? With your permission, he intends to make those border lands a separate state and give them a name: the Principality of Ferrano."

She looked at Royce again. "And in honor of Royce's service to both the crown of Thuringia and the crown of Châlons, Mathias wishes to bestow those lands on him. Along with a new title—prince of Ferrano." Turning back to her father, she shrugged. "I had already made him a baron, you see, and Mathias could think of no other honor suitable enough to reward him for all his help."

"If you approve, Your Majesty," Royce emphasized.

"The decision is yours."

"And of course, were Royce and I to marry," Ciara added, "our holdings would be joined, and our heirs would rule over both as one."

The king looked from her to Royce and back again.

And then he smiled.

And then he began to chuckle. "A wise man, this Prince Mathias. I think I will like him."

"I am certain you will." Ciara's heart was thrumming. "So…will you give us your blessing, Father?"

He slipped his arm around her shoulders. "Aye, Daughter. I give my blessing. To all of it. With all my heart."

She hugged him, her joy spilling over. "I love you, Father."

"And I love you, my sweet girl." He extended a hand toward Royce, and the two men grasped forearms. "And you, Royce Saint-Michel, prince of Ferrano." His smile widened. "Welcome home."

Chapter 22

Ciara stood at the entrance to the palace's chapel, feeling as if she were in a dream. Hoping no one would awaken her.

Joy filled her heart to overflowing, the feeling even brighter and more dazzling than the flood of morning sunlight that lit the small sanctuary. She glanced over her shoulder as Miriam gave the long train of her wedding gown a final adjustment. Ciara had chosen white silk because Royce said the cloth reminded him of snowfall.

After sharing a warm smile with her friend, she waited for Miriam to rejoin the other guests, then turned and started down the aisle toward the priest.

And her groom.

Standing beside her father, Royce gazed back at her, his dark eyes brimming with so much love that it brought an ache to the very center of her chest.

He looked so handsome, she had to keep herself from sighing aloud. His dark blue tunic and leggings made his hair gleam blue-black and set off the white ermine lining of the royal robes he wore casually thrown back over his broad shoulders. His new crown sparkled in the sun, as did his silver spurs and the gold hilt of his father's sword at his side.

Despite all the tingles coursing through her, Ciara did not allow herself to rush, wanting to savor every moment of this day. As she walked slowly down the aisle, the beams of silvery brightness pouring in through the arched windows danced between her and Royce—and she had a strange sensation that she had been here before, walking through the nave of a small chapel toward Royce and her father….

Then she remembered that she *had* experienced this moment before: on the day they had met in the abbey.

Almost every detail felt the same.

Except that this time, the look in Royce's eyes was one of love. His expression warmed the air all around her, made her feel as if she were floating, and promised that the feeling would last forever.

At the front of the chapel, she took her gaze from his long enough to steal a glance at the friends who had gathered to celebrate with them. She and Royce had decided to wait a fortnight for their wedding so that everyone could join them.

The pews were crowded with pardoned rebels and peasants and nobles from both Châlons and Thuringia. Including Bayard and Elinor. Prince Mathias. Karl and Miriam and Landers, whose arm was still in a sling. And Royce's friends from France, Duc Gaston de Varennes and his wife, Lady Celine.

And Thayne.

Or rather, *Sir* Thayne, she corrected herself, giving him a quick smile as he bowed his head toward her. Not only had the former rebel leader been pardoned but Mathias and her father had offered him so many honors and accolades, he had been overwhelmed and somewhat embarrassed by all the attention.

In the end, he had accepted only two of the rewards offered him: a knighthood and a small keep to go with it.

With her last step toward the altar, Ciara came to stand between her father and her groom. Royce took her hand, and the sensation that glittered through her made her catch her breath.

Shimmering rays of mountain sunlight danced around them as they exchanged their vows.

And gleamed on the gold band that he slipped on her finger, the same ring he had given her once before…except that this time it was truly a wedding band, and truly hers. As he was hers, and she his. Now and forever.

You and no other, the heart conquers all.

When they sealed their vows with a kiss, 'twas to the sound of the rebels cheering.

Ex-rebels, she reminded herself happily.

As her husband kissed her thoroughly, she wrapped her arms around his neck and did not care that she was making a shameless emotional display. Being a princess did not mean she had to be proper *all* the time.

"Out you go, fierce little Hera. Your mistress has no need of a protector tonight." Royce chuckled. "Besides, that duty was mine well before you came along."

Dislodging the frisky puppy, who had chomped onto his soft leather boot, he scooted her into the corridor. Then he closed the door to his wife's darkened bedchamber and leaned against it, throwing the bolt with a happy sigh.

At last, he had escaped. The wedding feast and dancing and revelry would have to continue without him. It was already near midnight.

As tradition demanded, after the guests had showered the bridal couple with handfuls of grain, the men had kept him occupied with overlong toasts—involving copious amounts of cassis, thanks to Bayard—while the ladies spirited the bride away to garb her for her wedding night.

That had been two hours ago. His friends had finally given up their mirthful efforts to pickle him, letting him go after he vowed revenge on all future grooms in the group.

With a wicked grin, he tucked that vow away in his memory and moved into the room, which was lit only by the glowing embers on the hearth. He caught the scent of sandalwood shavings that had been added to the flames, no doubt well over an hour ago, before they had burned down to almost naught. A large bathing tub filled with water had been set before the fire…and a sheer cotton kirtle lay draped over a chair beside it.

His breathing became heavy as he glanced around to see where his wife was hiding. Then he saw her: already in the bed, almost hidden beneath the covers.

Asleep.

A groan escaped him and he frowned over his shoulder at the door, thinking that revenge might not be enough for Thayne and Karl and all the rest. He might just have to kill them. They had kept him drinking in the hall so long that his bride had fallen asleep waiting for him.

But a moment later, as he turned with a sigh and walked closer to the bed, he did not mind so much after all. Looking down at his lady, his wife, so pale and lovely and innocent, he felt a warmth that had naught to do with the cassis he had consumed. And he knew that he would cherish this memory as he did all the others this day had brought him.

She lay on her side, snuggled beneath the silky-soft white sheets, her hair damp and dark against the pillow, a smile gently curving her lips. One of her hands curled around the wedding gift he had left here for her.

He had placed it in the middle of their bed earlier today, festooned with silk ribbons: a new mandolin.

His heart thudded against his ribs as he stood there, silent, watching her sleep. She looked so sweet, she reminded him of…

He smiled at the thought. She reminded him of a princess in a troubadour's tale, awaiting a kiss from her prince to awaken her.

He unfastened the chain that held his ermine-lined mantle in place, let it slide from his shoulders, then shed his boots and belt and the rest of his garments.

And when he lifted the covers and slipped into bed, he realized that she, too, wore naught but a smile. He moved closer, gently draped his arm around her waist to draw her against him, placed the lightest kiss on her shoulder.

She stirred, sighing in her sleep, then shivered as the bristly hair of his chest touched her back and his bearded jaw tickled the nape of her neck. "Mmmmm…" Her lashes lifted. "Oh, saints' breath…did I fall asleep?"

"Aye, wife," he whispered, nuzzling her neck, inhaling deeply as he caught the intoxicating scent of her perfume.

She tilted her head back with a drowsy sound of pleasure as he kissed his way along her throat. "I was waiting for you," she murmured, "and then I decided to wash the bits of grain from my hair…and then I was just so…sleepy…"

"Fear not, my love, you can stay just as you are for the moment. You do not even need to move." He heard her breath catch as she felt his arousal nestling against the lush curve of her bottom. "I have no intention of leaving this bed for at least two days." He nibbled at her earlobe.

"Mayhap three," she agreed with a soft moan.

"And then we will find a creative use for the tub…."

"And then in front of the fire?" she asked hopefully.

"Definitely in front of the fire."

She lifted her hand from the mandolin to reach back and caress his stubbled cheek. "Thank you for the wedding gift, Royce," she whispered sleepily. "Wherever did you get it?"

"I left instructions with Landers before we left Thuringia. He picked it up at a little shop in Gavena that Karl and I are familiar with."

"It is beautiful."

"No more so than its owner." He kissed her jaw.

"But I do not have a gift for you."

Reaching across her, he set the mandolin on the floor. "I am sure you will think of something."

She grinned sleepily as he settled back beside her, as he slid his hand downward to press her hips against him. "Oh, aye," she whispered. "Aye, I think I will. If I told you some of the dreams I have been having the past fortnight…"

He groaned, his palm moving down her body in a long, slow caress. "No doubt they would match the ideas that have been running through my mind while I lay awake at night, in my guest chamber on the opposite side of the palace, thinking of you here…in bed…"

"What sort of ideas?" she asked huskily.

"Unspeakable ideas," he growled, his hand stroking upward slowly, over her knee, her thigh, her hip. "I was contemplating another midnight raid through milady's window, but I discovered one problem." He lifted his head just long enough to shoot a glare at the thick panes of glass built into the window on the opposite wall. "Whoever designed this keep intended to make ravishing any damsels within damnably difficult."

She giggled, and laughter rumbled from deep in his chest as he brushed kisses through her hair, over her jaw, his arm circling her waist again. "Of course," he added, "when we rebuild the keep at Ferrano, I will no doubt want to do the same, to protect our daughter."

"Our daughter?"

He smiled, remembering the dream he had had in Gavena: of the two of them together, in front of the hearth at Ferrano, watching their children at play…a little girl with her mother's eyes, and a dark-haired boy just learning to walk. "A daughter first, and then a son, I think."

"You are quite certain, my prince?"

"It is just something that I"—he paused, tracing the curve of her mouth with his thumb—"wished. What is that secret little smile, wife?"

"Oh, I was just"—she sighed, snuggling closer to him—"thinking." She closed her eyes with a look of bliss as his hand moved downward again, over her flat belly, lower. "About how long it has been since that night, that first time you and I—"

"Five weeks, four days, twenty-one hours, and fifteen minutes, more or less." He nudged her thighs apart, moving his hips to position himself against her feminine heat. "Not that I have been keeping count."

His fingers glided into her silky curls, and he heard the soft music of her excitement as he stroked her.

And then there were no more words. Only her yearning sighs and his deep groans as he pleasured and teased her with his touch, drawing out the anticipation, the tension until neither of them could bear it any longer.

And when he slipped into her from behind, claiming her fully with a single, smooth stroke, the low sound that dragged from her throat was a gentler echo of his own. He withdrew slowly, only to push forward with swift, deep thrusts, rocking her against him. His fingers sought the bud of her desire, massaging until she bit her lip to hold back cries of abandon.

The two of them swept higher, faster, their bodies ebbing and flowing together until they came to the crest …

And plunged into the hot sea together. Release swept down upon them both, rippling through them as one, flowing on long after his essence spilled into her.

He lost all sense of time as they loved one another again and again through the night, their breathing and their heartbeats and their bodies and souls all joined. Made one. Now and forever.

The darkness beyond the window began to lighten, the stars winking out, and still they had not slept. Ciara lay atop him, her cheek pillowed by his chest while his fingers moved lazily up and down her spine.

Then she sighed and lifted her head, crossing her arms to prop her chin up on her hands. "I have been thinking, my love…"

"Have you any more dreams I can make come true?" he asked in a low, wicked whisper.

"Later," she promised. "Actually…I was thinking that I do have a wedding gift for you. But my gift will take a little longer to arrive."

"Hmmm?" he murmured, his hand moving through her hair, his attention distracted by the silky texture of her thoroughly mussed curls.

"I was going to wait…" she said haltingly. "It is too early to be certain…but I simply cannot keep it to myself anymore."

He shook his head in bemusement, not understanding.

"Our first night together, Royce, that magical night when you made me yours…it was almost six weeks ago…" Her smile was a little bit shy. "And I have missed my monthly time."

His hand went still. His heart seemed to stop, then started pounding.

"You…" He cupped her face in his palms, stunned by her announcement. "I-I…y-you…I…"

"Aye. You. Me. We…are going to have a baby." Laughing, she reached out to trace the curve of his smile with one fingertip. "What are you thinking, husband?"

Beaming at her, overwhelmed by the rush of joy and love that poured through him, he drew her closer and murmured his answer against her lips as the first rays of dawn shimmered through the window. "That sometimes wishes do come true."

Acknowledgments

I want to express my deepest gratitude to my critique partners, LaVerne Coan, Elizabeth Manz, and Linda Pedder, for their creative insights, helpful suggestions, and endless support as I wrote and revised the original manuscript of *His Forbidden Touch*. Now that we're scattered across the country, I miss you like crazy. You truly are the sisters I never had.

Dear Reader,

I hope you enjoyed spending time with Royce and Ciara in the pages of *His Forbidden Touch*. I'd love to keep writing books that touch your heart for many years to come. Readers like you make it possible, and I'm so thankful for your support and enthusiasm.

If you enjoyed *His Forbidden Touch*, could I ask you for a small favor? I'm just getting started in indie publishing, and with hundreds of new books published every month, it's difficult to stand out in the crowd. I need a little help (actually, a lot of help) getting the word out about my books. If you'd be willing to share your enthusiasm with other readers, I'd really be grateful.

The easiest way is to post a reader review on Amazon, Barnes & Noble, the Apple iBookstore, or wherever you bought the book. Just visit this book's page on that site and scroll down to where it says "Customer Reviews." Your review doesn't have to be long. Short and sweet is fine—just a line or two about why you enjoyed the story. The more reviews a book has, the more it encourages other readers to sample an author they've never read before. My goal is to always deliver stories worthy of five stars and a place on your keeper shelf.

If you're active on Facebook, Twitter, Pinterest, book sites like Goodreads or Shelfari, or review blogs, those are also great places to post a little note about the author you just discovered and the book you enjoyed.

Thanks so much for your support. I really appreciate your kindness!

Warmest wishes and happy reading,
Shelly

Website
http://www.shellythacker.com

Facebook
http://www.facebook.com/AuthorShellyThacker

Twitter
http://twitter.com/#!/shellythacker

Pinterest
http://pinterest.com/shellythacker/

About the Author

Reviewers use words like "exquisite" and "stunning" to describe Shelly Thacker's unique blend of powerful emotion, edge-of-your-seat adventure and steamy sensuality. Shelly's historical and paranormal romances have earned her a place on national bestseller lists and lavish praise from such diverse media as *Publishers Weekly*, *The Atlanta Journal-Constitution*, *Locus,* and *The Oakland Press*, who have called her books "innovative," "addictive," "memorable" and "powerful."

A two-time RWA RITA Finalist, Shelly has won numerous other honors for her novels, including a National Readers' Choice Award, several *Romantic Times* Certificates of Excellence, and five straight KISS Awards for her outstanding heroes. The *Detroit Free Press* has twice placed her books on their annual list of the year's best romances.

When she's not at the computer, you'll find Shelly reading with her kids, knitting in local cafes, or kickboxing at the gym. She lives in Minnesota with her husband and two daughters. For the latest news and sneak previews of upcoming books, visit www.shellythacker.com

Made in the USA
Middletown, DE
22 September 2015